M000013334

CONSEQUENTIAL
DAMAGES

Joseph Hayes

ISBN: 0615819710
ISBN 13: 9780615819716

DEDICATION

To Susan, With All My Love.

DEFINITION

Consequential Damages: Loss, harm or damage that, while not an immediate or direct result of a certain initial act, is a foreseeable consequence of such act.

PART ONE

PROLOGUE

Present Day
Suburban Chicago

Jake McShane shivered as the bitter November wind lashed into him. At some other point in his life, he might have felt different about this place. It was a setting unlike any other, where nature, history and spirituality were prominently on display, woven into one seamless and harmonious fabric. It was a place revealing the strongest connection between humanity and nature, where man truly became one with the earth. It was a place where restless souls found themselves, drawn by its promise of solace and serenity. However, to Jake McShane, at this moment, it was none of those things. It was just a cemetery.

It was Sunday, late afternoon, but darker than it should have been, as ominous storm clouds hung low in the sky. Large raindrops began to fall, announcing their presence with loud splats. Jake had neither overcoat nor umbrella. He stood there motionless, staring down at the grave, as if in a trance. The intermittent jabbing of the icy raindrops quickly became a downpour, yet he remained transfixed, quietly absorbing nature's blows. Perhaps his physical discomfort would numb the agony he felt inside. Perhaps it would sharpen his senses and draw him out of the daze that had possessed him for weeks, and bring him some clarity of thought and understanding.

He needed that clarity. The trial was just one week away. Without question, it would be the biggest trial of his career—if he could pull himself together in time to handle it. In terms of preparation and knowledge of the case, he was ready. He had twenty-eight months of his life invested in this case and he knew it cold. But this was not just another lawsuit he was defending; there was so much more involved here, and he was plagued by a crippling combination of indecision and self-doubt. Could he possibly summon up the passion, intensity and fortitude that a trial like this would require?

If he didn't try the case, his client would almost certainly lose, and lose badly. The verdict could be hundreds of millions of dollars, and the company could be driven into bankruptcy. But it wasn't his company or his money, so why should he care? This was not what he had bargained for when he enrolled in law school. He had learned the hard way that high-stakes litigation was not a gentlemen's game, where honor and integrity mattered and all players respected the rules. It was all-out war, which resulted in serious casualties, and his exposure to it had cost him dearly. It had rocked his faith in the legal system to its very core, along with his faith in human nature and in himself. And it had brought him here, to this cemetery and this grave.

He needed to think and to make a decision, and had come to this spot hoping to find resolution, yet as he stood there gazing upon the grave marker, all of the anguish he had been trying so hard to tuck away came rushing back. Tears streamed down his face, and he wept quietly for a long time. How long, he had no idea. He had no sense of time and no sense of the world around him. He felt completely alone, separated from the rest of the universe by an invisible wall of grief.

As the rain slowed to gentle drizzle, a burst of thunder jolted him and caused him to look around. Jake felt his awareness returning, and with it, a growing sensation that something was amiss. It began as a vague feeling of uneasiness and slowly evolved into a conscious thought—clear, lucid and unmistakable: Something was out of place here. He looked around nervously, and saw nothing unusual. No one was in sight, which was not surprising, given the rain. He moved toward his car, carefully surveying the surrounding area, absolutely convinced that trouble was lurking nearby. Still, he saw nothing.

He reached his car, which was parked on the narrow blacktop road that wound through the cemetery. Then he saw it. Although not visible from the grave, from the roadway he could see the gaudy white Cadillac with the gold trim and maroon roof, parked just across the street from the cemetery's entrance. He'd seen that car before, outside the courthouse after jury selection. He recalled being unnerved at the time because the driver—a huge, muscular black man dressed like a gangbanger—seemed to be watching him. The pimped-out vehicle was clearly out of place in this well-to-do white-bread suburb.

Jake hobbled purposefully toward the Cadillac on his crutches, anger and curiosity crowding out all fear. The rain had stopped and the driver's window was down. Despite the doo rag and the mirror sunglasses, Jake recognized the face. It was definitely the man he'd seen outside the courthouse. He reached the cemetery gate and stopped. They stared at each other from across the street as cars cruised by between them. There was something familiar about the face. He had thought so at the courthouse and was even more convinced now, but he couldn't place it. Jake waited impatiently for a break in traffic. The dark glass of the driver's window began rising silently.

"Wait! Who are you? Why are you following me?" Jake yelled as traffic cleared and he began limping rapidly across the street. Tires screeched, and the Cadillac sped away, leaving Jake standing in the middle of the road, bewildered and exasperated.

CHAPTER 1

Ten Years Earlier
San Francisco Bay Area

As the van pulled away from San Francisco International Airport, Jake McShane thought back on his first impressions of California, formed while watching the Rose Bowl Parade every New Year's Day as a young boy. He and his brothers would hunker down in front of their television, sheltered from the bitter cold and snow of the Chicago winter, and stare longingly at the sun-drenched parade-goers basking in the balmy Pasadena weather. It seemed like such a magical place—so different from his world. Now, as he beheld the Golden State with his own eyes for the first time, he was struck by a wave of exhilaration mixed with awe. The newness of the surroundings signaled beyond any doubt that he had left his former life far behind.

Jake stared out the window, mesmerized by the scenery, as the van cruised south on Highway 101. This was his first hour in California, and he had never seen mountains before. The locals might refer to them as hills, but to a young man accustomed to the unending flatness of the Midwest, they were certainly mountains. They were golden in hue that time of year, not green as he expected, but still stunningly vibrant beneath a cloudless sky that seemed almost unnaturally blue and bright.

Less than an hour later, the van rolled onto the campus and stopped at Weston Hall, a graduate student dormitory populated mostly by law students. It was a modern looking six-story structure of white stucco. Jake stepped out of the vehicle and checked the room number on the small brown envelope containing his key, even though he had no doubt about the number: 306. He took the elevator to the third floor and easily located the room. The door was wide open, and several partially unpacked suitcases were strewn around the floor, but their owner was not in sight. Jake surveyed the surroundings with a feeling of approval. The room was spacious, for a dorm room, with twin beds on either side. In between were two large desks made of light colored wood, with matching bookcases above them. Thick carpeting, which looked and smelled new, covered the floor. "Greetings!" A cheery, confident voice came from behind him. "If this is your room, then I guess we're roommates. I'm Tony Scarano," said the tall, dark-haired young man, extending his hand.

"Jake McShane. Nice to meet you," replied Jake, feeling a sense of relief. Moving in with an unknown roommate was a dicey proposition and Jake had been concerned about the possibility of getting a bad draw. This fellow seemed entirely normal, and Jake's first impression of him was a good one.

"Where you from?" Tony asked.

"Chicago," replied Jake. "How about you?"

"New York. Born and raised on Long Island. Doesn't the accent give me away?"

"Actually, it does," said Jake with a chuckle, quickly feeling at ease. "Where'd you go for undergrad?"

"Harvard," Tony replied matter-of-factly. "You?"

"I went to Illinois—its branch campus in Chicago," said Jake, suddenly feeling self-conscious about his commuter school background.

"So, did we make the right decision?" asked Tony. "Stanford Law School, I mean. The Left Coast, land of the fruits and nuts, etcetera?"

"Sure beats the hell out of where I come from. I can't wait to get a better look at the place."

"Let's go have a look around," Tony suggested eagerly. "We can unpack later."

"Hi guys!" A perky young woman entered the room. "I'm Kelly Conrad—room 303, across the hall." She was petite, with short blond hair, impeccably groomed and stylishly dressed.

Tony and Jake introduced themselves. Kelly proceeded to explain that she had grown up in nearby Sunnyvale, in the heart of Silicon Valley, and had graduated from Stanford three months earlier. She happily agreed to act as tour guide, and for the next two hours, the three of them strolled the bustling campus. Kelly provided a running commentary about the various buildings and spots of special interest, adding a touch of history now and then, as well as pointers on things to do in the area. Her enthusiasm and affection for the place were unmistakable.

The tour concluded with a stop at the law school. She led them to the library, where a large picture board displayed the names and photographs of the one hundred seventy members of this year's entering class, along with their hometowns and undergraduate schools.

Jake couldn't help but focus on the schools represented rather than the faces. The board was dominated by big-name universities, such as Harvard, Stanford, Yale, Berkeley and MIT. The University of Illinois at Chicago definitely seemed out of place. Those thoughts vanished as Jake noticed a familiar face. "Hey, I know this guy!" he said with surprise, pointing to a handsome looking student by the name of Richard Black.

"Wow, he's hot! Is he a friend of yours?" asked Kelly.

"No, I've never met him, but he's from Chicago. He was an all-state basketball player in high school, then he went to Indiana. He was the starting point guard on the team that made it to the NCAA championship last spring."

"I remember him," said Tony. "He was the heart of that team. Great playmaker, tenacious defender, and tough as hell. Couldn't shoot, though. If he could, he'd be in the NBA instead of here."

After scouring the picture board for several more minutes, Kelly spoke up. "I'm going to head back to the dorm, guys. I want to get a jump on my studies and be ready for tomorrow."

Tony and Jake looked at each other. "Are there assignments already?" Tony asked.

"No, I just like to be well prepared," said Kelly, as they headed back to the dorm.

They compared schedules and learned that they shared most of the same classes, including Contracts with Professor Farris first period. "See you in class," said Kelly, as she excused herself to spend some time with her books, leaving the new roommates to their unpacking.

The next morning, Jake and Tony arrived at their Contracts class ten minutes early. The corridor outside the classroom was buzzing, as students made acquaintances and shared information about Farris and the other first-year professors. As Jake was visiting with several of his new classmates, he was approached by a tall, athletic looking student with perfectly coifed blond hair and an unmistakable air of confidence. "Jake McShane," he called out, offering his hand. "I noticed you on the picture board. You and I appear to be the only Chicagoans in this crowd. I'm Rick Black."

"Hi Rick," said Jake, feeling flattered that someone of Rick Black's stature would seek him out. "I watched you play ball for the Hoosiers, so I feel like I already know you. Are you in this class?"

"Yep. I hear Farris is one tough customer. They say he's a maniac with the Socratic Method. He selects one victim at the beginning of each class and barrages that poor bastard with questions for the entire ninety minutes."

"I've heard that too, but I've also heard he's a decent guy and not at all nasty about it," chimed in Kelly, who had just joined them.

They entered the classroom, and sat near the front, since most of the other seats were already occupied. Promptly at eight thirty, a lanky, middle-aged man with a well-trimmed gray beard strode into the classroom and proceeded briskly to the simple wooden desk situated at the front, facing the class. He sat down, staring at the desk for a few moments while an abrupt hush fell over the room. Still looking downward, Professor Farris began speaking in a deep, resonant voice that seemed inconsistent with his thin frame. "Welcome to Stanford

Law School," he began. Looking up, he continued. "My guess is that many of you feel somewhat surprised to be sitting here today. You may feel like you've done a good job fooling people for a long time, and now you're wondering whether you really belong here and whether you have what it takes to succeed at a place like this." There was a slight ripple of nervous laughter at this insight.

"Let me make one thing perfectly clear: There were no mistakes in our admissions process. In the entire universe of law school applicants, you represent the elite. Look around you. You are looking at the future leaders of the legal profession. You've got what it takes, or you wouldn't be here. Don't ever doubt that."

He paused for several moments and looked around the classroom at the eager faces before him. "Your legal career starts today. The law will test your intellect and your resourcefulness, as well as your patience and your perseverance. It will confound you and exasperate you, but it will also thrill you and excite you. It will give you a sense of purpose, and a sense of accomplishment. It is a powerful force; therefore, it must be wielded with care. It can be used to work great good, but it can also be used to work serious injustice.

"As the future leaders of this profession, you will be entrusted with a tremendous responsibility. Use your talent, training and leadership to serve the greater good. Hold yourselves and your profession to the highest standards of ethics at all times. You will be the stewards of a noble calling with a rich history and tradition. You will occupy positions of influence, and the profession will be counting on you to use that influence wisely and responsibly.

"But first things first—you need to get through law school, and you will quickly realize that law school is hard work. It is stressful. But it can also be one of the most exciting and rewarding experiences of your life. For the next three years, you will be surrounded by the brightest, most talented group of people you will ever encounter. Learn from each other; challenge each other; inspire each other. Keep the work and the stress in perspective and make the most of this experience.

"I am delighted that you're here, and I consider it a privilege to be one of your professors." He paused again, and a trace of a smile flashed across his face for just an instant. "Now, let's get down to business. Let's talk about Contracts." He looked down at his roster and chose a name. "Mr. Black, what are the essential elements of a contract?"

Rick sprang to his feet, brimming with confidence. "In my opinion, the essential—"

"Your opinions are not relevant to this particular conversation, Mr. Black."

"Yes sir," Rick replied, undaunted. "In order for there to be a binding contract, there must be a bona fide offer by the offeror, coupled with an acceptance communicated by the offeree."

"What do you mean by a bona fide offer?" Farris demanded, his tone more curt than it had been just a few minutes earlier.

Rick responded and the sparring continued for the entire period. When class adjourned, Rick looked at Tony and Jake and exclaimed, "Damn, that was fun!"

"You've got a sick sense of fun," replied Jake.

"I agree, but great job! You were awesome," said Tony. "How much time did you spend preparing for that class?"

"Not a minute. I was flying by the seat of my pants. What a rush! I've got to run. Time for Torts. See ya." He dashed off.

"That guy is impressive," said Tony. "He was so quick on his feet and never got the slightest bit flustered, even when Farris was really pounding on him."

"That will be a tough act to follow for tomorrow's victim," said Kelly, as they hurried to their next class.

Jake spent the remainder of the morning attending Torts and Civil Procedure, and marveling at the impressive array of new classmates he had been meeting. He dove eagerly into his studies early in the afternoon, after classes were finished. By nine o'clock that evening, the intense studying and the excitement of the day had caught up with him, and he returned to his room, weary yet elated. Within minutes, there was a knock on his door. He opened it to find Rick Black standing there smiling, a bottle of champagne and a small stack of plastic cups in hand.

"Well Jake, we've made it through our first day of law school. I'd say a little celebration is in order. Everyone on my floor is still grinding away in the law library, so I was hoping your floor has a little more spirit."

"Great thinking," said Jake. "Let's see who's around."

They walked down the hall, in opposite directions, knocking on doors. A bleary-eyed Kelly responded to Jake's knock, and began to decline his invitation until she heard Rick's voice, then quickly changed her mind. Kelly introduced her roommate, Claire, a large girl with a friendly face, who enthusiastically accepted the invitation. Rick had found only one other soul at the far end of the hall, a short, rotund student named Phil, who had an advanced degree in engineering from MIT. It appeared that everyone else was still at the law library, preparing for Day Two at Stanford Law School. Tony emerged from the elevator just as Rick popped the cork.

"Looks like I got here just in time," he said, eyeing the champagne. "Only one bottle?"

They stood together in the hallway as Rick filled the cups with cheap champagne.

"So, how do we like law school so far?" Rick asked.

"I don't know about you guys, but I'm scared shitless," replied Phil.

"Oh come on, Phil," said Rick. "You're the closest thing to a rocket scientist we have around here. What's to be scared of?"

Rick raised his glass and looked at the group. "Well gang, I think old Professor Farris knows what he's talking about. We are the elite. This will be a great experience. Let's make the most of it. Here's to the future leaders of our esteemed profession. Cheers!"

CHAPTER 2

"I really wish you'd consider staying, Grandma," said Amanda Chang as she busied herself emptying drawers and packing her grandmother's things in an old leather suitcase. "Mother and Daddy would love to have you here, and there's plenty of room."

"No, I'm well now," replied the elderly woman seated by the window. "I've imposed on all of you for almost six weeks now. It's time for me to go home. I miss my apartment, and I miss Chinatown."

Amanda stopped her packing, walked over to her grandmother and gently took her hand. She stared deeply into the older woman's eyes and smiled. "I know you do," she said softly. She turned toward the window, and they both stared in silence at the stunning view. It was a view Amanda had never taken for granted, despite having lived with it since she was five years old. The house was perched high in the Berkeley Hills, overlooking the University of California directly below them and the City of Berkeley gradually sloping westward toward San Francisco Bay. Beneath the brilliant blue sky, sailboats dotted the water, darting between Angel Island and Alcatraz. The Golden Gate Bridge stretched majestically in front of them, connecting Marin County with San Francisco, or "The City," as everyone in the area called it. The striking natural beauty was complemented perfectly by the bold and elegant skyline of downtown San Francisco.

"You'll never find a view like this in Chinatown," said Amanda.

"There's no view like this anywhere," the old woman acknowledged.

"I used to stare out this window whenever I called you on the phone as a child. I'd picture you talking to me from your apartment. It was such a comfort knowing that you were right there across the water."

"You were such a precious child, Amanda. You have no idea how much those phone calls meant to me. No matter what was going on, those calls from you would always brighten my day. You were so special. You still are. I can't believe you gave up your vacation to spend time with your decrepit old grandmother. You shouldn't have done that."

"That's okay, Grandma. In a way, your pneumonia was a blessing. I was able to spend some real quality time with you this summer. I can take a nice vacation next year. Anyway, I got all the break I needed. I truly love what I do, so it's not like I was dying to get away."

"You must be the youngest doctor on that staff—certainly the youngest looking. How old are you now, twenty-three?"

Amanda laughed. "I wish. I'm twenty-five now. I feel like I'm getting old in a hurry!"

"Be careful you don't let life pass you by, dear. You should be looking for a husband, and starting a family of your own," said the elderly woman, a serious tone in her voice.

"Maybe someday. Right now, my career is very important to me. I don't have time for distractions."

"There are more important things in life than professional accomplishments. Like the people in your life. Like your family. You know that, don't you?"

"I know that," Amanda replied softly. "And when the right person comes along, I'll have no trouble changing my priorities. I haven't met that person yet, but I'm not going to worry about it. My life is good right now. I'm happy."

"I'm glad. You deserve to be."

They stared out the window again, silently, still hand-in-hand. After some time, Mrs. Chang broke the silence. "Do you still play the piano?"

"I haven't played in years. Susan and Jeffery have both kept it up and play beautifully," Amanda said, referring to her younger siblings.

"What about your singing? You always had such a lovely voice."

"Sure, I still sing all the time—in the shower, in my apartment, walking down the street." Amanda laughed. "People sometimes stare at me because I'm singing to myself and don't even realize it."

"That's good. It means you have a happy heart. You really should try to keep music in your life. It's good for the mind and the soul. It helps keep you balanced, and with all the pressures in your life, you need that balance."

"That's good advice, Grandma. I'll keep it in mind."

After another brief but comfortable silence, Amanda said, "I better go now. I promised to meet some friends in Palo Alto for dinner tonight. Daddy will be driving you back to the City in the morning. I'll come visit you as often as I can on weekends."

"You should be spending your weekends relaxing and having fun with your friends."

"Oh, I will, but I'll always find time for my grandma. You stay healthy, do you hear me?"

"Goodbye, child."

"Bye, Grandma. I love you," Amanda said, hugging the old woman and turning quickly so that her grandmother would not see the tears in her eyes. She was so frail now. Every time they parted company, Amanda experienced a wave of sadness, knowing that any visit could be their last.

CHAPTER 3

J ake McShane and the other first-year law students quickly settled into their new routines. For nearly everyone, that meant finding a way to devote massive amounts of time to studying—without losing their sanity. Just doing the bare minimum to keep up was a strain. Trying to do more than that and truly master the material seemed an impossibility.

Despite the crushing workload, Jake was determined to make time to enjoy the experience of life in California. The palm trees, the lush vegetation, and the constant sunshine filled him with a positive energy every moment he was outdoors. He was enthralled by this place, and had no intention of spending all of his daylight hours under the fluo-rescent lights of the law library.

He developed a routine that enabled him to spend time every after-noon enjoying the outdoor life California had to offer. He would awaken and be at the books by six o'clock. He would study hard until classes began, and would use every minute between classes as study time—until three o'clock rolled around. At that time, he would don his running shoes and take a leisurely jog around campus. That proved to be an excellent way to familiarize himself with the surrounding area and soak in the California scenery. He usually finished up at the gym and lifted weights for thirty minutes before casually strolling across campus back toward the dorm. Then he would shower, have dinner, and hustle back to the law library with a clear head for several more hours of study time. By nine-thirty or ten o'clock, he would pack it in and wind down by quietly playing his guitar for a short while before bed.

Most of the other first-year students had found their rhythm as well. Tony would take a break for coffee and a bagel after classes ended in the early afternoon and spend some time socializing with any classmates he could find lingering around, seeking a brief respite from their books. After an hour or so, guilt and anxiety would set in and he would trek back to the law library, where he generally would stay planted until midnight, with only a short break for dinner at the dorm.

Kelly seemed to be working every waking moment, and would make a point of announcing to anyone within earshot how many hours of study time she had logged for the day and for the week. Not to be outdone were the "Two Mikes," who lived in the room adjoining Jake and Tony. Mike Mitchell, also known as "Big Mike," was a mountain of a man and a former wrestler from Notre Dame. He had bushy, dark hair and a five o'clock shadow by noon. His size, coupled with his gruff, sarcastic demeanor, made him an intimidating presence. His roommate, Mike Martinez, was small and slight, and seemed perpetually nervous and preoccupied. The two of them spent virtually all of their waking hours at the desks in their dorm room, highlighting their textbooks and jotting down volumes of notes. Any time of the day or night, Jake could put his ear to their door and hear the sound of highlighters moving across paper. They, too, kept track of every minute of study time, and would boastfully blurt out their totals whenever they encountered Kelly. This usually caused her considerable consternation, because they simply did not need as much sleep as she did, and therefore were able to log more study time.

Rick Black was an anomaly. The prodigious work habits of his peers in no way rubbed off on him. To the contrary, he continually chided his classmates for being compulsive, workaholic bores. Despite his cavalier attitude, however, he was attentive and participative in class, and always performed exceedingly well when called upon.

One afternoon, early in the semester, Jake was leaving the dorm to begin his afternoon run when the elevator door opened and there was Rick Black, dressed in his gym clothes and holding a basketball.

"Hey, Rick. Going to shoot hoops?" Jake asked, observing the obvious.

"Yep. There's open gym at the Athletic Center every afternoon at three o'clock. Intramural basketball starts in February, and I want to start getting in shape. Do you play?"

Basketball was one of Jake's passions. Ever since learning that Rick Black was a classmate, he had hoped to have the opportunity to play on the same court with him. "I'm not Big Ten caliber, but I love to play," Jake replied.

"Then let's go. I want to see your game, Chicago boy," said Rick with a smile and a challenge in his voice.

As they walked from the dorm, a familiar voice called out, "Hey, is there a basketball game I wasn't invited to?" It was Tony, who hurried to catch up to them, carrying an armful of books. "Can I get in?" he asked.

"Sure," Rick replied. "Go change, we'll wait."

The court was occupied when they arrived, a game of five-on-five already in progress.

"We've got winners," Rick announced authoritatively, finding two players to join them. As they warmed up on a side court, Jake watched Rick with a feeling of awe. Six months ago, he had seen this guy on national television, leading his team to the NCAA championship. Now they were teammates in a pickup game.

The game going on before them was intense, and Jake could feel the beginnings of butterflies in his stomach as he watched. These guys were really good. They were mostly black, mostly tall, and extremely fast. There was a great deal of trash-talking. This was not the kind of group Jake expected to find at a place like this.

As they took the court against the winning team, Jake's butterflies intensified. The opposing team brought the ball up court first, and Rick immediately proceeded to strip the ball from his man and raced up the court for a silky smooth layup. The butterflies subsided just a bit.

The next time down the court, the opponents' big guy backed down low and fired up a short hook shot that rolled around the rim and out. Rick snatched the rebound and headed up the left side of the court, blowing past two defenders without even breaking stride. Jake raced up the right side of the court, and Rick rifled a perfectly placed no-look pass directly into his hands. In one fluid motion, Jake caught the pass, stopped in place and launched a graceful jump shot over the outstretched arms of the lone defender. Swish! The butterflies were gone.

The rest of the game was a fast-paced offensive clinic conducted by Rick Black and Jake McShane, leaving everyone else on the court breathless and mesmerized. Rick played a ferocious brand of defense, leaving his opponents frustrated and angry, with him and with each other. On offense, he relentlessly pushed the ball up-court at break-neck speed, rocketing through and around helpless defenders as he dished crisp, pinpoint passes to his teammates. Most of them went to Jake, who consistently finished the job with an impressive array of deadly jump shots, slashing drives to the hoop, and other acrobatic scoring efforts.

As they walked back toward the dorm, Tony gushed with exhilaration. "That was incredible! That was some of the best basketball I've ever seen in my life, and I've seen a lot. Rick, you dominated! You're even better in person than you are on TV. And Jake, where the hell did you learn to play? You're an absolute scoring machine!"

"No shit!" said Rick, looking at Jake with obvious admiration. "You were on fire. I had no idea you were a ballplayer. You must have played in college."

"Nah, I'm just a playground player," said Jake.

"Bullshit!" replied Rick. "You've got Division I game. I can't believe you didn't play in college. Why the hell not?"

"I got a late start," Jake explained. "I really didn't play much until my junior year in high school. Senior year I blew out my ankle in the third game. That was it. Career over."

"Why didn't you try out in college?" asked Rick, a look of disbelief on his face.

"You know the odds of making a college team as a walk-on. I figured I had no chance, so I didn't even bother trying out. I played a lot during college, but it was mostly intramurals, playgrounds, church leagues—that kind of stuff."

"Well, all I can say is that if you guys are anywhere near as good at law school as you are at basketball, the rest of us poor slobs don't have a chance," said Tony.

"You can count on it," Rick replied.

For the next several weeks, Jake, Tony and Rick made afternoon basketball part of their daily routine. Following their games, they would casually stroll past the law school on their way back to the dorm, basketball in hand. They delighted in the bewildered looks they received from their classmates, who wondered how these guys could be so relaxed about their studies that they had time for basketball in the middle of the day.

As they walked home following a game in late October, Rick asked the others, "Same time tomorrow?"

"Sorry, can't make it," Tony replied. "I really need to start gearing up for finals. I'm not as far along as I should be."

"Finals? Come on, Tony, finals are six weeks away," Rick said disdainfully. "You're not turning into one of those compulsive grinds, are you?"

"Hey, six weeks isn't much time," Tony replied. "Last weekend I looked over all the material we need to know, and the sheer volume is mind-boggling. I figure it'll take me four weeks to prepare my outlines and then I'll need the final two weeks to do some serious cramming."

Jake agreed. "I went through the same drill. I've put together a timetable for outlining each of my classes, and realized that I need to get started—now. I think most people already have a pretty good jump on us. I get a knot in my stomach just thinking about it."

"Me too," said Tony. "I'm not used to having my entire grade determined by the one exam, and these grades will really count when we're interviewing for clerkships next year. The stakes are high!"

The serious tone in his classmates' voices apparently made some impression on Rick, as his focus abruptly shifted from basketball to exams. "Sounds like it's time to get my game face on," said Rick, with newly found determination. "I've been coasting at a pretty easy pace, but I guess it's time to shift into high gear. I need to do at least well enough to kick your butt, McShane. You and I will be the only ones here vying for the top jobs in Chicago, and I have no intention of getting aced out by the likes of you!" Although he said it with a smile on his face, the look in his eyes and the tone of his voice indicated that he was absolutely serious.

"Don't worry, Rick, there will be plenty of jobs for Stanford Law grads in Chicago, even if I do smoke you," Jake replied with a grin.

"There won't be any room for Number Two where I'm going," said Rick. "There are two law firms in Chicago that are head and shoulders above all the other firms there—Samuelson & Reid is one and Cassidy, Burns & Nash is the other. They recruit from only the top ten law schools and hire just a small handful of lawyers each year. They like to spread those positions around, so they're not likely to hire two Stanford grads in the same year. I intend to be in the driver's seat and have my choice."

"Hell, what's gotten into you, Rick?" asked Tony. "I've never seen you so serious about school before."

"It's prime time, guys, and I'm a prime time player. Just watch!"

As November wore on, the intensity level steadily escalated. Basketball had come to a halt. Jake still allowed himself an afternoon exercise break, but it was limited to a thirty minute run, and then he promptly returned to the books, usually without taking the time to shower. He found himself using his running time to mentally review the outlines he was developing.

Everyone was in outlining mode. It was the universally applied method of preparing for law school finals. The basic concept was to take the massive amount of information covered during the semester and condense it down to its essential points in the form of an outline for each subject, which then became the primary study vehicle for the final exam. For many students, the outlines themselves turned out to be as long as a good-sized textbook.

Jake approached the outlining process with his usual sense of organization and discipline. He developed a study plan that covered every day between early November and the beginning of finals. Sticking to his plan proved to be more difficult than he anticipated, however. He still had to keep up with all of his classes, in addition to preparing his outlines. Even after giving up most of his afternoon free time, he found himself falling behind, so he began starting his day at five a.m. rather than six.

The atmosphere in the dorm was different now. Previously, it had always been pleasant and collegial, despite the workload and the self-imposed pressure. Now, it was tense, and the residents were often irritable and short-tempered. The Two Mikes were seen even less than usual, having taken to eating every meal in their rooms, to maximize study time. Kelly's perky demeanor had changed, and she seemed withdrawn, preoccupied, and just plain grumpy. For awhile, Jake made a practice of knocking on her door at meal times to give her a brief respite from the books and some social interaction, but he soon tired of hearing her yell "Go away!" without even opening her door.

On Wednesday evening, the day before Thanksgiving, few students were left in the dorm. Jake, Tony and Rick were among the small crowd in the dining room because they were either too far from home, too broke to afford the trip, or just too intent on studying to tear themselves away for the long weekend. The combination of study overload and having a Thanksgiving with nowhere to go had the three of them in a bleak mood.

"I need to get away from this place," Rick grumbled.

"Pressure getting to you, Rick?" asked Tony.

"I'll tell you what's getting to me," replied Rick. "It's that goddamn Elliott," he said, referring to his roommate. "He's driving me crazy! Every night he's on the phone with his parents, griping about how he hates it here and wants to quit. I'm sick of listening to it! I keep telling him he should quit if the pressure is making him that miserable, but he wants Mommy and Daddy to tell him it's okay."

"The pressure is getting to a lot of folks around here, Rick. It's not just Elliott," Jake pointed out.

"Well, he's losing it. I walked into our room yesterday and he was staring at the pictures in our class yearbook, mumbling, 'fat ... bald ... fat ... abnormal ... bald ...' He said he was counting the number of people in our class who are either overweight, losing their hair or just plain weird in some way. He told me that helps him realize that he's better off than a lot of people around here and that makes him feel better. What a nut! I told him that if he's trying to distinguish himself from the crowd, he better stick to just fat and bald because he's as goofy as they come. That sorry son of a bitch is driving me mental. I've got to get away from here. What would you guys say to a road trip? Lake Tahoe is less than four hours away. We could spend a night or two in the casinos and recharge our batteries."

"I can't take that much time," Tony replied. "I'm too far behind as it is."

"Same here," said Jake, sounding gloomy. Then his face brightened. "Hey, how about a shorter trip? We could head up the coast late in the morning, drive a couple of hours north of San Francisco, and still get back by early evening. I've heard that the coastal route there is spectacular."

"Fine with me," said Rick. "I've just got to get a break, even if it's a short one. Tony?"

Tony hesitated and looked troubled. Obviously, this was a deviation from his study plans.

"Come on," urged Jake, starting to feel some enthusiasm. "A little break will do you good."

"Okay, I'm in," said Tony. "We can get in a solid morning of studying and leave around noon. How does that sound?"

"Sounds like a plan," said Rick.

"See you guys in the morning," said Jake, as they all went their separate ways for an evening with their outlines.

They met in front of the dorm at noon. "Nice ride!" said Tony, as he surveyed Rick's shiny black BMW convertible. "How the hell did you afford this?"

"It was a graduation present from my old man," explained Rick. "My basketball scholarship saved him some hefty college tuition bills, so this was payback."

"What a great dad," said Jake.

"Nah, he's a real schmuck," said Rick. "But he's a rich schmuck!"

Traffic was light as they drove through San Francisco and then across the Golden Gate Bridge into Marin County. All three of them felt law school fading from their thoughts as they took in the spectacular scenery. A short time later, they had left the scenic marinas and hillside dwellings behind and found themselves driving north along the Pacific Coast Highway. To their left, the Pacific Ocean spread out in its vastness. To their right were the steep and rugged coastal mountains. The narrow two-lane road twisted and turned as it cut through the jagged wall of pine-covered rock, hundreds of feet above the crashing surf. Jake and Tony stared in quiet amazement, their silence punctuated only by a recurring chorus of awe-inspired utterances such as, "Wow, look at that!" or "Unbelievable!" or "Holy Shit!" as each turn in the road revealed even more stunning vistas.

Rick had been proceeding cautiously along the tortuous road, especially as he navigated the innumerable blind curves. Even at a modest pace, Tony and Jake could feel their fists clenching and their stomachs tensing as they beheld the precipitous cliffs just feet, if not inches, from their vehicle. Their right legs instinctively shot forward as if searching in vain for some imaginary brake pedal. Rick's confidence in his driving and in his vehicle quickly mounted, and he began putting the BMW through its paces, accelerating aggressively between blind spots and leaning into sharp turns, his face inches from the steering wheel. The fear felt by his passengers rose in direct proportion to the aggressive enthusiasm of their driver.

"Look how this baby handles, boys," Rick shouted exuberantly. "Nothing like a BMW!" He whooped and hollered with a gleeful yet maniacal look on his face as he gunned the engine and sped around hairpin turns, while Jake and Tony implored him to slow down. Eventually, the road descended to sea level, and they found a small cluster of buildings, one of which was a rustic looking café that happened to be open for business despite the slow traffic of Thanksgiving Day. As luck would have it, they were serving traditional Thanksgiving fare—sliced turkey, stuffing and mashed potatoes—so the three classmates had the unexpected pleasure of a holiday dinner in the middle of the afternoon. They ordered a round of beer before their food arrived and Tony exclaimed, "Jeez, Rick, I didn't think I would live to see my next meal. You drive like a goddamn maniac."

"Nothing like a little adrenaline rush to clear your head," Rick replied. "I'll bet finals don't seem so scary compared to that!" Rick laughed hard and drank half his beer in one gulp, then excused himself to use the men's room.

"Let's make sure that one of us drives home," suggested Tony. "I'd rather not entrust my life to that thrill-seeking son of a bitch again."

"Agreed. I'll drive," said Jake.

Rick returned just as the waitress arrived with their dinners.

"This was an inspired idea, Rick," said Jake. "Thanks for twisting my arm. Something about the great outdoors in California really helps me keep everything else in perspective."

"Yeah, so does a brush with death," said Tony.

Rick laughed. "You guys are wound way too tight. Shall we finish dinner and drive a little farther up the coast?"

"Well, as fun as this is, I vote we start heading back," said Jake. "We're a good three hours from campus, and I promised myself I'd get to my criminal law outline this weekend. I haven't even started it yet."

"I'm dreading that test more than any of the others," said Tony. "Rumor has it that Professor Preston always gives take-home exams."

"Isn't that a good thing?" asked Jake. "We won't be racing the clock for three hours."

"No, we won't," said Tony. "We'll be racing the clock for twenty-four hours. We pick up the exam at eight o'clock Tuesday morning and have to return it by eight a.m. on Wednesday. Virtually everyone taking that exam will use every minute trying to keep up with the pack. Who's going to stop after four hours when everyone else is putting in an all-nighter?"

"That's insane!" replied Jake. "I need my sleep. There's no way I'm staying up all night for an exam!"

"We'll see about that," said Tony. "You're just as competitive as the rest of us. You'll be putting the finishing touches on your exam at seven thirty Wednesday morning, like everyone else."

"Hey, look on the bright side," said Rick. "You won't have to spend nearly as much time memorizing your outline. You'll be taking the exam in your room, and you'll have all the resources you need right at your fingertips."

"Sorry to disappoint you, pal," said Tony, "but it's take-home, not open book. You're not allowed to use books, notes, outlines or anything else."

"That's crazy," said Rick. "There's no way to enforce that."

"It's the honor system," said Tony, shrugging his shoulders.

"Yeah right," said Rick. "How many people do you really expect to abide by the honor system?"

"I assume everyone will, Rick," said Jake. "These people didn't get into Stanford Law School by cheating. They didn't have to, and I don't expect they'll start now."

Rick looked incredulous. "You guys are dreaming. Our esteemed classmates are a group of ultracompetitive personalities within an ultracompetitive profession. Plenty of them will be using every resource at their disposal, looking for any advantage they can get. You'd be foolish not to try to level the playing field and do the same."

Tony leaned across the table, looking angry and indignant. "But that's just dishonest, Rick. It's unethical. Doesn't that bother you?"

"Look, there's no way to enforce that requirement; everyone else will be ignoring it; and there's no risk of getting caught. So why not?" asked Rick.

Jake stared at Rick, open mouthed, trying to decide whether he was actually serious. "There's an honor code here, Rick. Don't you think we have some responsibility to each other to play by the rules?"

"After all we've invested here, I think our primary responsibility is to ourselves—to do as well as we possibly can," said Rick.

"Well, try this one on," urged Jake. "Don't you really want to know how good you are, how you measure up with this bunch? Doesn't it cheapen your accomplishment if you get there by skirting the rules? What you're talking about sounds like cheating on your golf score."

"There are two flaws with your argument, McShane," said Rick smugly. "First, this is not like a day on the golf course all by yourself. Others are playing in this tournament and someone is definitely keeping score. The ones who advance are the ones with the best scores. It's that simple. Second, others will be bending the rules, so if you don't approach your game in the same way, you'll be giving yourself a real handicap. That makes it hard to win."

"Well, in my opinion, your entire premise is flawed," said Tony. "I don't share your cynical view of our classmates. I honestly believe that the vast majority of them are honorable and ethical. And if those of us who choose to abide by the honor code are at a disadvantage, so be it. Sacrificing one's integrity in the hope of scoring a few additional points on an exam just isn't worth it."

Rick looked from one to the other, a bemused smile on his face. "I hope I have the pleasure of meeting you guys in court someday—you have your heads in the clouds. Let me bring you back down to earth with a very practical example: If you approach a stop sign at a deserted intersection at three a.m. and you knew there were no other vehicles on the road, would you stop? Of course not. Nobody would."

"I disagree," Jake replied emphatically. "I would stop. I *do* stop in situations like that. I've never really thought about the reasons, but I suppose it's because it means something to me to live my life by a certain standard. That includes obeying the laws—even when nobody is watching."

Rick chuckled and threw up his hands in a gesture of surrender. "I give up," he said. "I'm sorry I even brought it up."

"So, Rick," asked Jake, with a serious tone, "I know you enjoy a good debate. I also know you like to yank our chain. You're not really saying you would use reference materials during a take-home exam, are you?"

"I never said that I would and I never said that I wouldn't," replied Rick. "I spoke only hypothetically."

"But you said it would be foolish not to use all the reference materials we can get our hands on," Tony pointed out. "So, reading between the lines, it sounds like you're prepared to do exactly that. Have I got that right?"

"I never said that," Rick replied. "But I will say this: You guys could really benefit from a dose of the real world. Let's go." He finished his beer, stood up, and headed toward the door.

"Hey Rick, I've never driven a Beamer before. Mind if I drive home?" Jake asked as they strolled across the parking lot.

"Not at all," Rick replied, flipping Jake the keys. "Don't trust me?" Rick grinned.

"You got that right," Jake answered, as they climbed into the convertible and began the leisurely drive back to campus.

CHAPTER 4

By December 1st, the level of intensity around the law school had reached a crescendo. Male students were mostly unshaven, and the women had largely dispensed with makeup, as even basic grooming had become a luxury few dared to spend time on. Social interaction was becoming rare, and what interaction there was consisted mostly of students grilling each other in preparation for the upcoming exams.

Jake finished his outlines precisely on schedule. After going through that exercise, he realized how invaluable they were, given the enormous quantities of subject matter they were expected to learn. His plan now was to spend as much waking time as possible poring over those outlines, which held the key to his success on these all-important first semester finals. The first exam was just ten days away.

Watching and listening to his classmates as they relentlessly quizzed each other and shared horror stories about finals only served to heighten Jake's anxiety. Not only did he have no desire to participate in that kind of interaction, he didn't even want to witness it, yet it pervaded the school, the law library and the dorm. Jake found refuge in the massive undergraduate library. He had discovered it during Thanksgiving weekend, when the law library was closed, and found it to be an ideal place to avoid the law school frenzy. He had been going there every day for over a week now and had yet to spot a single law student.

Shortly after lunch, Jake made his way to his usual spot, which was a study carrel among the stacks of books on the third floor. Although a few of the carrels around him were occupied by under-graduate students, Jake felt remote and isolated, since there were no law students anywhere in sight. He intended to devote the entire day to Contracts, since it was his first final. He quickly lost himself in the intricacies and nuances of contract law and became oblivious to everything around him.

By late afternoon, Jake found his concentration fading as he was distracted by the sound of his stomach growling. He glanced at his watch and realized that he had been there for nearly five hours. He needed a short break and some sustenance to energize himself for a long night of studying. He remembered that there was a delicatessen just around the corner. He could grab a cup of coffee and a bite to eat and be back in fifteen minutes.

Jake got up, stretched, rubbed his bleary eyes, and headed for the elevator. He did not want to lose his prime study spot, so he draped his jacket over the chair and left his study materials strewn all over the desk. He tucked his backpack underneath the desk, hidden from view.

It was dark already as he walked outside. Without his jacket, the December air felt chilly. He walked briskly to the deli, ordered a chicken salad sandwich and a large cup of coffee, and perused the sports section of the *USA Today*. As he did so, a dark thought quickly crossed his mind. Was it foolish to have left his outlines behind in the library, even for a few minutes? After all, his work for the entire semester was captured in those documents. He was just being para-noid, he told himself. Doing so might be risky at some of the cutthroat law schools back east, but not here. Besides, the third floor of the library was pretty deserted, and those outlines would be of no use to any undergraduate who happened to be studying there. He quickly calmed down and felt reassured, and congratulated himself on his decision to avoid the dorm and the law library.

The brisk walk, the food, and the caffeine had him feeling invigo-
rated, as he walked casually back to the library, psyching himself up for
another long night with his outlines. The third floor was utterly quiet.
Most of the undergrads who had been there earlier were gone. They
must be eating a nice leisurely meal, Jake thought with some envy.

As he approached his study carrel, he sensed immediately that
something was amiss. His backpack was on the chair. He was
certain that he had made a point of tucking it away under the desk.
He sprinted the last few feet to the carrel, panic gripping him. His
books lay exactly where he had left them, but the Contracts outline
was nowhere in sight. He cast aside the loose pages of notes covering
the desk, desperately hoping that his outline was buried among the
papers. It was not there. He looked under the desk. He scoured the
entire area surrounding the carrel. Feeling dizzy and nauseous, he
yanked the zipper on his backpack with shaking hands. Every one of
his outlines had been in there. They were gone.

CHAPTER 5

"Professor? Is this a convenient time?" asked Amanda Chang, as she knocked softly on Dr. Marsh's door.

Dr. Ellen Marsh looked up from her desk. "Amanda, so nice to see you. Please come in." She walked around her desk, smiling warmly as she extended her hand to her visitor.

Ellen Marsh was the dean of the residency program at Stanford Medical Center, and one of its leading neurologists. She also served on the faculty of the medical school. She was in her early fifties, but looked ten years younger. Her hair was short and sandy brown without a trace of gray. Although her features were plain, her skin was perfect, as were her teeth, which she displayed frequently through her quick, easy smile. Her demeanor was invariably calm and pleasant, and she exuded a confidence bred out of a lifetime of knowing that she was always the smartest person in the room.

Although Dr. Marsh was not Amanda's assigned advisor, she had informally assumed the role of mentor after Amanda had worked as her research assistant during her final two years of medical school. Their relationship now transcended that, and they had become good friends.

"I'd like to take you up on your offer to discuss career options," Amanda said. "After this year, I'll be halfway through my residency. I need to figure out what I want to be when I grow up."

"I'd be delighted to help in any way I can," said Dr. Marsh as she guided Amanda to the brown leather couch opposite her desk. They sat down, facing each other. "Knowing you as I do, I'm sure you've thought about this from every possible angle. Has a general direction begun to emerge?"

"Not really," replied Amanda, a look of concern crossing her face. "I feel torn. I've thoroughly enjoyed the research we've worked on together. I feel that I'm reasonably good at it and part of me thinks that I could do something meaningful along those lines, but—"

"Let's put all modesty aside, kiddo. You and I both know that you are a very gifted scholar. Many doctors who go into medical research are really just lab technicians or bookworms. You know the type. I don't mean to minimize what they do, but most of them lack real insight and perspective. You're different. You are not only a genuine scholar, you have great creative instincts and the ability to be a true visionary. I think it would be a loss to the medical profession if we were deprived of your academic talent."

"I think your impression of my academic abilities may be inflated," said Amanda with some embarrassment, "but I do love that part of my work. On the other hand, I went into this profession so I could make a difference in people's lives. The human interaction is what brings me the most satisfaction."

"You've got a gift for that, too. I've seen it. I've watched the way your patients react to you. Even when they can't be physically healed, their state of mind is invariably better because of how you treat them. But look, you don't have to choose one option and forego the other. There are ways to do both. Look at my situation. I'm directly involved in cutting-edge research projects; I teach; and I still spend time with patients at the clinic. You could follow a similar path. Are you still interested in geriatric medicine?"

Amanda nodded. "That's the one thing I'm sure of. I've felt that calling since I was a child watching my grandmother care for the elderly in Chinatown."

"That's an ideal situation. Unlike cancer research, and neurology and many other specialties, research in geriatric medicine requires a great deal of interaction with patients, as opposed to lab research. You could really use all your talents in that field. But, you should start by learning from the best. We have some fine doctors here at the Medical Center who specialize in geriatric medicine, but I'd recommend you try to work under the real leaders in this field." Dr. Marsh paused and looked steadily at her protégé. "How do you feel about snow?"

"Why do you ask?"

"Because there are two doctors doing some real pioneering work in this area, and they both happen to be in Chicago. One is at Northwestern and the other at the University of Chicago. If you want my advice, that's where you belong at this point in your career."

"But this is my home. My parents are here. My grandmother is here. Everyone I know is in the Bay Area. How could I leave?"

"It doesn't have to be forever. You could apply for a fellowship there, which would only last for a year or two. You can always come back. My guess is that, before too long, Stanford will be knocking at your door asking you to join the faculty here. But for now, you owe it to yourself to become the best you can be in your chosen field, and in my opinion, that means learning from the best."

Amanda pondered the suggestion for a few moments. "You're right, as always," she said with a smile, starting to warm to the idea. "How do I go about exploring those possibilities?"

"I don't think we'll have any problems making it happen. Your academic record speaks for itself. I have some good connections. Let me start making some contacts."

"You're my hero, Dr. Marsh. I can't thank you enough," Amanda said as she leaned over and hugged her mentor. "I hope you'll come visit me if I move away. The thought of leaving my family and friends is pretty scary."

"I will. I promise," said Dr. Marsh. "The AMA frequently holds its conventions in Chicago."

They stood up and walked toward the door. "I don't mean to be nosy, but how's your social life?" asked Dr. Marsh. "I worry that you push yourself too hard and don't have enough fun."

"You sound like my grandmother," said Amanda with an easy laugh. "The Chinese really stress balance in life, and she constantly reminds me of that. Anyway, there's no need for concern there. I have a lot of friends. In fact, I'm on my way to meet my college roommate for dinner right now. She's a law student here. Thanks for the chat, Dr. Marsh. I'll see you soon."

Amanda walked briskly down the hall and out of the building. Although her disposition was naturally cheerful, the visit with her mentor had her in even higher spirits than normal as she walked toward Weston Hall, singing softly to herself.

CHAPTER 6

F inding no trace of his outlines at his study carrel, Jake stormed around the stacks, looking for anyone that might be a suspect. There were only a few undergrads scattered around the third floor. He approached the one nearest his carrel, a young-looking student with thick glasses and bad skin, biology books piled high around him. Jake interrupted him unceremoniously and asked in an aggressive voice, "Did you happen to see anyone at that carrel over there in the last thirty minutes? I stepped away and now some of my things are missing."

The young man started at the sound of Jake's voice, which was far louder than typically heard in the library, and which had disturbed his deep concentration.

"Sorry," he replied. "I've been in a zone here. Didn't notice a thing."

Jake turned and quickly walked away without another word. He descended the stairs to the first floor and brusquely strode to the front desk.

"Who's in charge here," he demanded of no one in particular. One of the three people behind the desk approached him. She was an overweight middle-aged woman who very much looked the part of a librarian. "How may I help you," she asked.

"Some of my things were just stolen," Jake blurted out. "My study outlines. I was in one of the carrels on the third floor and stepped away for a few minutes, and when I got back, they were gone."

"I'm sorry, sir, but the library can't be responsible for lost belongings," she said matter-of-factly, pointing to a sign behind the desk that stated exactly that.

"I'm not trying to hold you responsible," Jake said with exasperation. "I was just hoping you could do something to help. Has anyone else reported thefts here recently? Has anyone reported seeing suspicious characters around here?"

"No problems have been reported, sir," she replied with obvious irritation. "What would you have us do?" The question was rhetorical, and it was clear that she had no desire to do anything.

"Hell, I don't know! Not a damn thing, I guess!" Jake stormed away.

He returned to his dorm room and frantically searched every inch of it, hoping that he had lost his mind and had really left at least some of his outlines in his room. They were not there. His head was spinning again, and he was chilled by a cold sweat. His emotions vacillated between rage and panic. He had to get a grip on things. He needed some air.

He headed outside and tried to bring some coherent thought to his situation. He knew that he was losing precious time and needed to focus on developing a new study plan, but he was not ready to accept that his outlines were gone. Trying to prepare for finals without those outlines seemed like a terrifying and hopeless task. He had to get them back. He tried to recall every detail of his trip to the library that day. He desperately hoped that somewhere in the recesses of his memory he would find a clue that could lead him to the culprit, and ultimately the return of his outlines. To his dismay, he remembered nothing useful. He had been so preoccupied with his finals preparations that he'd been oblivious to everything around him. The feeling of panic gradually evolved into one of despair, as he faced the grim realization that his outlines were likely gone for good.

Jake wandered through the campus, head down, barely paying attention to where he was going. He eventually made his way to the law library, where he roamed around for several minutes, looking for no one and nothing in particular. He couldn't help but notice the legions of law students there, calmly and intently absorbed in their outlines. Panic returned.

"Jake, is something wrong?" A familiar voice brought him out of his trance-like state. He saw Kelly approaching him, a look of concern on her face. She had noticed Jake standing motionless in the same spot for several minutes, staring aimlessly about, distress projecting from every inch of his body.

"My outlines are gone. Stolen. Every one of them," he replied in a shaky voice, unable to look at her.

"Oh, no! Oh, my God! Are you sure?"

"Yes," he said with quiet resignation. "What am I going to do?" He sounded pathetic and he knew it.

She took him by the arm and led him outside. "Tell me exactly what happened," she demanded. Jake told her the whole story.

"You need to report this to the Dean's office or the campus police— both. I can't believe this. This is terrible!" She could see that her words were not helping. "Don't worry, Jake, we'll help you. You'll be all right." Her voice sounded wishful rather than reassuring.

"Thanks," Jake replied dejectedly, "I don't think anyone can help at this point." He walked away, with no particular destination in mind. He just needed to be by himself to get his thoughts and emotions under control, and to try to overcome the panic that was gripping him.

After an hour or so of aimless walking did nothing to improve his mental state, Jake returned to the dorm. Tony met him as he approached the front stairs.

"I've been looking all over for you. Kelly told me what happened. Everyone's been worried about you. Are you okay?"

"Not really," said Jake quietly, touched by his friend's concern. He avoided making eye contact to conceal his watery eyes. "But don't worry, I'm not suicidal." He smiled ruefully, then looked up at Tony and his demeanor quickly changed, as the rage boiled up again. "I've never been so pissed in my life. It's just so ... wrong, so ... low," he said, groping for the right words to express the degree of depravity in this act, and not quite finding them.

As they rode the elevator to the third floor, Tony assumed a take-charge attitude. "I've called campus security," he said. "I also called Dean Sheffield at home. He was dismayed to hear about this, and said he's never heard of anything like it happening here before. He told me he would speak to campus security, and issue some sort of memo reminding students to be careful with their belongings—not that that will do you any good. He also pointed out the obvious: Your outlines are gone. It's not realistic to expect you'll get them back. You need to forget about that and do the best you can without them. And we're going to help you—all of us."

The elevator chimed as it opened on the third floor. Kelly and Claire burst into the hallway. Phil stuck his head out of his room and hurried toward the group as well. Even the Two Mikes dropped their highlighters and rushed to greet Jake. They all began speaking at once, expressing sympathy, indignation and outrage, but mostly offering to help.

"I'll head to the copy shop first thing in the morning and copy my outlines for you, Jake," said Big Mike. "And if they ever catch the bastard who did this, I'll personally break his neck!"

"Feel free to borrow mine, too," said Kelly. "Any time at all. You might find my handwriting easier to read than Big Mike's."

"Obviously, you know mine are at your disposal," said Tony. "They're on my bookcase. Just help yourself."

After the emotional roller coaster of the last several hours, the generosity and concern of his classmates was too much for Jake. He felt tears brimming up in his eyes and fought to suppress them, but soon they were rolling down his cheeks, much to his embarrassment. He wanted to say something to properly express his appreciation, but couldn't find the words. After a short, awkward silence, he looked up at his friends and managed a weak smile. "Thanks everybody. You guys are great." He hugged the girls and shook hands with each of the guys and then headed to his room, Tony's hand on his shoulder.

Drained by the evening's events, Jake slept deeply that night. Upon awakening, he was in good spirits for an instant due to the restful night's sleep. Then the memory of the previous day's events flooded back, and a feeling of dread quickly overtook him.

His first exam was only nine days off, and he knew that he had to quickly devise a new study plan. Big Mike knocked on the door and entered, carrying an overstuffed, messy looking three-ring binder. "Behold, my masterpiece," he said proudly. "Also known as *Mitchell on Contracts*. I realized it would be too much of a pain to copy this, so I thought I'd just let you hold onto it. I won't be getting to this one until the middle of the week, so it's yours until then. You're welcome to any of my other outlines whenever I'm not using them."

"This is super. You're a real pal, Mike," said Jake, trying to feign enthusiasm, while his heart sank at the sight of Big Mike's outline. It had to be four hundred pages long. His own had been only sixty.

Mike excused himself to get back to his studying, giving Jake an opportunity to peruse *Mitchell on Contracts*. To his eyes, it was a mess. Mike's handwriting was virtually indecipherable, and Jake had trouble making any sense out of Mike's organization. Jake's approach to outlining was the customary one—he tried to work through the vast amount of information covered during the semester and condense it down to the most important concepts. From what he could see, Big Mike had attempted to capture absolutely every scrap of material covered in class or in their textbooks. There was no way Jake could possibly get through this mountain of information in the time remaining before exams.

Jake grabbed Tony's Contracts outline off the bookshelf and walked across the hall to ask Kelly if he could borrow hers as well. She retrieved it from her desk and handed it to him without hesitation, although Jake couldn't help noticing that nervous look on her face.

"Don't worry. You don't even have to say it," he assured her. "I'll guard it with my life." He tucked the outline under his arm and hurried off to the law library.

Jake decided to begin his preparation by using both Tony's and Kelly's outlines so that he could compare them and choose the one that he found more helpful. It turned out to be an exercise in frustration. Reviewing his own outline had been easy because he could quickly skim a page and know exactly what was on it and what every notation meant. He knew exactly what had been in his mind and what concepts he was trying to document as he prepared his outlines. Trying to make sense of another person's outline was a painstaking process. Aside from the difficulty of deciphering another person's handwriting, abbreviations and other forms of shorthand, it was like trying to get inside another person's mind to fully grasp the idea that the notations represented.

Despite his determination to dedicate virtually every waking moment to his studies, Jake found himself repeatedly pushing the outlines away in frustration and taking numerous breaks to clear his head and refocus. By dinnertime, he had covered only a small fraction of the material he had hoped to cover. It was taking all of his powers of concentration just to translate the notes in his classmates' outlines, and he was spending very little time actually absorbing the material. As he looked at his watch and recognized that the precious hours were slipping away, panic began overtaking him once again. At this rate, it would take him a full week just to prepare for Contracts, and he had four other finals. This was not working. He had tried to deny that realization throughout the day, but now the unpleasant conclusion was inescapable: Using another student's outline was an exercise in futility. He was lost without his own.

As that realization set in, Jake slowly packed up his things and rose from his desk and left the library. He needed a different plan. He trudged back to the dorm, doing his best to keep the panic at bay so that he could think clearly enough to devise another approach. He had to be creative. He needed new ideas. He tried desperately to think clearly, but his thoughts seemed disjointed, and his brain seemed to be moving in slow motion. He tried to will himself to banish the panicky feelings, but panic was winning out over reason.

Jake realized that every hour spent not studying made his predicament more dire. However, he was useless in his present state and he knew it. He decided to go for a run, hoping that physical exertion would bring back mental clarity. He ran, and ran hard, until his heart was pounding and he was gasping for breath. His brain seemed to be functioning again. He could see things more clearly now, but what he saw brought him no comfort. He couldn't possibly recreate his own outlines in the short time left, nor could he use anyone else's outlines. The stark reality was that there was no way to efficiently master his subjects under these circumstances. Any hope of good grades was gone. His goals had to be adjusted, drastically. He had to hope that he just avoided flunking out.

With that brutal realization, Jake slowly walked back to his dorm room. The panic that had built throughout the day was gone, replaced by gloom and despair over the hopelessness of his plight. In his room, he could hear the sound of highlighters moving across paper, through the adjoining walls. He could visualize the Two Mikes poring over their precious outlines, highlighting almost every line in a rainbow of colors, each of which had some significance known only to the writer. He envied them, and pitied himself. He could not stay there, listening to those sounds, and there was no reason to return to the law library.

Feeling utterly defeated, Jake picked up his guitar and began strumming quietly. He realized that this might disturb the Mikes, so he retreated to the back stairwell where no one would hear him. Earlier in the semester, he had discovered that this stairwell was an ideal place to play his guitar. It provided solitude, since it was rarely used, as most students opted for the elevator or the stairwell near the front of the building. The area was soundproof, so he would neither disturb his fellow residents nor embarrass himself with his singing. Also, the acoustics actually made him sound halfway decent. The walls were cinderblock, painted white. The stairs were concrete. The doors were heavy black metal, and windowless. The narrow quarters, combined with the absence of any noise-absorbing material, amplified any sounds and caused them to reverberate off the walls. It made his modest guitar playing sound like studio-quality musicianship, at least in his mind, and it made his voice, which he considered barely pass-able, sound strong and resonant.

Jake seated himself on the landing between the third and fourth floors. He started and stopped several songs, searching for one that he really felt like playing. After a few minutes, he found himself finger-picking *Landslide*, by Fleetwood Mac. The notes rang off the walls, filling the small chamber with a rich, full sound. He began singing the words, softly at first, and then gradually building to full volume as his confidence was lifted by the sound-enhancing qualities of the deserted stairwell. He lost himself in his singing and playing, until halfway through the song he realized with a start that there was a clear female voice singing in perfect harmony. No one was in sight, and for a few short seconds, his mind tried to grasp whether he was imagining the sound or whether it was real. He quickly realized that it was indeed real, and abruptly halted. He heard footsteps above him and a voice called out, "Don't stop! That sounds great!"

Under normal circumstances, Jake would have stopped cold rather than risk further embarrassment. Tonight, however, he just didn't care. With all the other fears gnawing at him, he was not fazed by a little embarrassment. What the hell, he thought, and he continued with the song. As he did, a striking young woman rounded the corner on the fourth floor landing and walked toward him down the stairs. She resumed her harmonizing, smiling at Jake as she approached. Jake finished the song with confidence, feeling that her singing enhanced his modest musicianship to a level he had never before achieved. As the final note reverberated off the stairwell walls, she clapped softly and smiled at him.

"Wow! You've got an incredible voice," said Jake, with genuine admiration. "Welcome to my studio," he said with a slightly embar-rassed smile, gesturing at the surrounding stairwell.

"Thank you," she replied. "You play beautifully. I've always loved that song."

"Me too, although I've never been able to figure out what it means. *Landslide* just seemed appropriate today, since my whole world is crashing down around me." Jake immediately felt angry with himself for mentioning his troubles. This had been a nice moment, and he might have just ruined it with his self-pity.

"Oh, come on!" the girl replied cheerfully. "How bad can things be? You look like you're in good health. You're a student here at Stanford, which means you're a smart guy with a bright future. You are a student here?"

"Yes—first year law school."

"Let me guess. Stressed out about finals?" she asked, taking a seat a few steps above him.

"Well, it's a bit more complicated than that," replied Jake, giving her a brief account of the loss of his outlines and why they were so important to him.

"I'm sorry to hear that," she said. "It's really disheartening to think that somebody around here would do something so low. But you know what? You'll be fine. Get past the anger and despair and look at this logically. Isn't that what lawyers are supposed to do? Just look at the facts. First, you must be an extremely intelligent person, or you wouldn't have gotten into Stanford Law School."

"I don't know about that. Sometimes I still think they made a mistake when they let me in," said Jake, trying to be modest.

"No they didn't. You're here because you deserve to be here. Fact Number Two: You kept up with your studies during the semester, right?"

"Pretty well, I guess."

"Fact Number Three: You just told me you spent six weeks of very intensive work preparing your outlines?"

"Yes. Wasted effort, I'm afraid."

"Not wasted at all. So here's what it all adds up to: You're a smart guy, you've been studying hard all semester long, and you just finished a very thorough review of your materials as you prepared those outlines. You could take those exams right now and you'd do just fine."

Jake was struck by her words. They made sense. More than that, however, he was struck by her presence. She was perfectly still as she spoke. She didn't gesture, and didn't move her head or her eyes, which looked directly into his, conveying a sense of confidence and wisdom. Although she was casually dressed in blue jeans and a white sweatshirt, she was extremely attractive. More than just pretty, Jake thought. Exotic. She was clearly of Asian descent, with lustrous black hair and deep dark eyes, but her complexion and facial features suggested Caucasian ancestry as well.

Jake put his hand on his forehead and looked toward the ceiling. "God, I must sound pathetic. I'm sorry. I've been so wrapped up in my studies, and I'm surrounded by people in the same situation. It's hard to look at things objectively. Sometimes it helps to talk with someone from the outside world to get some perspective. Thank you."

"You're welcome," she replied, seeming pleased that perhaps she had brought some comfort to him. "You know, in my opinion, spending too much time studying before finals can be counterproductive. There's a point of diminishing returns. A lot of people put so much stress on themselves and get so exhausted with the preparation process that it actually impairs their performance come exam time. I believe you get more benefit from being well rested and relaxed than cramming in additional hours of study time at the end. There's an old Chinese proverb that says *When your mental faculties are put to a test, the state of your mind matters more than what's in it.*"

"Really?"

She laughed, a cheerful, hearty laugh. "No, not really. I just made that up. But there should be. Don't sweat it. You're going to do just fine, I'm sure of it. You should be, too."

"Thanks for the chat," said Jake. "And the song. It really helped. By the way, my name's Jake."

"Amanda," she replied, with a warm smile, extending her hand. "Good luck on your finals, Jake. You'll do great. If I were you, I'd spend more time playing your guitar and less on last minute cramming. Bye." Then she was gone.

Jake played a couple of upbeat songs, then returned to his room, his spirits buoyed considerably. He actually felt relaxed, and relished that feeling. That girl, that stranger who knew nothing about him, had somehow seen his situation far more clearly than he had been able to, and had changed his entire outlook. He would bring a new approach to his finals preparation. His first step toward developing the right mindset would be to take the night off and relax. It had been weeks since he had given himself the luxury of an evening off, and the thought of it made him almost giddy. It seemed reckless and daring.

Tony walked into their dorm room a short time later, in search of some aspirin, and was stunned to find his roommate lying on the floor in front of their tiny television, watching an episode of *The Andy Griffith Show*. His jaw dropped. "What the hell are you doing?" he asked.

"Watching Andy Griffith." Jake replied matter-of-factly, still staring at the TV. "This is a great episode. It's the one where Barney—"

"Are you out of your mind? We don't have time for Barney Fife! Finals are eight days away! If there's anyone here behind the eight ball right now it's you." His demeanor quickly changed from astonishment to concern. "You're not just giving up, are you? I know your outlines are gone, but that's no reason to throw in the towel."

"Do you believe in guardian angels?" Jake asked, turning away from Andy Griffith and looking directly at Tony.

"What are you talking about?"

"I spent all day trying to decipher other people's outlines, and it turned out to be a hopeless task. By six o'clock, I had reached a point of total despair. I needed a break to collect myself, so I went to the back stairwell to play my guitar for a little while. So there I was, sitting in that dingy stairwell, a place where I'd never seen another human being before, totally isolated from the outside world, when out of nowhere appears this beautiful woman. We sang a song together, and I told her about my plight. She talked through the situation with me and really helped me gain some perspective. Did you know that there's an old Chinese proverb that says something like 'your state of mind matters more than what you've crammed into it?'"

"Sounds to me like you've been hallucinating. Are you okay?"

"I feel great. I'm more relaxed than I've been in weeks."

"I can't believe this! Last night you were on the verge of despair, and now you're cool as can be, reciting some Far Eastern mystic crap. Are you serious about this girl? Who is she? What's her name?"

"Her name is Amanda, that's all I know. She's definitely for real. Relax, man, I'm not crazy. I'm fine."

"And you're not giving up on finals?"

"After all the work I've put in, hell no! I'm just planning on a more unconventional approach to my preparation, since I don't have much choice."

"Which is?"

"I don't know yet. I'll figure that out tomorrow. Right now, I need to see if Barney and Thelma Lou get back together," he said, turning back to the TV.

Over the next week, Jake developed a new study technique. He walked. He ran. Occasionally, he would stop and rest at scenic spots. All the while, he reviewed his courses in his mind. Each day was devoted to a different subject, and with each subject, he tried to remember everything covered during the first semester. He approached it chronologically, starting with the first day of class and working all the way through the end of the semester. He used no notes, no books, and no outlines. The only written materials he referred to was a table of contents from his textbook and the course syllabus distributed at the beginning of the semester. This enabled him to identify all of the subjects covered and make sure he hadn't forgotten any important topic. With that as his checklist, he tried to recall everything he could about each subject. To his surprise, Jake found that he had little diffi- culty remembering the essential points he had included in his outline, and often could visualize exactly what he had written in the outline on any particular subject. He was amazed at how much he was able to recall when he set his mind to this exercise.

This routine served two purposes. First, it was an effective and methodical way of reviewing the course material and reinforcing his grasp of it, as well as how it all fit together. Second, spending time in the great outdoors under the California skies continued to have a positive effect on his mental outlook. Unlike the draining effect he experienced from long days and nights surrounded by the sterile walls and the fluorescent lights of the law library, his long leisurely trips around campus left him feeling relaxed and in good spirits.

Another key element of Jake's new approach to exam preparation was building rest and relaxation into his schedule. He forced himself to get eight hours of sleep per night, a luxury he had not permitted himself since school began. He took a regular break around midmorning to pick up a newspaper and read the sports section. Late in the afternoon, he would shoot baskets for thirty minutes, and purposely avoid thinking about finals while he did so. And, at seven o'clock in the evening, he turned on the TV and watched the exploits of Andy Taylor, Barney Fife and the other residents of Mayberry. Something about that seemed so incongruous with the atmosphere surrounding final exams at Stanford Law School, that he took an almost perverse pleasure in it.

When he allowed himself a break from his mental exercises and cleared his mind of legal concepts, Jake's thoughts continually drifted back to his experience in the stairwell. He tried to recall as much as he could about his encounter with the mystery girl, as Tony called her. He remembered her words, and her voice. He vividly recalled her face—the fine features, the fetching smile, and the intelligent eyes. Most of all, he remembered her presence, and the effect she had had upon him. Dwelling on those thoughts became a source of pleasure, yet it also sparked another reaction—a compelling desire to see her again. He had no idea what he would say or do if he did. After all, he knew nothing about her. What he did know, beyond any doubt, was that there was something special about this girl. So he looked for her, everywhere he went.

When finals arrived, Jake felt well rested and relaxed. When they were over, he thought about what the girl had said. She was right. He honestly believed that he would have been no more prepared if he had spent every waking moment of the last ten days poring over his outlines. He was confident that he had done just fine.

As his plane soared high over the Sierra Nevada Mountains, taking him back to Chicago for Christmas break, Jake reflected upon the last four months. He had come to California without knowing a soul. Now he had an entirely new group of close friends. He had come there without ever having laid eyes on California and not knowing what to expect. He had developed a real love for this place—the stunning surroundings, the outdoor lifestyle, the weather—everything about it. He had come to Stanford not knowing how he would measure up with the most gifted law students in the country, and he thought about what Professor Farris said on the first day of class. Farris had been right. He belonged there.

He also thought about the girl—Amanda. Of all the memorable experiences during his first semester at Stanford, his encounter with her was the most memorable. Since the moment she walked out of the stairwell, Jake had rebuked himself for not getting her full name, or phone number or finding out where she lived, or anything about her. At this moment, however, he was just grateful for the encounter. Maybe someday he'd see her again, and be able to properly thank her. Even if that didn't happen, Jake was happy that their paths had crossed, if only for a few moments, and was grateful for the memory. Life is made up of special moments, he thought, and his meeting with Amanda would be a moment he would treasure, even if he never saw her again.

As he drifted off to sleep, Jake smiled to himself, knowing that, for the first time in his life, he was exactly where he wanted to be, doing what he wanted to do. The sense of restlessness and longing that had always been part of his consciousness had been appeased. Life was very good.

CHAPTER 7

T he First Years returned from the holiday break feeling confident and optimistic. The nervousness and uncertainty of the
first semester was behind them. They had survived their first
set of final exams, and proven to themselves and to each other that
they did indeed belong at Stanford Law School.

Jake dove eagerly back into his studies, and also resumed his
routine of afternoon exercise under the California skies. Promptly
at three o'clock, he would either set out on a five-mile run or spend
an hour cruising the area on the secondhand racing bicycle he had
purchased. Occasionally, as he was running or cycling, he would see
someone who, from a distance or from behind, looked like she might
be the girl from the stairwell. On each such occasion, he felt a surge of
hope, only to be disappointed when it turned out to be someone else.
In the evenings, after completing his studies, Jake would frequently
take his guitar to the back stairwell. He felt drawn there, not only
because it was an effective way to decompress, but also because some
part of him held out hope he might encounter the mystery girl there
once again.

In late January, Jake, Tony and Rick resumed their afternoon
routine of pickup basketball games at the Athletic Center, and several
weeks later, the law school team began playing intramural games on

Thursday evenings. Jake's game was soon as sharp as it had ever been. His prolific scoring, coupled with Rick's leadership and intensity, made the law school team a juggernaut within the intramural league. No one could touch them.

For Jake, playing as a teammate of Rick Black, the Indiana University superstar, was a thrill. Rick was spectacular, and yet Jake was able to hold his own. On the court, they clicked perfectly. There was an undeniable chemistry between them that was on display for all to see. After each game, the two of them felt like they had not only achieved another conquest, but had put on a show.

After going undefeated and winning the intramural championship, the law school team gathered at one of the local watering holes. It was early April, and about time to begin gearing up for finals, but the team felt entitled to a celebration. Rick poured Jake a cold beer from the pitcher and said, "Awesome season, man! It's great running the floor with you. We should get together and play in Chicago over the summer. Have you heard about the summer league at City College?"

The City College summer league was well known by Chicago basketball aficionados. The teams were made up largely of NBA hopefuls from major colleges, a few high school superstars, and players who had previously enjoyed brief stints at the professional level and still dreamed of getting back there. "I've heard about it," Jake replied, "but those guys are way out of my league."

"Bullshit! I've gotten into some games there over the past few summers. It's a kick! It's rough as hell but the talent is amazing—best anywhere outside the NBA. We'd never be able to enter a team, but what you do is you go hang out there, and sometimes you can get into a game if a team is shorthanded or someone gets hurt. Even if you don't get in, it's great just to watch. We've got to go."

"Sounds great," Jake replied. "Call me anytime."

As second semester finals drew near, the First Years approached them with less fear but all the intensity of the first semester. Although Jake had survived without his outlines the previous semester, he was not willing to test fate again, and so he diligently and methodically went about the outlining process once more. From his first semester experience, however, he did learn the value of balancing his study schedule with an adequate amount of rest and relaxation. When the two-week finals period arrived, Jake felt prepared, relaxed and confident. He expected that the Contracts, Torts and Constitutional Law exams would be the most difficult, and all three were scheduled during the first week. After finishing those exams, Jake felt that the home stretch would be like a walk in the park. Civil Procedure and Property were scheduled for the following Tuesday and Wednesday. Those were his strongest subjects, and he had plenty of time to prepare.

As he strolled back toward the dorm after his Constitutional Law final late Friday morning, Jake saw Kelly walking ahead of him, and hurried to catch up with her. "We're almost there, girlfriend!" Jake shouted exuberantly as he gave Kelly an enthusiastic high-five.

"I know. I can't believe it! We've got nothing until next Tuesday. I'll be celebrating tonight!"

"Good for you. What have you got planned?"

"My college roommate, Kathleen, is having a party. She's in medical school here, and they just finished their finals. Should be a wild time! Hey, why don't you come along? It's really a fun crowd."

"Thanks, but I'm wiped out. I don't think I'd be much fun. I'm going to sleep for about twelve hours, and maybe I'll party tomorrow night."

"Oh, you're such a bore." She shoved him playfully. "You need a life outside of law school, Jake. If you get a second wind before eight o'clock tonight, let me know. You'd really be perfectly welcome."

Jake arrived in his dorm room and flopped down on his bed, intending to rest his eyes for a few minutes. It was nearly three hours later when he awoke with a start, feeling disoriented but blissfully well rested. He donned his running shoes and briskly jogged into one of the nearby residential neighborhoods. His route took him several miles off campus, and he stopped at a supermarket for a cold drink. He noticed a shiny black BMW parked near the entrance and thought that it might be Rick's, and that perhaps he could get a lift home. Upon closer examination, he realized that the car was parked in a disabled parking space and had a disabled tag hanging from the rearview mirror. It must be somebody else, he thought, as he walked past the vehicle into the store. He found the refrigerated section and contemplated his choices among the various sports drinks.

"McShane! Forget the Gatorade, grab some beer! Even you aren't studying tonight, I hope!" The boisterous greeting came from Rick, who was standing at the other end of the cooler, accompanied by two attractive young women. He was pushing a shopping cart piled high with beer and wine and an assortment of snacks.

"Hi Rick. Save some for the rest of us, will you?" replied Jake, gesturing toward the grocery cart.

Rick stuck out his hand and gave Jake a hearty handshake. "Three down, two to go! We're almost there. Hey, meet my friends. This is Cheryl," he said, turning toward to the petite redhead to his right, "and this is Mary Ann," nodding toward the other, a well-built brunette, who looked like a runner. "Girls, this is Jake McShane, one of my classmates. When he doesn't have his head buried in the books, he's the best basketball player on campus."

"Yeah, right," said Jake, embarrassed, but appreciating the compliment. He changed the subject quickly. "Looks like someone's getting ready for a party."

"They're medical students," Rick replied, "and they just finished their finals, so they're having a little celebration tonight."

"Why don't you join us?" asked Cheryl, flashing a friendly smile. "We're a bunch of nerds most of the year, but we can really party when we put our minds to it. And tonight, we'll really be putting our minds to it!"

"I think there may be a shortage of good-looking guys there too," Mary Ann chimed in, smiling seductively. "You really should stop by."

"Thanks for the offer. Maybe I will. Where's the party?"

After they gave him the address, Jake said, "I better hit the road. I've got a long walk ahead of me. It's been nice meeting you."

"You're walking?" Rick asked. "It's got to be three miles. I'll give you a lift, if you don't mind stopping by Cheryl's place to unload this stuff."

Sure enough, the car parked right in front was Rick's. The four of them hopped in and drove a short distance to a tidy, one-story stucco house, unloaded the groceries, and left the girls to their party preparations. On their way back to the dorm, Rick explained, "I dated a medical student a couple of months ago—not either of those two. It only lasted a short time, but I got to meet their crowd and started hanging around with some of them. It's a fun group, and there are a lot more women than in law school—better looking too!" He laughed and slapped Jake on the shoulder. "A couple of law students hang out with this crowd, too. Their other roommate is a good friend of Kelly's, so she'll probably be there tonight."

"She will. I saw her earlier today, and she told me she was going to a party with a bunch of medical students. She invited me along, but I told her I'd probably pass."

"Well, now you've been invited twice. I think it's just meant to be, pal—you better go."

Jake looked hesitant, and Rick continued. "Listen, this crowd is going to be blowing off a lot of steam tonight. They'll be drinking hard. They'll be rowdy and uninhibited. I'd say the odds of getting lucky are pretty damn high—even for you!" Rick laughed hard, clearly in a jovial mood and looking forward to the evening.

"What's with this?" Jake asked, pointing to the disabled parking tag hanging from Rick's rearview mirror.

"You know what a bitch it is to park around here. And all those disabled parking spaces just going to waste. They're never used. I've made connections with people in the local medical community, and one of them fixed me up with this." There was a tone of pride in his voice as he flicked the tag with his finger.

"You're a piece of work." Jake felt indignant, but he was in a great mood and not about to argue.

"Hey, I would never take a disabled parking space if there's someone else who really needs it, but there never is. Really, how many disabled people drive cars? I'm just doing my part for the environment. I don't have to drive around burning gas looking for a goddamn parking space. Look at this—beautiful!" said Rick as he pulled into a disabled space directly in front of the dorm. "Door-to-door service! If you want to go to the party tonight, be down here at eight o'clock."

Jake generally did not like attending social events where he did not know many people, especially parties. Making small talk with a roomful of strangers was not his idea of fun. Ordinarily, he would've found some reason to avoid going to the party; however, the nap, the exercise, the sunshine, and the fact that he had just completed his three toughest finals, had him in high spirits. He would know at least a few people there, Rick and Kelly, and Cheryl and Mary Ann seemed friendly. So, what the hell, he thought. Why not?

Jake left the dorm with Rick promptly at eight o'clock. As they approached Cheryl's house, they could see that the party was already in full swing. Cars lined the street and the sound of music and boisterous voices could be heard from some distance.

Someone yelled Rick's name as they entered the crowded living room, and he made his way toward the voice, leaving Jake standing alone in the doorway, holding the bottle of wine he had brought for his hostesses. He headed toward the kitchen to deliver the wine, and saw Kelly talking with Cheryl and several other young women. Kelly stopped in mid-sentence when she saw him approaching. "Jake McShane! You made it! I never thought you'd come." She gave him a friendly hug. He'd never seen Kelly this animated, and suspected immediately that she was a bit tipsy.

"Hi Jake. I'm so glad you came," said Cheryl, also giving him a warm hug.

"So am I. Thanks for having me," said Jake. It seemed like a friendly crowd, and he immediately felt at ease.

Kelly poured him a glass of wine. "Come on, let me introduce you to my friends," she said, grabbing him by the arm.

"Do you know most of these people?"

"Yep, just about all of them. It's really a great bunch. You'll see."

Jake's circle of friends in Palo Alto was limited to his law school classmates. He was impressed, as well as a bit envious, to see that Kelly had so many friends and acquaintances outside of law school. Kelly introduced Jake to her former roommate, Kathleen, and the two of them escorted him through the living room, introducing him to a small army of exuberant medical students, most of whom were inebriated or well on their way toward that state.

Mary Ann found them and welcomed Jake to the party. He thanked her for the invitation and complimented her on the great party. "There's plenty of food in the next room, so help yourself," said Mary Ann, gesturing toward a large table of snacks and appetizers in the middle of the adjacent dining room. Jake's gaze followed her hand and he started to say something, but abruptly stopped. He saw a short, skinny young man in a Hawaiian shirt holding a plate of food, chatting with an extremely attractive young woman Jake recognized immediately: the mystery girl from the stairwell. Amanda.

Both his tongue and his feet froze momentarily. "I think I'll take you up on that," he replied, regaining his composure, as he walked casually into the dining room. Amanda saw him as he approached and flashed a welcoming smile.

"I hope I'm not interrupting. I just wanted to say hello," said Jake politely.

"Nice to see you again, and under happier circumstances," Amanda replied, extending her hand. "I see you survived your little crisis."

"I did, and I've been hoping ever since that I would see you again to say thanks. Your words of wisdom really helped."

She laughed. "I'm happy to hear that."

"So you're a medical student?" Jake asked.

"No, she's a doctor," interjected the young man in the Hawaiian shirt, looking impatient. Amanda introduced him as David, a second-year medical student. "You're halfway through your residency, right, Doc?" David asked.

"You seem surprised." Amanda said, addressing Jake.

"I don't know why I should be—you've got a great bedside manner." Jake could see that David was irritated by his presence, so he decided to politely excuse himself. "Well, sorry to interrupt. See you later."

"I hope so," Amanda replied brightly.

Jake walked away, trying to appear calm, despite the fact that his head was spinning. Although their conversation could not have lasted two minutes, her manner had completely captivated him once again, just as it had during their first encounter. She radiated cheerful friendliness, and at the same time, her voice and her eyes conveyed an impression of self-assurance and intelligence, the like of which he had never encountered.

Jake wandered back into the living room and found Kelly, who was in the midst of a heated debate over whether medical school was more taxing than law school. From where Jake stood, he had a clear view into the dining room and could see that Rick was now visiting with Amanda. He felt a twinge of concern. "Hey, Kelly, do you know that girl talking with Rick?" Jake asked.

"That's Amanda Chang. Why? Got your eye on her, Jake?" she teased him, and much too loudly, as far as Jake was concerned. Kelly was more than a little tipsy now.

"I met her briefly once. I was just curious. What's her story?" Jake asked, trying to sound nonchalant.

Kelly paused for a moment, collecting her thoughts. "Look around this house, Jake. Think about how much talent is right here. Stanford law students. Stanford medical students. Every person in this room is extremely gifted. But Amanda is in a league of her own. Really, I mean it. She began medical school when she was twenty. She hasn't even finished her residency yet, and she's already appearing as a guest lecturer at the medical school and making presentations before faculty and Medical Center staff on groundbreaking research projects. She's special. And despite all that, she's the most down-to-earth person you'd ever want to meet. She's fun, she's friendly, and she's really sweet. Come on, you need to meet her." Kelly grabbed his arm and began pulling Jake toward the dining room. His attempts to explain that they had already met went unheeded.

"Amanda, I'd like you to meet one of my classmates, Jake McShane." Jake tried to interrupt her to point out that they had already met, but Kelly would not be deterred. "Jake is a great guy, a real pal. He's one of the most well liked guys in our entire class. Everyone admires him. He's kind of quiet, but very confident and poised. He's thoughtful and articulate in class. And thoughtful outside of class, too. He's nice to me even when I'm a total bitch during finals, right, Jake?" Jake looked at Amanda and shrugged a helpless shrug, as Kelly went on. "I'd be throwing myself at him, but I hear he doesn't like to date law students. What a shame!" She looked at Jake with an exaggerated pout-face, then broke into a loud, drunken laugh.

Jake was embarrassed, and looked it. "You're too kind, Kelly."

Kelly then began her introduction of Amanda. "Amanda has already graduated from medical school. She—"

Amanda interrupted Kelly before she had a chance to get rolling again. "Jake and I have already met, several months ago."

Kelly gave Jake a look of surprise. "Why didn't you tell me?" Then she laughed again and said, "Sorry, I'm a little buzzed," and hurried off in another direction.

"Well, that was embarrassing," said Jake sheepishly.

"She obviously has a high opinion of you. That's nothing to be embarrassed about," Amanda said with a smile. "I trust finals are going a little better this time around?"

"Much better. I'm a lot more relaxed. Actually, I did get my act together last semester after you saw me. I took your advice and put a little positive mental attitude to work, and everything turned out okay. So tell me about your residency program. How do you like it?"

Jake was thrilled to actually have some time alone with Amanda, and looked forward to getting beyond party chitchat and having a real conversation. He learned that she'd gone to Stanford as an under-graduate, but had grown up about an hour away, in Berkeley, where both of her parents were professors. She was halfway through her four-year residency program at Stanford Medical Center, where she was focusing on geriatric medicine. She started asking about his background, and as Jake mentioned that he was from Chicago, David returned and began a discourse on the Chicago political scene. Soon several other revelers joined the group, bringing an end to the private conversation Jake had been enjoying. After a few minutes, he politely excused himself, not wanting it to appear to Amanda or anyone else that he was hovering around her.

Jake mingled with the celebrating medical students, although he continually glanced around the room, subtly watching Amanda. He felt somewhat dismayed to see that Rick was spending a great deal of time with her, as was David. Jake kept his distance, not wanting to make a nuisance of himself. He wandered into the living room and spent several minutes browsing through the collection of CDs. "I like that one," he heard a voice behind him as he picked up a Jimmy Buffett CD. It was Amanda. "Can you play any of those songs on your guitar?"

"No, but I'd sure like to learn some of these."

"I like your taste in music. You didn't happen to bring your guitar, did you?"

"No, I don't play much in public."

"Stage fright?"

"No, a more fundamental problem—lack of talent. I'm just not very good."

"Oh come on, you're being modest. I'm sure you have loads of talent."

"I really don't, honestly. I don't think I have a musical bone in my body. Whatever skill I've acquired is based on sheer stubbornness and perseverance. A few years ago, I made up my mind that I'd learn to play, and forced myself to practice virtually every day for about two years. I've developed some proficiency just by working at it, but it's not something I have any natural gift for. The stairwell at the dorm makes me sound much better than I really am. But you, you can really sing! You're a natural."

"Oh, please, stop." She laughed again, that easy, natural laugh.

Jake noticed that her wineglass was empty. "Can I get you a refill?" he asked.

"Thank you. I'd love one," she replied, handing him her glass.

Jake walked onto the back porch, where a makeshift bar had been set up on a picnic table. He poured a glass of Chardonnay for Amanda, then walked to the nearby ice chest in search of a beer. "Grab one for me while you're at it, pal." Rick had just walked out looking for another cold beer. Jake handed him one. "I'm on a roll, man," said Rick in a low voice. "I'll be getting lucky tonight, that's for sure. That Chinese chick is crazy about me. You know what they say—you ain't a man 'til you get a Chan!" He laughed loudly and slapped Jake on the back.

"You're a pig."

"I know. I admit it," Rick replied, as if that were a compliment. "Just watch and learn, pal." He strutted back into the house.

Jake followed Rick inside and brought Amanda her wine. Rick was already talking with her, and turned his back toward Jake in a not so subtle attempt to cut him out of the conversation. After a few moments of watching Rick trying to lay on all his considerable charm, Jake walked back into the kitchen, where he found Mary Ann and Cheryl comparing notes about which guest was the most drunk. The debate was settled as David tottered toward them, spilling his red wine as he walked. "We've got a winner," said Cheryl, and they both laughed heartily, leaving Jake alone with the drunken know-it-all. David looked at his glass and launched into a lecture about the nutritional properties of the various types of red wine. Just as Jake was trying to think of a polite excuse for walking away, Amanda appeared and asked, "Can I steal you away for a few minutes? I'd like to get your thoughts on a legal matter." She gave him a look that made it perfectly clear that she knew what he had been enduring.

"Certainly," Jake replied, hoping his sense of relief was not too obvious. "Excuse me, David. I'd love to hear more about the superior nutritional qualities of French wines, but that'll have to wait."

They walked away, back toward the living room, leaving David swaying as he walked off in search of another patient soul.

"Thank you," Jake said. He didn't need to explain why. "Now, regarding my legal advice, just remember that free advice is worth what you pay for it."

"Sorry, I just made that up. You were being very patient with David, but I thought you could probably use a break."

"Thanks again. I owe you."

"I've been visiting with Rick. Are you and he close friends?"

"I've gotten to know him pretty well. We're classmates, and we live in the same dorm. We play basketball together. But I wouldn't say we're close."

"He seems like a pretty impressive guy," Amanda remarked.

Jake's heart sank. "No question about that," he agreed, trying to sound matter-of-fact.

"He's also pretty impressed with himself, isn't he?"

"What makes you say that?"

"Well, within five minutes of meeting him, he told me that he was a basketball star in college, his father is loaded, and he plans on graduating at the top of your class. Also, I hear from my friends that he's quite the ladies' man."

"I'm sure you can take care of yourself," Jake said, with a grin, feeling relieved.

They picked up where they had left off in their prior conversation. Jake attempted to explain his impressions of the differences between life in Chicago and his experience thus far in California. He talked about Chicago's ethnic communities and his own Irish Catholic neighborhood and upbringing. He was surprised to learn that Amanda was raised Catholic also. Her mother was of Italian descent and a devout Catholic, and had passed her faith along to her daughter. He listened with keen interest as Amanda spoke in reverent tones about her paternal grandmother, whose parents had sent her to San Francisco from China at the age of fourteen in search of a better life. She quickly learned English, became a nurse, and went to work at San Francisco General Hospital. However, her true calling, Amanda explained, was caring for the residents of her Chinatown community, who were not comfortable dealing with the American medical establishment. As a child, Amanda had often accompanied her grandmother on her visits to the sick and the elderly in Chinatown, and it was that experience that had inspired her to pursue a career in medicine.

After a while, they both found themselves straining to speak over the noise, which had been steadily increasing. They stepped outside onto the back porch, hoping to escape the din. Before long, the music was cranked up louder as the living room became a dance floor.

Jake had been thoroughly enjoying his conversation with Amanda, and was thrilled that she seemed to be enjoying his company as well, and had actually sought him out a couple of times during the evening. He was eager to continue their conversation, but the raucous partying was becoming a hindrance. She seemed to be reading his thoughts.

"How would you like to take a little walk and get away from this noise for awhile," she asked, a bit shyly.

"Great idea. I'd love to."

They worked their way through the crowded house toward the front door, passing Rick on their way out. He said nothing, but looked at them with obvious surprise, which to Jake seemed to transform into an angry glare as they walked out the door.

"What a great party," said Jake as they walked from the house. "I'm really glad I came."

"So am I," said Amanda.

They walked at a leisurely pace toward campus. Beyond the immediate vicinity of the party, all was quiet, since it was well past midnight. The sky was clear; there was no breeze; it was neither warm nor cool; just another perfect night in Palo Alto.

They walked for some time, and eventually found themselves back on campus, looking up at Hoover Tower, Stanford's most famous landmark. The moon shone brightly and illuminated the pale walls of the three-hundred-foot-tall structure. The normally bustling locale seemed eerily quiet and deserted as they sat on the edge of the circular fountain in the plaza beneath the tower. They sat there talking deep into the night, oblivious to the passing of time. They talked about their families, places they had been, and places they wanted to go. They spoke of their childhood and college experiences, and their professional aspirations. They talked about faith and religion, and countless other subjects, light and deep. Jake had never found it so easy to converse with anyone, and he had never found it so pleasurable just to be with someone. He was enthralled just listening to her, and looking at her. More than once during the evening, as he stole a glance at her striking face, he thought to himself, I could spend the rest of my life with this woman. He didn't know whether it was a premonition or wishful thinking, but it felt good just contemplating that notion.

It was still dark when they heard birds beginning to chirp, and before long the sky to the east began to brighten. "I can't remember the last time I stayed out all night," said Amanda.

"I've done far more all-nighters than I care to admit," said Jake. "With the books," he added quickly, so that she wouldn't get the wrong impression. They walked back in the general direction of the party, but veered off toward Amanda's apartment before they got there. Jake walked Amanda to her door. "I've had a great evening, Amanda. Can I see you again?" he asked.

"I'd like that," Amanda replied.

"I finish finals on Wednesday. There's a new play at the Student Center Wednesday evening. How would you like to meet for pizza at Milano's around six, and then see the show at eight?"

"That sounds great, but can we make it a bit later? I'm working until six o'clock on Wednesday, but I could meet you at the restaurant by six thirty."

"Perfect. See you then."

Amanda pulled a small leather bound notebook out of her pocket and made a note of it: "Wednesday 6:30—Jake at Milano's." Jake extended his hand, feeling rather awkward, but not wanting to seem too forward or presumptuous. She laughed and gave him a warm hug. "Goodnight, Jake. See you on Wednesday. And good luck with finals!"

Jake leisurely walked back to the dorm. It was nearly six o'clock by the time he reached his room. He knew he should try to get some sleep, so that he would be sufficiently rested and alert to study for finals, but he was wide awake. He laid down anyway, and dozed lightly. The previous night's events replayed themselves in his mind, over and over, preventing him from achieving any sort of deep sleep. After a few hours, he gave up trying.

He had missed breakfast at the dorm, so he decided to grab an omelet at a nearby café. He sang softly to himself as he walked, basking in the feeling that life was very good at this moment. He noticed the spring flowers all around him, and the fragrance of jasmine in the fresh morning air. California had never seemed so enticing. He congratulated himself on the wisdom of his decision to move there. He thought about law school, how much he truly enjoyed it, and complimented himself for choosing a profession that suited him so perfectly. He thought about all of the close friends he'd made over the past year, and how Stanford had really become his new home. Mostly, however, he thought about Amanda.

He tried to recall as much as he could about his time with her at the party and afterwards. He thought about things she had said, the way she looked, the way she smiled and laughed. He remembered how good it felt to talk with her. He had never had a conversation like that with anyone. They had talked all night long, and it was effortless. The image of her face kept flashing through his mind, and he did his best to keep it there. Wednesday could not come soon enough.

His musings were interrupted when he saw Rick standing in line at the café, ordering a large cup of black coffee. "Late night, McShane? I left at four o'clock and you weren't back yet."

"Sorry, Rick, I hope you weren't waiting for me. It did turn into a late night. It was almost six o'clock by the time I got home."

"I saw you leaving with that Chinese girl. What do you think you're doing, horning in on my action like that?" Rick said, with a pretense of jesting, although the edge in his voice was not lost on Jake.

"She asked me if I wanted to take a walk. How could I say no?" Jake replied casually, trying hard not to gloat.

"Yeah, right. That must have been a pretty long goddamn walk," Rick muttered as he walked out the door.

Amanda slept soundly for several hours and awoke feeling cheerful and energetic. She had planned on devoting the day to her latest research project, but just now she was not in the mood. She wanted to spend some time with people rather than books. She couldn't wait to tell someone about last night.

She put on a running outfit, and jogged back to the scene of the party, arriving just before noon. The inhabitants were moving slowly. Cheryl and Mary Ann were dressed in shabby sweat clothes, seated at the kitchen table drinking Cokes, and munching on leftover hors d'oeuvres. They were sharing observations about the previous evening's events and had made no movement toward beginning the massive cleanup effort that would be necessary to undo the night's damage.

"Good morning, ladies," Amanda called out cheerfully as she walked in. "Just thought I'd drop by to help you put your house back together."

"Why are you so chipper this morning? Weren't you up all night like the rest of us?" asked Cheryl in a hoarse voice.

"Look at you! You look like you're ready to run a marathon. This isn't fair," said Mary Ann, noticing Amanda's jogging attire, as well as her clear eyes and obvious perkiness.

Kelly staggered out of a bedroom, still wearing last night's outfit, which she had obviously worn to bed. "Rise and shine, sleepyhead! It's past noon already," Amanda sang out as she busily picked up bottles and cans that littered every surface in the house.

"Where's the aspirin," Kelly moaned, rubbing her temples. "And why are you so annoyingly happy?"

Cheryl, Mary Ann and Kelly looked at each other, then looked at Amanda as she scurried about the kitchen, tossing empties into a large trash bag and singing to herself as she did so.

"You got lucky last night, didn't you?" shouted Mary Ann, suddenly becoming animated. "That's what it is!"

"Holy Shit! Who was it?" Cheryl asked.

Amanda stopped her cleaning and faced them, beaming.

"You and Jake? Are you serious?" asked Kelly.

"Let's just say I had a wonderful evening," said Amanda coyly, still beaming.

"You and Jake?" Kelly asked again, her astonishment quickly transformed into excitement. "Amanda, that is so great! Two of my favorite people. He's such a great guy. What a perfect match. I can't believe it!" She let out a shriek and gave Amanda an exuberant hug. "Details, I want details!"

"Yeah, lay it on us," Cheryl demanded. "We want the complete play-by-play, the whole night."

"Well, we left here a little after midnight, and stayed out until dawn, just walking and talking."

"And what else? Did you invite him back to your place?" asked Mary Ann.

"Nothing else. We just walked and talked, all night long. He walked me home and we said goodnight around six o'clock this morning."

"And that's all? He didn't even make a pass at you?" Cheryl asked.

"He was way too much of a gentleman. I had such a great evening. I can't remember the last time I was able to talk with a guy like that. In fact, I never have. It just felt so right. And no, that's not all. We have a date Wednesday night."

Amanda's three friends looked at her, speechless for a moment. Then all three simultaneously shrieked in delight and wrapped her in a group embrace.

As Amanda walked toward the Medical Center early Monday morning, she saw Dr. Marsh getting out of her car, and waved from across the parking lot. "Good morning, Dr. Marsh," she called out enthusiastically as Dr. Marsh approached her. "How was your weekend?"

"Hello, Amanda. My weekend was just fine. How was yours?"

"It was super!"

Dr. Marsh looked at her with curiosity. The tone of Amanda's voice was a giveaway. This was no ordinary weekend. "Really? Did you do anything special?"

"I met someone."

Dr. Marsh stopped in her tracks and peered at Amanda over the rims of her glasses. "Someone with potential?"

"I think so," said Amanda, feeling like a schoolgirl revealing a new crush. "I really think so."

Amanda made her rounds cheerfully that morning. Her patients and colleagues noticed nothing unusual, since she was always a bundle of positive energy. But inside, she felt different. Wednesday evening was never far from her mind.

Just as she was about to break for a quick lunch, she heard her name being paged over the public address system. She picked up the nearest phone, and the operator connected her to an outside caller.

"Amanda?" She recognized her father's voice, and immediately became alarmed. He had never called her at work before.

"Hi, Daddy. Is everything okay?"

"I'm afraid there's been an accident. Grandma fell on some stairs this morning. She's just been admitted to San Francisco General. It looks like she broke her hip."

"Oh no," Amanda gasped, knowing instantly how devastating this would be to such an active woman who thrived on her independence. "How bad is it?"

"We don't know. They haven't taken x-rays yet, but the ambulance driver and the emergency room staff seemed certain that it's broken. She's in a lot of pain and is really upset, as you might imagine."

"I'm on my way, Daddy. I'll be there as fast I can," she said, tears welling up in her eyes.

"Are you able to get away from work?"

"It's Grandma. I have to be there," she stammered, her voice breaking. "They'll just have to do without me for awhile."

Two hours later, she was in her car, heading north toward San Francisco.

CHAPTER 8

J ake tried hard to focus on his exams, but found studying difficult. By Tuesday afternoon, he had finished his Civil Procedure exam and was doing his best to get in one more solid study session that afternoon for his Property final, which was the following morning.

He was engrossed in his Property outline in the dorm's study lounge when Rick approached him in his gym attire, in high spirits, since he had already completed his last final. "McShane! How about some hoops? Give that massive brain of yours a little break."

"Sorry, Rick, can't do it," Jake replied, barely looking up. "I need a few more hours of study time."

Rick teased and cajoled for a few minutes, and then realized he was not going to change Jake's mind. "Mind if I borrow your basketball?"

"Help yourself," said Jake, tossing Rick his room key. "It's in my closet."

Rick ran up the stairs to the third floor. He heard a telephone ringing as he put the key in the lock. He ignored the ringing phone and found the basketball in the closet. As he closed the closet door, an answering machine clicked on, and Rick listened as the caller left her message. "Hi Jake. It's Amanda. It's Tuesday afternoon. I've been really looking forward to tomorrow night, but something just came up. My grand-mother broke her hip and I've had to run up to San Francisco to be with her. I'm really sorry, and I hope we can reschedule soon. If you'd like to call, you can reach me at my parents' house in Berkeley. Good luck with finals. Again, I'm really sorry and hope to hear from you soon." She left her parents' phone number as well as her cell phone number.

Rick walked over to the answering machine, searched for the erase button, and pressed it. "Take that, you son of a bitch," he whispered to himself. Then he casually walked out of the room dribbling the basketball.

Jake was seated at a table in Milano's Pizzeria by six o'clock on Wednesday evening. He was feeling jubilant to be finished with finals, but even more excited at the prospect of another evening with Amanda. He had arrived early, hoping that she might do the same, giving them more time together.

Jake was surprised when she had not arrived by 6:30. Amanda struck him as someone who would be punctual. By 6:45, she still had not arrived, and Jake's excitement was turning to concern. "Dammit!" he muttered to himself. Why hadn't he gotten her phone number? Seven o'clock came and went. Still no Amanda. It just didn't make sense. Did he have the date wrong? Did she? No, that couldn't be it. He clearly remembered her saying, "Wednesday—6:30," as she wrote it down in her notebook.

By 7:15, despair started setting in. Jake left the restaurant and walked hurriedly to the theater, hoping that perhaps she had forgotten about dinner and was waiting for him there. A small crowd was milling about in front of the box office. Amanda was not there. Maybe there was an emergency at the hospital, he thought. That would be a logical explanation. He called the Medical Center from his cell phone. After being passed around to several different stations, he was finally connected to the right one, but was dismayed to hear that she was not there. He sat glumly on a bench outside the theater until 8:00, at which time he gave up and went home, utterly dejected.

The next morning, Jake called the hospital again. He reached Amanda's station and spoke with a pleasant sounding receptionist. "Is this a medical emergency?" she asked.

"No emergency. It's a personal call. I'm just a friend." The receptionist took his name and number and promised to pass the message along.

Where was she, Jake wondered? Why hadn't she shown up? Why hadn't she even called? A feeling of panic set in. He was heading back to Chicago the next day and he had to speak with Amanda before then. He realized that during their many hours of conversation, he had not mentioned to her that he would be spending the summer in Chicago. It seemed so stupid now, but some part of him had feared that she would not be interested in striking up a relationship if she knew he was about to leave town.

On Friday morning, Jake picked up the phone in his dorm room and tried calling Amanda at the hospital again before leaving for the airport. To his dismay, the phone service in the dorm had already been disconnected. He called from his cell phone on the way to the airport, but was told that Amanda was not available. He left another message. He felt helpless, and depressed. A grim realization was setting in: For whatever reason, Amanda Chang had decided she was not interested in seeing him.

Amanda felt a deep and pervasive sadness. Her grandmother had indeed fractured her hip, rather severely as it turned out. Amanda knew the statistics. A large percentage of patients over seventy-five who fracture their hips would die within six months. On top of that depressing realization, she had broken her date with Jake, and he had not returned her call. That didn't seem to fit. He seemed so kind and understanding, how could he be angry over this? Why wouldn't he give her the courtesy of a return phone call? Friday afternoon, she decided to call him again, not caring if she came across as too forward. She found his phone number at the dorm and dialed it. A recording advised her that the number she had dialed was no longer in service.

A short time later, Mary Ann called Amanda to check on her grandmother. After providing a status report concerning her grandmother's condition, Amanda told Mary Ann about her broken date with Jake, and her inability to reach him by phone. Mary Ann mentioned that she was planning to see Rick that evening, and promised to see what she could find out.

That evening, as she and Rick drove toward one of the local music clubs, Mary Ann asked, "Where's your friend, Jake? Amanda has been trying to reach him and found out that his phone has been disconnected. She's worried. Do you know where he is?"

"Nothing to worry about," Rick replied casually. "He just went back to Chicago for the summer. He has a fiancée there, I think."

The following Monday, the new receptionist, Mrs. Norris, received a briefing on her responsibilities. The floor administrator explained the phone system, message-taking protocol, and who was who, among other things. Mrs. Norris noticed two messages taken last week for Dr. Chang, and asked about them.

"Dr. Chang has taken a leave of absence," explained the administrator. "We don't know when she'll be back. Let me see whether these are urgent and need to be passed along to someone else." She examined the messages and noted that they were both from a Mr. Jake McShane. The messages each bore the notation, "Personal call—a friend. Not urgent."

"No need to worry about these. They're just personal calls, and I'm sure her friends have figured out by now that Dr. Chang is on leave." She tossed the messages in the trash bin.

CHAPTER 9

J ust a few days before, Jake had expected to be returning home feeling like a conquering hero. Instead, a dark mood enveloped him. On the Monday following his return home, he began his employment as one of the twenty summer associates with Taylor, Martin and Moretti, one of the top-tier law firms in Chicago. This was considered a plum position, particularly for a first-year law student, and his fellow summer clerks seemed eager and excited to be there. Jake did his best to appear upbeat and positive, although it required considerable acting talent. Day and night, regardless of his surroundings or activities, thoughts of Amanda haunted him.

On Thursday afternoon of his first week, he received a call from Rick, who had just arrived home to begin working at his father's law firm for the summer. "I'll bet you're tired of that grind already. How about we head over to the City College tonight and watch the summer league play," Rick suggested.

Jake's first impulse was to make some excuse. Being around Rick might be a painful reminder of recent experiences in Palo Alto. On the other hand, he knew from past experience that basketball was a great way for him to clear his head and forget about anything else. "What the hell, why not?" he responded, warming to the idea.

City College was on the far south side of the city. Measured in miles, it was not a great distance from Jake's old neighborhood, but in other respects, it was a universe away. Like most Caucasians who knew their way around the city, Jake avoided the area, for the simple reason that it was just plain dangerous. Although the immediate vicinity was a reasonably well kept, working-class black neighborhood, it was surrounded by some of the toughest areas of the city, and there was no way to get to the college without driving through gang infested, crime-ridden slums. For hard-core basketball fans, however, there was no better place to be on a warm June evening than watching the City College summer league in action. As Jake entered the dingy gym, he was comforted to see that there were at least a few other white faces in the crowd. Some were certainly college or professional scouts. A few were guys like Rick, whose love of the game outweighed their fear for their own safety.

Jake and Rick were quickly caught up in the fast-paced battle going on before them. Rick was right, Jake thought. These guys were amazing. Rick recognized many of the players, and explained to Jake who was who. Some were enrolled in college programs around the country and had come to sharpen their game for next season. Others were former collegiate players, not ready to give up on their dreams, still hoping that the NBA would come calling. A few had briefly lived the NBA dream, and were clinging to some hope for a second chance.

Rick had been trading observations about the players with an elderly black gentleman in a White Sox baseball cap seated next to him in the bleachers. "Pretty tough brand of basketball out there, ain't it." The old man spoke in a low, gravelly voice, without taking his eyes off the game.

"No shit," Rick agreed. "I was hoping to get in on it."

The old man continued looking straight ahead, and laughed quietly, a raspy wheezing laugh. "I don't know where you've played, son, but I don't think you're ready for this shit."

"I've played here before, trying to keep my game sharp while I was in college."

"You don't say?" The old man turned and looked at Rick skeptically. "Where'd you play in college?"

"Indiana. Made it to the Final Four last year. Lost to UCLA in the championship game."

A look of recognition crossed the old man's face. "You was the point guard. I remember you now. That was a hell of a team. I don't remember seeing you out here before."

"Oh, I've played here a few times. Best basketball anywhere, outside of the NBA."

"No, it ain't. It's good—awfully damn good. But it ain't the best. I've seen better and it ain't far from here."

"Come on, better than this? No way! Where?"

"Just a couple miles from here. There's an outdoor court at an old abandoned school called St. Simon's. They got some real ballplayers there. Better than the pros, some of them."

"If they're so good, then why aren't they in the NBA?"

"I'll tell you why. These dudes got all the talent in the world, but they're fuck-ups. Most of them dropped out of school, or got thrown out. A lot of them done time. Some are gangbangers. These are guys that can't handle authority—schools, coaches, whatever. They can't play by the rules. No discipline and no character. But amazing talent, man, just amazing."

"That's where we need to go," said Rick confidently, slapping Jake on the knee.

"Oh, no. You don't need to be going there, son," said the old man. "It ain't safe. It ain't safe for nobody, but it really ain't safe for guys that look like you."

"He's right," Jake chimed in. "You're not from the South Side, Rick, but I know that area. It's as rough as it gets."

"Aw, don't be a wimp, Jake. We're not seeing any action here. We'll try there next week, Wednesday night," Rick said as if the matter had been settled.

"Sure we will," Jake replied, to bring the conversation to an end. Even a crazy thrill-seeker like Rick couldn't be serious about that proposition.

Another week went by, and Jake's mood had not improved. If anything, it had gotten worse. Every day, he thought about calling Amanda, and every day he decided he couldn't. He had left her two messages and she had not returned his calls. If he continued calling, she might consider it harassment. Obviously, for some reason he could not fathom, she had chosen to ignore him.

His job situation was not helping either. He had been under the impression that most law firms did their best to make the summer clerkship experience an enjoyable one. It was essentially a tryout for both parties. The law clerks had an opportunity to demonstrate their skills, in the hope of receiving an offer of employment following graduation. The firms did their best to sell themselves as a great place to work, so that they would have their pick of the best and brightest. With that goal in mind, most of the major firms spent a great deal of time and money entertaining the impressionable young clerks. Dinners at the city's finest restaurants, lavish parties at the elegant homes of senior partners and other less extravagant forms of entertainment such as ballgames and happy hours were all part of the routine. The firms were also careful not to overwork their summer clerks, for fear of creating the wrong impression and potentially losing bright young prospects.

Unfortunately for Jake, his experience was not off to an auspicious start. Although the firm's attorneys had been asked to be sensitive to workload issues, Jake was subject to the beck and call of any lawyer in the firm, and within a matter of a few days, he was overloaded with work. One of the young associate attorneys advised him that he needed to find tactful ways of making it clear that he was too busy to take on more assignments. When he was approached with a massive research project by Mr. Pritchard, a humorless senior partner in his late fifties, Jake politely stated that he had so many other projects pending at the moment that he would not be able to do justice to Mr. Pritchard's assignment. His words fell on deaf ears, and he found himself spending all day on both Saturday and Sunday working frantically to meet Mr. Pritchard's ambitious deadline. The following Tuesday, he missed the firm's baseball outing at Wrigley Field, as he struggled to meet another one of Pritchard's unrealistic deadlines. Feeling irritable and sorry for himself, he answered the phone brusquely when it rang late Wednesday afternoon. It was Rick.

"It's Wednesday. Remember our plan?"

"What are you talking about?"

"Basketball. At St. Simon's."

"Are you crazy? You heard that old man—we'd never make it out of there alive."

"Oh, come on, Jake. You can't go through life being a chickenshit. I do stuff like this all the time. Once they realize we're just there to play ball and they see that we can hold our own, we'll be fine."

"You haven't played anywhere like this place, Rick. I'm serious. I know the area. Believe me, it would be suicide. Why don't we just go back to City College tomorrow night? I've got a lot of work to do tonight."

"This'll be a great tune-up for tomorrow night. Come on, Jake, you're not selling your soul to that firm already, are you? I hear summer clerkships there are pretty cushy."

That touched a nerve. "They're supposed to be," Jake replied with obvious bitterness. "I'm not having much fun yet." Talking about it made Jake angrier about his situation. "What the hell," he said feeling reckless. "Alright, I'm in. Just give me some time to draft my will."

Rick picked up Jake in front of his office at 6:00 and they drove toward the South Side. Traffic was bad until they exited the expressway at 63rd Street to travel the few remaining miles by side street. Jake looked around at the urban wasteland surrounding them. The buildings were old, constructed of dark brick for the most part, and made even darker by nearly a century's worth of dirt and grime, with windows that were either boarded up or just gaping, glassless holes. Very few appeared to be occupied. Graffiti was everywhere. The streets seemed to have been as neglected as the neighborhood's inhabitants. They were strewn with litter, curbs were crumbling or simply gone, and potholes were everywhere. Small groups of boys and men of all ages loitered idly in doorways, and an assortment of lost souls wandered aimlessly down the streets, oblivious to traffic.

Jake thought that once Rick had surveyed the neighborhood, he would come to his senses and suggest finding a game elsewhere. To the contrary, Rick seemed to be enjoying the adventure. "Are you sure you want to do this?" Jake asked, as the bleakness of the setting took hold of him.

"Hell, yes! How many guys like us do you think have played at this place? What a kick! Don't you want to see how you measure up?" Rick slowed down before a crowd of tough looking youths to ask for directions.

"Keep driving!" Jake ordered between clenched teeth.

Rick ignored him. "Hey, where's St. Simon's?" he yelled toward them.

Several of them started moving toward the shiny BMW. "Get your sorry ass out of here," one of them yelled, hurling a beer bottle toward the car. Rick sped off, as the bottle sailed overhead.

"I think it's a block or two this way," he said, making a left turn onto a street that looked even bleaker, if that were possible.

Sure enough, two blocks ahead, they found an old church, adjacent to what looked like an abandoned school building. At one end of the asphalt parking lot were two basketball goals facing each other, chain nets hanging from the rims. A raucous game of four-on-four was in progress in front of a dozen or so highly vocal spectators. They watched from the car for several minutes. Jake could hear the trash-talking, shouting and swearing. He felt a flurry of emotions, none of which were positive. He felt like a trespasser. He felt out of place. He felt pure, unadulterated fear. He realized he was shaking. He also realized that Rick seemed to be experiencing no such feelings. To the contrary, he seemed excited and ready for action.

"Don't worry," Rick said, sensing Jake's apprehension. "These guys are basketball junkies, right? If that's the case, they surely follow the NCAA tournament. They'll know who I am and they'll want a chance to prove they're better than me. Trust me. Let's go."

They exited the car, and walked toward the court, Rick bouncing his basketball and seeming perfectly at ease.

"What the fuck is this?" A loud voice rang out from the crowd.

The game stopped. Everyone stared in astonishment. Two clean-cut white boys, BMW in the background, calmly walking up to the court at St. Simon's. It didn't compute. The group stared in silence for a few moments, assessing the situation, trying to decide if these guys were undercover cops, basketball scouts or just plain crazy. They didn't appear to be cops or scouts.

The player with the basketball, shirtless and wearing a white bandanna, took a few steps toward them and yelled, "You boys lost?" Jake sized him up. He looked menacing. He also looked like he intended to have a little fun at their expense.

"Don't think so," Rick shot back coolly, as they approached the court. "Is this St. Simon's?"

"Maybe. What the fuck do you want?"

"Just hoping to play a little ball. We've been told this is the best game around."

"You're damn right, sucker. But you ain't ready for our game," said a tall, muscular man covered with tattoos. "Go back to your own neighborhood."

A smaller, slightly built boy of about fifteen wearing a gold Lakers jersey walked to the front of the crowd and stared harshly at the visitors. "Let's fuck these dudes up. We need to teach 'em to respect our turf."

A giant of a man with a shaved head and a goatee stepped forward. Jake thought he must have been the largest human being he had ever seen in person. He had to be at least seven feet tall, on a rock solid frame. He flashed a menacing smile, revealing a gold front tooth. "I say, if they want to play, let 'em play. But you gotta pay to play here." He lowered his face to within inches of Rick's. "Gimme your wallet, motherfucker."

"I don't have a wallet. Look—I'm in my basketball clothes," Rick replied casually.

"Bullshit! White boys like you always carry wallets. It's in your car, ain't it? Tell you what; I'll just take your car keys instead. I'd look gooood in that BMW." He laughed, giving high fives to several of his cohorts, who were obviously enjoying this.

Rick joined the laughter, then said, "Hey, I know you, don't I?" The big guy stared at him, a puzzled look on his face. Rick continued, "You played at Michigan State. I remember playing against you." That brought a chorus of hoots and jeers from the crowd.

"You a college boy, T?" one of his pals asked with mock surprise.

"Shit," said another. "The closest T ever got to Michigan State was doing time with the Michigan Department of Co-rections!"

Clever approach, Jake thought. Change the subject. Flatter the big guy and make it known that you played in the Big Ten. That may appeal to their egos. They would relish the opportunity to thrash a Big Ten player on their court. The big guy took the bait. "So you played against Michigan State, huh? Sounds like bullshit to me. Where'd you play, boy?"

"Indiana. Went to the Final Four last year."

The kid in the Lakers jersey was obviously unimpressed. "This guy is full of shit, man. Come on, let's fuck these dudes up. What do you say, Shooter?" he asked, glancing at the guy with the basketball.

They all looked toward Shooter. "I remember you," Shooter said, recognition setting in. "Couldn't shoot worth shit, as I recall." He paused for a moment. "Alright, let's see if these guys can handle our game." He paused again for effect. "Then we'll mess 'em up!" The crowd roared its approval.

Jake and Rick walked toward the far end of the court. "Brilliant idea, man." Jake muttered in a low voice. "I can't believe I let you talk me into this." His fury at Rick was beginning to replace the stark fear he had felt moments earlier.

"Hey, just stay cool," Rick shot back. "Just play your game. We'll earn their respect and everything will be cool."

They would play full-court, they were told; four-on-four. Jake and Rick were assigned two teammates from the crowd, who seemed none too happy with their mission. The opposition consisted of Shooter, T, a tall skinny guy named Curtis, and the young kid in the Lakers jersey, whose name was Jerome.

The game began, and within seconds, the talent level was obvious. Shooter displayed some ball handling wizardry, and then worked the ball inside to T, who finished the play with a rim rattling, two-handed dunk, yelling ferociously at the top of his lungs as he did so.

"Nice play," said Rick as he retrieved the ball.

"Fuck you."

Rick confidently dribbled up court, despite having Curtis hanging all over him and passed to Jake on the wing as he crossed half court. Jake felt a vicious bump just as the pass hit his fingers. He wound up on the asphalt watching as Shooter led a fast break up the court. Jake felt like he was watching a professional team drill, as Shooter and his pals exchanged three lightning quick passes, leaving Rick helpless as the young kid completed a layup.

Jake quickly felt out of his league. Whenever he or Rick took the ball inside, they wound up flat on their backs. During a battle for a rebound, amidst a flurry of flying elbows and darting hands, Jake felt a jarring blow to his jaw and tasted blood from his split lip. He and Rick were powerless to stop the two big guys, and their teammates were not interested in providing much assistance. Rick was covered tightly by the lanky Curtis, and it seemed doubtful he would be able to launch a clean shot. Jake, on the other hand, was being guarded by the kid, who was quick and agile, but gave up a good deal to Jake in height and bulk. That was probably intended as an insult, Jake surmised. Getting beat by a skinny teenager would make it abundantly clear that he had no business trying to play with this crowd.

Fifteen minutes into the game, Rick called a timeout. "Look, this is getting out of hand," he said at his teammates. "This guy isn't giving me an inch. You're going to have to do the scoring," he said looking at Jake. "Light up that kid from the outside. We'll set screens for you."

It worked. Within the next few minutes, Jake scored on three long jump shots, after his teammates set the screens. After the third shot, the crowd on the sidelines began riding Jerome.

"You're gettin' burned, little man," teased one.

"You gonna take that shit?" another taunted him.

"Jerome, shut his ass down!" Shooter snapped, all business.

Jake could feel himself getting into that familiar groove. He knew that if he got the ball in his hands, he could beat this kid and put it into the net. He launched another shot over the kid's outstretched hands. The kid crashed into him roughly after Jake released the ball. Swish! The next time down the court, the kid draped himself all over Jake, determined to deny him the ball, but Rick still found a way to get it to him. The kid had both hands on Jake's back as Jake started to move toward the basket. The kid stepped in front of him, grabbing Jake's arms as he extended to shoot. Jake gripped the ball tightly, overpowered the young defender, and banked a shot in off the backboard as the kid sprawled to the pavement.

"That's a foul, sucker!" Jerome shouted, springing to his feet and pushing Jake in the chest.

"On you, pal," Jake shot back, turning away.

Jerome rushed at Jake, fists flying, pummeling the back of his head. In an instant, Shooter roughly pulled Jerome away from Jake. "Cut the shit, little brother," he demanded glaring at the younger player. "I'll cover this dude."

"Keep shooting, man," Rick encouraged Jake as they walked back to their end of the court.

Shooter played a much more physical game, and Jake found it was all he could do just to get his hands on the ball. Rick managed to make that happen, and Jake's hot streak continued. He shot from behind screens when they were available, and when they weren't, he launched an array of long-distance shots, most of which found their mark. The game, which had been a blowout earlier, was getting closer, and their two reluctant teammates were now becoming engaged as both Jake and Rick started finding them with crisp passes.

As Jake's team closed the gap, Shooter turned up the physical intensity. Whether Jake had the ball or not, Shooter was pushing, shoving and banging him all over the court. Jake did his best to give it right back. They were roughly the same height, at just over six-foot-one, but Jake outweighed Shooter by a good twenty pounds and tried to use that to his advantage. The spectators gave Shooter a hard time whenever Jake got the better of him, and Jake could see the escalating intensity and frustration on Shooter's face.

With his team's lead slipping away, Shooter drove hard toward the basket. Jake leaped, and blocked the shot squarely, hitting Shooter hard as he did so. "I've had enough of this shit!" Shooter shouted, shoving Jake roughly in the chest. "You're hacking me every time down the court, man. You want a piece of me? Come on, let's go!"

Jake's mind raced. The last thing in the world he wanted was to get into a fight with this street hardened thug, who could probably beat him to a pulp. Even if by some miracle he managed to hold his own, reinforcements almost certainly would join in. They could have weapons for all he knew. He had to think fast.

Jake took a step toward Shooter and grinned at him. "You're scared, aren't you?" he said in a taunting voice. "You're afraid you're going to lose, so you're looking for a way to quit. You can't stop me and you know it."

"Kick his ass, Shooter! Don't take that from him. Fuck that dude up," yelled Jerome.

Jake glanced quickly at Rick, who for the first time since Jake had known him, looked panicked. Rick was shaking his head and mouthing the word "Don't!"

Shooter pointed a finger in Jake's face. "I can shut your ass down anytime I want. You ain't seen nothin' yet."

Jake pushed the ball into Shooter's midsection. "Yeah? Prove it. You and me. One-on-one, right now. Let's see what you got."

Most of the crowd was enjoying this. "Ooooeee, we got us a live one here!" yelled a voice from the crowd. "Time to teach that cocky sucker a lesson, Shooter."

Jerome still wanted blood. "Fuck that shit, man! Let's cut his ass to pieces."

"Shut up, Jerome. Clear the court!" Shooter commanded. He flipped the ball to Jake and grinned maliciously. "You're on. Up to ten, by ones. Time for you to get schooled, chump!"

Their one-on-one contest picked up where the previous game had left off, with constant pushing, shoving, and banging. Shooter quickly went up two-to-nothing, as he drove to the basket and eluded Jake's blocking attempts with impressive aerial acrobatics. Jake found his shot again. Although Shooter was draped all over him, he resorted to a series of fade-away and turnaround jump shots that found the bottom of the net. Both players were soon breathing hard. There was no trash talking now, just intense focus and concentration. Every shot was contested. Every step toward the basket met bruising resistance.

"Kick his ass, Shooter! Kill that motherfucker!" Jerome became increasingly vocal and hostile as the game progressed. Jake's shooting touch stayed true, and soon he had pulled away. The score was eight to five, in his favor. He could see Rick on the sideline, looking pale and sick.

Okay, you've made your point, Jake thought to himself. Don't be stupid here.

Jake missed his next several shots, and Shooter relentlessly drove the ball to the hoop. Within a few minutes, the score was tied nine – nine. Jake had the ball. "Showtime, Shooter," he grinned. He dribbled to his left, spun in a half circle, changing directions, and drove hard to the hoop. He leapt as high as he could, and cradling the ball with his right hand, tried to slam-dunk it home. He came up short, and the ball bounced off the front of the rim. As Jake struggled to maintain his footing, Shooter chased down the long rebound and fired up a graceful fifteen-foot jump shot. He watched it rattle around the rim and drop through. "Yeah! Ballgame!" Shooter yelled, pumping his fist in the air.

Jake bent over, put his hands on his knees and sucked in long gulps of air. He straightened up, walked slowly toward Shooter and held out his hand. "Good game," he gasped.

Shooter glared for a moment, then slapped his hand hard. "Now get your ass out of here. And don't come back!"

Jerome wasn't finished. He strutted toward Rick and yelled, "Let's kick their asses now!"

Shooter gave Jerome a look that terminated the discussion. "I just did," he said, still breathing hard. "You're done," he said looking at Rick and Jake. "Leave."

Jerome walked up to Jake, stared at him coldly, and in the most menacing voice his teenage body could muster, said, "Don't come back, motherfucker. If I ever see you again, you're a dead man."

"Thanks for the game, guys," said Rick, trying to sound cheery and nonchalant, but the swagger was gone from his step as they hurried back to the car.

Jake was pleasantly surprised to see that the BMW was still there and unharmed. He flopped down into the passenger seat. The adrenaline rush that had sustained him over the past hour had subsided, leaving him feeling utterly exhausted – physically and emotionally. He turned his head sideways and said in a tired voice, "Rick, I love playing ball with you, but this was a really stupid idea. We're lucky to be alive."

Rick took offense, his feistiness returning now that he had reached the relative safety of the BMW. "Stupid? Who the hell was being stupid? I can't believe you called that Shooter bastard a chickenshit. That's what almost got us killed!"

Jake didn't stir. His head leaned back into the plush leather of the passenger seat. "That was a calculated move. I was in complete control," he said quietly.

"Yeah, right. If that's your idea of staying in control, I'd hate to see you when you lose it."

"Hey, I got him focused on whipping me in basketball instead of killing me. I'd say that's a good thing."

"Until you started beating him. It's a good thing your game fell apart at the end."

"That's okay," Jake said softly, looking straight ahead and smiling to himself. "Shooter was able to save face in front of his homeboys, so we're still in one piece. And everyone there, including Shooter, is wondering whether I let him win."

Rick looked astonished. "You *let* him win?"

"Like I said, I was in complete control."

CHAPTER 10

On Thursday of the following week, Rick picked up Jake after work, and they drove to City College together to watch the summer league play. Jake wore his basketball shoes and gym shorts, but after his previous experience, had no expectation of getting into a game.

They found a seat in the bleachers and watched the warm-ups. There did not seem to be nearly as many players on the floor as there had been last time. Rick nudged Jake with his elbow and nodded toward the far end of the court. "Look who's here—your buddy."

It was Shooter, warming up with a group of players wearing green jerseys. An uneasy feeling settled over Jake. Over the past week, he had thought a great deal about their visit to St. Simon's, and with the passing of time, he came to realize how foolish that trip had been. He had no desire to encounter Shooter or any of the other characters from that playground ever again.

As game time approached, it appeared that the green team was going to be shorthanded. Shooter scanned the hopefuls in the crowd, looking for a stand-in. His gaze fell upon Jake and Rick, and he paused for a moment, staring at them. "Hey, Stanford," he yelled, referring to the name on Jake's T-shirt. "You wanna run?"

Jake was flustered. "Me?" he asked, pointing to himself.

"Yeah, you. Come on."

"Go on," urged Rick, shoving him toward the court. "That's why we're here."

Jake wandered onto the court, feeling shaky. Shooter tossed him a green jersey and introduced Jake to his three teammates, none of whom he had seen at St. Simon's. They looked at him doubtfully. "I've played with this dude. He's alright," Shooter announced, in an attempt to allay their skepticism.

The game was starting, and Jake had no time to warm up. He'd seen the caliber of play on his previous visit, and felt sure he had no business being in the same court as these guys. Although his shooting had been red hot when he played at St. Simon's, he knew that was not a performance he could duplicate at will. His primary goal was to avoid embarrassing himself or hurting his team.

The game was a blur, fast-paced and physical. Shooter and his pals put on an impressive show, and Jake contented himself with playing solid defense and getting the ball into the hands of his teammates. His team won handily. While he felt that he hadn't added much, Jake was pleased that he had gotten through the entire game without embarrassing himself. He hadn't shot much, but scored on most of the shots he did take.

As Jake walked off the court after the game, Shooter called out after him, "Hey, Stanford! Good game," he yelled, pointing a finger at Jake's direction. He walked toward Jake, extending his hand. "Thanks for playing."

"Any time," Jake replied.

"You gonna be here next week?"

"Probably."

"You ought to come, man. If we're shorthanded again, you're in."

"Sounds good."

"So, did you play at Stanford?" Shooter asked.

"No. I just go to school there. Law school."

"No shit? You're gonna be a lawyer? That's cool. I'll probably need a lawyer someday." He laughed.

"Call me any time," Jake said lightly. "So, where are your pals from the playground? Don't they play up here?"

"Nah. Most of them have too much attitude. I stopped inviting them because they embarrass me. They have a way of starting fights and getting thrown out."

Jake looked puzzled. This was the same guy that had seemed ready to tear him apart last week. Now he seemed perfectly friendly, and reasonably well-spoken. Shooter must have sensed Jake's confusion. "Look, man. I need to act a certain way around my homeboys, on our turf. It's just the way it is," he stated with a shrug, as if that explained everything. "That was a stupid goddamn stunt you and your pal pulled last week—really stupid. Don't go back there. If I hadn't been there, that could've been a bad scene. You'd have gotten hurt—bad. I mean it, don't go back there."

"Don't worry. I thought it was a bad idea to begin with. I have no intention of going back."

"Good. So tell me your name again, Stanford."

"Jake McShane."

Shooter repeated it, as if trying to commit Jake's name to memory. "Nice playing with you. See you next time."

Jake watched Shooter strut out of the gym, slapping hands and shouting out greetings as he went. Halfway to the exit, he stopped and turned around. "Hey, Stanford," he called out. "When was the last time you dunked a basketball?"

Jake paused for a moment before answering, then responded truthfully. "Never."

Shooter stared back at Jake, nodding his head slowly, as he reflected on the final minutes of their one-on-one contest. "Didn't think so." He smiled, as he turned and walked away, shaking his head. "Later, man."

CHAPTER 11

For the remainder of the summer, Jake and Rick continued their visits to City College on Thursday evenings. Jake played with Shooter's team on only one other occasion, but that was fine with him. Just watching the action was a treat, and being able to say he played in the City College summer league felt like an accomplishment in itself.

Conditions gradually improved at the law firm. Paul Doherty, an enthusiastic and sincere young partner who oversaw the firm's summer clerkship program, had become concerned by Jake's repeated absences from the firm's social functions. Jake's fellow clerks explained to Doherty that the cause of those absences was the mountain of work continuously heaped upon Jake by Mr. Pritchard. Doherty must have intervened behind the scenes because Jake was approached by a junior associate, who informed him that he had been asked to assume all of Pritchard's pending projects. The workload eased considerably, and Jake finally was able to partake in the social activities. He actually began enjoying the work and the camaraderie.

On weekends, Jake spent time relaxing at his parents' house and reconnecting with old friends. His parents lived in Beverly, an old neighborhood on the southwestern outskirts of the city. When he had a free evening, he would often visit one of the neighborhood's drinking establishments on Western Avenue, where he was certain to run into friends and acquaintances he had known since childhood. There was a smattering of young professional types, but for the most part, it was a working-class bunch—policemen, firemen, other city workers, and a variety of tradesmen. Many of them drank too much, and would never amount to anything, but Jake still felt a strong connection to these people. He had grown up with them, gone to school with them, and played sports with them. They shared a common history and a bond that would never be broken, no matter how wide the gulf between their lives might otherwise become.

After the final game of the City College summer league season, Rick suggested that they go out for a beer to toast their Chicago summer. Since City College was closer to Jake's neighborhood than Rick's, Jake suggested they go to Riley's Pub, which he considered one of the least seedy of the Western Avenue bars.

Jake waved to the bartender as they walked in. "How's it going, Jimmy?" The bar was crowded for Thursday evening.

"Jake! Good to see you," Jimmy replied. "Back from California?"

"I've been here for the summer. Heading back next week," Jake said as he pulled up a couple of barstools. "This is my friend, Rick. He's from the North Side, but don't hold that against him."

"Hey, I've got nothing against North Siders, as long as they're not Cub fans."

Rick shook hands with Jimmy and laughed. "Hell, no. I was when I was a kid, but I don't have it in me to support a bunch of perennial losers. It would be bad for my self-image."

"Good! What'll you have, fellas?"

They ordered a couple of beers and chatted with the steady stream of old pals who came by to visit Jake.

"It seems like you know everybody in this place," said Rick, obviously impressed. "I feel like a party crasher at somebody's reunion. Friendly bunch though, no doubt about that."

Jake had felt some apprehension about bringing Rick to one of his neighborhood hangouts. He was quite sure that Rick wasn't accustomed to this type of crowd. His fears turned out to be unfounded, as

Rick easily fit right in, talking sports with the guys and flirting with the girls. Jake felt a bit ashamed for having been embarrassed by his friends.

"Jake McShane! Hey everybody, Jake McShane is in the house! Let's partyyyyy!" The booming voice belonged to a big redheaded man with a baseball cap on backwards, staggering toward them.

"Friend of yours?" asked Rick with amusement.

"That's Eddie Mullins. I've known him since we were ten. Looks like he's added about fifty pounds since I saw him last."

Jake stood up and offered his hand to Eddie, who ignored it and wrapped him in a huge bear hug. "Jakey! How the hell are ya?"

"Hi Eddie. Nice to see you. You look good."

"Aw, kiss my ass. I look like a fat drunk. But I love you for saying so, anyway."

"This is my friend, Rick," said Jake. "We go to law school together in California."

"Damn glad to meet you, Rick. Welcome to Riley's!" Eddie bellowed, as if he owned the place. "Law school … I forgot you were in law school, Jake. Maybe you can help me. I need some legal advice." He looked at them hopefully, through bleary eyes.

"We're not lawyers yet, Eddie, but maybe we can help out. What's the problem?"

"I got fired by the city a few months ago. I worked for the police department for three years, and they up and fired my ass with no warning. I want to sue those bastards."

"They fired you for stealing, Eddie," said the diminutive man on the bar stool next to Rick, in a loud and irritable voice. He was wearing dirty work clothes and stared intently at his beer mug as he spoke. "He's told his sad story to everyone in this place a hundred times," the little man explained to Rick and Jake without taking his eyes off his beer. "He arrested some scumbag and emptied the guy's pockets for evidence. Found a wad of hundred dollar bills and decided to keep it for himself. Seems the city had a little problem with that. Go figure."

"Hey, the guy was a lowlife drug dealer. I found a bag of weed on him, too. You didn't mention that. The way I see it, that money was obtained from his illegal activities. It would've been forfeited if he'd been convicted. I just helped the judicial system work a little faster. Anyway, my partner ratted me out and the guy walked. The prosecutors dropped the case. What a joke!"

"I hate to be pessimistic, Eddie, but I don't think you have much of a chance," said Jake, trying to sound at least a bit sympathetic. "If—"

"Wait, that's not the whole story. I had a perfect record. Well, almost perfect. They wrote me up a few times for missing too much work, but nothing like this had ever happened before. Don't they have to give me a warning?"

"Not for stealing, you mope," said the man at the bar.

"But if I were black or Mexican, they wouldn't have fired me. That's discrimination!"

"Do you know of any minorities that were treated more leniently for this type of issue?" asked Jake.

"Not personally, but that shit happens; it happens all the time."

Jake searched for a way to let his old friend down easily. "Eddie, my advice is to get past this and move on with your life. Whether you think it's fair or not, the Chicago PD is unlikely to change its mind."

Rick spoke up. "But, if you *can* prove discrimination, you might have something worth talking about. If that's the case, and if you find the right kind of lawyer who can push the right buttons, you might be able to convince them to give you your job back."

Eddie looked indignant. "The hell with that! I don't want to work for those assholes again. I want to take them to the cleaners. I want to score some cash!"

"You're dreaming, Eddie," said the man on the bar stool. "Just stick with your lottery tickets. Your odds are better."

As Eddie shuffled away muttering to himself, a man in tennis clothes who had been listening from a few feet away approached the group. He looked familiar to Jake. "Hi guys. Pat Corcoran." He looked to be about thirty, had thinning blond hair and a dark tan. "You may have known my brothers. I think they're about your age. Paul and Kevin."

"Kevin and I were classmates," said Jake, realizing why Pat looked familiar.

"I've got a legal question, too. Mind if I run it by you?"

"Not at all. Fire away."

"Great, thanks. I'm having trouble with my back, and I'm trying to find out if I can take time off from my job and still get paid. Do you know anything about workers' compensation laws?"

"Just a little, not much. How did you hurt your back, Pat?" asked Jake.

"It's been bothering me for several years. I play a lot of tennis. A few years back, I was serving during a match, and I stretched a little too far and felt a twinge in my lower back. I couldn't finish the match, and it was really stiff for a few days. It's bothered me off and on since then."

"But you still play," asked Jake, noticing Pat's tennis bag under his barstool.

"Yeah, but my back's always sore and I think my job is making it worse."

"What does your doctor say?"

"He told me to give up tennis for awhile."

"What kind of work do you do?"

"I'm an assistant manager at a pharmacy. I'm on my feet all day long. Sometimes I have to move boxes. I know it's aggravating my back."

Rick had not said a word during the conversation. He watched Jake intently, with a look of amusement on his face. "How long have you worked there?" asked Jake.

"About nine months."

"Look Pat, I'm really not an expert in this area, but I think the injury has to occur on the job for workers' comp to apply."

Jimmy spoke out from behind the bar. "Still looking for a way to get paid for playing tennis, Pat?" he asked with a grin.

Pat ignored him and continued pleading his case. "No, this is really bothering me. I need some time off."

"I'd suggest you talk with your boss and see if he's open to some sort of leave of absence. Maybe he'll let you use sick time or vacation days so you can still get paid. Or maybe he'll agree to an unpaid leave of absence. It might be worth it if it helps you get better."

Pat looked defeated. "I've already used up all my sick time and I haven't worked there long enough to have vacation time. Thanks, anyway. I figured I was probably out of luck, but just thought I'd ask. Can I buy you guys another round?"

"No thanks, we really need to be shoving off," replied Jake.

After leaving a generous tip on the bar for Jimmy, Jake and Rick walked out into the muggy Chicago evening. Rick was in a jovial mood as they walked toward his car. "What a friendly bunch! Not the kind of crowd I pictured you hanging out with, but certainly an interesting group. Hell, that place could be a gold mine for a plaintiffs' lawyer."

"What do you mean?"

"I mean it's the kind of place that attracts plenty of losers who believe the world has done them wrong, and they're just dying to sue someone."

"The only problem is that they usually don't have a case."

"You need to think more creatively, Jake. Things aren't always black and white. Even those two yo-yo's we spoke with tonight could probably cash in if they find a lawyer who's smart and aggressive. Like my old man always says, in the hands of the right lawyer, any case can be a winner."

"But why would any self-respecting lawyer take a case like that?"

"Because it's good sport. It's a challenge. And more importantly, you could make some real money. Hell, I'm going to need to remember this place if I ever need to troll for clients." Rick climbed into his BMW. "Hey, it's been fun. See you back at school next week." He sped off into the night.

CHAPTER 12

Amanda and Ellen Marsh sat side-by-side on the old leather couch in Dr. Marsh's office. It was Amanda's first day back at work after her leave of absence.

"I'm glad you're back, Amanda. How's your grandmother doing?" asked Dr. Marsh.

"Not very well, I'm afraid. It's been a rough few months." Amanda looked down as she tried to blink away the tears filling her eyes.

"I'm sorry to hear that. Has her rehab been difficult?"

"Extremely. While she was staying in the rehab center, she picked up a dreadful staph infection. She spent nearly a month in the hospital battling the infection, and was so weak she couldn't rehab her hip. We finally brought her home—to my parents' house—but she's still really weak."

"How are her spirits?"

"Not good, and that concerns me even more than her physical condition. She's always been so active and independent. She lives in a third-floor apartment in Chinatown, with no elevator, so she knows she won't be going back there anytime soon. That has her depressed, and she's really struggling to keep going." A tear rolled down Amanda's cheek, and she paused to keep her voice from breaking. She took a deep breath and composed herself. "I feel like I've done all I can do.

I've spent the last several months at her side, being her nurse, and her cheerleader, and her personal trainer. Now it's just up to her. She has to look within herself and find the will to live—or not." She forced a smile. "Anyway, I'm glad to be back. Thanks for letting me take time off to be with her."

"You're a good person, Amanda Chang. You need to get on with your own life. I'm sure that's what your grandmother would want."

"I know. I'm ready to do that."

"Good. So tell me, how's your personal life otherwise? Last time I saw you, you were very excited about a new man in your life."

"Unfortunately, that hasn't been a bright spot in my life either," Amanda replied glumly. "When we met, I really thought there was potential. It just didn't pan out."

"I'm sorry."

"Me too, but I'm ready to dive back into work. I think that will help me get my act together again."

"I'm sure it will. By the way, I've been in touch with my contacts in Chicago. They would love to meet you. Why don't you plan on visiting there sometime this fall? I'm sure you'd be impressed. Something fresh and exciting may do you a world of good."

"I'd like that," said Amanda, smiling again. "I may wait a month or two, so I can settle in here again, but I'll definitely make the trip sometime this fall."

CHAPTER 13

As the second-year students returned to school in late August, there were three principal topics of discussion: what they had done over the summer; what they knew about their new classes and professors; and the upcoming interview season. Commencing in early October, law firms, corporations and government agencies from across the nation would descend upon campus for several weeks of interviews. Second Years would be interviewing for coveted summer clerkship positions, and Third Years would be interviewing for permanent positions that would start following graduation.

"Do you guys understand how this works?" Tony asked, as he, Jake and Rick sat in the shady courtyard adjacent to the law school.

"I've been talking to some of the Third Years," Rick replied. "Here's the scoop: There will be hundreds of potential employers coming through here this fall, mostly big law firms. Each one generally spends a day here interviewing whatever students have signed up to meet with them. The interview lasts about half an hour. If they like you, you'll get a callback within a week or two, which means they invite you to visit the firm at their office for an entire day's worth of interviews. If you pass that test, they'll make you an offer. You can interview with as many firms as you like."

"What if a firm is from out of town?" asked Tony. "I plan on going back to New York after law school."

"I'm sure all the major New York law firms will be here," Rick replied. "If they like you, they'll fly you back to New York for more interviews. They'll put you up in a nice hotel and take you to some expensive restaurants, all on their dime. They call that a flyback."

"Will any Chicago law firms be recruiting here?" asked Jake.

"Yep. I saw last year's list. There must've been at least twenty Chicago firms on it. All the top-tier firms will certainly be here."

"Excellent! So I may be able to get a couple of free trips home this fall?"

"Absolutely. If you're smart, you might even be able to make a few bucks." Rick grinned slyly, as if he already had a plan.

Tony looked suspicious. "Make money? What are you talking about?"

"It's easy. You plan your flybacks so that you visit several firms on the same trip. Then you bill each of them for all your expenses—airfare, hotel, taxis, the works."

Tony and Jake exchanged glances. "Bullshit!" Tony blurted out. "You can't do that!"

"You're not serious, are you?" Jake asked.

"Of course I'm serious," said Rick. "Look, each one of these firms would be willing to pick up the entire tab if I were visiting only them. It's part of the process. It's a cost they're willing to bear."

"Yeah, but their intention is to reimburse you for your expenses, so you don't take a financial hit by going to see them," Jake replied, still unsure whether Rick was simply having fun at their expense. "You're not out of pocket anything once one firm reimburses you. How can you bill another firm for those same expenses? They're not paying you for your time. Clearly, you should be dividing the costs among whatever firms you're seeing on that trip."

"I disagree," said Rick. "They're in recruiting mode. They want me to take the time to travel to Chicago, and they're willing to pay for it. There's no reason any particular firm should receive a windfall just because I choose to interview with another firm while I'm there."

Tony shook his head. "That's just not right."

"Again, I disagree," said Rick. "I would avoid making any representation to any one firm that I will be spreading the expenses around. Unless they explicitly limit the terms of their reimbursement—which they don't normally think to do—there's a clear understanding on their part that they will be picking up the entire tab. So what's the harm?"

"It's just not right," Tony said again. "Besides, what if one of those firms were to find out that you were treating the interview process as a profit-making opportunity? It might hurt your chances of getting hired."

Rick's face darkened at that thought. "Well, you may have a valid point there," he acknowledged reluctantly. "Maybe it's not worth running that risk. But I'll tell you this—it isn't as black and white as you seem to think." Rick looked from one to the other. "You guys are spending way too much time in the ivory tower. You need an education in how the real world works. We're joining a profession where the most successful practitioners are the ones who are the most aggressive and creative, the guys who aren't afraid to push the envelope."

"Within limits," Jake corrected him. "There are ethical rules governing our profession, and we need to play within those rules."

"Granted, but those rules are flexible. There are very few situations that are truly black and white. Mostly, we deal with shades of gray, and we deal with arguments. Sometimes an argument can be made that a certain course of conduct is against the ethical rules, but there's almost always a legitimate counterargument that it's not. Our overriding obligation as attorneys will be to zealously represent our clients. Our system is built on that foundation, and I don't plan on letting my clients down. I play to win—whether it's basketball or law or anything else."

Jake was warming up to the debate. "You raise a good example: basketball. Sure, professional basketball players play to win, but there's a rulebook. If they violate the rules, they get called for a foul or they get ejected. Those are the rules of the game."

"Wrong again, pal," Rick countered. "It's not so simple. Yes, there is a rulebook, but there are unwritten rules, too. Just watch any professional basketball game and look at what goes on underneath the basket. There's pushing, shoving, holding—all the time—even though it's technically against the rules. It's accepted. More than that, it's expected. And the most successful players are the ones who are best at it. The same principle applies to the legal profession. If you want to be successful, you need to understand the unwritten rules, and you need to understand that even the written rules are elastic. You can't fight your battles with one hand tied behind your back. Your mission is to win. You do what it takes."

"You do what it takes to win, eh?" Tony scoffed. "The ends justify the means? I'm not buying that crap. The only way that theory works is if the end result somehow serves the greater good. What if your client is wrong and undeserving? Your whole theory falls apart."

Rick looked annoyed. "You're missing my point entirely," he replied. "The end game is winning—that's all that matters. It's not up to us to weigh the moral or social value of the cases we handle. We're hired to win. That's the goal, and we need to do what it takes to accomplish that goal."

"You're missing *my* point!" Tony shot back. "We spend ninety-nine percent of our time living in the realm of the means. It's the journey we travel during most of our waking lives, while our arrival at the destination—the ends—is just a fleeting moment. The way we conduct ourselves on that journey defines who we are, and that's far more important than the outcome of any particular case."

"I agree with Tony," said Jake. "Holding ourselves to the right standard of ethics is an end in itself, and that should be what guides us throughout our careers."

Rick looked amused. "I disagree. In this country, we keep score, and the only thing that counts is the end result. That's how our world will judge us. Like I said, you guys need a good dose of the real world. I got plenty of that this summer, working for my old man's firm. The lawyers there understand that the rules are elastic, and they know how the game is really played."

"Sounds like bullshit to me," Tony replied. "So, how do lawyers in the real world apply this elasticity? Give me an example."

"Sure, that's easy. Take the whole universe of personal injury law. Do you really think that every client who walks into a lawyer's office is hurt as badly as he says he is? Of course not. But how does an attorney make that assessment? He can't, and it's not his place to do so. So he sends the client to someone better qualified to make that evaluation—a medical expert he happens to know—a doctor to whom he sends a lot of business. The lawyer, if he's got half a brain, would never instruct the doctor as to what his findings should be, but guess what? Time after time, the doctor will issue an expert opinion confirming the patient's complaint."

"That's because the doctor is a sleazebag with no conscience," Tony replied. "He knows that if he doesn't provide the diagnosis the lawyer wants, then the lawyer will stop sending business his way."

"Precisely. But the end result is that the lawyer gets what he needs—support for his client's claim—without doing anything outside the rules."

Jake was disturbed, both by the reality of what Rick was describing, as well as the fact that Rick seemed to be defending it, even embracing it. "You're painting a pretty grim picture of our profession."

"Hey, if you look beneath the surface of any well-oiled machine, you'll find some grimy parts, but those parts are essential to the machine's operation."

"I don't know about that," Tony responded glumly. "If there's too much sludge in an engine, it just stops working."

"Well, get your heads out of the clouds, boys. Your summer clerkships will give you a firsthand glimpse of the legal profession in action. Watch and learn. A couple of smart and ambitious guys like you will figure it out in no time. Before long, you'll be bending the rules with the best of them."

CHAPTER 14

Although Jake had seen Kelly several times during the first week of classes, he'd had very little conversation with her. He greeted her cheerfully and enthusiastically when he encountered her, but she seemed distant. Their conversations had been short, and she didn't seem to be in the mood for chatting whenever he spoke with her. Jake assumed something must be troubling her, but didn't feel it was his place to pry.

Toward the end of the second week, Jake saw Kelly sitting in an outdoor café by herself, sipping tea and reading a newspaper. He decided to try to cheer her up. He snuck up behind her, put his hand on her shoulder, and leaning close to her ear, said in his most suave voice, "Hey good-looking, come here often?"

She turned around with a start. "You're real smooth, McShane," she said without smiling.

"Mind if I join you?"

"If you like," she said, looking back at her newspaper.

Jake ignored the snub. "We miss you at the dorm, Kelly. It's not the same without you. How's apartment living?"

"It's okay."

"How was your summer?"

"Fine."

"I hear you worked at Watkins & George in the City. How was that?"

"About like any other big law firm, I imagine." Her eyes remained fixed on the paper.

"Kelly?" She looked up. "It feels pretty frosty around here. Are you upset with me about something? What's going on?"

She glared at him. "If you don't know, then you're not as smart as I thought you were."

"I have no idea what you're talking about. Please, clue me in," Jake pleaded.

She leaned back in her chair, folded her arms, and gave him a harsh look. "I hate it when guys act like inconsiderate bastards, and have no regard for how their actions may really hurt someone. I didn't think you were that type, but obviously I was wrong."

The sharp words caught Jake by surprise. "What have I done to hurt you, Kelly? I honestly have no idea. Whatever it may have been, I can assure you it wasn't intentional, and I apologize. Just talk to me. I don't like this silent treatment. How have I offended you?"

She looked at him with contempt. "Not me—I'm talking about Amanda. That was really rotten of you to lead her on like that. She's one of the sweetest people I know. She's been going through a very difficult time and you've made it a lot worse."

Jake stared at Kelly with his mouth open, utterly dumbfounded.

"You never told me you had a fiancée in Chicago. And you sure never told Amanda that either. You—"

"What? What in the hell are you talking about?" Jake demanded in a loud voice that turned the heads of those seated nearby.

It was Kelly's turn to be taken aback. She had never seen Jake like this. Every inch of his body projected shock and outrage. Her tone became less confrontational, as a look of uncertainty crept over her face. "I heard you had a fiancée in Chicago. Isn't that why you gave Amanda the brush-off?"

"Are you nuts?" he shouted, his face turning a deep shade of red. Then, doing all he could to exercise self-control, Jake lowered his voice and continued. "How long have you known me, Kelly? Have you ever heard me mention any fiancée? Where did you get that crazy idea?"

"That's the word that was going around shortly after the party at Kathleen's place," Kelly replied, sounding defensive and less sure of herself.

"Look, I don't have a fiancée. I don't have a girlfriend. I've been driving myself crazy all summer long trying to figure out what went wrong with Amanda. We had a date arranged right after finals ended. I was ecstatic. She never showed up. I called her several times. She never returned my calls."

Now it was Kelly's turn to look totally confused. She stared silently at Jake for a few moments, struggling to absorb this information. "Oh shit, Jake!" She raised her hands to her cheeks. "I don't know what happened. I know she tried to reach you before she left town. She thinks you just decided not to call her again."

"She left town? Where did she go?"

"She went home to Berkeley for the summer. She took a leave of absence from the hospital after her grandmother had an accident."

"That's where I was calling her—the hospital. Maybe she had already left. What happened to her grandmother? Is she okay?"

"She broke her hip, and then had some pretty serious complications. She's not doing very well, but Amanda returned to work a couple of weeks ago. Here, look at this." She handed him the campus newspaper she had been reading, pointing to a notice in the health section. It referred to a series of luncheon seminars being conducted at the Medical Center covering various topics of interest to the medical community. The topic for the next seminar was the difference in the incidence of Alzheimer's disease among Asian cultures as compared to others, and a discussion of research being conducted to identify the reasons. It was scheduled for the following day, and the speaker was Dr. Amanda Chang.

"I need to fix this," Jake said. "Is she really angry with me, Kelly?"

"I wouldn't say angry. More sad and disappointed. And confused. She just couldn't understand it."

"I've got to go," said Jake, abruptly getting up from the table.

"Jake, I'm really sorry. Let me—"

He was gone before she could finish.

Jake hurried away from the café, and found himself walking in the direction of Amanda's apartment. What a mess, he kept thinking to himself. How could communications get so fouled up? Yet, despite his anger and frustration, he had a new sense of purpose. There was hope now, where yesterday there had been none. He needed to make this right.

Within a few minutes, he found himself in front of Amanda's apartment. He realized he didn't know what to say to her. He had to have a plan. He might only have one chance to fix this and he was determined not to blow it. He turned and walked in the opposite direction, back toward the dorm.

Wheeler Auditorium was a modern lecture hall located within the medical school complex. Because of its proximity to the Medical Center, it was frequently used for lectures and seminars that were of interest to the doctors, nurses and other health care professionals at the Medical Center, as well as students, professors and researchers from the school.

The auditorium had a seating capacity of approximately five hundred, but only about a quarter of the seats were occupied. Jake walked in and seated himself in the back row, feeling out of place, but doing his best to appear as if he belonged. The moderator was just finishing her introduction. "If you have any questions for Dr. Chang, jot them down on the index card on your chair. We will collect them toward the end of our program and Dr. Chang will answer as many of your questions as time permits."

Jake listened with rapt attention as Amanda delivered her presentation. She came across as a polished and accomplished speaker. She was confident, and engaging. She spoke without notes. He soon found that, although his eyes were glued to her, and he heard every word she spoke, he was not paying attention to what she was saying. He was focused on how she looked, the sound of her voice, her manner as she moved about the stage in complete command of her subject and her audience.

As Amanda was concluding her presentation, she offered to take questions from the audience. The moderator walked down the aisle, collecting index cards. Jake hastily scribbled something on a card and passed it to the aisle.

The moderator handed Amanda several cards. She read the first question aloud and proceeded to answer it without hesitation. She answered two more questions and then picked up the final card. She looked hard at the question and then scanned the audience. For the briefest moment, she seemed flustered. She quickly regained her composure and said, "I'm sorry, I can't make out the handwriting on this last question." She paused, then said, "Whoever submitted it can see me privately afterwards and I will do my best to respond. Thank you all for coming." She walked off the stage to polite applause, stopping to read the note again once she was off the stage. It read: *An old Chinese proverb says "When your mind doesn't understand, listen to your heart." Can we talk? Jake.*

Jake remained seated as the crowd dispersed. Several people approached Amanda and cornered her near the stage while they asked questions and shared observations. After a few minutes, she excused herself and walked toward the exit at the back of the room. She saw Jake as he stood and made his way toward the aisle.

"Hi Amanda," Jake said with an uncertain smile. "I enjoyed your presentation."

"Hello Jake. I didn't expect to see you here."

Jake stood before her, hands in his pockets, feeling awkward and uncomfortable. "Amanda, I—"

"I spoke with—"

They spoke at the same time, and shared an embarrassed laugh.

"How's your grandmother? I just heard about her accident. I'm really sorry."

"She's struggling, I'm afraid. Thanks for asking."

"I didn't know you had left town. I tried reaching you at the hospital ... I thought about ..."

Get a grip, he thought to himself. Stop stammering like an idiot. He paused and took a deep breath, looking up at the ceiling as he groped for the right words. "Amanda, I hope you don't think I'm a jerk for coming here, but I had to see you. I've been thinking about you all summer long, thinking I must have done something to offend you. I truly hope I haven't. There are some things that need explaining."

He paused, still searching for the right words, which seemed impossibly elusive. Amanda interrupted gently. "Kelly called me last night. She explained some things."

"She did?" Jake had not asked Kelly to intervene, but was happy to hear that she had.

"Yes. It sounds like there were some communication breakdowns."

"Amanda, I honestly don't know what happened, but I'd love to have the opportunity to try to find out."

Amanda avoided his gaze and stared at the floor. "Just answer one question for me. You don't have a fiancée in Chicago, do you?"

Jake looked exasperated. "I don't know where that came from. The only time I've ever been engaged was when I was twelve years old, and she dumped me before I turned thirteen! Can we start over and try this again? A fresh start?"

Amanda smiled gently. She nodded her head, still looking down, unable to speak. Then she found her voice, looked up and said, "I believe there is a lot of wisdom in the old Chinese proverbs. I'm listening to my heart, and it's telling me that would be an excellent idea. I'm free this evening. How about a movie?"

"That would be great." His voice was calm, but his spirit was soaring.

"But only if you let me pay. After all, you got stuck with the theater tickets last time we tried this." She laughed, the hearty, carefree laugh Jake first heard in the dormitory stairwell.

"Deal!" he replied.

"Great! Why don't we meet at Milano's for pizza at six o'clock? I promise, I'll be there this time," she assured him, smiling brightly. Then, glancing at her watch, she said, "I've got to get back to work. See you tonight." She began walking away, with a bounce in her step.

After about ten paces, she stopped, turned around and trotted briskly back to Jake and gave him a quick embrace. "It's really good to see you again, Jake," she whispered, and hurried off.

That evening, they picked up where they had left off. The awkwardness they felt that afternoon was gone, replaced by an eagerness to make up for lost time. They discussed their summer experiences over pizza and strolled to the movie theater. As Jake sat next to Amanda in the dark theater, he found himself stealing subtle glances at her face, and experiencing the same sensation he had felt during their last evening together: a powerful and unmistakable feeling that this was the perfect girl for him. He could not allow himself to lose her again.

After leaving the theater, they stopped for ice cream and walked slowly toward Amanda's apartment, neither of them in any hurry to end the evening. "I know you have to work in the morning, so I won't keep you out all night like I did last time," Jake said as they neared her apartment. "Can I see you this weekend? Saturday perhaps?"

"I have to drive up to Berkeley on Saturday, to visit my grandmother."

Jake did his best to hide his disappointment. "I understand."

"Have you ever been to Berkeley?" Amanda asked.

"Not yet. I'd love to see it, but not having a car, I'm somewhat grounded."

"Why don't you come with me? It's a fabulous place. There's nowhere else like it. 'Berserkley,' many people call it. I need to spend some time with my grandmother, but we could leave early and make a day of it. I'll show you around."

"That sounds great. Count me in! Will I get to meet your grandmother?"

"I'd like that."

"Me too."

They stopped in front of her apartment. "Would you like to come in?" Amanda asked.

There was nothing that could have sounded more enticing at that moment, but he did not want to appear too forward. He wanted to be a gentleman. "It's getting late, and you have to work tomorrow. I'll see you on Saturday."

He leaned forward and kissed her softly on the lips. It lasted only a second, but it was sensuous and left them both longing for more. Like everything else with her, it was easy and natural. He gave her hands a tight squeeze and walked away.

CHAPTER 15

Traffic was light between Palo Alto and Berkeley Saturday morning, and they made the trip in a little over an hour. Amanda parked the car and they began a stroll through the campus. She acted as tour guide, identifying the various buildings and providing facts about the University, the city and local history. They walked through a large bronze gate, green from the passage of time, and into a wide concourse at the center of campus. Amanda explained that this was Sproul Plaza, the site of raucous sit-ins and protests several decades earlier. It was very serene now. They walked along winding paths that snaked through groves of ancient trees, grassy knolls and over a gurgling stream, which Amanda identified as Strawberry Creek. The buildings were mostly gray stone or concrete structures, old but well-maintained. The entire campus was built on an incline, sloping gently upward to the east, into the majestic Berkeley Hills. They passed a few students walking purposefully across campus or lounging on the ubiquitous concrete benches, reading or visiting. For the most part, the campus was quiet and sleepy.

They made their way to the southern edge of the main campus. Bancroft Way was the main artery stretching from East to West, with university buildings on the north side of the street and shops and eateries on the south side. Looking westward, Jake could see the terrain gradually sloping downward until it reached San Francisco Bay, glistening in the distance.

Telegraph Avenue intersected Bancroft Way at the midpoint of the campus, and provided a jolting contrast to the serenity of the campus grounds. Bustling crowds of people jostled past each other on both sides of the street. The sidewalks were lined with card tables and blankets, where street vendors hawked cheap jewelry, artwork, and psychic readings, among other things. Clean-cut students, scruffy street people, middle age professorial types, and scary looking teenagers blended comfortably together in a colorful mosaic of humanity.

It was an effort to stay together, as they navigated the crowded sidewalks. Amanda took Jake's hand and guided him through the shifting maze. They walked for some time with no particular destination, hand-in-hand, just watching the people. After an early lunch at an outdoor café, they returned to Amanda's car and drove up into the hills toward her parents' house.

As they ascended the winding roads up into the Berkeley Hills, Jake stared at the stunning panorama before him. Within minutes, they were overlooking the University of California campus, San Francisco Bay and the Golden Gate Bridge. "Wow! What a view! Your parents must be loaded."

"No, they're professors, and they live very simply," Amanda replied. "They bought their house twenty years ago, before property values went through the roof."

High up in the hills, Amanda pulled into a driveway in front of a modest looking house made of dark wood, with forest green shingles, which blended perfectly into the wooded surroundings. "Anybody home?" Amanda called out brightly as they entered. The house looked like the home of two professors, Jake thought, as he looked around. The walls and floors were dark wood, and the furnishings were simple, yet tasteful. Books were everywhere. The place had a warm and cozy feeling. They walked past the kitchen and down a flight of stairs into a comfortable family room, which was dominated by floor-to-ceiling windows framing the most spectacular view Jake had ever seen: San

Francisco Bay glimmering in the sunshine in all its glory, spreading out into the vastness of the Pacific Ocean beyond.

"Hello?" Amanda called, walking in the direction of the windows and opening a sliding glass door that led onto a cedar deck. "There you are," she said as she found her parents having lunch on the deck. Jake could see their faces brighten at the sight of their daughter, as they stood up to embrace her. "Dad and Mom, I'd like you to meet someone. This is Jake McShane."

"It's a pleasure to meet you both," Jake said, shaking their hands.

"The pleasure is ours, Jake," said Mr. Chang, as he greeted Jake warmly. He was a short man in his late fifties, with a confident yet soft-spoken charm about him.

"I'm so glad you could come," said Mrs. Chang. She had lively eyes and an energetic manner about her. Jake was struck by the resemblance between mother and daughter. It seemed that he was looking at two versions of the same face, Amanda's unmistakably Asian in appearance, while her mother was fair skinned and blue-eyed.

"This is a stunning view," Jake remarked.

"It is marvelous, isn't it?" Mrs. Chang agreed. "We've been here over twenty years now and I never take it for granted. We were very fortunate to have found this place when we did."

For the next fifteen minutes, Jake received a lesson in Bay Area geography, as Mr. and Mrs. Chang together identified the various sites before them. After the lesson concluded, Amanda changed subjects. "How's Grandma?" she asked, a look of concern crossing her face.

"I think she's coming along physically," her father replied, "but mentally, she's still not herself. She's really struggling. It's hard getting her interested in anything. She reads a bit, and watches TV occasionally, but mostly she just stares out the window," he said sadly. "She'll be glad to see you, though. Your visits always lift her spirits."

"Come on, Jake, I'd like you to meet her."

"I'd like that," he replied, as they excused themselves and headed upstairs.

"Knock, knock," Amanda called out cheerfully as she opened the bedroom door and peeked in. Her grandmother was sitting in a wheelchair next to a large window with the same view Jake had seen from the floor below.

"Hello kitten," the old woman said, smiling weakly.

Amanda walked across the room and hugged the old woman for a long time, then pulled back and looked directly into her grandmother's eyes. "I've missed you," she said. "You're looking better."

Grandmother Chang gave her a skeptical look.

"You really are, Grandma. You must be getting your appetite back." Then, looking toward Jake, who was standing awkwardly in the doorway, she said, "I've brought a friend along. I'd like you to meet him. This is Jake."

Jake approached and shook the frail hand. "Hello, Mrs. Chang. It's an honor to meet you." She looked at Jake for a few moments, as if assessing him, but did not speak. Jake continued. "I was very sorry to hear about your accident. I hope your rehab is going well."

"It's hard getting old, really hard," she replied, in a faraway voice.

"Oh come on, Grandma. You're the youngest seventy-seven-year-old I know. You'll be fine. It all starts up here." Amanda pointed to her temple. "How about if I make some tea?"

"That would be nice."

Amanda left Jake alone with her grandmother as she excused herself to prepare the tea. The situation felt familiar to Jake. During high school and college, he had worked at a neighborhood grocery store, where he spent much of his time delivering groceries to housebound customers. Most of them were elderly women, many were infirm, and almost all were lonely. At first, he had found it intimidating and uncomfortable because he didn't know how to deal with them. He quickly learned that he had it within his power to lift their spirits, and made it a challenge to do so with each visit. He discovered that the littlest things could really brighten their day. Sometimes he would do simple chores for them. Sometimes he would tell them a joke. Sometimes he would ask about their families. If he was able to get a smile out of them before he left, he felt like he had accomplished something.

He had another trick that was tried and true, and he had come prepared to use it if the opportunity presented itself. He pulled a chair alongside Mrs. Chang's, produced a deck of cards from his pocket and smiled at her. "I know a card player when I see one, Mrs. Chang. What do you say?"

Amanda returned a short time later with a tray of tea and crackers. "Tea time," she called out as she opened the door. She stopped dead in her tracks and stared in amazement at the unexpected scene before her. Her grandmother was sitting up straight in her chair, looking very much like her old self, lively and alert.

"Three eights," Jake announced, spreading out his cards.

"Three jacks!" Mrs. Chang replied, rubbing her hands together gleefully.

"Son of a gun, how did you pull that off?" Jake demanded, feigning shock and surprise.

"Young man, I come from Chinatown, where we take our poker play very seriously." She sounded boastful and cheerful at the same time.

Neither of them looked up when Amanda came in. She set up a folding tray next to them and laid out the refreshments. "Well, well, you two seem to be getting along famously."

"Your grandmother thinks she can take me at poker. We're going to see about that! Pull up a chair, I'll deal you in."

Amanda poured the tea and then joined in the game. Jake needled Mrs. Chang in a good-natured manner as they played. She chattered constantly, obviously enjoying herself. Amanda was overjoyed to see her grandmother in good spirits. She caught Jake's eye as her grandmother dealt the cards and silently mouthed, "Thank you," admiration and gratitude beaming from her face. Jake smiled back and mouthed, "You're welcome."

After Mrs. Chang beat Jake's straight with a full house, he announced, "You're killing me! I surrender. You win."

The old woman beamed. "Well, thank you for the game. I enjoyed that," she replied, obviously pleased with herself.

"Okay, let's change the subject now," Jake suggested, a trace of mischief in his voice. He looked at Mrs. Chang, then at Amanda. Then, looking back at Mrs. Chang, he said, "Tell me about Amanda when she was a little girl. I'm sure you've got some great stories."

"Oh no, you'll embarrass me, Grandma," Amanda pleaded, with a good-natured laugh.

Mrs. Chang ignored her, clearly thinking that this was a great idea, as Amanda was without a doubt her favorite subject. She proceeded to regale Jake with story after story about Amanda as a baby, Amanda as a young child, and Amanda as a teenager. Most of the stories were opportunities for Mrs. Chang to comment about how smart, talented, pretty and kind her granddaughter was. Amanda's embarrassment was obvious, but she endured the accolades, because she could see how much her grandmother was enjoying the conversation. After some time, Jake spoke up. "I really should give the two of you some time to catch up. I think I'll go for a walk and check out your neighborhood."

Jake walked for over an hour. It was late afternoon when he returned to the Chang house, where he found Mr. and Mrs. Chang beginning to make dinner preparations.

"If you don't have plans, we'd love to have you join us for dinner, Jake," said Mrs. Chang, just as Amanda entered the kitchen.

"Would you mind if we ate here, Jake?" asked Amanda. "I know we were planning on going into town, but Grandmother is in such great form that I hate to leave her right now."

"That sounds great. I'd love to," Jake replied.

Amanda wheeled her grandmother into the dining room and they sat down to a delightful dinner of Cantonese food, the like of which Jake had never tasted on the South Side of Chicago. Grandma Chang chatted happily throughout the meal, and Amanda and her parents found their own spirits buoyed as a result.

After dinner, Jake and Amanda cleaned the kitchen together, and then excused themselves to start the drive back to Stanford. Amanda's parents and grandmother remained at the dinner table, drinking tea and sharing their impressions of the young man they had just met. As

Amanda's parents exchanged observations, Grandma Chang spoke up in a tone that left no room for argument. "He's the one."

"What do you mean, Mom?" Mr. Chang asked.

"I mean, he's the one—the man Amanda is going to marry. No question about it."

"What makes you say that?" asked Mr. Chang. "They haven't known each other very long."

"I just know it. I can tell by the way she looks at him. And by the way he looks at her. He's the one. And do you know what? That's a good thing. He's the right one."

Amanda and Jake climbed into her Honda, and she started the ignition. Then she turned it off, and turned to face Jake. "I hope you don't mind that we wound up spending almost the entire day here. I know that's not what we had planned."

"I don't mind at all. Your family is great. I'm really glad I had the chance to spend some time with them."

She looked at him silently for a long moment. Her eyes became misty. "You're a very special person, Jake McShane. I'm glad I met you." She leaned over and threw her arms around him. Then she quickly kissed him on the cheek and started the ignition.

CHAPTER 16

Over the next two months, Jake and Amanda were virtually inseparable. While their respective workloads remained demanding, finding time for each other became their highest priority.

Fortuitously, their career paths seemed to be converging, and pointing both of them in the same direction: Chicago. Amanda had heeded Dr. Marsh's advice and made arrangements to visit both Northwestern and the University of Chicago during the first week of November to learn more about their fellowship programs and meet the people in charge. Jake had begun the fall interview process on campus and received flyback offers from several of Chicago's elite law firms. He was able to schedule those interviews during the same week Amanda had scheduled hers. They decided to stay for the weekend following their interviews so that Jake could show her around the city.

After four grueling days of nonstop interviews, they were able to spend all day Friday together sightseeing. They visited the Art Institute of Chicago, Navy Pier and the Willis Tower. Late in the afternoon, they browsed the glamorous shops on Michigan Avenue, had a casual dinner of authentic Chicago style pizza, and then went to a blues club on Rush Street for the evening.

At breakfast on Saturday morning, Jake began making suggestions about other notable Chicago sites they could visit. Amanda stopped him. "Let's not play tourist today. I'd like to see the real Chicago. I want to see where you grew up."

"Sure, we can do that, but I have to warn you, it's nothing like this," Jake replied, gesturing toward the glitzy hotels and high-rises along Lake Shore Drive.

They drove south, through downtown, and then through some of the more blighted areas on the city's South Side, before arriving in Beverly about thirty minutes later. Jake took Amanda on a brief driving tour of the neighborhood. For starters, they drove along Longwood Drive, a winding street at the bottom of the only real hill in the entire city. Perched atop the hill, looking out over spacious, well-manicured lawns, were large stately homes designed by some of the most renowned architects of the early and mid-20th century. They traveled up the hill and proceeded to drive back and forth through the gridlike pattern of the neighborhood streets. The homes were mostly old brick structures, with an occasional stucco or frame house here and there adding a bit of variety. Many of the homes were quite large and impressive, remnants of a time years ago when this was an exclusive neighborhood for the well-to-do. Just as many homes were more modest, bungalow style structures that had sprung up in the post-World War II era, providing affordable housing for city workers and tradesmen within the city limits. While there was great disparity among the size and appearance of the neighborhood's homes, the grand and the simple were seamlessly bound together by the innumerable trees lining every street. Maples, oaks, chestnuts and elms dominated the landscape.

"These are my old stomping grounds," Jake said as Amanda marveled at the brilliant fall colors. "I've got to take you to a very special place."

He pulled up in front of a smallish grocery store with a 1950s vintage sign that simply read "Quinn's Fine Foods." The parking lot was full, so they parked half a block away and made their way on foot. "This is one of the real nerve centers of the neighborhood," Jake explained as they joined a throng of shoppers entering the old but well-kept building. "I worked here all through high school and college."

The inside of the store was a flurry of activity. Unlike the large supermarket chains Amanda was accustomed to, Quinn's had only three aisles, each of which was barely wide enough for a pair of shopping carts to pass in opposite directions. Customers were lined up several rows deep in front of the butcher counter, where half a dozen butchers carved up fresh meat on large wooden butcher blocks and then wrapped their orders in crisp white paper for the waiting customers. A small army of women in their fifties and sixties wearing pale blue smocks scurried around, filling grocery carts from shopping lists and then disappearing into a back room.

Jake recognized nearly everyone, customers and employees, as he strolled through the store with Amanda, exchanging warm handshakes and friendly hugs with old friends and acquaintances.

As they made their way toward the produce section, they observed a short, trim man with a shock of white hair walking briskly and purposefully toward a customer. "Mrs. Callahan," he called out in a strong voice with a thick Irish brogue. "You forgot your pastries." He held up a small white bag as he chased a customer down the third aisle. "Hello, Jacob," he said casually as he hurried past them, as if he were used to seeing Jake on a daily basis.

"That's Mickey, the owner. He's my former boss." Jake explained. "He must be nearly seventy by now, but he still runs around like a kid."

A moment later, Mickey was back. "Jake! Great to see you, lad!" He beamed and shook Jake's hand enthusiastically. "Who's your lovely friend?" He turned toward Amanda, and Jake made introductions. They made small talk for a minute or two until Mickey noticed an overweight middle-aged woman searching for something she was obviously unable to find in the frozen food section. He gave Jake and Amanda a look that said, "duty calls." "Can I help you, dear?" he called out in a strong, friendly voice, as he hurried off.

They squirmed through the crowd in front of the butcher counter. "I can't believe how busy this place is," Amanda said. "Are they giving something away?"

"Nope. To the contrary, Mickey can't compete with the big chain stores on price, but he's still fabulously successful. He's built this place into a neighborhood institution, even though he breaks all the traditional rules of business."

"How does he do it?"

"It's simple. Mickey's goal is serving the community rather than trying to maximize his profits. His store is the vehicle that enables him to do that. He truly couldn't care less about how much money he makes. And because he places such importance on community service, people flock to his store, and the business thrives even though he does things that many business owners would consider utterly foolish."

"Like what?"

"For one thing, he provides a delivery service. There are a lot of elderly people in this neighborhood who don't drive, or have health problems or who otherwise have difficulty getting out to the store. They can phone in their order and have it delivered to their door—at no charge. Mickey employs a small army of people who take the orders, do the shopping, box up the groceries and then deliver them. His accountant continually harangues him because he loses his shorts on that service, but taking care of those shut-ins is very important to Mickey. He doesn't care what it costs. Not only that, he employs lots of high school and college students, probably twice as many as he really needs. Mickey believes he's providing gainful employment and valuable job experience that prepares them for the working world. Keeps them off the streets, too. Because of that, he's got a tremendously bloated payroll, but he doesn't care. He's making a positive difference in people's lives."

"Sounds like quite a man."

"He's a special person. I can't think of anyone I admire more. Come on, I'll give you the private tour," Jake offered, as they walked into a narrow entranceway leading to a swinging door. He led Amanda through it into the back room, which was bustling with activity, as the ladies in the blue smocks packed their groceries into boxes, which were then lined up along the floor leading to the back door. Two young men were busily carrying the boxes out the door and loading them into an old van. Jake looked at the names and addresses taped to the boxes and recognized most of them.

"Hi Kenny," Jake called out as one of the young men burst through the back door and lifted another box.

"Jake! What the hell are you doing here?" Kenny asked, winded from the exertion.

"Just stopped in for a visit. Looks like you're on your way to the Waiting Room. Say hi to all my girlfriends there."

"Will do. Gotta run now. See ya!" Kenny hustled out.

"Girlfriends?" Amanda asked with amusement. "What's the Waiting Room?"

"It's short for 'God's Waiting Room.' It's a big apartment building about a mile from here. A lot of the residents there are elderly, and never leave their apartments. It's as if they're just passing time, waiting to meet their maker. Somebody dubbed it 'God's Waiting Room' years ago. Pretty crass, huh? It's been shortened to just the Waiting Room."

"That's terrible," Amanda said with mock indignation.

"We take great care of them. Sometimes, we're the only person from the outside world they see all week. I'm not sure what they would do if Mickey didn't provide this service."

"I can't believe how many people you know around here," Amanda remarked as they made their way out of the bustling little store.

Jake shrugged. "I've lived my entire life in this neighborhood, and spent almost six years working at this store."

They spent the remainder of the afternoon visiting with Jake's parents at his childhood home, a few blocks up the hill from the grocery store. Of Jake's four siblings, only his youngest sister, Colleen, still lived at home. She was a senior in high school, and like Jake, was enamored of the idea of going to school on the West Coast. She eagerly peppered Amanda with questions about colleges in California, and seemed equally interested in hearing about the beaches, the mountains, and the California lifestyle.

Mrs. McShane prepared an elegant prime rib dinner, and they continued visiting into the early evening, until Jake announced, "We'd better be going now. I promised Amanda I would show her the neighborhood's primary form of entertainment."

"Oh no, you're not going to take her to the dive bars on Western Avenue, are you?" asked Colleen. "Talk about a way to ruin her impression of our great city!"

Jake looked at Amanda. "You wanted to see the real Chicago, right? Drinking beer at the local taverns is the primary form of social activity around here."

"Yeah, for lowlifes and drunks," said Colleen. "You can't take Amanda to a place like that!"

Jake was unconcerned. "Too late. I've already committed us. I told Johnny we'd meet him at Riley's." Then looking at Amanda, he asked, "You're still up for this, right? It may be a bit of a culture shock."

She laughed. "I think I can handle it. I may be living here someday, so I better do my best to learn the local customs. When in Rome ..."

They said their good-byes and walked toward Western Avenue. It was chilly and looked like it might rain, but it was only a few blocks. Western Avenue was the only commercial street in the Beverly neighborhood, and formed its western boundary. The east side of the street was lined with retail shops, fast food restaurants and small office buildings. The west side of the street hosted similar occupants, along with a wealth of drinking establishments. From 99th Street to 115th Street, there were bars on every block. At the moment, their names included Riley's, O'Brien's, Kelly's, and McSweeney's, but they changed frequently, usually from one Irish surname to another.

As was typical for a Saturday night, Riley's was crowded and noisy, although a bit less crowded and noisy than most of the other nearby taverns. For that reason, Jake preferred it to the others. One could actually carry on a conversation without too much exertion.

On their left as they walked in was a long bar with a shiny brass rail around it, and two bartenders behind it, hustling to keep up with drink orders. On the opposite wall were tall circular tables surrounded by high barstools, every one of which was occupied.

"Hi Jimmy!" Jake yelled to the bartender as they approached.

"Jake! Good to see you! Who's your friend?" The bartender had a booming voice and a friendly face.

"This is Amanda. She's visiting from California."

"Welcome, Amanda! I hope you're enjoying the Windy City. Drinks are on me. What'll you have?"

Jake ordered for them both. Amanda was not much of a beer drinker, but gamely sipped at the brew Jake handed her. They made their way toward the back of the bar. As in the grocery store that afternoon, Jake knew almost everyone in the place. He shook hands with many of the guys, hugged a few of the girls, and introduced Amanda to them all.

"I can't believe you know all these people," she said.

"It's a very close-knit neighborhood. Many of these people I've known since grade school. Most of those I didn't go to school with are brothers or sisters of my classmates. Large families are the norm here in Beverly—it's the Irish Catholic influence, I guess. Even if you don't know a particular person, chances are that you know someone in his family. Anyway, this is what people do to socialize on the weekends around here. I suppose it may seem a bit decadent if you're not used to it, but for many people here, this is a way of life."

"It doesn't strike me as decadent at all. Everyone seems friendly and well behaved. And they come here every weekend?"

"More often than that, for some of them."

They found a table near the back and sat facing the door. "So tell me about Johnny," Amanda asked.

"Sure. He's my cousin, and we've been best pals our entire lives. I'd have to say that, along with Mickey Quinn, Johnny is one of my real-life heroes. I've never met anyone that has such a way with people. He's generous, outgoing, charming and friendly, with everybody. In high school, he was the ultimate jock and definitely part of the 'in crowd,' but he would go out of his way to be friendly to the kids that were quiet or nerdy or misfits for whatever reason. He has a way of always finding the good in somebody—even when it's hard to find. I saw that long before high school. When we were eight or nine years old, a disabled kid moved into our neighborhood. He was in a wheel-chair and had real difficulty talking. I was freaked out by this and tried to avoid him, but Johnny went out of his way to talk to the kid and treat him like anyone else. When we became teenagers, Johnny started going to a summer camp for kids with muscular dystrophy and other disabilities. I went to visit a few times and always felt uneasy around them. I know that sounds terrible, but I did. I had trouble understanding their speech and that embarrassed me. But Johnny was their best pal, totally at ease in that situation."

"So what's he doing now?"

"He could have done anything. He was the star of our high school football team and as smart as any kid in the class. He just wasn't very motivated. He never studied, never cared about grades. He received a football scholarship to Wisconsin, but quit after two years. So now he's a painter. Not the artist kind – he paints houses. Does a little carpentry and remodeling work, too. He works for himself, and that gives him the flexibility to do what he really loves, which is running a camp for disabled kids in the summertime, and spending a lot of weekend time doing similar things."

A tall, dark-haired young man in a white fishermen's sweater walked in and looked around.

"Let me guess. That must be your cousin." As Amanda said that, he saw them, and waved.

"Yep. That's Johnny."

"Jake! Hey everybody, Jake McShane is back in town!" Johnny shouted as he strode across the room. Shouts went up from the bois-terous crowd.

"Let's hear it for Jake!"

"Here's to Jake!"

"Beers are on Jake!"

Johnny threw his arms around his cousin. "Great to see you, man! This must be Amanda. You're right, Jake, she's gorgeous!"

"Hi Johnny." Amanda extended her hand. Johnny shook it briefly, then embraced her in a bear hug as well.

"I can't believe you brought her to a dive like this!" Johnny said. "Don't you have any class? Or brains? You'll probably never see her again after this kind of treatment."

Jake laughed. "You too? Colleen said the same thing." Then looking at Amanda, he asked, "Am I in trouble?"

"We'll see. The night is young yet. I'll withhold judgment for now." Then, looking from one to the other she said, "Wow, you two really look like brothers. The family resemblance is striking."

Jake heard that frequently, and took it as a compliment, since Johnny was clearly a good-looking guy. He was tall, with a muscular build, and had the same distinctively Irish looking combination of fair skin, pale blue eyes and dark hair as Jake, only his hair was thick and curly, to the point of unruliness. He had an easy-going manner and an air of confidence about him.

They spent some time catching up, Jake and Amanda briefing Johnny on their recent interviews, and Johnny explaining that life was pretty much the same for him. He was working as much or as little as he wanted and enjoying the free and easy single lifestyle. He dated a lot of girls, but none of them seriously, he assured them.

Throughout the evening, old friends and acquaintances stopped by to chat. Jake was struck by how easily and gracefully Amanda fit in, even though, in his mind, she seemed totally out of place in a joint like Riley's. As the evening wore on, the crowd became louder and more boisterous, and it was clear that more than a few patrons had been overserved. Just as Jake was thinking it was about time to make a polite exit, a familiar face approached.

"Hey McShane, I thought you moved to the land of fruits and nuts." It was Danny Flynn, formerly one of the star athletes of their class, now an unemployed or sometimes employed truck driver, who spent most evenings cruising the bars on Western Avenue.

"Hi Danny. How's it going?" Jake tried to be polite, but this was one fellow he generally tried to avoid.

"Doing great, man. Partying all the time," Danny replied, hoisting his beer mug. Then leering at Amanda, he slurred, "And who's this hot little number? Can I buy you a drink, babe?"

Amanda was unfazed, and just smiled politely. "No, thank you."

"Amanda is a doctor, visiting from California," said Johnny casually, attempting to ignore the boorish behavior.

"No shit? I think I need a checkup. Wanna check me out, Doc?" Danny roared at his own attempt at humor.

Jake stepped forward quickly and took Danny by the arm. "Come on, Danny, let's take a walk."

A sneer crossed Danny's face. Jake pointed to his beer mug. "You're empty. Let me buy you a refill." He led Danny to the bar, ordered a drink for him, and then returned to Johnny and Amanda, feeling embarrassed. "Sorry about that. Danny's had a few too many. Don't take it personally. He's got a bit of a drinking problem."

Johnny was clearly incensed. "He's got a lot of problems, the biggest of which is that he's a selfish, inconsiderate prick, pardon my language. He married Cory Miller, one of the sweetest girls in our class, and he treats her like dirt. She's at home with two little kids, and that scumbag is up here every night getting drunk. He's just as mean and nasty when he's sober. That son of a bitch!"

"Johnny and Cory were high school sweethearts," Jake explained under his breath.

"She doesn't deserve this," Johnny said, still fuming. He took a deep breath, shook his head rapidly, and regained his composure. "I'm sorry, Amanda. I shouldn't let that guy get to me. It's just part of our colorful life on the South Side of Chicago."

It was well past midnight when Jake and Amanda decided to call it a night. Cold air blasted them as they stepped outside, and a light rain was beginning to fall. "Don't worry, it's a short walk," Jake assured her as she looked up at the ashen sky.

They walked briskly, hand-in-hand, heads down to avoid the bitter wind. Before they were halfway home, the skies opened.

"Okay, maybe walking wasn't such a good idea," Jake said. They ducked underneath a roof overhang protruding from a small garage, which provided adequate shelter from the rain, if not from the cold.

"Welcome to Chicago," Jake laughed, spreading his arms, palms up toward the sky.

She laughed with him, and they quietly watched the rain, snuggling close together for warmth.

"Well, what do you think? Of Chicago, I mean?" Jake looked at her seriously.

"There's so much to see, and so much to learn. It's so different from what I'm used to."

"Good different or bad different?"

"Neither. Just plain different." There was less enthusiasm in her voice than Jake had hoped for. She looked like she wanted to say more. Jake gave her a look, encouraging her to go on. "What if I really don't like it?" she asked. "What if I can't handle being this far from home? I know I'll miss my family terribly." She looked troubled.

Jake put his hands on her shoulders and looked deeply into her eyes. His voice was soft, yet firm, as he said, "Then we'll move back to California."

"We?"

"Yes, we."

"But you'll be starting your career here in Chicago. Your family is here, and all those friends that think so much of you. You belong here."

His gaze was steady, as he shook his head gently. "Amanda, I belong with you. I know we've only been together for a few months, but I've never been more sure of anything in my life. Wherever you go, that's where I want to be." This thought had been lurking in the back of his mind for some time, but he didn't expect to be vocalizing it this soon. Talking about their future together seemed far enough off that he had never given serious consideration to when and how to bring it up. He had never considered what words to use, or given any thought to the right setting for a romantic and dramatic proposal. But now, the words just came out. Not very eloquent he thought, feeling some chagrin, but heartfelt and sincere. He hoped he hadn't come on too strong or shocked Amanda with the suddenness of his suggestion.

She looked down. "Do you mean..."

"I mean I want you in my life—always. I mean, I think we should get married. I don't know when or where. I haven't thought about the details. I hadn't even thought about bringing the subject up until just now. But I know it's right." He paused, looking for a reaction. "What do you think?"

She continued looking down, and Jake saw a tear roll down her cheek. She looked up at him, through watery eyes, and nodded her head, slowly at first and then vigorously, laughing and crying at the same time. She couldn't find words. She threw her arms around him and squeezed as hard as she could. "I love you so much," she whispered in his ear, her tears wetting his cheek. "I can't wait to marry you!"

Jake lifted her off the ground and twirled her in circles as they embraced. Their spinning took them out from under the overhang and rain poured down upon them. They didn't care. They kissed, a deep, long, passionate kiss, in the dark, pouring rain. Then they stepped back and looked at each other, hands clasped, smiling and laughing—joyous, unrestrained laughter, as the rain mixed with tears on their faces.

"When should we tell people?" Jake asked, feeling giddy. "I don't think I can keep this bottled up inside."

"Let's figure that out tomorrow. We have a long plane ride back to California. We can talk it over then."

"We've got to tell somebody. I feel like I could burst. Let's go back to the bar and tell Johnny. Hell, let's have a glass of champagne!"

"Don't you think we should tell our parents first?"

"You're right, we should." Jake knew she was right, but didn't like the answer.

"Would you trust Johnny with a secret like this?" Amanda asked, looking as if she, too, couldn't wait to tell someone.

"I'd trust him with my life."

"Then let's go." She grabbed his hand and they marched purposefully back to the bar, making no attempt to shield themselves from the rain.

"Jesus Christ, look at you two! You look like drowned rats," Johnny shouted as they reentered the bar. "Did you forget something?"

Jake and Amanda stood there dripping, hair matted, clothing completely soaked through. They were shivering. They said nothing and stared at Johnny, with enormous smiles on their faces.

"What? You just found the winning lottery ticket? What's with you two?"

They looked at each other as if to say, "Who should tell him?" Then they looked back at Johnny, still smiling, but unspeaking.

Understanding suddenly set in. "Holy Shit! You son of a bitch! How long have you been keeping this a secret? You're getting married, aren't you?"

They both nodded their heads, their giddiness returning. Johnny hugged them both—rough, affectionate, drunken hugs, and started to shout to the bartender for champagne. Jake cut him off. "We've only been engaged for ten minutes. Nobody knows except you. You're sworn to secrecy for now, got it?"

"Got it, pal. This is fantastic! You two make such a great couple. I couldn't be happier for you!"

"I'm the luckiest man alive, Johnny," Jake gushed. "I really am." And then looking at Amanda, he said softly, with wonder in his voice, "I can't believe I get to spend the rest of my life with Amanda Chang."

PART TWO

CHAPTER 17

Grandmother Chang was right. Jake and Amanda were married the following summer. After finishing their final year at Stanford, they moved to Chicago, where Amanda began her fellowship at Northwestern and Jake began his legal career with Samuelson & Reid.

Amanda threw herself into her work with her customary passion and enthusiasm, quickly making a name for herself in the Chicago medical community. Jake's work did not provide the same level of excitement or fulfillment. Samuelson & Reid handled sophisticated, high-stakes litigation and cutting-edge business transactions; however, as a new associate, Jake was typically the junior-most member of a small army of lawyers on any given project. His work consisted primarily of long hours of legal research, and drafting lengthy legal memoranda, briefs and pleadings. He recognized that was a necessary and unavoidable part of the career path at a major law firm, and took solace in the fact that he had the opportunity to work with, and learn from, the finest lawyers around.

Their life outside of work as a young married couple was everything either of them could have hoped for, and they cherished their time together. Each took great interest in the other's professional life, and they shared their experiences, their thoughts and their hopes for the future. Life was good, and Jake was acutely aware of that. He often found himself gazing at his wife while she was sleeping, or at her desk reading, or walking toward him on the street, and saying a silent prayer of thanksgiving.

Shortly after completing her fellowship, Amanda gave birth to a baby girl. They named her Anna, after Amanda's grandmother. Amanda took a leave of absence following Anna's birth, and then returned to work three months later, on a reduced schedule. Fortunately, the hospital had an on-site day care center, which enabled Amanda to stop and visit Anna periodically throughout the day. Jake changed his hours to accommodate family life also. Although he had little flexibility regarding the amount of billable time he was required to log, he began arriving at work very early in the morning so that he could be home by early evening to spend time with his wife and daughter. It was a busy schedule, but they made it work. They were stressed, but happy.

Sunday was family day. No matter what demands their careers placed on them, they made a point of treating Sunday as their own time. They went to early morning Mass, and then Jake would fix breakfast. In the afternoon, they would try to enjoy one of the many sites and recreational opportunities the city had to offer. Sometimes it was a museum, sometimes a park or the zoo, and oftentimes it was the lakefront, their favorite destination. At least once a month, they had Sunday dinner at Jake's parents' house.

Jake had settled into a routine at the office as well. He would generally arrive no later than seven o'clock in the morning, and try to leave before six o'clock in the evening. He made a point of leaving the office for an hour at lunchtime no matter how busy he was, to break up the long day.

On a gray Thursday afternoon in early December, Jake returned to his office after his lunchtime break and was handed a stack of phone messages his secretary had taken while he was out. He recognized all of the names but one. "Darnell Tucker? Who's he?" Jake asked Alice, his secretary.

"I don't know," Alice replied. "He wouldn't tell me what it was about." Knowing Alice as he did, Jake was confident she would have politely pressed the caller for information. "He said it was important and sounded kind of upset. He wants you to call right away. He told me you might know him as Shooter. Seemed kind of strange."

Jake's mood darkened. He hadn't thought about Shooter in a long time. He walked slowly into his office, staring at the message. With considerable apprehension, he dialed the number.

"Cook County lockup," a brusque voice answered. It seemed more like an expression of annoyance than a greeting.

"May I speak with Darnell Tucker, please."

"You his lawyer?"

"I'm an attorney. I don't know what this is about. I'm just returning his call. He called me about ten minutes ago."

"Hold on."

Jake waited for several minutes, then he heard a familiar voice, but it was missing the cockiness that had accompanied it on past occasions.

"That you, Stanford?"

"Shooter?"

"Yeah, man, it's me. I'm in a jam. I need some help."

Jake glanced at his door, confirming that it was closed. He suspected that the partners at the firm would not look favorably on his association with someone they might perceive as a street thug. "You're in jail?"

"Yeah. Can you help me out?"

Jake hesitated as he groped for a tactful way to avoid involvement. "Shooter, I'm not sure I'd be of much use to you. I don't practice criminal law. You'd be better off with someone who really knows that stuff."

"Man, I don't know any other lawyers," Shooter replied, urgency in his voice. "You can handle this. It's not a big deal. They charged me with possession, but the shit wasn't even mine. I swear it. I just need to get out of here and then we can get this straightened out."

"Look, Shooter, I work for a big law firm; I don't practice on my own. I don't know if the firm would even allow me to handle your case. Besides, the rates here are really high. How about if I make some phone calls and try to find someone who's better equipped to handle this, and a lot more affordable?"

"Aw, come on man! You owe me!" Shooter was angry now and raising his voice. "Do you think you would have walked away from that playground if I hadn't been there? No way! No way, man." He stopped for a moment and regained his composure. "I'm sorry. I've got no right to talk to you like that. Can't you at least come down here so we can talk? I'm asking you as a favor. Please, help me out, Stanford."

Jake paused, thinking it over. His instincts told him that getting involved would be a bad idea, but he was reluctant to turn his back on a desperate soul who was pleading for his help.

"I did nothing wrong," Shooter said, enunciating every word, clearly and forcefully, in an adamant whisper. "I swear to God."

"You're at Cook County Jail, on 22nd Street?"

"Yeah."

"Alright, sit tight. I'm on my way."

As Jake sat in the taxi, he thought about how he might extricate himself from this situation. He was certain that Shooter could not afford his hourly rate. The firm did have a pro bono program, through which it provided legal services free of charge in certain instances; however, those matters typically involved legal representation of civic and charitable organizations, which provided a vehicle for the firm's lawyers to make contacts with well-connected community leaders who might steer business their way. He was certain that the firm's leadership would not condone his representation of an accused drug dealer, whether he was a paying client or not.

Twenty minutes later, the cab pulled up in front of Cook County Jail. Jake knew of it by reputation, but had never seen it in person. It was a massive concrete structure, almost completely devoid of windows. Jake informed the harried woman at the reception desk that he was there to visit Darnell Tucker. He had to look at the phone message to remind himself of Shooter's real name. "Take a seat over there," she snapped, without looking up, motioning to some grimy wooden chairs, most of which were occupied by people who looked and dressed nothing like any of the people in Jake's usual circles. "They'll call you when they're ready."

The place was loud and crowded. Many of the visitors smelled bad. "What in the world am I doing here?" Jake muttered to himself.

After what seemed like a very long wait, he was ushered into a small, stark cell. Except for two metal folding chairs and an old wooden table, the room was empty. He took a seat in one of the chairs, and Shooter was escorted in by a surly looking prison guard. "Thanks for coming, Stanford. I really appreciate it," said Shooter in a humble voice as he sat down across the table from Jake.

"No problem. So tell me what happened."

"We were up at St. Simon's last night, shooting hoops. The usual crowd was there. Two dudes come walking up—black dudes—and ask to get in the game. We let 'em play. They couldn't play worth shit, but they seemed like okay guys. They hung out with us afterwards and we were just bullshitting with them and Jerome asks them if they want to get high. He grabs his jacket off the ground and pulls out some weed, and guess what? They whip out their badges."

"Then what?"

"Jerome's my little brother, and I didn't want to see him get busted. He doesn't have a record and I don't want to see him get one. So I told them the shit was mine. It was only enough for a few joints, so I figured I could talk these guys into just confiscating it and leaving us alone. I knew if they went after Jerome, he'd lose his cool and make it worse. He's got a bad temper, and besides that, he's been doing the shit himself—pot and crack—way too much. He ain't thinking straight."

"So then what happened?"

"Jerome loses it, and tells those dudes to fuck off. Tells them they can't make a case on just a few joints, and they should just leave before they get hurt."

"Wrong thing to say to a couple of narcotics cops."

"No shit. They ask him if it's his stuff and he gets all defiant and tells them they can't prove shit. Next thing I know, one of them pulls a piece and the other handcuffs both of us. The guy with the gun says there must be more where that came from, and he asks us to take them to our crib. Jerome tells them they can't search our place without a warrant, so they say fine, have it your way. They bring us down here last night, and lock us up. Then they get a search warrant and search our apartment. They just told me they found a huge stash there: pot, cocaine and heroin, half a million dollars' worth. I don't know whether they're lying or what. If they did find anything, I don't know nothing about it, and that's the honest truth."

Jake looked at Shooter silently. "Oh, there's one more thing," Shooter said, looking down and speaking more softly. "I've got a record. I've done time. When I was nineteen, I got into some bad stuff. Started selling drugs. Never did them, and I was never a big player, but I know a lot of people and it was an easy way for me to keep in spending money. It went down just like yesterday. I tried to sell to the wrong guy and got busted. Had a good-sized stash and they nailed me. I served twelve months. But I ain't done it since, I swear. I've stayed clean."

Jake leaned back in his chair, folded his arms and took a long look at the young man on the other side of the table. Shooter seemed sincere, but he was a street hardened ex-convict. He could be lying through his teeth. Jake realized that he did not know this person at all, and that made him uneasy. "Here's how I see it," he said authoritatively, surprised at his own confidence, given the unfamiliar setting. "We tell the truth to the State's Attorney's Office. You had nothing to do with this. The drugs weren't yours. You know nothing about them. You explain to the prosecutor that you initially spoke up to help your brother out – just like you explained it to me. But," he paused for emphasis, "this only works if Jerome steps up and tells the truth also. If he takes responsibility for this, they have a hard time making a case against you."

"I don't like that plan," Shooter said. "You expect me to turn on my little brother? Make him take the rap? I can't do that! We need a Plan B."

"Shooter, there is no Plan B, and you're not turning on him. He needs to be a standup guy. He needs to take responsibility for his own actions, and not drag you down with him. You'll be in no position to look out for him if you're in jail. Don't forget, you've got a prior conviction. If you take the rap, you'll be looking at serious jail time. How old is Jerome?"

"Seventeen."

"Then there's at least a chance he could be prosecuted as a minor. Even if he's tried as an adult, he may get some leniency because of his age and the fact that it's a first offense for him. In any case, he'll certainly get off a lot easier than you would if you took the rap."

Shooter looked troubled. He stood and began pacing. Jake continued. "Maybe doing some time will actually help Jerome straighten himself out. If you go to jail, and he's back on the streets, how much confidence do you have that he'll stay out of trouble?"

"Not much. He's wild, man. Probably wouldn't be long before he's hanging with the gangbangers. His attitude will get him in trouble. He's always trying to pick a fight with somebody. You get hurt that way." Shooter looked sullen and dejected as he pondered his choices.

Jake spoke up. "You asked me for my help. I'm here, and I'm giving you my best advice. If you choose not to take it, that's up to you. It's your life. If you want my help, I'll talk to the State's Attorney's Office and see if we can get this straightened out. If you don't want me involved, that's your call. They'll assign you one of the public defenders and you can take your chances in court."

"I know you're right," Shooter said with quiet resignation. "This is tough, man." He shook his head sadly. "I'd like your help. I can't pay you right away, but I'm good for it. Just give me a little time."

"I'll tell you how you can repay me, Shooter, and it's not with money. I don't want a dime from you. What I want is a commitment that you will do everything within your power to straighten out your life. No more drugs; no stealing; no fighting. Do something constructive with your life. Look at you – you're young, you're strong, you're healthy. You're the kind of guy people look up to. I've seen it—at the gym and at the playground. Use those gifts to make something of yourself."

There was an angry tone in Jake's voice as he lectured the dejected young man across the table. Shooter listened quietly, staring at the floor. Jake knew he must have sounded naïve and self-righteous, but he didn't care. He felt entitled to issue a stern lecture, if for no other reason than to make himself feel like he wasn't completely wasting his time by being there. Aside from that, the sight of this healthy, talented young man so close to the brink of squandering life's precious opportunities just got to him, and he felt compelled to speak his mind.

"Listen, Shooter," Jake continued in a softer voice. "I realize I don't know anything about your world and all the challenges life has thrown your way. But we all have choices. You can choose to do what it takes to improve your situation and live a life that you can be proud of. Or you can choose to be mad at the world and find lots of excuses for why you can't succeed. Graveyards are full of people with good excuses who wasted their lives and never amounted to anything. Don't be one of those people. Promise yourself you won't. That's how you can repay me."

Shooter continued looking down and nodded his head. "You're right, man. I need to do that." He looked up at Jake. "So what now?"

"I need to talk to Jerome. Getting you out of this mess will depend entirely on him. Will he talk to me?"

"I don't know. He's pissed at the whole world right now. Blames me for letting those cops into our game. He's hard to reason with under any circumstances, but he'll probably be even worse now."

"I'll see what I can do. I'll be in touch."

"Thanks, Stanford. I won't forget this."

As the guard returned to escort Jake out of the cell, Jake informed him that he needed to see Jerome Tucker. After another excruciatingly long wait, Jake was escorted back to the room where he had met with Shooter. As Jerome was led in, Jake could see that his face was just as he remembered—youthful, tough and angry, but the rest of him had changed considerably. He was no longer short and skinny. He was several inches taller than Jake, with a rock solid frame. He walked slowly, shoulders slouched, and had a menacing air about him even though his hands were cuffed in front of him.

"Hi Jerome. Remember me?"

Jerome looked at him sideways for a few moments, then grunted as recognition set in. "I remember you. What do you want? You a cop?"

"No, I'm a lawyer. I just met with your brother."

"You his lawyer?"

"I don't know yet. I'm hoping he won't need a lawyer. That really depends on you."

"What the hell are you talking about?"

"Do you want to help your brother?"

"Why should I help his stupid ass? It's his fault we're locked up. If he hadn't made friendly with those cops, we wouldn't be here."

"But the fact is, you are here, Jerome. And so is Shooter. And from what I've heard, he doesn't belong here. If the stuff was yours, you ought to take responsibility for your own actions, and not make your brother take the rap for this."

"Who the fuck are you to tell me what to do?" Jerome yelled, glaring at Jake and stepping toward him in a threatening manner. "I don't have to talk to you. Why don't you get your ass out of here?"

Maybe it was because Jerome was in handcuffs, or maybe it was because he'd had a long day and was irritable and impatient, or maybe he was just incensed that this kid would actually let his brother pay for his transgressions. Whatever the reason, Jake was not about to be intimidated. He stepped toward Jerome, coming within inches of his face. "Listen, hard ass, I'll go when I've said what I came to say, and here it is: I was hoping some part of you would want to do what's right. I was hoping you had it in you to be something more than a coward, trying to save your own skin. I was hoping you wouldn't be the one to send your brother to jail for something you did. It's in your hands, Jerome. You can send him to jail or you can set him free."

Jerome glared back for a few minutes, then turned his back on Jake. He shuffled a few feet in the opposite direction and stopped. "Fuck!" he shouted, at no one in particular. "Son of a bitch!" he shuffled around the small cell, trying to assess the situation. "So you want me to confess—tell the cops the shit was mine and Shooter had nothing to do with it?"

"That's the truth, isn't it? That's what it will take to get Shooter out of this."

"But if I confess, then I go down. I could take my chances at trial. I could say I didn't know anything about the stash in the apartment. They can't prove it was mine. It could've been anybody's."

"Think about it, Jerome. If you do that, Shooter goes down. He told the cops the stuff in your jacket was his. He's got a prior conviction for possession. And, they found the stash in the apartment where you both live. The jury will nail him in a heartbeat, and he'll go to jail, maybe for a long time. It would be a second conviction. There's no way around this. He goes down, unless you come clean."

"There's got to be another way!" Jerome shouted. Anger and desperation contorted his face as he walked in circles around the tiny cell. Jake sensed that he might be making some progress, and that Jerome was close to coming around. His hope vanished in an instant as Jerome stopped and approached him, saying in a low, venomous voice, "Here's how it's going to work, motherfucker. You're Shooter's lawyer. You figure this out. You find a way to get us both off. People walk on technicalities all the time. Figure it out! If you turn on me, I'll make you pay. Someday, someway, I'll get you. If I do time, you better watch your back, man. I'll find you."

Jake turned and walked away, fuming. "Get us out of here!" Jerome shouted after him. Jake looked at his watch and realized that he'd lost his entire afternoon. He hoped he hadn't been missed at the office. He needed to get back. He did not want to endure another long wait to see Shooter again. He would find out how to reach him by phone tomorrow.

On the cab ride back to the office, Jake tried to formulate a strategy—an exit strategy. He had tried to help. He'd given it his best shot and it just didn't work out. He would call Shooter in the morning and describe his meeting with Jerome. He would call the State's Attorney's Office and try to convince them that Shooter was not their guy. It would be a futile gesture, but then he could back out of this mess with a clean conscience.

CHAPTER 18

Approximately eighty lawyers sat in the windowless conference room of the downtown hotel, eating a lunch of tasteless chicken and overcooked asparagus, listening to the guest speaker drone on about the new legislative efforts to bring tort reform to the State of Illinois. The thought of punitive damage caps made the meal even more unappetizing for the majority of the audience, who earned their living as plaintiffs' attorneys.

Rick Black looked around the room, hoping to identify someone who might be worth getting to know, such as a prominent personal injury or medical malpractice attorney. What he saw was a sea of unknown faces, looking as bored as he was. He wolfed down what passed for chocolate pudding, and walked impatiently out of the room, not caring whether it was bad form to leave in mid-speech. This was a waste of time.

It had been about a month since he left Robbins & McKee, one of Chicago's largest and most prestigious law firms. It was a bad fit, he told himself. He was a born trial lawyer and belonged in the courtroom. Spending years in the bowels of the firm's law library, researching and writing, and being the junior member of the oversized team of lawyers assigned to any given case was a waste of his talent. He was a warrior who craved combat; a performer who needed to dominate center stage. Therefore, his career needed a sharp detour from the road he had initially chosen.

As he considered his talents and his temperament, his path became clear. He was smart and aggressive. He was creative. He was a gifted communicator, who could charm any jury. And he had a burning desire to be fabulously successful, both through his courtroom victories, and through that ultimate and unambiguous measure of success—money. He would be a plaintiffs' lawyer, the bane of the existence of firms like Robbins & McKee and their wealthy corporate clients. They would assign armies of lawyers to defend the cases he would bring, and he would vanquish them. Those were the thoughts that tantalized and motivated him. He could do it, and he vowed to himself that he would do it.

He was on the right path now, he told himself; he just needed some traction. For the time being, he had set up shop in his father's office. Neither of them viewed this as a long-term arrangement. He had the use of an office in his father's suite, and access to secretarial support, but beyond that, he was expected to be self-sufficient. You eat what you kill, his father had told him, meaning he had to generate his own business, because his father did not plan on sending work his way.

Rick had spent the last month attending lunches, bar association meetings, and other functions that would enable him to meet other attorneys and pass out his business cards. He frequently met lawyers who remembered him as a basketball player, which was a good conversation starter. However, despite having thrown himself headlong into the networking circuit, those efforts had yielded nothing in the way of business.

Rick walked briskly across downtown toward his office. He had no appointments and no reason to be in a hurry other than to get out of the harsh, December wind that whipped his face. His father was ushering a disheveled looking woman in her early forties out of the office as he walked in.

"Who was that?" Rick asked.

"Someone who wanted to waste my time," the elder Mr. Black replied, looking annoyed. "She got fired for failing a drug test at work and wants to sue her employer. Dead loser. I told her I don't handle those kinds of cases."

Rick never passed up the opportunity to needle his father. "Business must be good, Dad. You used to tell me that any case can be a winner with the right lawyer."

"Well, almost any case—but not that one. I think she was stoned when I interviewed her." He walked abruptly into his office and slammed the door.

Rick casually strolled toward his office, stopping briefly to flirt with Amber, his father's well-endowed secretary, who was fond of low cut blouses even in December. He sat at his desk and looked out the window at the light snow that was beginning to fall. The words he had just spoken to his father were stuck in his head. He remembered using them on another occasion, when living examples of their truth seemed to be present in abundance. It was at that bar on the South Side, McShane's hangout. He thought about it. It was Friday. He had no plans that evening. Why not?

Rick donned blue jeans and his red Indiana sweatshirt. There were bound to be plenty of sports fans there, and some of them would certainly remember him as an Indiana University basketball star. It would be a good icebreaker.

He arrived at Riley's Pub around nine o'clock. It was packed. As luck would have it, Jimmy was still tending bar, and he immediately recognized Rick from their prior meeting. He introduced the former basketball star to the handful of people at the bar, and Rick was welcomed like a visiting celebrity. He chatted with his new friends, played darts and shot a few games of pool. He found that he was actually enjoying the evening.

After several hours of this, Rick decided it was time to get to work. He walked up to a crowded table that included several people he had shot pool with earlier in the evening. "I guess pool's not my game," he announced with a broad smile and a modest shrug. "Lost again."

"Better stick with basketball, Rick," said Robbie, a skinny guy wearing a striped rugby shirt, with a tone of good-natured superiority. He had beaten Rick at pool earlier in the evening.

"I don't know, I think Rick might be hustling you guys. He's probably the best pool player in this joint," said Kim, a flirtatious blonde who looked too young to be in a bar, flashing a becoming smile.

"I wish," replied Rick. "No, I'm done. I'm tired of losing!" he laughed.

A balding, round-faced man gestured to an empty chair. "Have a seat, Rick. Let me fill you up." He grabbed Rick's half-empty glass and poured beer from a pitcher.

"Thanks, don't mind if I do."

Someone asked Rick what had brought him to Riley's. He explained that he was supposed to meet a friend, but the guy hadn't shown up. Someone else asked about basketball, and why he hadn't gone pro. He did his best to sound modest, and said he simply wasn't good enough. Then Rick decided it was time to steer this conversation in the right direction.

"So Curt, what kind of work do you do?" he asked the round-faced man who had invited him to sit down.

Curt explained that he worked for a small accounting firm. His father and two brothers were partners in the business, and they officed about a mile up the road.

"How about you, Robbie?" Rick asked.

"I'm a fireman," Robbie replied. "The pay's not great, but you can't beat the hours. Lots of free time—I love it."

Rick looked at Kim. "Let me guess. You must be a model, right? Haven't I seen you in the Victoria's Secret catalog?" They all laughed.

"I like the way you think. I'd love to get paid for parading around in my underwear." She looked at him suggestively. "Unfortunately, I work for the IRS. I don't think they would approve of that."

That prompted an onslaught of teasing, which she handled graciously. "How about you, Rick? What do you do now that you've moved on from basketball?" Kim asked.

Sounding as nonchalant as he could, Rick replied, "Well, I'm like Robbie. I'm lucky enough to have a job that I truly enjoy. I'm a lawyer."

"A lawyer? That sounds worse than working for the IRS," Curt remarked. Other good-natured ribbing and bad jokes followed. "You actually like that?" Curt asked.

"It's great," said Rick with as much enthusiasm as he could muster. "Partly, I like it because it's like sports. It's competitive, the stakes are high, and I love to play the game. But there's another reason, too. I like it because I can really make a difference for people. When someone gets hurt or is treated unfairly, I can help. I fight for them. Sometimes I can win big bucks for them. It's like being Robin Hood."

"What kind of cases do you handle?" asked a young man named Larry, who had been listening quietly until that point. He had greasy black hair and several days of stubble on his pale face.

"I focus on representing the little guy who's been wronged by someone bigger and more powerful. The type of wrong doesn't really matter. If someone's been fired unfairly or otherwise treated badly by his employer, if someone has gotten hurt, if a doctor's been negligent, I'll fight that fight. And I love it, I really do. I play to win, and there's nothing more satisfying than winning big bucks for your client. I can really change their lives for the better." He said this with such sincerity that no one dared make any more lawyer jokes. Then he quickly changed the subject. "Well, enough about me! Who needs a refill?"

He walked up to the bar, bought a few drinks, carried them back to the table, and politely excused himself. He had planted some seeds, now he needed to circulate through the bar and plant a few more. It was easy. He was good at working a crowd. His good looks, charm, and friendliness made it easy for him to start conversations with total strangers. By the time the conversation concluded, the person he was chatting with would believe that he was a very successful plaintiffs' lawyer, without ever feeling like he was hustling for business.

Later in the evening, Rick was sitting at the bar chatting with the bartender when two young men approached. One was Larry, whom he had met earlier. The other was a carrot-top with a ruddy complexion and crooked teeth, who introduced himself as Ace. "Mind if we pick your brain for a few minutes?" Larry asked. He seemed hesitant and nervous, looking around as if he didn't want to be overheard.

"Sure thing, fellas. What's up?"

"We were hoping for a bit of legal advice," said Larry, under his breath.

"No problem," Rick replied in his most accommodating voice. "What's going on?"

"We've both gotten screwed by our employers," said Ace. "We'd like to know if you think either of us has a decent case."

"I'd be happy to talk about it," said Rick. "Let's move over there, so we can have a little privacy." He pointed to a booth near the window that had just been vacated.

Ace was eager to tell his story, and launched into it even before they had sat down. "I work in construction, for a local home builder." His demeanor was dark and angry as he began reliving his story. "There's this Mexican guy that was just hired as foreman. Thinks he knows everything. Thinks his shit don't stink, you know what I mean? He drives all the guys crazy, he's so goddamn particular. He's always on our case, and he's on me more than most. So a couple of weeks ago, I show up at work one morning and he jumps all over me for leaving the construction site a mess the night before. How was I supposed to know the owners were coming by? No one told me. That's what I say to him, but the guy gets right in my face and he won't let it go. So I shoved him and told him to get out of my face. I didn't hit him, I just shoved him. The son of a bitch fires me right there. It's not right, man. I'd been working there almost two years and never had no problems until this asshole came along. He provoked me!"

Rick look steadily at Ace, then at Larry. "Look guys, here's how it works. You've got to put yourself in the jury's shoes. You've got to make sure that they see it your way. Nothing in this world is black and white—not much anyway—especially when it comes to employment decisions. If a guy gets fired because he loses his temper, or because he doesn't get along with his boss or co-workers, there's almost always more to the story. You've got to be able to tell the jury what the rest of the story is. Is there some subtle form of discrimination going on? Is the employee being retaliated against because he was trying to do the right thing? Those things happen all the time. You've got to make sure the jury hears those reasons, and if you tell your story the right way, they will. When that happens, they'll become furious with the company and want to dole out some serious punishment. You know what that translates to in our system? Big piles of cash!"

Ace was fired up. "I want to nail that bastard!"

"Then you need to think hard about all the facts leading up to this incident. Like I said, if your story is that you just got mad and shoved your boss, that's not likely to impress a jury. Think about anything else your boss did before your termination that was unfair. Also, remember that litigation is war. You need to exploit your opponent's weaknesses. Think about what pressure you could apply that will make him want to avoid a very public fight." Then reaching into his wallet, he pulled out a business card and handed it to Ace. "If you want to talk further, feel free to call me."

"So, do I have a case?" Ace asked.

Rick looked at him, unsure whether anything he had just said had sunk in. He lifted his beer mug and clinked glasses with Ace. "In the hands of the right lawyer, any case can be a winner. Just think about what I said."

"What about you, Larry?" asked Rick, looking across the table. "You mentioned that you've got an issue, too." Larry had been silent throughout the exchange between Rick and Ace, but despite his bleary eyes, had listened with keen interest.

"Yeah, I got fired, too. I worked for a … retail establishment. It was just like you said. They fired me and gave me some bullshit reasons, but something else was going on." He seemed reluctant to talk about it. "Can I have one of your cards?"

"Sure, call me anytime." Rick handed him several business cards.

"I don't have a lot of money, Rick," Larry said, looking troubled. "I haven't worked since I got fired. How much do you charge?"

"Don't worry about that," Rick said dismissively. "I handle cases on a contingent fee basis. That means that if I agree to take your case, it costs you nothing. My fee comes out of whatever money we recover. If we don't win, you pay me nothing. If we do, I get thirty percent of any settlement, forty percent if the case goes to trial. So there's absolutely no risk to you, and you know I'll be motivated. I've got every incentive to score as big as we can because my fees are based on what we recover. So if you've got a case, even if it's a long-shot, there's no reason for you not to pursue it."

"That sounds great," said Larry. "I'll give you a call. I'm a little smashed right now and want to be sure I'm thinking straight when we get into this."

"Call me anytime, pal. I'll be in the office most of next week."

Rick drove home thinking about the evening, Larry and Ace in particular. It was obvious to him that they were a couple of losers who probably deserved exactly what they got from their employers. Nevertheless, he had tremendous confidence in his own resourceful-ness. If he heard from them, why not take their cases? It would be a real challenge, a test of his ability. He liked playing against long odds. Good practice, too. Anyway, it was a moot point, he thought. He would probably never hear from them again.

CHAPTER 19

I t was Monday, four days after his trip to Cook County Jail. Alice
buzzed Jake on his intercom and announced that Mr. Tucker was
holding. With considerable reluctance, Jake picked up the receiver.
"Hello?" He had difficulty concealing the irritation in his voice.

"I'm out, man. You did it! They dropped the charges."

Jake was astonished. "Are you serious?"

"Jerome stepped up. He told the prosecutor the real story. He ain't
happy, man. He's still pissed at me and he's really pissed at you, but
he stepped up. You must have gotten through to him. They released
me about an hour ago."

"That's great. I'm happy for you, Shooter. I hope Jerome can learn
from this and turn his life around. I also hope that next time I see you
is on the basketball court and not in jail!"

"Me too," Shooter replied. "Hey thanks, Stanford. I really mean
it. I owe you, big time."

"Don't mention it, Shooter. Best of luck to you. Stay out of trouble!"

Jake wondered who would be representing Jerome. It sounded
like he had confessed, which meant there would be a plea bargain
rather than a trial. In any event, his curiosity about that subject was
outweighed by his distaste for it, and his desire to put these people in
his past as quickly as possible.

CHAPTER 20

Larry Doyle sat in the waiting room of the downtown law office, looking at his worn jeans and dirty boots, feeling self-conscious. He had never had an appointment with an attorney before, so the setting felt foreign. On the other hand, Rick Black struck him as a decent guy, and after all, he had encouraged Larry to come see him.

Larry thought carefully about his story. His boss had told him that his attitude had been lousy for some time. The boss said he had become unreliable, because he frequently arrived at work late or called in sick. That was bad enough, his boss had told him, but when his bad attitude resulted in rudeness to customers, that couldn't be tolerated. So he was fired after a customer called the store to complain about him.

Well, the boss didn't have the complete picture. Those crotchety old ladies were insufferable. They ordered him around, they were condescending, and they complained incessantly. He was hired to make their deliveries, which he did. No one told him that he was expected to unpack their boxes, or take out their trash, or stand there and listen to them drone on when he was in a hurry. It had been a bad morning. He was hung over and that nag, Mrs. Leonard, just pushed his buttons, and he snapped. It could have happened to anyone. He should have been given another chance.

Rick strode through the glass doors in a charcoal pinstriped suit, looking very much the part of a successful trial lawyer. Larry immediately felt self-conscious again, but Rick greeted him enthusiastically and immediately put him at ease. Rick appeared to be treating him like an important client, which bolstered his confidence.

Rick escorted Larry to his office and invited him to have a seat in the dark leather chair facing his desk. The office was impressive. Rick's Stanford and Indiana University diplomas adorned the paneled walls, surrounded by pictures and newspaper headlines of his glory days as a college basketball star. Larry was a fanatic about college basketball, and they chatted briefly about the teams and players who were likely to be the standouts this year. After several minutes of this, Rick leaned back in his chair, folded his hands and looked directly at Larry. "So, let's talk about why you're here, Larry. I believe you told me on Friday that you lost your job."

Larry told his story, just as he had rehearsed it in his head. Rick listened attentively, jotting down notes on a yellow legal pad.

"Is that it?" Rick asked when Larry had finished. Larry detected disappointment in Rick's voice. "I'm afraid it's going to take more than that to get a jury fired up, Larry."

Larry started to say something, but stopped. He had been afraid he would hear that. His eyes darted around the room. He had heard every word Rick said Friday night about having a claim that would incense a jury. He had heard what Rick had said about identifying your adversary's pressure points. Larry hadn't been the smartest guy in school, but he was street-smart, he told himself. He could play this game.

"Larry?" Rick was staring straight at him, eyebrows arched. "Is there more to this story?"

"Yeah, there is," Larry replied, looking at the floor. "It's just like you said the other night. The owner of the store was looking for a reason to fire me. Bitching out that old lady was just a convenient excuse. He had it in for me because of something else."

"What else?"

"This is hard to talk about." He took a deep breath. "The guy was making passes at me. You know, coming on to me. I ain't no fag, man, so I wouldn't give him the time of day. I think that's why he really fired me."

Rick was sitting bolt upright now, looking intensely at Larry. "This is important, Larry. Tell me exactly what he said."

Larry's eyes darted around the room again. "I don't remember exactly, it's been a few months now," he stammered.

"Then tell me the gist of it, if you don't remember the exact words," Rick demanded.

"I don't remember, specifically, I mean ... I was so shocked. He basically made clear that he wanted to perform ... some kind of ... sex act with me." Larry fumbled for his words. "I'm sorry, this is really embarrassing."

Rick ignored the apology. "What kind of sex act, Larry?" His tone was impatient.

"Shit, I don't remember. I was so stunned."

"Where did this happen? And when? Did you tell anybody?"

"Hell no, I didn't tell anybody. Would you? It's embarrassing, and humiliating. Who knows what they might think of me. It was in the store. It started a few months before I got fired. It actually happened several times."

"Where in the store? Precisely where did it happen, on any of those occasions?"

"Hell if I know, I can't remember—in the back room, I think, when no one was around. Does it matter where?"

Rick put his pen down and leaned back in his chair, studying the man across the desk from him, skepticism written all over his face. He stood, walked toward the window and stared out at Lake Michigan. After a long silence, he turned around. The skeptical look on his face had transformed to one of eagerness and intensity.

"Larry, first of all, let me say that I'm really sorry for what you had to endure. That's absolutely terrible. But that's why we have laws and a court system. You and I are going to make that bastard pay! But we've got to put together a game plan. And you need to do exactly as I say. Got it?"

The surprise was evident on Larry's face. The story sounded like bullshit, even to him. Yet here was this hotshot lawyer ready to take on his case. "That's great, Rick. Awesome! I really appreciate it. Just tell me what we need to do."

"First, let me get some background information." He proceeded to ask Larry about the business where he'd worked, its owner, and Larry's employment history, among other things. "Tell me more about your former boss, Larry. What kind of guy is he? What makes him tick? What things are most important to him?"

"Well, most people don't know what I know. They think he's a saint. He's active in the local church, he's chairman of the neighborhood planning committee, he's worshiped by all the customers who shop in his store. The neighborhood loves him. He's been a goddamn institution there for years."

"Has he had any legal problems? Extramarital affairs? Any dirt you know about?"

"No. Like I said, he's a pillar of the community. Everyone loves the old bastard. Sorry, I wish I could think of something scandalous, but I just don't know of anything."

"Don't be sorry. This is great. If his reputation is what you say it is, he's got a lot to lose. Once he sees what we've got in store for him, he won't want a public battle. There's a good chance he'll pay up without much of a fight, just to keep this quiet and preserve his reputation. If he doesn't, he's a fool."

"So what happens next?"

"Here's the plan. You need to write down your story for me. Don't spare any of the gory details. You need to be very specific about what he said and did. Remember, the story needs to make the jury feel absolutely shocked and disgusted."

Larry looked worried. "But how can we prove all this? There were no witnesses."

"You're the witness, Larry. You'll be selling your story to the jury, so it better be good. Remember, this guy screwed you. Our mission is to make sure that justice is done and he pays for what he did. If you have to embellish your story to make sure the jury reaches the right conclusion, then do it! Words are our weapons here, Larry. Don't hold back. We need to do what it takes to make sure that the jury does the right thing here—punishes that son of a bitch and makes you rich! That's the right result, so whatever it takes to get us there is okay."

"I understand," said Larry. "I'll get to work on that. Then what happens?"

"Then we go to war. First, I'll send a demand letter, letting the old fart know that I'm representing you, and that we will be pursuing a claim for sexual harassment and retaliatory discharge. I'll tell him that we will be initiating formal legal action if he doesn't agree to a quick settlement. He probably won't, so then we'll start ratcheting up the pressure. We'll file a complaint with the EEOC, the Equal Employment Opportunity Commission. That's the federal agency that handles employment complaints involving sexual harassment and retaliation. They'll assign an investigator, who will interview your former boss and get his side of the story. It ought to shake him up when an investigator representing the federal government starts questioning him. And, what'll shake him up even more is that the investigator will talk to his employees to see whether any of them have observed anything inappropriate. It doesn't really matter what the employees say—the mere fact that they are being interviewed about this will stir things up and get the rumors flying."

"I love it!" said Larry, his eyes gleaming. "But what if the EEOC doesn't buy our story?"

"It doesn't matter. The EEOC investigates these matters, but they don't render any final judgment. When they finish their investigation, they'll simply render an opinion stating whether or not they concluded that there's probable cause for believing that the law was violated. Regardless of their conclusion, you then have the right to file a lawsuit in federal court. Then comes the really big blow."

"What's that?"

"We get the local press involved. They can be our greatest ally."

"Will they take our side?"

"Not overtly, but just by doing what they do, they'll be a huge help. If the allegations are juicy enough, they'll see the potential for a great story. They'll make some pretense of trying to be objective, but the reality is that they'll want to sensationalize this. When that happens, the old boy is done for. Everyone who knows him will be wondering about this. By that time, he'll really be feeling the heat, and he may be forced to settle before all of his business dries up and blows away."

"So how much should we ask for?" asked Larry, trying unsuccessfully to suppress his eagerness.

"If you want there to be any hope for a quick score, without a battle, we need to keep it reasonable. If the opening number is too high, he'll have no choice but to fight. If he does decide to fight us, then our price goes way up. What kind of money do you think this guy has anyway?"

"Shit, he's loaded. That business is a gold mine. You ought to see the traffic that flows through there. He's got to be worth millions."

After some discussion, they settled on an opening demand of $250,000. Rick then escorted Larry to the elevator, both of them caught up in the excitement of what was to come. "I'll be ready to go as soon as I get your written summary, Larry, so get to work on it. And Larry—make it good!"

CHAPTER 21

◆

"Listen, Jerome, you've got to be careful in there. You've got to watch your back every second. Be careful who you hang with." There was an urgency in Shooter's voice as he spoke to his younger brother. It had been two days since Shooter was released from lockup, but he had not been allowed to visit Jerome until now.

"Let me tell you how I got by," Shooter continued. "I tried to make sure that people in there thought I was one dangerous son of a bitch. I talked tough. I acted tough. I made up stories about things I had done on the outside, but I didn't boast about them in public. I'd tell things to one or two guys, like it was a secret. Before long, everybody heard about it. But here's the key: Except for one time during my first few days, I never actually got into a fight. If you do that, you make enemies. You don't want enemies in the joint. They'll find a way of getting to you. Also, fighting ruins your chances for an early parole. So control your temper, man. Be smart!"

Jerome looked tired, like he hadn't slept much lately. He was sullen, the usual bravado and defiance gone. By instinct, he had been acting pretty much like Shooter had suggested since he'd been locked up, but he was eager for any advice Shooter could provide. Jerome had always looked up to his older brother. Shooter was smart, and he knew how things worked. Shooter had been here before. "You gonna come visit once in awhile?" Jerome asked glumly.

"Yeah, I'll be around. And when you get out, things will be different. I've got plans. But first, you've got to get through this. What I'm saying is important, Jerome. There are some bad dudes in there, and I mean real bad. You've got to do your best to avoid them, but don't let anyone think you're afraid or weak. Shit, look at you. You're as big as an NFL linebacker now. People won't mess with you unless they think you're afraid. But if you are, they'll sense it, and they'll be all over you."

"I can take care of myself," Jerome replied, sounding more like he was trying to convince himself than like he actually believed it.

"Another thing, Jerome." Shooter stood up, and his voice rose in intensity. "Watch out for the gangs. They'll try to get their hooks in you. Big, tough looking dude like you – they'll want you on their side. They'll promise you protection. They'll promise you all kinds of shit. But don't go for it. You've got to get along—don't make them mad. It's even okay if you get tight with some of them, because you don't want them as enemies. But don't join up with them. If you do, you'll have a built-in set of enemies on the inside, and the gang you're with will expect your allegiance once you get out. Like I've been telling you your whole life, if you get in with the gangs, you'll wind up dead or right back in here. Don't let that happen! Got it?"

"Yeah, I got it." Easier said than done, Jerome thought. Shooter had survived prison okay, but he only had to do twelve months. Jerome was looking at five very long years.

A week later, Jerome was in the prison weight room finishing his workout. The bell had sounded, signaling an end to the exercise period. The weight room cleared out much faster than usual. As Jerome moved toward the door, three inmates blocked his path. Two of them had been working out and had the physiques of serious weightlifters. A third had just appeared from somewhere else, apparently just for this occasion. He was small and slight, but had a malicious look about him.

"Is this the new meat?" the small man asked, a sinister smirk on his face.

"I think he'd make someone a nice wife, what do you think? said the smaller of the two weightlifters. The three of them laughed harshly.

"Fuck you," Jerome shot back, glaring at them angrily. He hoped the guard would show up to shoo them out of the weight room, like he normally did at that time. He did not.

"He talks dirty. I like that," said the bigger weightlifter.

"I don't like it," scowled the little man. "Let's teach this punk some respect."

All three moved toward Jerome, menace in every step. The big man was in front of the others. Jerome saw the glint of a shiny metal object in his hand, just as he lunged at Jerome.

CHAPTER 22

Thoughts of Shooter and Jerome continually drifted through Jake's mind in the days following Shooter's release, like a bad dream that a fitful sleeper cannot escape. He couldn't stop thinking about the contrast between his life and theirs, and the accidents of fate that placed him where he was and them where they were. He was grateful for the life he was living: his prestigious, well-paying job, his comfortable downtown condominium, and most of all, his precious wife and daughter. Life was difficult for many, but for Jake McShane, right here, right now, life was very good and he was determined not to lose sight of that.

As the weeks passed, Shooter and Jerome faded from Jake's consciousness. He was too focused on living his own life to dwell on such matters. Work kept him extremely busy. He was getting high marks from his superiors, which was gratifying, but he was still a long way from being put in charge of any significant cases. A generous raise at the start of the year had him feeling even better about his employment situation; however, it was accompanied by an increase in the billable hours quota that he and the firm's other associates were expected to meet.

Although the time demands imposed by the firm were increasing, Jake did his best to keep family time sacred. He tried to make it home by seven o'clock in the evening, and was generally able to accomplish that by arriving at work earlier in the morning. Sometimes he would work at home late at night, after Amanda and Anna were asleep, but he made sure that the early evening hours were devoted to the two women in his life.

Their evening routine typically started with a carryout dinner, since neither of them had time to cook. They used mealtime to discuss anything notable from the day. Jake always felt a sense of admiration and pride as he heard about Amanda's work—her interactions with patients; the new treatments that were being explored and developed; and her efforts to build her practice. She was making a difference in people's lives, and he derived some vicarious sense of balance in his own life through his wife's accomplishments. He was often struck by the contrast between Amanda's professional life as a caregiver and his own work as a litigator, which often left him wondering what difference he was making.

After dinner, they were both entirely devoted to Anna. Most evenings, weather permitting, they would walk the path along Lake Michigan. Rollerbladers, bicyclists and joggers sped by as they leisurely pushed Anna in her bright blue stroller. Ambling along the stunning lakefront under the Chicago skyline in the company of the woman he loved and their happy little child made it easy for Jake to forget his life at the office and focus on how fortune had smiled upon him.

After their walk, Jake would plop Anna on his lap for their bedtime reading ritual. This had become a special time for both of them, and only the most dire emergency could interfere with it. Amanda had teased him for starting this routine when Anna was far too young to have any comprehension of the words, yet she was touched by the bond that was obviously being formed between father and daughter.

On weekends, they usually found time to visit Jake's parents on the South Side. Both Jake and Amanda enjoyed watching his parents light up in the presence of their little granddaughter, and do everything they could to spoil her within the space of a few hours.

St. Patrick's Day fell on a Saturday that year, so Jake took Amanda and Anna to see the raucous South Side parade in his old neighborhood.

There was no other gathering quite like this, where one could count on seeing virtually the entire neighborhood in one place at one time. It was a great opportunity to share a uniquely Chicago experience with Amanda during her second springtime in Chicago, and introduce her to dozens of friends and neighbors he had known since childhood.

They walked the four short blocks from his parents' house to the parade route on Western Avenue, and elbowed their way through the crowd, Anna stuffed tightly into a backpack strapped around Jake's shoulders. Amanda gamely got into the spirit of the event and sipped on the green beer that was handed to her as they watched the floats and cars full of neighborhood leaders, city politicians, local business owners, Boy Scouts, marching bands, Little League teams, and the occasional drunken nobody with the Irish cap, just trying to be part of the action.

Like most St. Patrick's Days in Chicago, it was chilly and damp, so Jake and Amanda walked back toward his parents' house after the parade ended, rather than join in the massive post-parade street party. They switched from green beer to hot chocolate and sat at the kitchen table with Jake's mother, while Anna played on the floor. Mrs. McShane had always enjoyed the parade, but did not feel up to the crowds and the cold weather this year. She listened attentively as Jake recounted the afternoon's festivities and named the various dignitaries and old friends they had seen.

"I didn't see Mickey there," Jake mentioned to his mother. Then turning to Amanda, he explained, "Mickey is usually there every year, right up front, driving his shiny old Model T."

"I'm not surprised, under the circumstances," said Mrs. McShane. Then, noticing the quizzical look on Jake's face, she said, "Oh my! You haven't heard, have you?"

"Heard what? Is he okay?"

"No, the poor chap is far from okay. I'll be right back." She walked into the living room and returned with a copy of the *Southside Review*, the local newspaper. She handed Jake the paper, opening it to the second page. There was a picture of Mickey Quinn, a startled expression on his face, below the headline which read, "Local Grocer,

Community Leader Accused of Sexually Harassing Male Employee."
Jake seized the newspaper, and his eyes raced over the article. It
began,

> "Mickey Quinn, owner of Quinn's Fine Foods and
> longtime community leader in the Beverly area, has
> been accused of sexually harassing a 24-year-old male
> employee. A lawsuit was filed in federal district court
> last week alleging that Quinn made unwanted sexual
> advances toward the employee and terminated him
> for refusing to accede to those advances. The lawsuit
> alleges other serious improprieties, including accusa-
> tions that Quinn exposed himself to the employee …"

Jake was stunned. "I don't believe this," he said angrily. "I don't
believe a word of this! Mickey? No way. Absolutely no way!" He
handed the newspaper to Amanda.

His mother's face was sad. "I find it hard to believe, too. The
whole neighborhood is talking about it. After the scandals involving
the Catholic priests, everyone around here is really touchy about these
types of issues. I think the poor man is afraid to show his face."

"Do you know Larry Doyle, the accuser?" Amanda asked.

"Yeah, I know him. In fact, I trained him to be my replacement. I
had reservations about that guy from the start, and I told Mickey about
them. We gave him a short trial period, and I recommended to Mickey
that we pass on the guy, but as usual, Mickey thought this might be
another lost soul he could help."

Jake looked at his watch. It was five-thirty, and Quinn's was open
until six o'clock. "I think Mickey may need a little legal advice. I'm
going to go pay him a visit. Do you mind?" he asked, looking at
Amanda.

"Not at all. He could probably use a friend about now."

Jake made the short walk to Quinn's and arrived about twenty minutes
before closing. The store was normally bustling with last-minute shoppers at this time, but business seemed slower than usual. He walked

through the aisles, looking for Mickey, and even before he finished making the rounds, he could tell that Mickey was not in the store—it was too quiet. When Mickey was there, his presence was obvious. Even when he couldn't be seen, his strong, chipper voice could be heard incessantly as he greeted customers: "Hello, Mrs. Palmer. You're looking lovely today... Mrs. Barry, how nice to see you... Rita darling, can I help you find something? ... Good morning, Lucy. How are the little ones?" The voice was accompanied by the sound of his heels clicking across the tile floor at a brisk pace. That was just part of the sound Jake associated with a visit to Quinn's, and it was conspicuously absent.

Jake recognized the tall middle-aged man wheeling a cart of produce past him. "Hi Bob. Is Mickey around?"

"Hi Jake. In the back," he replied without slowing down.

Jake walked into the back room. In contrast to the quiet of the store, the back room was a flurry of activity as the crew swept the floors, took out the trash and otherwise tidied up so they could make a quick exit after closing.

Jake found Mickey ensconced in his tiny office, absentmindedly looking at some invoices. It was the only place in the building that provided any semblance of privacy, and even that was limited by the paper-thin walls and the large curtainless windows. Two gray metal desks littered with inconsequential paper formed an L shape against the walls and left barely enough room for two people. Mickey rarely spent time there, except when he needed private time with an employee and when it was time for his quarterly meeting with Vern Snyder, Mickey's sourpuss bookkeeper.

"Mickey?"

The old grocer looked up and offered a weak smile. "Hello Jake. How are you, lad?" He seemed pensive and his voice was subdued.

"Mind if I sit down?"

"Not at all," Mickey replied in his Irish brogue, motioning toward the gray metal chair beside him.

Jake stepped inside the cramped office and closed the door. "I just saw the newspaper article about the lawsuit. I hadn't heard until now. If there's anything I can do—anything at all—let me know."

"Scandalous, isn't it?" He looked hurt. "Why would he do something like this, Jake? I really tried to help that boy. I could have fired him a dozen times before I finally did, but I tried to work with him."

"Two motives, I suspect: revenge and money. He's angry with you because you fired him, and this is his way of retaliating. Aside from that, he sees this as his chance to play the litigation lottery. Unfortunately, a lot of undeserving people have gotten big paydays, thanks to our legal system."

"Well, he's not going to get away with this, I can tell you that," said Mickey emphatically, becoming feisty. "Mickey Quinn doesn't shy away from a fight. The gloves are off and that little bastard will see that he's messed with the wrong guy! Look at this shyte," he said, flinging across the desk a copy of the complaint that had been served on him the week before. "Lies, every word of it. He's trying to destroy my reputation. First thing I'm going to do is sue him and the Southside Review for defaming my character. They won't get away with that!"

Jake perused the complaint as Mickey ranted. He found himself getting as angry as Mickey as he read the scurrilous accusations, which included allegations that Mickey had made vulgar and explicit sexual propositions, had exposed himself, and had attempted to fondle Larry's private parts. "This is nasty stuff," Jake remarked, shaking his head. "I don't believe a word of this, Mickey, and neither will anyone who knows you, but you'd be wasting your time and money trying to sue Larry or the newspaper for defamation."

"Why is that, for Chrissakes? Every word is a malicious lie. He's obviously trying to ruin my good name, and the newspaper is helping him do exactly that." Mickey had raised his voice and was growing red in the face. Jake was sure that, despite the closed door, anyone within fifty feet would have no trouble hearing him.

"Unfortunately, Mickey, you can't make a defamation claim based on the content of a lawsuit. A person can put whatever they want in the complaint. It's considered protected speech. You can't sue them for that, even if every word of it is untrue."

Mickey looked at him in disbelief. "How can that be? You mean someone can fabricate horrible stories about another person and publish them in a lawsuit for the entire world to read, and there's no recourse for the victim?"

"I'm afraid so. But, if a person makes false statements publicly, outside the context of a formal legal complaint, that's another matter, and you may be able to prevail on a defamation claim."

"So then I'll go after the newspaper. They published this rubbish for the entire South Side to read. They're not part of the lawsuit!"

"No, but they were very careful about how they reported the story. They didn't make any false statements. They reported the facts. They said things like 'a lawsuit was filed against Mickey Quinn' and 'the lawsuit alleges that Mickey did such and such.' All of that is perfectly true."

Mickey looked incredulous. "How can they get away with that? Regardless of what words they used, they passed along these outrageous allegations and gave everyone who read the story the impression that I'm some kind of pervert. Don't they realize what they're doing by publishing malicious lies like that? Don't they care?"

"I'm afraid they would try to justify their actions by simply saying that this is news, and it's their job to report it. They would say that the public has a right to know, that kind of crap."

Jake picked up the complaint and scanned it more closely. He stopped dead when he reached the last page.

"Damn!"

"What is it?"

"I know this guy—the lawyer who filed this lawsuit."

"He must be trash, if he represents a slimy little worm like Larry."

Jake looked worried. "Have you hired a lawyer yet, Mickey?"

"Sure, I've asked Vern to represent me. He handles all my legal affairs."

Jake was dismayed by that piece of news. Vern had obtained a law degree from night school, but he was primarily a bookkeeper. He dabbled in legal matters from time to time—prepared a few wills, handled some simple probates and real estate closings, and a divorce now and then—but he was certainly not a seasoned trial lawyer. "Look, Mickey, this is serious. This lawyer you're up against is no slouch. He's smart and he's aggressive. You need a real pro here. Vern is a nice guy, but he's out of his league. Nothing personal against Vern, but this just isn't the kind of work he normally handles."

Mickey bristled. "Vern has been my lawyer for over twenty years. I trust him. He's been a loyal friend, and that's important to me—loyalty. I'm finding that many people I thought were my friends don't know the meaning of that word," he said sadly. "But I do. Vern is my lawyer."

Jake could see that Mickey was resolute, but pressed anyway. He could envision Rick Black walking all over this mild-mannered accountant. "Mickey, you really should reconsider that."

"My mind is made up," Mickey snapped in a voice that left no room for further discussion.

"Okay, I understand. But I want you to know that I'm prepared to help in any way I can. Just let me know what I can do. And tell Vern that, too. If he wants to discuss tactics or strategy, any time, I'm available."

"I appreciate that, lad. We'll get through this. This is America—innocent until proven guilty—right? And I'm not guilty. The system will work. Anyway, what choice do I have?"

Jake looked at him glumly. "You do have choices, Mickey. Unfortunately, none of them are good ones. Still, you should carefully consider all your options. The way I see it, there are three ways this can go, and they all have serious downsides. First, you could go to trial and win; second, you could go to trial and lose; or third, you could settle. You could pay him to just go away so you can get on with your life. You—"

"I'll do no such thing!" Mickey interrupted. "The whole world would think I was guilty. I couldn't live with that, and I couldn't live with myself if I surrendered."

"All I'm saying is that it's an option, and you shouldn't rule it out too quickly, without thinking through all of the ramifications."

"Look Jake, think about the message a settlement would send. These guys are like muggers on the street, trying to use force to take what's not theirs. If their victims just open their wallets and hand over their money, we make it easy for them and their kind, and we encourage that behavior. I won't do that. There's still a tough Irish streetfighter in here," he said, pointing at his heart. "No one is going to take me down without a fight!"

"You're right, Mickey. This is like a mugging. You just need to remember that most muggers have weapons, and if you choose to fight them, you can get hurt—badly sometimes. Fighting these guys may leave you bloody, even if you win. The fight will be a long one. It will be expensive. And it will be fought in a very public arena. The local press has already latched onto this. All of these horrible allegations will be made public in the courtroom and in the newspaper. People will talk. They will wonder what really happened. Even if you win in court, people will always wonder."

"I've got no choice. It's the only way I have any hope of clearing my name."

"I know," Jake said quietly. "But there's also the possibility that you won't win. If that happens, not only will your reputation be shot, you could be ruined financially."

"Jesus H. Christ, Jakey, you're a basket of sunshine, aren't you? How can I lose? There's no proof, because I did nothing wrong. I have to trust our legal system. It's not perfect, and I resent being forced into it this way, but it'll work and I'll be exonerated. I believe that."

"It's an imperfect system, Mickey. It's only as good as the people in it. Plaintiffs, witnesses, and sometimes even lawyers may be dishonest. Jurors may be gullible or incompetent. It doesn't always work like it should." Jake looked morose.

Mickey leaned toward Jake, an earnest and hopeful expression radiating from his face. "Look, lad. When I was a boy in Ireland, I saw America as the Promised Land, a land of endless opportunity for those with energy and ambition. I saw it as a land whose people valued honesty and integrity, and respected the rights of every man, woman and child. Fairness and justice matter here. That's the way I saw this country when I came here forty years ago, when I was about your age. And do you know what? That's the way I still see this place. Liberty and justice for all, that's what our Pledge of Allegiance says, right? Well, I for one believe that. I have faith in our judicial system—justice will prevail."

Jake felt bad. He had come to offer Mickey support. Instead, all he had accomplished was painting a grim and pessimistic picture for his old friend. He was glad to see that he had not completely squelched Mickey's natural optimism. "You're a great man, Mickey. You've always been an inspiration to me, and to countless others. I hate seeing this happen to you. I just hope the system you're so proud of doesn't let you down. And I'm sorry. I didn't mean to discourage you or sound pessimistic. All I was trying to do is point out that the stakes are very high here, and that you have a formidable adversary."

"I know that, lad, and I appreciate it. I really do. And Jake, I'm getting old, but I'm not stupid. I heard every word you said. I understand my options, and I understand the risks, but for me, there's no choice. I have to fight this with everything I've got, even if it means spending my last penny. And if I lose, here's how I see it: I've spent my entire life trying to do the right thing, trying to help those in need, trying to make our community a better place. I will go to my grave knowing that, no matter what anyone else thinks. That's something no one can ever take away from me."

The customers and employees had long departed by the time Jake walked through the empty store, like he had done hundreds of times in his life. In the past, he had always enjoyed the after-hours stillness. It was a striking contrast to the beehive of activity that marked most of his time there, and it also meant he'd completed a good day's work. Tonight, it just felt lonely, as Mickey walked him to the front door and unlocked it.

Jake trudged uphill toward his parents' house, feeling a profound sense of sadness. Mickey was right—he'd made a tremendous contribution to the neighborhood, and no one could take that away. But Jake understood the power of the press. People would believe what they read in the papers and heard on TV. They shouldn't, but they would. Media statements were given the status of fact. If this case proceeded, Mickey's good name would be tarnished forever. His reputation would never recover. That was a fact, and Jake knew it.

CHAPTER 23

"**Y**ou need to join, man. Become part of our gang—the Street Sultans. It'll make life in here a lot easier for you. It'll help you when you get out, too." Jerome looked at the lanky inmate across the table from him, as they ate their cold oatmeal. He knew him only as Snake. He was probably no more than thirty, but looked much older. Every inch of exposed skin was covered with tattoos. Snake had spent most of his adult life as a resident of various penitentiaries. He knew how things worked on the inside. "Besides, Carlos likes you," Snake said. "He wants you in."

"That crazy sucker likes me, huh? He's got a funny way of showing it. He almost had me killed down in the weight room."

"He was just testing you. He liked what he saw."

"Well, I didn't like it none," Jerome replied bitterly. "It cost me a month in solitary, and ruined my chances for early parole."

Carlos had indeed been impressed with what he saw. He had taken Jerome for an easy mark. He was big and strong, but he was just a kid. He almost certainly had never come up against ruthless, experienced street fighters like Bear and Jamaal, the two weightlifters who had confronted him in the weight room with Carlos. When Bear had lunged at Jerome with the shank, the kid had deftly dodged the weapon, grabbed Bear by the throat and viciously slammed his head into the wall, rendering him instantly unconscious. As Jerome turned around, he caught a powerful blow from Jamaal square on the jaw, and barely flinched. Jerome proceeded to pummel Jamaal mercilessly and within moments, Jamaal lay on the floor next to his comrade, immobilized and bleeding profusely. Carlos had just watched. Jerome then turned to him and screamed, "You want a piece of me, too?" Carlos had eyed him coolly and just said, "Maybe later," and casually walked away.

Word spread quickly that Jerome was one very dangerous inmate. Other rumors had begun to circulate, suggesting that Jerome had been involved in the demise of a big-time drug dealer. Jerome did nothing to squelch those rumors.

"Think about it, man," Snake urged. "You're one bad dude, but in here, it helps to have someone watching your back. And like I said, when you get out, you could have a bright future with the Sultans. Carlos has connections. He'll hook you up. Shit, man, a dude like you could be a big-time enforcer."

"And why would I want to do that?"

"Hell man, big money, women, drugs ... anything you want. And you'll have respect. People won't mess with you."

"If it's so great, then why don't you do it? Why doesn't everyone do it?"

"Because, only the baddest dudes around can be enforcers. You got what it takes, man, I'm telling you. Only you got to make the right connections, and that starts here."

"If I wanted to do this—become an enforcer—what happens when I get out of here? What comes next?"

"First, you meet the leadership. The big dogs need to be convinced you're the right kind of dude. The reputation and connections you build in here will help. Then there's the initiation."

"What's that?"

"You've got to prove that you'll do whatever the gang asks, even if it means taking someone out."

"Yeah? How do you do that?"

"Easy—you take someone out. That's the only way. And it can't be some lowlife crackhead. You got to prove that you've got the balls to go after a real target—and the smarts to get away with it. So you go after a banker, or a lawyer, or a tourist, and whack someone like that."

Jerome stirred his oatmeal slowly. "I'll think about it. Don't rush me, man. And if I decide I'm in, I've got just the target in mind."

CHAPTER 24

S pending four days in jail had served as a jarring wake-up call for Shooter. He had barely slept the entire time, partly out of fear, but mostly because his circumstances had forced him to do some serious soul-searching. He had always considered himself smart and talented, yet there he was, sitting in a jail cell, facing the very real possibility of doing serious prison time. He was wasting his life, and he desperately wanted to change course.

He'd had plenty of time to reflect upon his past and the road that had brought him once again to the brink of incarceration. Growing up, basketball had been his life. His identity and his future aspirations were inextricably tied to the game of roundball. In high school, he had been recognized as a star with almost unlimited potential—until he was expelled. He continued playing wherever he could, hoping he might someday draw the attention of the professional scouts, but he'd learned the hard way that they generally had no interest in someone who couldn't prove himself in high school and college. He was twenty-four years old now, and had to face the harsh realization that, despite his talent, his chances of landing in the pros were all but gone.

Despite the lack of any future in basketball, he was still passionate about the game, and it was a big part of his life. Even though he wasn't playing on a big stage, he was known in South Side basketball circles as one of the best around. Because of his talent, he had respect, and that was important to a person who had little in the way of material possessions or accomplishment.

Respect. He craved it. It motivated him and made him feel good about himself. He had attained it through his basketball prowess, but he had earned it in other ways as well. He was smart. Everyone in the neighborhood could see that. But he was also tough. He could use his fists better than anyone around, and growing up, he had rarely passed up an opportunity to prove it. He had earned a reputation as a dangerous character. No one would mess with him. Even the gangs kept their distance. They made overtures from time to time, but he made it clear that he was his own man, and had no interest in being part of any street gang. And they respected that.

As he took a hard look at his life from the vantage point of his prison cell, it all seemed so meaningless and inconsequential. He had to admit to himself that he'd done nothing productive with his life. What did it matter if he was respected for his basketball abilities and his fists? Of what value was the respect of the lowlifes and street thugs in his neighborhood? Where had that gotten him? To a prison cell, looking at the possibility of wasting even more of his life behind bars. It made him sick, and it made him angry—with himself. And it scared him. It just flat-out scared him.

He had spent twelve months in prison when he was nineteen years old, and had survived largely based on his ability to play the role of the ultimate bad-ass. He had displayed his fist-fighting prowess on a single occasion early on during his incarceration, and his reputation as a skilled and ruthless fighter quickly spread. In addition, rumors circulated that he was called "Shooter" because of his proficiency with firearms rather than because of his jump shot, and he did nothing to squelch those rumors. Mostly, however, he survived because his sentence was short enough that he could sustain some measure of hope, to which he desperately clung to keep his sanity and his soul intact. The pervasive meanness and constant proximity to truly evil human beings drained his spirit. The inhumane existence in a setting completely devoid of hope and joy was almost more than he could bear. He could not go back there. He feared for his safety, and he feared for his future, but most of all, he feared for what an extended prison term would do to his heart.

As he contemplated his dismal prospects during those four dark days, Shooter vowed that things would be different if he were spared that fate. While he had never considered himself a criminal, he had dabbled in illicit activities with some frequency: selling small amounts of drugs from time to time; fencing stolen property; even stealing, when an easy opportunity presented itself. It seemed so foolish now, and needlessly risky, not to mention just plain wrong. The irony was that he found himself sitting in a prison cell for something he didn't do. Regardless of how he got there, he needed to turn his back on that lifestyle, and he was prepared to do so—if he only got the chance.

Shooter didn't know whether he believed in God or not, but he prayed constantly while he was in that jail cell. He promised the Almighty that he would do something productive with his life if he were able to walk away a free man. He didn't know what that would be, but he would figure it out, and he would pursue that goal relentlessly. Like the lawyer said, he had what it takes. He just needed another chance.

And then the lawyer came through. He was freed. He would have that second chance, and he was determined to make the most of it. He had promised the lawyer he would do so, and he would keep his word. He had also made a promise to God, and while he still didn't know whether he believed in God or not, it seemed inadvisable to break that promise, just in case he was really out there. And he would do it for Jerome. He had always considered Jerome to be his responsibility, and did what he could to exert some level of control and influence over his wild younger brother. He kept him out of fights when he could, and did his best to keep him away from the gangs, but beyond that, he hadn't succeeded in having much of a positive influence. That was obvious, since Jerome was now in jail.

But Jerome would be out of jail in a few years, and Shooter was determined to be in a position to make a difference then. Jerome looked up to him, and if he was doing something legitimate and productive, and making a steady income, perhaps Jerome would see that a better way of life was possible. If he were making decent money, they could live somewhere else, away from the bad influences that had surrounded both of them for their entire lives. That would be his mission.

With that goal in mind, Shooter thought for the first time in his life about entering the job market. He applied for work with the Chicago Fire Department, as well as several other branches of the city and county governments. He hoped that their commitment to diversity and affirmative action was more than lip service and that they would be willing to take a chance on a twenty-four-year-old black man with no history of gainful employment. They took his applications, but gave him little reason for optimism. There were long waiting lists, he was told, and he was starting at the bottom.

He took buses to neighborhoods that had shopping malls and department stores. He had difficulty envisioning himself wearing a uniform and working in a retail establishment, but he was willing to start just about anywhere. Wherever he started, it would be a stepping stone to something better.

Months went by, and Shooter's efforts had gone unrewarded. No one seemed willing to take a chance on a young black man who had spent time in prison on drug charges. His optimism was fading. He was running out of ideas—and hope. Then another thought occurred to him. There was one thing he was really good at, as good as anyone, and it was something he loved: basketball. He now realized that he would never make a living as a professional player, but he knew the game. He could use his knowledge and experience. He could coach. He could teach young men the game, and be a positive influence on them. He could help them avoid the mistakes he had made as a teenager.

With renewed hope, he went to see Coach Foster, his former high school coach. Coach had once told Shooter that he had more potential than any player he had ever seen. He had stood by Shooter when the administration sought to have him expelled. Unfortunately, Coach had not succeeded in keeping Shooter in school, but he was definitely someone Shooter could talk to now. Coach understood life in this neighborhood, and might be willing to help give a person like Shooter a second chance. Maybe he would let him help out as an assistant, or at least put in a good word for him at another school.

Coach Foster had been pleased to see him, and seemed genuinely enthused by Shooter's desire to make something of himself. He promised to make some inquiries. But Foster was also a realist, and he was brutally honest. He told Shooter that, in the present legal climate, schools were reluctant to expose their students to a staff member with a criminal record. Getting hired by the Chicago public school system, or any other school, was a longshot. Nevertheless, Shooter left his meeting with Coach Foster trying his best to think positively. It was a longshot, Coach had told him, but he hadn't said it was impossible. Sometimes longshots paid off. For the moment, Shooter lost all interest in pursuing any other possibilities, since this one seemed so perfect. It was worth waiting for.

The basketball court at St. Simon's was empty when Shooter arrived late in the afternoon, after his meeting with Coach Foster. That was not surprising, since it was cold and had been drizzling intermittently throughout the day, making the court too slick for a game. He was actually glad that the courts were deserted. Shooting baskets in solitude was his favorite form of meditation.

After he had been shooting for about twenty minutes, he noticed a black Ford with two occupants pull up nearby—clearly an unmarked police car. Undercover cops had been coming around with some frequency since he and Jerome had been busted. Shooter did his best to ignore them. He knew he had nothing to be afraid of, yet he still felt uneasy. After a few minutes, the doors of the Ford opened and two cops approached him. He recognized one. It was the cop who had arrested him.

"What's up, Darnell? Mind if we shoot around with you?" He held up his hands, in a silent request for the ball.

Shooter looked at him coldly. "If you want," he replied, sending the ball to the cop with a short bounce pass. These guys clearly were not interested in shooting hoops. They were both wearing dress slacks and shiny black street shoes.

"How's your brother?" asked the cop.

"How do you think? He's in jail."

"Oh yeah, I forgot." He took a few shots, missing badly.

"Say Darnell, do you know a guy named Julius Jefferson?"

"Nope."

"Maybe you know him by a different name. Ever heard of The Priest?"

Everyone around knew The Priest. He got that nickname years ago, after he had somehow obtained a priest's outfit—black shirt and pants and a white collar—and spent his time masquerading as a man of the cloth. He roamed the more affluent parts of the city and nearby suburbs asking for donations for underprivileged inner city youths. He made good money, and being a true entrepreneur, used those funds as seed money to finance a drug trafficking business, and quickly became a successful dealer. As his success grew, he tried to make the leap from small-time dealer to major league player. The gangs made it clear that they did not appreciate him encroaching upon their turf and cutting into their business. Like any good businessman, The Priest cut the best deal he could, and joined forces with the area's largest street gang. They provided him protection and an opportunity to expand his trade, and he provided the gang with a hefty share of the profits. He soon became the biggest dealer on the South Side.

"I've heard of him," Shooter replied. He was not going to be foolish enough to antagonize these guys, but he had no desire to be of any help either. The cop continued shooting as he resumed his questioning.

"How about Freddy Fontaine? Heard of him?"

"Yeah."

"He was a pretty good friend of Jerome's, wasn't he?"

"They knew each other."

"Seems like old Freddy was trying to break into the drug business."

"I don't know anything about that," Shooter responded, his anxiety rapidly increasing.

The cop stopped shooting. He picked up the ball and walked toward Shooter, stopping a few feet in front of him. "The Priest was murdered," he said, looking Shooter directly in the eyes.

"I heard that."

"Have you heard that Fontaine was killed too? Caught a shotgun blast right in the face."

"I heard."

"Do you remember when this happened, Darnell?"

Shooter was silent.

"I'll remind you," said the cop, his voice becoming threatening. He tossed the ball over his shoulder, and folding his arms across his chest, took a step closer. "It happened just before you and your brother got busted, just before that big stash wound up in your apartment. Now I wonder," he said in his most sarcastic voice, "Jerome is a seventeen-year-old kid with no apparent source of income. How the hell would someone like him come to have a stash worth over half a million bucks?"

CHAPTER 25

The Kensington was a stately old hotel in the heart of downtown Chicago. It had recently undergone major renovations after being purchased by one of the large hotel chains, but the new owners had done a nice job of retaining the look and feel of the pre-World War II era. The floors and walls of the cavernous lobby were white marble, accented by gleaming brass trim, fine artwork and stunning crystal chandeliers, authentically capturing the cool elegance of a bygone era. Jake had chosen the spot because he knew it would not be crowded at six o'clock on a Wednesday evening.

He entered the hotel bar and looked around. Rick was not there yet, so he seated himself in a corner booth, facing the door. He had not seen or spoken with Rick since law school graduation, nearly two years before. Rumor had it that Rick had left Robbins & McKee after less than a year, under some sort of cloud, although he had not heard any particulars.

Rick had sounded pleased when Jake called that afternoon and invited him for a drink. Jake had not mentioned the reason for his invitation, and wondered whether Rick suspected. He could not recall whether he had ever mentioned to Rick that he had worked in a grocery store. Even if he had, how would Rick have known it was Quinn's? He wondered whether Larry would have spoken to Rick about him, but couldn't think of any reason why it might occur to Larry to mention his connection with Jake or Jake's connection with the store.

He saw Rick stop in the entryway and look around the bar, as his eyes adjusted to the dim light. Jake waved and caught Rick's eye.

"Hello Jake! Great to see you. It's been way too long." They shook hands and Jake was reminded of the effect Rick could have on people, with his good looks, confidence and charm. There was no question that he had a certain presence about him that seemed even more powerful now that he was an experienced attorney and not merely a law student.

"Hi Rick. You look great. I'm glad you could make it on such short notice."

Rick looked at his watch. "It's only six o'clock. I can't believe Samuelson & Reid would let you off the clock this early. Shouldn't you be getting in a few more billable hours before you call it a day?" he asked with a grin. "I'm sure glad I got away from that grind."

They ordered a couple of beers and brought each other up to date on their career progress. Rick had not kept up with any of their law school classmates, so Jake filled him in on what he knew. As they finished their second beer, Jake decided to come to the point.

"Rick, I'd like to talk with you about one of your cases. I've heard that you're suing Mickey Quinn on behalf of Larry Doyle." He handed Rick a copy of the article published in the Southside Review when the suit was filed.

Rick looked pleased with himself as he glanced at the headline. "What's on your mind?"

"I know these people, Rick. I used to work at Quinn's. I was the one who trained Larry when he started working there. I know Mickey Quinn like I know my own family. Your lawsuit is off base. Larry's feeding you a crock of shit."

Rick did not act surprised. He seemed neither offended nor defensive. "Look, Jake," he said in a calm and sincere voice. "You have no way of knowing what happened. All you can do is speculate. You're obviously fond of Mr. Quinn, and probably have never witnessed anything like this from him, so you want to believe him. That's perfectly understandable. But people we know and respect surprise us all the time. They let us down. It happens. We never really know people like we think we do."

"I know Mickey. I worked with him almost every day for six years. I know the man. There's no way these allegations could be true. I've spoken to him about it, and I'm absolutely convinced he's telling the truth when he tells me that this whole sordid story is a complete fabrication."

"You know I can't discuss the particulars of this case with you or anyone else, Jake. That would be improper. I'll just say this: My client tells me this is what happened. I have no basis for doubting him, and have a duty to provide him with the best representation I can. That's what I intend to do."

"There's a difference between providing good representation for your client and pursuing scorched earth tactics designed to ruin someone, and that's what you're doing here," Jake said angrily, pointing to the newspaper article he had previously shown Rick. "There's no need to whip the press into a frenzy over this. You're attempting to try your case in the media, and they've found him guilty already. His reputation is being destroyed."

"I don't control the media. They print what they want to print. This is news. They're going to print it, whether you like it or not."

Jake suspected that Rick had been working the media, and the lack of any denial on that point confirmed his suspicion. "Maybe, but you don't have to solicit their involvement. You don't have to feed them your side of the story, and keep them stirred up."

Rick clearly looked irritated now. "Is there a purpose to this conversation? What do you want? What do you expect me to do?"

Jake stared at his beer, with a look of resignation. "All I can ask is this: Remember that a man's life is being ruined over this. Remind your client of the consequences of his actions. Remind him that there are laws against perjury. And take a hard look at your client and his story and don't encourage this if you're not convinced of its truthfulness."

Rick looked sincere again, even a little hurt. "Jake, do you honestly think I would involve myself in a case that I thought was bullshit?

Now, let me ask something of you. Keep this in mind: There are three sides to every dispute—the plaintiff's side, the defendant's side and the actual truth. Each side has its own biases and perspectives, which invariably color its version of what really happened. The truth usually lies somewhere in between. What that means in a case like this is that your guy may not be as bad as Larry thinks he is—but he's probably no saint either. Who knows exactly what happened? That's why we have juries, and it's their duty to decide where the truth lies. But something must've happened to set Larry off on this course. You asked me to keep an open mind, and I will, I really will. But you need to do the same thing."

He sounded so sincere, Jake thought, and so convincing. He even had Jake starting to second-guess himself. Rick would have the jury eating out of his hands.

CHAPTER 26

"Can you come by the gym today? I've got some news." It was Coach Foster. It had been over a week since Shooter had met with him, and he had about given up hope of hearing back from the coach.

It was around noon when Shooter arrived at his former high school. The corridors were teeming with students as they moved from one classroom to another with varying degrees of hustle. Shooter walked past the noisy, crowded cafeteria. The shouts and laughter made the place hum with a positive energy. Shooter had hated high school, or at least thought he did, while he was there. All those authority figures, rules, and discipline were just not for him. Almost as soon as he had left, however, he missed it. Walking through the school now, he thought about what he had missed: the camaraderie, the social opportunities, the girls, and yes, even the education. It all seemed like such a positive environment now. He wanted so badly to be part of it. He felt certain he could contribute and make a difference, if only he were given a chance. As those thoughts passed through his mind, he felt a surge of hope. Coach Foster would not have asked him to stop by in person just to give him bad news.

"I'm afraid I have some bad news, Shooter," said the coach. "As I suspected, the school district has a strict policy against hiring people with a criminal record. The lack of any other employment history is a big strike against you, too. I'm sorry."

Shooter's shoulders drooped and he looked downward. "I would do a great job, Coach. I really would. Doesn't anybody believe in giving a guy a second chance?" he asked with quiet exasperation.

"That's why I asked you to stop by. The public school system may not be an option, but there's another possibility. It probably won't pay much, but if you really want to work with kids and get into coaching, it might be a good place to start."

Hope sprang up within him again, mixed with curiosity. "All I want is a chance. I can handle it from there."

"Have you ever heard of Lonnie Cole?"

"The football player? Sure, who hasn't?"

"Do you know what he's doing now?"

"He's a preacher, isn't he?"

"That's right. He's a friend of mine, too. We went to high school together. After getting out of football, he became a minister. He's got his own church now, over on the West Side. He's been working hard to build his congregation, and it's growing fast. One of his goals is to help steer young men in the right direction and away from the gangs. He knows that the unchurched won't just walk into his chapel to hear him preach or attend Bible study meetings, but if he offers them an outlet—like sports—that may get them off the streets, and maybe some of them will eventually want to learn more about his ministry."

Shooter looked doubtful. "Coach, I haven't been to church since I was a kid. I don't think I'm the kind of guy he's looking for."

"You may be exactly what he's looking for. He doesn't need another minister. He's looking for someone to help with his athletic program. Someone who can coach, and more importantly, someone who can relate to these kids. He's been able to raise a lot of money, mostly from a small handful of professional athletes who grew up around here. He's used it to refurbish the old gym, put in lockers and showers, and is even in the process of developing a first-class baseball field. His athletic program will be a big draw for the kids, but he's too busy to run it himself. He needs someone who can be dedicated to that part of his ministry."

"And you think he'll consider me?"

"I know he'll consider you. Hell, I've talked to him. He's already considering you. Will you go see him?"

Three days later, Shooter sat across a desk from Lonnie Cole, in a cramped but comfortable office in the back of Holy Redemption Church. There were few occasions where Shooter could remember meeting someone who made him feel nervous or intimidated, but Lonnie Cole certainly did. He was an NFL legend, both for his ferocity on the field and his wild lifestyle off it. At forty-eight years of age, he still cut an imposing figure. He was massive—six-foot-six, rippling with muscles, and not an ounce of fat on him. He looked just as intense in person as he did in the pictures Shooter had seen of him on the football field years earlier.

"I understand you've done time, and no one wants to hire you," said Reverend Cole in a booming voice. "What makes you think you can handle this position, Mr. Tucker?"

"I've played basketball all my life. I know the game. I think—"

"Have you ever coached before?" the Reverend asked sharply. "There's a big difference between coaching and playing, you know."

"Well, Reverend Cole—"

"Everyone around here calls me Reverend Lonnie, or just plain Lonnie. You can call me that too." It sounded more like a command than an invitation. "Yes sir," Shooter replied, feeling off-balance. "Like I was saying, I know the game and can play it at a high-level. I think that will be evident to the kids and it will help me earn their respect. I think they'll listen to me."

"Son, it takes more than talent on the basketball court to earn respect, especially with the kind of kids we have around here."

"I realize that, Reverend. But I think that these kids will relate to me because I'm just like them. I grew up like they're growing up. I had nothing. I lived in a gang-infested, crime-ridden neighborhood—just like them. I still do. And I've made mistakes. Hopefully that'll make me seem human to them, someone they can relate to. Maybe I can prevent at least some of them from making the same mistakes I've made."

Reverend Cole nodded his head and smiled. As he smiled, he seemed to transform into a gentle giant, rather than a ferocious intimidator. "Amen, Brother Tucker. That's my hope too. That's why I asked Coach Foster to send you over here."

Shooter squirmed in his chair and looked downward. "Reverend Lonnie, there's something you need to know. I don't go to church. I haven't been in years. If this is a religious ministry, I'm not sure I'm what you're looking for."

Reverend Cole put his elbows on his desk and leaned forward. "Listen, son, you can't force people to come to God. They need to come to Him willingly, on their own. I don't pressure anyone to find religion. I try to do God's work and lead by example. I tell people my story when they're ready to hear it—when they ask me. If I hired some religious fanatic to work with these kids, that would backfire. They would resent it and stay away. I just want to get them off the streets and in here. If they feel comfortable coming here, then eventually some of them will open their minds and their hearts to the Lord. If you come to work here, I will never push religion on you. I will insist that you act as a good role model, but as for religion, all I ask is that you avoid being judgmental, set aside whatever preconceived ideas you may have, and keep your mind and heart open. Do you think you can do that?"

"I can do that, Reverend. If you give me a chance, you won't regret it, I promise you. Just a chance is all I ask."

"The Almighty gives all of us a second chance for redemption. That's what the bible teaches us. Put our sins behind us and lead a better life. I've been given many chances, and I'm now blessed with the ability to give others a new start. That's what I see before me now. I'm giving you a chance. It's up to you to make the most of it."

Shooter sprang to his feet and extended his hand. "Thank you, Reverend. I really mean it. You won't regret this. I'll make you proud."

"I believe you will, Shooter. Now, it's time for my workout. How about a game of one-on-one? I want to see if your game is as good as I hear. They tell me your turnaround jumper is unstoppable. We'll see about that."

"Go easy on me, Reverend. I may be a little rusty." Shooter laughed, feeling a sense of elation for the first time in a long while. "By the way, can I ask you something?"

"Sure."

"How come there's nothing in your office to remind you of your football days? No pictures, no trophies, no helmet or jersey. What's up with that?"

Reverend Cole put his arm around Shooter's shoulder, and guided him out of the tiny office. "That's because it ain't about me, son. When I was playing ball, I was as self-centered as a guy could be. I craved attention, money, drugs, women—and I had it all. I lived a wild, hedonistic, selfish life. I had everything money could buy, and do you know what? I was empty inside. Then I found the Lord and I learned that I had it all wrong. I found purpose and meaning by turning away from myself and trying to make things better for others. That's what it's all about. It ain't about me, and I don't need any reminders of when I made it all about me. Does that make sense?"

"It makes perfect sense."

CHAPTER 27

As with most federal courts, the wheels of justice in the Chicago court system moved slowly. Almost two years had elapsed since Jake had visited Rick in the Kensington bar, and the trial was just now approaching. For the most part, the press had ignored the situation, since there was nothing new to report. However, the ordeal had taken a significant toll on Mickey Quinn. He could hear the whispers and the snickers when he walked past his friends at the country club or in the local restaurants. People stared. He was the butt of jokes and gossip and he knew it. Friends who had once been eager to golf with him or dine together were no longer calling. He had been asked to resign his position as chairman of the neighborhood planning committee, not because anyone thought he was guilty, he was told, but because he was a "distraction" and a "source of controversy." Just until he was exonerated, they told him, and then they would be delighted to have him resume his duties.

The atmosphere at the grocery store was markedly different. Business was steady, but it was not the booming, bustling place it had once been. Mickey's ubiquitous presence—greeting customers, helping them locate the hard-to-find items, advising them on their meat and produce selections—was no longer evident. He had become reclusive. Most of those still shopping there were his loyal supporters and told him so, but even those words of encouragement were bitter reminders of his bleak situation.

Vern, in his accounting capacity, had been advising Mickey that the business was in dire straits. Margins in the grocery industry were razor thin under the best of circumstances, and Mickey had always tolerated even thinner margins than most due to his bloated expenses—primarily, the employment of a staff whose size was grossly out of proportion to the revenues generated by the business. But now, business was down significantly, and financially speaking, he was bleeding. Let it bleed, Mickey instructed Vern, much to the latter's dismay. When the trial was over, everything would be back to normal, Mickey assured him.

Two weeks before trial, Rick summoned Larry to his office to begin the intense preparation for his testimony. They went over his story in excruciating detail, point by point. Rick prepared Larry for the questions he would likely hear from Mickey's counsel, and they carefully rehearsed their answers. Rick played the role of opposing counsel and put Larry through a brutal cross-examination, barraging Larry with questions in a rapid-fire style, badgering him, taunting him, even mocking him. Rick looked and felt like a frustrated football coach, rebuking, cajoling and pushing to get his player to perform at a level that he just did not seem capable of achieving. By the end of the afternoon, they were exasperated with each other.

"For Chrissakes, Larry, you've got to be believable! The only way we win this is if you can convince twelve jurors that every word you're saying is true. You're stumbling and stammering, you're hesitant, you're groping for answers. You look like an unprepared student trying to bullshit his way through class. That's not going to cut it!"

"Hey, get off my case, man," Larry snapped back. "You're supposed to be on my side. Stop giving me such a hard time. I know the story. You're just getting me flustered, that's all."

Rick fought hard to control his frustration. "Larry, it's better to get flustered here and now rather than in front of a jury, so don't be defensive. Just listen to me and try to learn. This preparation is critical. Let's break for today and try again later in the week. But here's what you need to do in the meantime. Pretend like you're an actor, preparing for the biggest performance of your life. Think about every detail of your story, over and over again. Relive it in your mind every waking second between now and the trial, so it comes out naturally in front of the jury. Think about any possible holes in your story, and how the other side may try to use them to cast doubt on you, and make sure you have an answer that comes out as natural and convincing."

Larry looked worn out and irritable. "Okay, I hear you. I'll work on it." He paused and turned to a more appealing subject. "So Rick, realistically, how much do you think I could win here?"

"Goddammit, Larry," Rick exploded. "We're not going to win shit the way this is going! To be honest, I was hoping we'd never have to go to trial with this. I did everything I could to pressure this guy into settling. I got the EEOC after him. I got the press involved. I took depositions of his employees and got them all stirred up. His business is hurting, and his reputation has been demolished, but the stubborn son of a bitch won't settle. I've done more than most lawyers would have or could have done for you, but now it looks like we're going to trial, and it's all going to be up to you. You've got to sell this story to twelve strangers. If they don't believe you, we lose. It's that simple."

"I can do this," Larry said, sounding defensive and unconvincing.

Rick ignored him. His own words were sinking in, and he did not like his predicament. He hated the fact that his chances of winning rested almost entirely on the credibility and persuasiveness of this lowlife sitting before him. He looked hard at Larry. "Right now, all we have is your word against Quinn's. It's a credibility contest. You know what we really need here?" he asked rhetorically. "We need to tip the scales in our favor. We need a witness. Someone the jury will believe. Someone whose testimony will bury this guy. Someone other than you."

"But there were no witnesses, I've told you that."

Rick looked at him coldly. "Then you better find one. Do what it takes. It doesn't have to be someone who saw him harass you. There's got to be someone out there who has some other dirt on this guy, someone else who wants a piece of him. We find that person and I like our chances. We could score big. If we don't, we're sunk. Go find that person, Larry. Get me a witness."

On Saturday evening, two days before the trial was to begin, Jake met Johnny at Riley's for a beer.

"Did you see the *Review* this morning?" Johnny asked.

"I saw it," Jake replied, disgust in his voice. "They just won't let up. They act like this is a sporting event. They have no regard for the damage their stories are causing Mickey. They didn't have anything new to report, other than that the trial starts on Monday. It's just a rehash of the same old sordid allegations."

"Your old pal Larry was in here last night, acting smug and confident," Johnny informed his cousin. "He had pictures of the Porsche he plans on buying with his winnings, and was talking to a real estate agent, asking her to keep an eye out for high-end homes going on the market. He isn't really going to win, is he?"

"Not unless he draws a really gullible and incompetent jury. Larry has the burden of proving his case, and he's got no proof. It's just his word against Mickey's. Who would you believe, a pillar of the community like Mickey or a scumbag like Larry?"

"Seems like a no-brainer to me."

"It should be. I'm just worried about the mismatch between the lawyers. Larry's lawyer is really smart and really smooth. The jury will like him. And Mickey's got Vern. That concerns me."

At that moment, Johnny looked toward the door, and said, "Well, well, look who's here."

Jake followed his gaze. It was Larry Doyle.

For the next thirty minutes, Jake did his best to keep his mind off the trial, yet he found himself repeatedly glancing at Larry across the crowded bar.

"Did you hear what I just said?" Johnny was speaking, but Jake's eyes and mind had wandered.

"Huh? Oh, sorry Johnny. I just can't stop thinking about that guy," Jake replied, nodding in Larry's direction. He took a deep breath and drained his beer mug in one gulp. "I'll be right back," he said, standing up and walking purposefully across the bar.

Larry was seated with two companions, and the three of them were attempting to flirt with a group of college girls sitting nearby. Their attention turned to Jake as he stopped at their table and glowered at Larry. "We need to talk." Jake spoke directly to Larry and ignored his companions.

"Hi Jake. Nice to see you too."

"Can you guys give us a minute?" Jake asked. It was more of a command than a question.

One of Larry's companions looked at Jake defiantly. He was a big guy, with bulging, tattooed forearms showing beneath a Chicago Bears football jersey. "I'm pretty comfortable right here," the big guy replied.

Jake glared at him. For an instant, he thought about getting into the guy's face, but quickly decided not to let himself get distracted from his mission. He looked back toward Larry. "My business with Larry is private. Let's take a walk, Larry," Jake said, gesturing toward the men's room.

Larry got up hesitantly. "What's on your mind?" Larry asked as he followed Jake into the dark, narrow corridor leading to the restrooms.

"The trial."

Larry stopped just outside the men's room door. "I got nothing to say to you about that."

Jake's anger had been gradually building throughout the evening, as he had watched Larry from across the bar. Now, confronting him face-to-face, it seethed forth. He roughly shoved Larry against the thin plywood wall, thrusting his forearm across Larry's throat. "Then I'll do the talking," he said through clenched teeth. "Mickey Quinn is a friend of mine. He's a good man, and what you're trying to do is despicable. If you ask me, it's criminal, and you ought to be behind bars. I don't believe a word of your bullshit story, Larry. If you have any conscience at all, you'll drop this charade right now before any further damage is done. If this goes forward, and by some miracle you convince a jury to believe you, think about this—you're a goddamn liar. You know it, and I know it. And I won't let it go. Not for a second."

Larry's eyes were wide with fear, and he was shaking. Jake released him just as his two comrades hurried to his aid. The big guy in the Bears jersey yelled, "You looking for trouble, pal?" Jake took a step toward him, fists clenching. Suddenly, Johnny was at his side, and Jimmy the bartender came racing toward them.

"Not in here, guys! Knock it off!" Jimmy ordered.

Jake and Johnny stood shoulder-to-shoulder, facing Larry's pals. Jimmy inserted himself in between. "Don't be stupid, fellas. Larry, tell your friends to cool it."

"We were just minding our own business until this asshole started harassing me," Larry shouted, his confidence returning now that reinforcements had arrived.

Jake took a step in Larry's direction and pointed a finger at him. "Remember what I said, Larry!"

"Screw you, McShane! I'm going to win this case. We'll see who has the last laugh." Then, looking at his drinking buddies, he said. "Come on, let's get out of this dump." He strode away quickly, looking at the floor. His companions glared at Jake and Johnny, shouted a few obscenities, and then followed Larry out the door.

CHAPTER 28

Monday morning, Jake arrived at the federal courthouse twenty minutes early. Although he had been laboring under a crushing workload, he was determined to sit through the entire trial, which was not likely to last more than a few days. Vern had thus far declined his offer to provide assistance, but now that the battle had moved into the courtroom, Jake felt confident that he could offer Vern observations and suggestions as the trial proceeded. Even if Vern was not interested in his help, he would be there to support Mickey.

Mickey and Vern were seated at the counsel table near the front of the courtroom. No one else was there yet. Jake approached them and offered words of encouragement to Mickey, who seemed nervous and distracted. What struck Jake most was how frail he looked. As long as Jake had known him, Mickey had always looked and acted a good ten years younger than his age. Today, he looked every one of his seventy years.

Within a few minutes, Rick walked in with Larry, who was dressed in an ill-fitting gray suit and clearly looked uncomfortable in it. Jake and Rick exchanged polite greetings, but nothing more. Mickey glared at Larry, who avoided looking in his direction. Jake could not tell which of them seemed more nervous.

By nine thirty, only four other spectators had arrived. Apparently, this case was not of much interest to anyone outside the Beverly neighborhood, and even those residents were content to read the newspaper and listen to the gossip, but did not care enough to actually attend the trial. Jake knew that was the case with most lawsuits; nevertheless, he was disappointed that none of Mickey's friends or neighbors had bothered to attend to show their support.

Jake looked up as the jury was ushered in. He studied their faces, and recognized no one, which was not surprising. In a big city like Chicago, a jury of your peers did not necessarily mean people from your own neighborhood.

The silver-haired bailiff walked briskly into the room from the door behind the judge's desk. "All rise," he ordered in a booming voice that required no amplification. "This court is now in session. Case number CV 03—1224, Larry Doyle versus Michael J. Quinn and Quinn's Fine Foods, the Honorable Christopher Gray presiding."

Judge Gray entered, robes billowing around him as he walked quickly to the bench. He was a scholarly looking man in his late forties, with dark hair, and wire-rimmed glasses. Jake had handled several matters before Judge Gray and had found him to be intelligent and fair, with a no-nonsense attitude about him. He derived some comfort from the fact that the case was in the hands of a very competent judge.

After discussing some preliminary procedural issues with the attorneys, Judge Gray invited Rick to proceed with his opening statement. In his navy suit and yellow tie, with his perfectly coifed hair and chiseled good looks, Jake thought he looked as much like a movie star as a trial lawyer, something that would not be lost on the eight female jurors.

"Good morning, ladies and gentlemen," Rick began. "I would first like to extend my sincere thanks to each of you for being here. I realize that jury duty is an inconvenience, and sometimes even a hardship, but it's a vitally important part of our judicial process and you are to be commended for being here to do your civic duty.

"As a jury, you have a tremendous responsibility. Your job is to listen to all of the testimony and consider all of the evidence, and decide what really happened. That responsibility rests entirely with you—not with me, not with defense counsel, and not with Judge Gray. You will decide the outcome of this case."

Jake watched the jury closely. They were looking at Rick with rapt attention. Rick was smooth and natural, and they were certain to like him. He continued. "What you are about to hear, you will undoubtedly find disturbing. I apologize in advance for the graphic nature of the testimony you will be hearing, but in order to really understand what happened, we need to describe the facts exactly as they occurred, even though hearing that may be unpleasant and distasteful. But the reality is, what happened to my client was unpleasant and distasteful—more than that—it was despicable. It was detestable. And, it was illegal.

"Larry Doyle worked for a grocery store owned by the defendant, Mr. Quinn. As Larry's boss, Mr. Quinn was in a position of power and authority. He abused that position. Larry will tell you, in graphic detail, how Mr. Quinn made unwelcome sexual advances toward him. Mr. Quinn propositioned Larry. He exposed himself to Larry. Larry was forced to endure inappropriate touching that no person should have to endure from his boss or anyone else. And what happened when he objected to all of this? He was fired."

Mickey's face turned crimson, and he seemed about to jump out of his chair, when Vern put a hand on his forearm and whispered something to him. Jake noticed that a few of the jurors were poker-faced, but most of them looked repulsed.

Rick continued. "Fortunately, we have courts in this country to deal with such situations, and there are laws against sexual harassment and retaliation. You will undoubtedly hear that Mr. Quinn was a civic leader in his neighborhood. You will hear that he was an employer to many people over the years. Be careful not to read too much into that. Yes, he absolutely was an individual of some power and influence in his little universe. But people in positions of power sometimes abuse their positions. Think about the recent scandals involving Catholic priests. For years, unscrupulous men of the cloth were allowed to get away with the most egregious types of conduct, but finally they were held accountable—because our legal system works.

"Listen carefully to the evidence, and the truth will be obvious to you. We don't like to believe that our leaders, those who enjoy our trust, could betray that trust. But we've seen it happen time and time again in our society—with politicians, priests, bosses—it happens. Set aside any preconceived notions that people in positions of power and influence deserve our trust, and simply consider the evidence. All I ask is that you listen to every word with an open mind and be guided by your conscience. If you do that, you will undoubtedly conclude Mr. Doyle is telling the truth. No other explanation makes sense. Thank you in advance for doing your duty."

Jake felt sick. Rick came across as the picture of sincerity. It was obvious that he was connecting with this jury.

Vern shuffled his papers and walked toward the jury, looking at the floor as he gathered his thoughts. "Good morning," he began, without making eye contact with the jury. "Mr. Black just got through telling you that you must believe Mr. Doyle's story because no other explanation makes sense. Well, there's a very simple explanation that makes perfect sense—Mr. Doyle is a liar."

Not a great start, Jake thought. Build some rapport with the jury. Lead them to that conclusion tactfully and subtly; lashing out may be perceived as overly defensive. Not surprisingly, several jury members seemed to bristle at such a bold and stark allegation.

"Larry Doyle was a lousy employee. That's why he was fired. He was unreliable; he had a pattern of missing work, or coming in late; his attitude was poor, and that negative attitude resulted in rude behavior toward the store's customers. No reasonable businessman can tolerate it when an employee antagonizes his customers. So Mr. Quinn fired him. It's that simple.

"So why are we here? Mr. Doyle is angry, like most people are when they get fired. He wants revenge. Beyond that, he wants to play the litigation lottery. He thinks he can just come in here and tell a disgusting sounding story and that you'll believe him. Don't let him get away with that.

"I do agree with Mr. Black on one point," Vern said. "Your job is to consider the evidence and decide what really happened. Mr. Doyle must prove his case. Other than his own story, he has no case. He has no witnesses, no supporting evidence, nothing. Don't let him con you with this completely unsubstantiated fish tale. It's just not true."

Jake cringed. Vern spoke the truth, but it was awkward from start to finish. He had difficulty finding his words. He stammered. There were long pauses. He looked mostly at the floor, with only the occasional fleeting glance at the jury. All things considered, he just wasn't very convincing, even to someone like Jake, who desperately wanted to believe him. Jake's throat was dry. The mismatch he feared was materializing at the very outset of the trial.

As Jake expected, Rick's key witness was his first: Larry. His mission was to turn the jury against Mickey from the very start by letting Larry tell his story, painting the most graphic and disgusting picture he possibly could. Rick didn't trust Larry to give a thorough, coherent narrative account of his claims, so he led Larry through the story with a series of short, carefully sequenced questions. Through that process, Larry told the jury of three separate instances where Mickey had made sexual advances toward him.

Larry first described an incident where Mickey called him into his office one evening after closing. His deliveries had kept him out late and everyone else had already gone home. Mickey invited Larry into his office, explaining that he wanted to give Larry something special for working late. As Larry entered the office, Mickey shut the door and dropped his trousers, saying, "Here's your bonus. Come and get it."

Every person on the jury looked disgusted.

Larry then recounted an incident that allegedly occurred at the lunch counter in the back room. According to Larry, he and Mickey were sitting side by side when Mickey spilled his coffee. Although none of it had actually landed on Larry, Mickey said "Sorry, looks like I got some on your pants," and reached under the table with a napkin and attempted to rub it against Larry's crotch.

Jake noticed that several jurors were casting contemptuous glances in Mickey's direction as the stories unfolded. They were sporadic and subtle at first, but gradually became more frequent and openly hostile.

Finally, Rick asked Larry about his termination. "Larry, did you have an encounter with a customer by the name of Mrs. Leonard on your last day of employment?"

"Yes. I'm afraid I lost my temper and snapped at her after she yelled at me for being late."

"Did you frequently lose your temper with customers?"

"Never, until that day."

"What made you lose your temper on that particular occasion?"

"I was upset. It was just before that delivery run that Mickey propositioned me for the third time. He told me that if I didn't start showing some respect for my employer, I could start looking for another job."

"What did you take that to mean?"

"I took it to mean that if I didn't respond to his advances, I'd be fired, so I was agitated all morning. When that old lady got on my case, I just lost my cool. I shouldn't have, but I did."

"What happened next?"

"When I got back to the store, Mickey told me that Mrs. Leonard had called and complained about me. I got in his face and told him I was upset because he kept coming on to me, and that I just took it out on the wrong person. I told him that he'd better not come on to me ever again. I'd had enough and I told him so."

"And then what happened?"

"He fired me."

"He fired you?"

"Yes, but first he told me that he would give me one more chance. If I showed my willingness to please the boss, he'd give me another chance."

"And then?"

"I refused, and he fired me."

"No further questions."

Judge Gray looked at Vern. "Your witness, Mr. Snyder."

Vern approached the witness, looking at the notes he had scribbled on a yellow legal pad. "Mr. Doyle, were there any witnesses to any of these events you just described?"

"No. He was always careful to make sure we were alone."

"Did you tell anyone about these alleged incidents after they happened?"

"No. I was embarrassed, and I was afraid of losing my job."

Good, Jake thought. Stop there, Vern. But Vern pressed on. "So you have no evidence whatsoever to support a single thing you've said. Why should the jury believe you?"

"Because I'm telling the truth," said Larry earnestly. "This is tough for me. I've never sued anybody. I'm intimidated by this whole legal process. Do you think I'd really just make this up out of thin air and have to go through this ordeal? I hate this, but I knew I had to speak up. If I didn't, he'd go after some other guy, and I wouldn't want to live with that."

Vern looked unsure about how to proceed. He stared blankly at Larry for a few moments and then said "No further questions."

Jake winced. Larry had scored points with that one.

Rick then introduced two experts. The first was a psychologist, who testified that it would not be at all unusual for a victim to keep silent about harassment of this nature, based on a combination of embarrassment, humiliation, guilt and fear. She also testified that these events could cause lasting psychological damage in the form of self-esteem issues, which could affect Larry's personal relationships as well as future employment prospects. Vern offered no cross-examination.

The second expert witness was an economist, who explained the financial statements of Quinn's Fine Foods as they were displayed on a large screen in front of the jury. The purpose of this testimony was to educate the jury about Mickey's financial condition, so they would be in a better position to know how much it would take to inflict meaningful punishment if they concluded he was guilty. The economist explained that Quinn's average annual revenues for the past five years exceeded three million dollars. Based on that revenue stream, he opined that the business itself was worth between five and six million as a going concern. Jake noticed that the expert failed to mention that Quinn's actually operated at a loss during the past year, and that during the four preceding years, its net profit never exceeded $120,000. Vern noticed these points as well and addressed them during his cross-examination.

That was Rick's entire case. He finished by mid-afternoon. Jake was relieved that nothing new had emerged, but was disturbed by his observation that Rick seemed to have the jury clearly on his side. Now it was up to Vern and Mickey to change that.

Vern began with his character witnesses. That struck Jake as odd. He would have put Mickey on the stand first, in an effort to get the other side of the story before the jury as early as possible.

Vern first called Father Reichert, the pastor of St. Francis Church, who testified about Mickey's long-time involvement in church activities, as well as his generosity with both his time and his money. Next, Vern called Tim O'Connor, the acting president of the Beverly Planning Commission, who told of Mickey's many years of service to that organization and to the community at large. Both men portrayed Mickey as a man of the highest character and integrity. On cross-examination, both acknowledged that they had no knowledge of his relationship with Larry or how he treated his employees.

Since it was late afternoon by the time O'Connor's testimony had concluded, Judge Gray adjourned the proceedings for the day and informed the parties that the trial would resume at nine thirty the following morning. Jake walked out of the courtroom with Mickey and did his best to offer words of encouragement to his former boss, who appeared dazed and shell-shocked.

As Jake arrived in the courtroom the following morning, Vern handed him that morning's edition of the *Southside Review*. Splashed across the front page was the headline, "Day of Reckoning for Quinn," and a picture of Mickey leaving the courtroom with a stunned look on his face. The story recounted the most graphic and inflammatory portions of Larry's testimony. It described Larry as "a clean-cut young man with a respectful and sincere demeanor." According to the article, Mickey listened to the damning testimony "in stone-faced silence, revealing no emotion or reaction whatsoever."

Mickey was sworn in promptly as the proceedings resumed. He bore little resemblance to the cheerful, confident man who ran around the store greeting customers and marched at the head of neighborhood parades. He seemed nervous and unsure of himself, as his eyes darted around the unfamiliar courtroom.

Vern spent the better part of the morning leading Mickey through a series of questions about his background: his immigration to this country; his start in the grocery business; the history of Quinn's Fine Foods; and the myriad of community activities and organizations he supported. Vern spent considerable time bringing out information about the store's delivery business and Mickey's commitment to serving the elderly. He had Mickey talk about the countless young people who were provided invaluable employment experience at Quinn's.

Jake had difficulty reading the jury during this testimony. For the most part, they stared impassively as Mickey's background was brought to life. Jake wondered whether they looked that way because they were skeptical and biased toward him already, or because the information was simply not very exciting.

By late morning, Vern turned his focus to the core allegations of the case. "Mr. Quinn, would you please describe for us your relationship with Larry Doyle?"

"He was an employee of mine at the store."

"Was he a good employee?"

"No."

"In what way was he deficient?"

"Lots of ways," replied Mickey, flashing an angry look in Larry's direction. "He had a bad attitude. He was surly to his co-workers and to our customers. He often came in late, bleary-eyed and smelling of alcohol. Sometimes he wouldn't make it in at all. He'd call late in the morning and claim to be sick, but more likely he was hung over or just playing hooky."

"And as a result of these deficiencies, you ultimately terminated his employment?"

"Correct. My patience with him had been wearing thin, and the last straw was a phone call I received from a long-time customer, complaining that he was rude and nasty to her. I can't tolerate that in my business."

Jake was encouraged to see that Mickey was speaking with confidence and forcefulness now. There was anger in his voice, which was a good thing. He had every right to be angry. The jurors were sitting straight up in their seats, paying close attention. A few were taking notes.

"Mr. Quinn ..." Vern paused, struggling with how to broach this next subject. "You heard Mr. Doyle testify yesterday that there was another reason for his termination. More specifically, he claims you terminated him ... because he refused to submit to ... uh ... uh ... sexual advances you had been making toward him. What's your response to that?"

"It's a bold-face lie!" Mickey shouted, his face turning crimson, as he glared at Larry with clenched fists.

"So there is no truth to—"

"No truth whatsoever. He's an unscrupulous scoundrel." He stood up, shouting now, pointing at Larry. "He's got no conscience. He's a—"

"Objection!" Rick's voice boomed, cutting Mickey off in mid-sentence.

Judge Gray turned toward Mickey and said sternly, "Mr. Quinn, please take your seat. I will not tolerate personal attacks in this courtroom. Just answer the questions your attorney is asking."

Mickey sat down, struggling to control himself. "I apologize, Your Honor."

Vern continued. "So, is it your testimony that Mr. Doyle's termination had nothing to do with any sexual advances?"

"He was terminated for the reasons I mentioned earlier. I never made any ... sexual advances." Mickey looked disgusted, and seemed to have difficulty even uttering the words.

"Did you ever expose yourself to him, or touch him inappropriately?"

"Absolutely not. Never." He glared at Larry disdainfully. Larry was looking down, as he had been throughout Mickey's testimony.

"I have just one final question, Mr. Quinn. If you never did any of these things, why do you suppose Mr. Doyle would say you did? What motive would he have?"

"Objection," Rick shouted. "Calls for speculation."

"I'll allow the witness to answer," Judge Gray replied.

"I don't understand it," Mickey replied sadly. "I don't know what could be in a man's heart to make him act that way. Revenge, I imagine. He's angry that he lost his job. Beyond that, what motivates most people? Greed, I suppose. Like a lot of people, he must think that filing a lawsuit is a legitimate way to make money, whether you're deserving or not." Mickey was not looking at the jury now. He was looking down, trying to hide the tears of frustration welling up in his eyes. "This has destroyed my life. It's a travesty," he said in a voice barely above a whisper. "A travesty."

After breaking for lunch, Mickey returned to the witness stand. "Cross-examination, Mr. Black?" asked Judge Gray.

"Thank you, Your Honor," said Rick, standing and approaching the witness. "I have just a few questions, Mr. Quinn." He folded his arms and looked up at the ceiling for a moment, then he looked directly at Mickey. "You testified that my client's job performance was unsatisfactory, is that correct?"

"That is correct."

"Did you ever provide any disciplinary memo, or any other type of written communication, advising him of these alleged deficiencies and what he needed to do to correct them?"

"I had plenty of conversations with Larry about his performance, and—"

"That wasn't my question, Mr. Quinn. Did you provide him anything in writing?"

"In writing? No."

"Is there any written documentation at all describing these alleged deficiencies, a memo to his personnel file, perhaps?"

Mickey looked puzzled. "No, I communicate with my employees face-to-face."

"So there's not a shred of written evidence to corroborate your claim that my client had performance problems?"

"Nothing in writing, but like I said—"

Rick cut him off. "It was a yes or no question, Mr. Quinn. You've answered my question. Now, let me ask you this: Were you ever alone with my client in the workplace?"

"I don't know—probably. I'm at the store every day, all day long. Larry worked there for over four years. I'm sure there were any number of times when we were alone together. That would not have been unusual at all."

"Let me be more specific. Do you ever recall being alone with Larry in your office, with the door closed?"

"Actually, yes, now that I think about it. When I had performance issues with an employee, I dealt with them face-to-face, in the privacy of my office."

"So you do acknowledge being alone with Larry in your office, behind closed doors."

"Yes."

"More than once?"

"Several times, I'm sure. Like I said, I had plenty of problems with Larry. He—"

"On any of those occasions, did you expose your genitals to my client?"

"I most certainly did not!"

"Are you a homosexual, Mr. Quinn?"

Vern stood up. "Objection." It sounded more like a question than a forceful interjection.

"Absolutely not!" Mickey blurted out simultaneously, before the judge could respond.

"Withdrawn," Rick replied. "Mr. Quinn, have you ever instructed any employee to do something unethical?"

"Of course not."

"Have you ever told any employee to keep quiet about your own unethical behavior at the risk of losing their job?"

Mickey looked irritated and confused. "I don't know what you're talking about. I would never do any such thing."

"So you never told my client to keep quiet about your overtures to him?"

"Certainly not. Like I said, I never made any overtures."

"And you never asked any other employee to keep quiet about any other type of inappropriate conduct on your part?"

Vern looked as puzzled as Mickey. "Your Honor, I object. I don't see the relevance, and besides, that question has already been asked and answered."

"He's right, Mr. Black. Move on, please," instructed Judge Gray.

"I have no further questions for this witness, Your Honor."

"Very well," replied Judge Gray. "You may step down, Mr. Quinn. You may proceed with your next witness, Mr. Snyder."

"I have no further witnesses, Your Honor," Vern replied.

"Any rebuttal witnesses, Mr. Black?" asked the judge.

"Yes, Your Honor. I have one rebuttal witness. We call Kenny Oliver to the stand."

Jake was taken by surprise. By the look of it, Vern and Mickey were surprised as well. Kenny was a current employee of Mickey's. His primary job was stocking the shelves, but he also handled deliveries when the regular driver was off or when he needed assistance on busy days. Jake and Kenny had known each other since fifth grade, and had started working at Quinn's about the same time. Jake had his doubts when Kenny began working at the store because he had gotten into more than his share of trouble when he was younger. It wasn't that Kenny was a bad kid at heart, but more that he was eager to please and easily led astray by the rougher crowd—and not smart enough to avoid getting caught. Despite that history, Kenny wasn't a bad employee. He was lazy—no question about that—and not particularly bright, but he was amiable and reasonably reliable.

Vern spoke up in a hesitant voice. "Your Honor, this person is not on the plaintiff's witness list, and I'd like to know what relevance his testimony will have to these proceedings."

Judge Gray looked at Rick. "Certainly," Rick replied. "Mr. Quinn has testified that he has never previously engaged in inappropriate conduct and then asked an employee to conceal it. This witness will testify about behavior of exactly that nature on the part of Mr. Quinn. It shows a pattern of behavior, and therefore is highly relevant."

"Alright, I'll allow it," said the judge.

Jake slipped a note to Vern, suggesting he ask the judge for a recess, so that he would have time to prepare. Since Kenny was not on the witness list, the judge would almost certainly be open to such a request.

Vern showed the note to Mickey. Although they were whispering, Jake could clearly hear Mickey say, "I want this over with—now!"

Kenny walked ponderously to the witness stand, breathing heavily as if the walk required too much exertion. He was considerably over-weight, his expansive belly hanging over his belt. He had thinning brown hair, combed over a large bald spot on the top of his head.

Rick began with a number of routine questions about Kenny's background, primarily his job duties and his employment history with Quinn's Fine Foods. Mickey, Vern and Jake were all on the edge of their seats, listening intently and wondering where this was going.

"Mr. Oliver, when was your last day of employment with Mr. Quinn's store?" Rick asked.

"I haven't worked since last week, and I don't plan on going back."

"Why not?"

Kenny looked from Rick to Mickey and back to Rick. "Because of him," he said, looking back at Mickey.

"Do you mean Mr. Quinn?"

"Yeah."

"Would you please explain what you mean by that?"

"He was doing things—things that weren't right."

Every eye in the courtroom was riveted on Kenny Oliver.

"What things?"

"I have a video."

Rick turned to Judge Gray. "With your permission, Your Honor, I would like to show the jury Mr. Oliver's video recording."

"Any objection, Mr. Snyder?"

Vern conferred with Mickey. It was clear that neither of them had any idea what this was about. "No objection," Vern mumbled, after Mickey again made it clear that he wanted the trial concluded quickly.

Rick wheeled in a large TV on a black metal stand, positioning it near the jury, but on an angle so that everyone in the courtroom could see it. "Mr. Oliver, please narrate for the jury as we play this video."

"Okay. This is Quinn's," Kenny began, as the video showed the front of the store. The picture became jerky, as the cameraman walked into the store and down the first aisle.

"Who's filming this?" Rick asked.

"I am." Kenny replied, as the screen showed a typical looking grocery store aisle with canned foods on one side and cereal on the other. At the end of the aisle, was a narrow pathway that extended past a refrigeration unit containing lunchmeats and cheeses. The image stopped briefly before a swinging double door, then turned sideways into the wall as a cameraman had apparently turned and opened the door with his body rather than his hands, so that he could keep filming. The image moved past a sink and a couple of restrooms, and showed a counter along a wall with a number of tall stools under it. "This is the back room," Kenny explained. "This is where the staff has lunch and takes their coffee breaks." The floors were gray concrete and the walls were cinderblocks, painted a pale yellow. The image rounded a corner and moved into another room. The middle of that room was a large empty space. The camera panned to a rear door with a red exit sign hanging over it. "That's the back door leading to the loading dock in the alley. The door next to it is the dairy cooler. The next door, right here, is the freezer, where we store the frozen food, and that little door there is Mickey's office." The camera moved in the direction of the office, the image bouncing as the camera moved. The camera ran continuously, with no breaks in the footage. No people were visible anywhere.

The video then displayed the interior of the office. There were pictures of Mickey on the desk with local political figures, and the walls were adorned with plaques paying tribute to Mickey for his involvement in various civic and charitable causes. A hand could be seen moving some books off the shelf above the desk and reaching behind them to remove a shoebox. The shoebox was placed on the desk and the hand could be seen removing the lid. "This was filmed last week. I had been in the store late a few days earlier after my delivery run. I was supposed to lock up that night and I couldn't find the keys so I began looking through the office. I found this box."

The camera remained fixed on the contents of the box. There were several credit cards, a few pads of blank checks, a string of pearls, a necklace, and several rings. The hand lifted up the credit cards and checks one at a time and placed them before the camera. The images went from blurry to clear as the camera automatically adjusted its focus. Kenny read the names: "Esther Hamill. Lucy Palmer. Margaret Finn."

"Do you know these names?" Rick asked.

"These were delivery customers," Kenny replied.

"Do you know anything about the jewelry?"

"I've seen Mrs. Hamill wearing pearls before. I think those might be hers. I believe that necklace and the rings are Mrs. Finn's. Anyway, I was looking through this box, and Mickey walked in behind me. He surprised me, and I think I surprised him too."

"Did he say anything to you at that time?"

"He asked me what I was doing and I told him I was looking for the keys to lock up. He grabbed the box and told me that I could go home, and that he would lock up."

"Did he say anything else?"

"Not that night. The next morning, he called me to his office and told me I shouldn't mention that box to anyone else. He told me to keep it to myself."

"Did he say anything else?"

"Yeah. I started to ask him why he had those things and he cut me off and said 'Kenny, you've worked here a long time. I've been good to you. You have a good job here – don't piss it away.'"

"What was your reaction to that?"

"I didn't know what to think. At first, I thought there must be a good explanation for why he had those things, but the more I thought about it, the more nervous I got. I remembered that, more and more, he had been making deliveries himself. When people called in their orders late in the day, he would drop them off on his way home. He also asked me to try to get keys from the customers. He said I should tell them it would be convenient if they were not home or were unable to get to the door. Then when he told me to keep quiet about the box, and that I might lose my job if I didn't, I knew something wasn't right."

"So what did you do?"

"I quit. I didn't want to be part of anything shady."

"By the way, did any of those delivery customers give you keys to their apartments?"

"A few did. Most were nervous about it and wouldn't do it."

"Do you remember which customers gave you keys?"

"Mrs. Hamill and Mrs. Finn did. One or two others, but I'm not sure which ones. But those two for sure."

"Was there anything else that made you think something wasn't right?"

"I remember Mickey grumbling a lot lately about how these people owed him. He'd been delivering to them for years and losing money on it. They owed him, he kept saying."

Rick looked triumphant. "No further questions," he said.

Judge Gray looked at his watch. It was nearly five o'clock, and he rarely asked the jury to stay beyond that time. "Mr. Snyder, would you like to begin your cross-examination, or shall we pick this up tomorrow?" It was an obvious invitation to take some time to prepare for this cross-examination, since this testimony was clearly a surprise.

"I'll proceed now, if I may, Your Honor. This shouldn't take long."

Vern paused for an uncomfortably long time, staring at his yellow legal pad, then stood up and slowly approached the witness stand.

"Mr. Oliver, were there any eyewitnesses to these conversations with Mr. Quinn you just described?"

"No, we were alone."

"Did Mr. Quinn explain to you why these items were in his possession?"

"No."

"Did you tell anyone about these conversations immediately after they occurred—excuse me, allegedly occurred?"

"Not at first. I didn't want anyone to think I was mixed up with something bad. Then I ran into Larry and he told me about his case, so I told him what happened to me. Then I met with Larry's attorney just a few days ago to talk about testifying here."

"Do you know for a fact how Mr. Quinn acquired the items in the box?"

"No."

"Do you know for a fact that he should not have been in possession of those items?"

"No, but why would he be holding some old ladies' jewelry, and hiding it?"

"Just answer the question, Mr. Oliver. The fact is that you don't know how or why these items came to be in Mr. Quinn's possession, isn't that right?"

Kenny glanced quickly at Rick, who ignored him. "That's correct," Kenny replied.

Mickey had been struggling to control himself, fidgeting and shaking his head and muttering quietly to himself every time Kenny finished a response. Finally, he exploded, red-faced, rising from his chair and pointing at Kenny.

"Of course he doesn't know because it never happened! This whole thing is a set-up! I've never laid eyes on that stuff. That man's a goddamned liar, just like his friend!"

"Order! Order!" shouted the judge, pounding his gavel. "Mr. Snyder, control your client! I will not tolerate any more outbursts, Mr. Quinn. You'll have your turn to speak. Now sit down and let your lawyer do the talking!"

Vern gently put his hand on Mickey's shoulder and guided him back into his chair. Mickey silently fumed as Vern quietly stressed the importance of heeding the judge's admonishment.

"One last question. Mr. Oliver, did you plant this evidence?"

Rick was on his feet in a flash. "Objection!" he shouted angrily.

"I'll allow it," replied the judge.

Kenny looked at Rick again, hesitating. Judge Gray looked hard at the witness. "Mr. Oliver, I have overruled the objection. Answer the question, please."

Kenny hesitated another moment, and then, looking offended by the question, replied, "I didn't plant anything. It happened just like I said."

"I have no further questions," Vern said.

"Mr. Oliver, you are excused," Judge Gray announced. "Do you have any further witnesses, Mr. Black?"

"No, Your Honor."

Mr. Snyder, your client may take the stand again first thing tomorrow if he wishes to respond to Mr. Oliver's testimony. After that, we will proceed with closing arguments."

Rick Black strode into his office, feeling excited and confident. The day's testimony had gone even better than he had hoped. He felt like he was back on the basketball court, leading a late game rally that was about to result in a huge upset. He loved that feeling.

His secretary followed him into his office, handing him a handful of phone messages. "Hold all my calls," he instructed her. "Call these people back and tell them I'm in trial. I'll get back to them later in the week."

"Yes, Mr. Black. But there's one person who insisted that you call her tonight. A Mrs. Helen Wright. She said it was urgent."

"I don't know her. I'll get back to her later in the week."

"She said she has information regarding the Quinn case that you'll want to hear."

That got Rick's attention. He looked at the message slip, closed his door and dialed her number. The woman who answered the phone had the rough voice of a heavy smoker. "I'm glad you called, Mr. Black. I've got information about Mickey Quinn—information that proves what a devious, manipulating dirtbag he is. Can we meet?"

The next morning, Rick began the proceedings by asking the judge for permission to call another rebuttal witness. This time Vern objected, and the judge summoned the two attorneys to his chambers to discuss the issue outside of the jury's presence. "Why are we just hearing about this witness now, Mr. Black, and what is the nature of her testimony?" Judge Gray was clearly annoyed.

"I just learned of this witness late yesterday, after court had adjourned," Rick explained. "She will testify that the defendant took advantage of an elderly relative of hers."

"Even if true, that has no relevance to the issues in this case," Vern protested.

"With all due respect, I disagree, Your Honor," Rick replied. "First, the evidence has probative value because it is consistent with the testimony of Mr. Oliver, thereby lending greater credence to his story. Second, the defense has made the defendant's character a significant part of its case, through the character witnesses it has produced. We are entitled to rebut that evidence."

Judge Gray looked sternly at both of them. "I don't like last-minute surprises, Mr. Black. However, I will allow this one final witness. Mr. Black is correct, Mr. Snyder, you pushed the door wide open on the issue of character and the plaintiff is entitled to rebut on that point. Mr. Black, you may proceed with your witness. After that, Mr. Snyder, you may recall your client if he wishes to respond to any testimony from this witness or from Mr. Oliver."

Rick called Helen Wright to the stand. She appeared to be in her early fifties, but working hard not to show it. Her hair was bleached blonde, and her makeup had been applied thickly, but couldn't cover the wrinkles around her lips and the dark circles under her eyes, which spoke of hard living.

After she was sworn in, Rick flipped on a projector and displayed a picture for the entire courtroom to see. It was a picture of an elderly woman, propped up in a hospital bed, a toothless mouth wide open, drooling, as she stared vacantly ahead. The left side of her face sagged noticeably.

"Can you identify this woman, Ms. Wright?"

"Yes, that is my aunt, Nancy Shadel."

"How old is she?"

"Eighty-two."

"What is the state of her health?"

"Lousy. You can probably tell from the picture that she's suffered a stroke. That was about three months ago. Her mind is gone—completely."

"How was her health before her stroke?"

"Not good. She had Alzheimer's. Once in a while she was lucid, but mostly she was confused and really out of it."

"How long had she been that way?"

"Several years."

"Do you know Mickey Quinn?"

"I know who he is."

"What was the relationship between Mr. Quinn and your aunt?"

"He was her grocer. She bought her groceries from his store and had them delivered to her apartment. She's been too feeble to get out and do her own shopping for a long time. I understand that he started visiting her on Sundays not long before she had her stroke."

"What do you know about your aunt's will?"

"I just looked into that. Since she's had a stroke and her health is declining, I thought I should make sure that all of her affairs were in order. I found her will in a file she kept on her desk. I have it right here." She held up a document in her right hand.

"Anything unusual about it?"

Ms. Wright glared at Mickey. "I'll say. Since I was her only living relative, her will provided that I was to be the sole beneficiary. Then, earlier this year, she changed it. I've been cut out of the will completely, and she's left everything to him." She pointed an accusing finger at Mickey.

"Why do you think she would do that?"

"I'll tell you why. Because he coerced her. He manipulated her. She didn't know what she was doing—her mind was gone. Visiting her every Sunday like that, pretending to be a good neighbor—right! He had only one thing on his mind and that was to get his greedy paws on her money." She turned to face Mickey. "You won't get a dime from her estate, mister," she shouted belligerently. "I'll see to that."

Again, Mickey looked stunned, as did Vern. Most of the jury members had the same look of disgust that had framed their faces when they listened to Larry's testimony.

Rick walked over to the picture of the decrepit old woman, and looked at her for a long time. The jury's gaze followed his. "So, you don't think she would have knowingly cut you out of her will and named Mr. Quinn as the beneficiary?"

"No way! Not a chance! Look at her, will you? She doesn't even know her name!"

Rick turned to Vern. "Your witness, counselor."

Vern asked for a few moments to examine the will, then approached Ms. Wright, studying the document as he did so. "Ms. Wright, would you please read Article Three of this will?"

He handed the document to Ms. Wright, who held it at arm's length to bring the words into focus. She read it aloud, in a halting voice, "I hereby bequeath my entire estate to Michael J. Quinn. It is my suggestion that he distribute my estate among such charitable and religious organizations as he deems worthy; however, all decisions regarding the identity of such organizations and the amount of any such distributions, or whether to share my estate with any such organizations at all, shall be entirely within the sole and unfettered discretion of said Michael J. Quinn."

"So, Ms. Wright, would you agree that your aunt's motivation is to see that her estate be distributed to charity and that she is entrusting Mr. Quinn with the responsibility for identifying appropriate recipients?"

"I don't agree with that at all. It's just a sneaky way for him to get his hands on the money. He's free to keep everything for himself, and I'm sure that's his plan. But I have no intention of letting that happen!"

Vern was able to get Ms. Wright to grudgingly admit that the date of her aunt's most recent will was prior to the time of her stroke, although she insisted that her aunt did not have the mental capacity to understand the consequences of her actions, even at that time. After that, Vern excused her and brought Mickey back to the witness stand.

Guided by Vern's questioning, Mickey explained that he had no idea that he had been named as a beneficiary under Mrs. Shadel's will. He mentioned that he was a special minister at St. Francis Church, and that, as such, he took Holy Communion on Sunday afternoons to parishioners who were unable to attend Mass, including Mrs. Shadel. He had been visiting her for that purpose for well over a year before her stroke. Since he had known her as a customer for over twenty years, and since she was obviously lonely, he frequently stayed and visited with her for an hour or so each Sunday. During many of those visits, Mrs. Shadel complained about being alone, and mentioned that her only living relative was a niece who never called or visited except when she needed money. Mickey testified that, on one occasion, Mrs. Shadel indicated that she wanted to change her will so that all of her property would go to charity rather than to her niece, but that she did not know what charities were deserving. Mickey testified that he had suggested to Mrs. Shadel that she discuss the matter with her attorney, and stated that there were no other discussions between him and Mrs. Shadel on that subject.

Jake thought Mickey looked defeated and resigned to a bad outcome as he finished his testimony. He spoke softly, without passion. That demeanor became more pronounced when Vern questioned him about Kenny Oliver. Mickey looked utterly bewildered. He denied any knowledge of the hidden shoebox or its contents. He denied any conversations with Kenny about that subject. He denied any threats or even suggestions that Kenny's job was at risk, and claimed that he didn't even know that Kenny had quit until hearing him say so in the courtroom.

Rick was entitled to one final cross-examination of Mickey regarding his latest round of testimony. His calm, folksy demeanor was gone. He had become the picture of bottled-up intensity. He approached the witness stand like a boxer in the late rounds of a prize-fight, circling a wounded opponent, looking to finish him off with a devastating and decisive knockout punch. "Mr. Quinn, you just testi-fied that you know nothing whatsoever about this shoebox and its contents, correct?" He touched the remote control and an image of the shoebox appeared on the screen.

"That's correct," Mickey replied softly.

"So in other words, Kenny Oliver is lying?"

"I don't know why he would do that, but what he said is simply not true."

"So he's lying, right?"

"Yes."

"And when Ms. Wright testified that you deliberately tried to take advantage of her aunt, she's lying too?"

"She's mistaken. She wasn't there and can't possibly know what happened."

"But you're saying that the version of events she described here in this courtroom is not true, is that correct?"

"That's correct."

"Okay, let me see if I've got this straight. You would have us believe that Larry Doyle is lying, Kenny Oliver is lying, and Helen Wright is lying. Basically, Mr. Quinn, you're expecting this jury to believe that every person involved in this case is lying, except you, is that right?"

"I'm telling the truth, as God is my witness."

Rick looked at Mickey with contempt. "We'll let the jury decide that, Mr. Quinn. No further questions."

"In that case, we will recess for lunch and begin closing arguments promptly at 1:30," Judge Gray announced. The jury filed silently out of the room, heads down, avoiding any eye contact with the defendant.

Jake, Mickey and Vern walked across the street to a sandwich shop and ordered lunch. They nibbled at their food, none of them having any real appetite. Jake tried to be encouraging. "Let's stay positive, Mickey. They have the burden of proving their case. They can't win unless they do, and they haven't come close to proving anything. You can't just walk into court and present a bunch of completely uncorroborated bullshit to a jury and expect them to buy it."

Mickey looked morose. "I don't understand this. Why would Kenny turn on me? I understand Larry's motive. He hopes the jury will award him a pile of money. But Kenny? He's got no stake in this. And that wretched Helen Wright? Clearly, she's got a beef because she was cut out of her aunt's will, but what does that have to do with Larry Doyle's lawsuit? Why was she allowed to come here and try to poison the jury with that nonsense?" He stared silently at his uneaten sandwich. "I have a bad feeling about this."

"I just can't believe any jury would buy into their story," Vern said, trying to sound upbeat. "We have to have faith in these jurors. We have to trust that they're not gullible or stupid and that they will see this case for exactly what it is—a calculated, unconscionable attempt to game the system at your expense. It's not over yet, my friend."

The judge granted each side one hour for closing arguments. Rick went first. He carefully led the jury through all of the key elements of the testimony from Larry Doyle, Kenny Oliver and Helen Wright. While summarizing Larry's testimony, Rick pointed to a flip chart that listed, in bullet-point format, each of the alleged incidents with approximate dates of occurrence. The written summary of graphically described transgressions painted a compelling picture—a clear and disturbing pattern of highly offensive behavior. While recounting Kenny's testimony, a blown-up photograph of the shoebox and its contents was displayed on the flip chart. During his reiteration of Helen Wright's testimony, an enlarged picture of the drooling, decrepit old woman with the lifeless eyes was prominently displayed. The jurors' eyes alternated between Rick and the pictures as he recounted the testimony.

After summarizing the evidence, Rick made his final appeal to the jury. "Ladies and gentlemen, as I mentioned at the outset of this trial, you have a vitally important task before you. The facts here are in dispute, and it's your responsibility to sort through them and determine where the truth lies. I believe that when you carefully consider the evidence, the truth will be clear.

"Mr. Quinn would have you believe that everyone who testified here—other than himself—is a liar. Unfortunately, there are some people in this world who choose to disregard the truth, but I believe that most people are honest. Most people do not lie, particularly when they're under oath. Trust your instincts here. Trust in the basic honesty within people, and the weight of the evidence points to one thing— there's only one person in this courtroom who is trying to deceive you; only one person who has reason to conceal the truth; and that is the defendant. Don't let him get away with that.

"In our society, we place a great deal of trust in certain people. Our bosses, for example. They have power over us, and we trust them to use that power fairly. We also place great trust in the people who occupy positions of responsibility within our churches, as well as the people who care for the elderly in our communities. We trust them not to abuse their positions and take advantage of those who have placed their faith in them. When that trust is betrayed, great harm can result. But who is there to protect the weak and the vulnerable against that harm? You are. Our legal system is. We protect those people by holding our leaders accountable. We make them pay for their mistakes and send a message to the world that such conduct will not be tolerated. You have that power, and it is your responsibility to wield it—justly and forcefully.

"Mr. Quinn occupied numerous positions of trust. He was an employer to many, including Larry Doyle and Kenny Oliver. He was a representative of St. Francis Church and interacted with elderly parishioners in that capacity. He served other elderly shut-ins with his delivery business. He enjoyed great trust from his community. Mr. Quinn abused that trust, and you must tell him and the world that type of behavior is not acceptable. How do you send that message? You do it by punishing him financially.

"You heard testimony about Mr. Quinn's income and the value of his business. You should consider that as you reflect upon what it would take to send him a strong message, and to compensate Mr. Doyle for all he has endured. Larry Doyle has been unable to sustain gainful employment since this awful incident over two years ago. He's been embarrassed and humiliated. He may be emotionally scarred for the rest of his life. He deserves to be compensated. Ladies and gentlemen of the jury, do what you think is right. That's all I can ask."

Despite the feeling of revulsion over what was happening, Jake could not help but admire Rick's skill as a litigator. He did a masterful job of succinctly and forcefully summarizing the evidence in the light most favorable to his client. He was smooth and articulate. He seemed genuinely sincere and passionate about his client and his case, and he was convincing. He never came across as nasty or arrogant or condescending, as so many trial lawyers with big egos are wont to do. Any jury would like this guy, and it was clear that this one did.

Vern was not possessed of the same ability to connect with the jury. He was neither articulate nor polished, and certainly did not come across as personable. In fact, he was boring. He spoke in a monotone, without passion. Despite his lack of flair, however, he did a decent job of summarizing his case.

He emphasized that there was not a shred of evidence to support Larry's testimony. He portrayed Larry as a disgruntled former employee who was obviously angry over his termination and was out for revenge. As for Kenny, there was no independent evidence to support his story either, other than the video, which could easily have been a setup. Why would a man of Mickey's means need to stoop to stealing jewelry from his customers? No explanation had been provided about what use, if any, had been made of the credit cards and blank checks. Clearly, Mickey could not expect to use them for illicit purposes without getting caught. It just didn't make any sense, and it was highly suspicious that this story should surface for the first time, through an acquaintance of Larry, just days before the trial.

Vern proceeded to point out that Ms. Wright had her own motive for coming forward—she had been disinherited. Her theory that Mickey was somehow trying to coerce or manipulate her aunt for his own gain was pure conjecture. In fact, his reasons for visiting with her on Sunday afternoons were motivated solely by his desire to be a Good Samaritan, by bringing her Holy Communion and spending time with her to alleviate her loneliness—something her niece never bothered to do. Vern also emphasized that Mrs. Shadel changed her will before she had her stroke. At that time, she was not the helpless, mindless creature portrayed in the picture repeatedly shown to the jury.

After summarizing the evidence, Vern walked back to the counsel table, picked up a legal pad and studied it for a few minutes. Then he proceeded with his final pitch to the jury. "As you consider the evidence presented to you, I ask you to keep in mind that the plaintiff has the burden of proof here. That means that there must be a preponderance of the evidence in his favor. The fact is that he hasn't proven anything. He has egregiously harmed Mr. Quinn and his business through these very scandalous and public allegations. He has done so for his own greedy and spiteful purposes, and he is counting on you to finish the job for him by forcing Mr. Quinn to pay him a considerable sum of money. There is a victim here, but it's not Larry Doyle. It's Mickey Quinn. Don't let Mr. Doyle con you. Show him that our jury system really works."

It was late Wednesday afternoon when Vern finished, and the judge instructed the jury to commence to deliberations first thing the following morning, and to continue deliberating until they had reached a verdict. He advised the attorneys that they would be contacted by telephone when the jury had reached its decision.

Late Friday afternoon, the call came in, and all parties scurried back to the courthouse. The tension was palpable, and evident in the faces of both parties and their attorneys as the jury filed into the courtroom. Jake tried to read their faces and body language, but could not pick up any clues.

Judge Gray looked at the parties and announced, "Gentlemen, the jury has reached their decision. Mr. Foreman, may I have the verdict please?"

A short, bald gentleman in the first row of the jury box rose and handed a piece of paper to the bailiff, who in turn delivered it to the judge. The judge read it silently to himself, then took a deep breath and read aloud, "We the jury find in favor of the plaintiff, Larry Doyle, on all counts, and order defendant, Michael J. Quinn, to pay plaintiff the sum of 2.2 Million Dollars."

CHAPTER 29

J ake and Amanda walked hand-in-hand along the lakefront, beneath the luxurious high-rises on Lake Shore Drive. It was Saturday morning, the day after the jury had rendered its verdict in the Quinn case. Jake had stayed with Mickey until late the previous evening, trying to console him and help him sort through his limited options. He had phoned Amanda to tell her the dismal news and that he would be home late, but they hadn't yet discussed the outcome of the case in any detail.

They walked in silence for a long time, under an overcast sky. After some time, they stopped and Jake wrapped his arms around his wife in a tight embrace. He held her like that for a long moment, then stepped back and looked into her eyes. He smiled at her, but it was a sad smile. "I'm so lucky to have you and Anna. I think about how good life is for us today, and how good it will be tomorrow, and on into the future. Then I think about Mickey. He's been through a living hell for the past two years. He woke up this morning to a world that must seem bleak and hopeless. It's so wrong! It tears me up to think about it. He's such a good man. He doesn't deserve this!"

Amanda leaned back and looked at her husband, her arms still around his neck. "You're a good soul, Jake McShane. I love the fact that you care so deeply for your friends. You've been so loyal and supportive to Mickey throughout this ordeal." She kissed him on the cheek and they resumed walking. "He can appeal, can't he?"

"He can, and probably will, but he has no realistic chance of prevailing. He'd have to be able to show that there was some fundamental procedural flaw that affected the outcome of the trial, and I don't know what that could possibly be. This judge knows what he's doing, and I don't see any basis for arguing that the process was flawed. The jury just reached the wrong conclusion. They were fooled. An appellate court won't second-guess a jury on the facts. At best, filing an appeal may buy Mickey some time and give him at least a little negotiating leverage. Larry won't want to wait two more years to get his money, so he'd probably agree to settle for something less than the full amount of the verdict, to speed up his payday."

"So what'll Mickey do? Does he have that kind of money?"

"No, the store brought in a lot of revenue, but he barely eked out a profit because of his bloated payroll. As a result, he's got very little money. All he really has is the business. He'll have to sell it, and even then he may not have enough to satisfy the judgment."

"So financially, he's ruined?"

"Financially and just about every other way. His good name and reputation are shot. The press has seen to that. Everyone will assume that he must really be the perverted scumbag that Larry described. But he's not the only one who'll be seriously hurt by this. Think of all the employees whose lives will be disrupted. He employed six butchers—even the large chain stores usually employ only one or two. He employed seven or eight people to support the delivery business. Anyone who buys the store will almost certainly eliminate all of those jobs. Most of those people are in their fifties and sixties. It'll be tough for them to find other employment. And what about all those shut-ins? How will they get their groceries? And the neighborhood will lose an institution. We already have. People came to Quinn's because of Mickey and the way he treated them. There was a certain magic touch there. Because of that, it was the place to shop in Beverly—a place to meet your neighbors and catch up on neighborhood events. That's been disappearing already. The business is dwindling. Even if a new owner makes a go of it, something special has been lost forever."

"How can this happen, Jake?"

"Back in law school, Rick used to say that the jury system is a complete joke. He said that juries are just like sheep, waiting to be led, and that a good lawyer can almost always lead them exactly where he wants them to go. I think he just proved his point."

"Do you really believe that?"

Jake gazed out over the lake and sighed deeply. "Much as I hate to admit it, some part of me believes that he's absolutely right. Think about it. Some jurors just aren't very bright. Others may be lazy—they just want to get the matter over with and go home. But even the ones who are smart and conscientious don't have what it takes to competently perform that job. They're expected to evaluate complicated and contradictory evidence and figure out what really happened. That's a very difficult task, and they just don't have the skills, the experience, or the training to carry it out effectively. And yet this completely unqualified group of people is given the power to drastically alter someone's life, or many lives for that matter. A person who is a good actor or a skillful liar can put on a persuasive performance and lead a jury to the wrong result—with disastrous consequences."

"But juries have been a fundamental part of our judicial system from the beginning. We've been relying on them for hundreds of years. The system must have some merit."

"In criminal cases, it makes perfect sense. Where the government is seeking to prosecute someone, a jury of your peers is a safeguard against abuse of governmental power. But in civil cases, the government's not a party, so that justification doesn't apply. Maybe years ago, when laws and business and society were less complicated, a jury might have had a better chance of adequately understanding the facts and the implications of their decisions. But now ..." His voice trailed off, and he shook his head sadly.

They stopped walking and sat on a bench overlooking the lake. Amanda looked troubled. "Obviously, there will always be some people who want to game the system, but don't the lawyers have an ethical obligation to avoid filing frivolous lawsuits? Aren't they supposed to prevent their clients from committing perjury?"

"Absolutely, and if the system is to work, the lawyers have to act as gatekeepers and keep out those frivolous lawsuits. But, if the lawyers themselves aren't burdened by a conscience, it all breaks down."

"Are there really that many lawyers who are so willing to ignore their ethical obligations? Can't they get into trouble with the State Bar if they do?"

"Our system provides a strong incentive for both attorneys and clients to play fast and loose with the truth. Greed is a powerful motivator. A lawyer who is skillful and aggressive can make a lot of money pursuing baseless cases, and our system makes it easy for lawyers to handle those cases without any risk to themselves. It's almost impossible to prove that they knew their clients were lying, and they can always argue that they were simply fulfilling their professional obligation to zealously represent their client's interests. Even if they have serious doubts about the merits of their client's case, many lawyers find it convenient to set aside any ethical considerations. They make the excuse that they're simply playing a necessary role in the system by being a good advocate and leaving it to the jury to make the ultimate determination of the case's merits. It's an easy cop-out."

"And a client who pursues a false or fraudulent claim, is there no risk to him?"

"Practically speaking, none at all. The plaintiff generally pays nothing if he loses because he can find a lawyer who will take the case on a contingent fee basis. So there's no downside and a huge upside – he could convince a jury to pay him millions of dollars. The potential reward is so great that many people succumb to the temptation and set aside their moral compass. Pursuing a bogus claim is really just another form of robbery or extortion – someone uses force to take something from an innocent victim. Yet people don't look at it that way. I guess they can sleep at night because they do it through the courts, so they can rationalize their action as something legitimized by our legal system."

"You're depressing me, Jake. Is our system really that broken? Surely, what happened to Mickey must be an aberration?"

"I wish it were, but I'm confident that court dockets across the country are clogged with countless lawsuits that have no merit whatsoever. And I'm afraid that juries make mistakes all the time. We were able to visit with these jurors when the trial concluded, and it just confirmed my reservations about their ability to reliably carry out their duty. One juror said that Mickey just looked guilty, and several others agreed. What kind of basis is that for making a decision that could ruin a man's life? Another said that he was persuaded because Larry produced more witnesses supporting his story than Mickey did. How can Mickey produce witnesses to prove that nothing happened? You can't prove a negative! Another juror said she wasn't sure what really happened, but she believes that where there's smoke, there's fire. She was willing to destroy a man's life over that. One woman said she just liked Rick better than Vern, and thought Rick was more credible. Well, it's not about the lawyers! And juries like that make tremendously important decisions every day. They often arrive at the wrong result and don't even think about the far-reaching effects of their decisions, or how many lives could be affected."

Jake was getting both angrier and more dejected as he spoke. "I wish I knew how to make it better. I wish I had some hope that it actually could get better." He spoke softly, a despondent look on his face.

Amanda turned to her husband and put her hands on his. "It can, Jake. I believe that. My grandmother always told me that one of the great things about this country is the way we deal with our problems. We have great freedoms here and sometimes those freedoms allow bad conditions to arise and flourish. The Industrial Revolution and free enterprise led to sweatshops and child labor, but our society responded with unions and legislation and we dealt with it. Racism has been a problem in this country for a long time. As a society, we've recognized that and made significant strides in the area of equal rights. More recently, corporate America has been plagued by financial and accounting scandals, and again, our society responded. Laws were changed and bad guys were held accountable. If our legal system is broken, it can be fixed too."

"But there are so many flaws, how do we even start to address them?"

Amanda thought quietly for a few moments. "I have no idea what changes would be effective and viable. Maybe the incentive to file frivolous lawsuits could be eliminated by prohibiting contingent fee arrangements, or by capping punitive damages, or making the loser pay. Maybe there should be other ways to punish wrongdoers besides forcing them to make some private citizen obscenely wealthy. I realize it's complicated and I'm in no position to even guess what the right solutions may be, but there is one thing I am sure about. Like any other major societal challenge, the starting point is to bring attention to the problem. If the system is really in peril, people need to hear about it. Leaders of the profession should write about it, speak about it, get the media involved, get the legislatures involved. That's how change happens. The good guys need to do their part by speaking out."

"I agree that some improvements could be made through legislation, but that's not enough," Jake mused. "The best legal system in the world can only be as good as the people in it. Somehow we need individual lawyers to take their ethical responsibilities seriously. But how do we accomplish that? Look at someone like Rick Black. He's as smart as they come. He has the skills to be the most effective trial lawyer I've ever met. He went to one of the best law schools in the country, where they truly did emphasize the importance of ethics, yet he feels absolutely no compunction to live by any value system other than his own, and that doesn't include a commitment to ethics. As long as people like that are able to flourish within our system, we will have problems."

"You're absolutely right. That's why people like that must not be allowed to flourish. When they skirt the rules, they should be reported and held accountable. That's what happened recently with unscrupulous corporate leaders and it can happen with attorneys. The profession needs to deal with ethical infractions publicly and forcefully. And each lawyer must do his part. When an attorney faces an ethical dilemma or witnesses inappropriate conduct on the part of a fellow attorney, he needs to have the courage to stand up and do the right thing. The bad guys won't be stopped unless the good guys make it their personal responsibility to stop them."

They stood and continued their stroll in silence for several minutes. Jake put his arm around Amanda's shoulder and said, "Thanks. I'll try not to lose hope."

She smiled at him. "There's always hope, as long as there are people like you in the profession."

They arrived at Navy Pier, which was crowded with tourists. They walked silently through the crowd toward the end of the pier, holding hands again. As they gazed out over the steely gray waters, Amanda asked the question that had been nagging Jake all week. "Is there any way the jury could've been right? Is it possible that Mickey actually did those things?"

Jake shook his head slowly. "I've asked myself that question a hundred times. I've looked Mickey in the eye as we've talked about the allegations. I don't believe Larry for a minute. His motives are obvious. And the other witnesses who showed up at the last minute— they were like vultures circling a wounded animal. Helen Wright has an obvious motive. She was cut out of her aunt's will and, lucky for her, this trial happened along and gave her the opportunity to publicly challenge the new will. After what he's been through, Mickey won't fight it, so she'll probably be able to get that will thrown out and the previous will reinstated without a challenge. But Kenny Oliver? I just can't figure him out. What motive would he have to say what he did? He worked for Mickey for a long time. He had nothing to gain by supporting Larry. That's the one part of this entire case that confounds me."

"Could they have bought his testimony?"

"Bribed him? I've wondered about that, but I can't imagine even Rick would be that brazen. He wanted to win this case badly, but I can't believe that he would risk his law license over it. But something's not right about it. I just can't figure it out."

PART THREE

CHAPTER 30

ickey filed his appeal, but within six months he had sold his business and put an end to the litigation. Vern had advised him that the value of the business was dropping precipitously as volume continued to decline, and that by selling at that juncture, Mickey might be able to satisfy the judgment and still have at least something of a financial cushion. If he stayed the course, he would likely lose the appeal, and the value of the business a year or two down the road might not be enough to satisfy the judgment. Bankruptcy loomed as a very real possibility, and the stigma and personal shame that held for him, on the heels of what he had already endured, was more than Mickey could bear.

Aside from the damage to his pride and reputation, not to mention his finances, Mickey's health was declining. He had lost weight. He'd been experiencing anxiety attacks and chronic headaches. His physical and mental well-being demanded a change of scenery, so he decided to take up residence in Naples, Florida, where he had purchased a small condominium several years earlier. He would try to leave this nightmare behind and clear his mind and heart of the bitterness that was consuming him. He was convinced that a fresh start in a new environment was his only chance of living out his remaining years in anything resembling peace.

Mickey was gone even before the sale of Quinn's Fine Foods was consummated. He wasn't there to witness the termination of the butchers or the entire staff that supported the delivery business. He wasn't there to receive the angry phone calls from the elderly shut-ins, complaining that they now had no means of obtaining the basic necessities of life. And he wasn't there fourteen months later, when Quinn's was closed for good, then bulldozed and replaced by new townhomes.

For Jake McShane, these events were also a source of bitterness and resentment—against the jury, for being gullible; against the *Review*, for being vicious and irresponsible; and against the system that made this tragedy possible. Mostly however, his resentment was directed toward the individuals who were directly responsible, primarily Larry Doyle, who was shamelessly flaunting his newfound wealth, and Rick Black, whose misguided talents had made this implausible and unconscionable outcome a reality. Jake also was unable to shake the suspicion that Kenny Oliver played some part in this dirty conspiracy, and that suspicion was heightened when he heard reports that Kenny had recently purchased a new Mercedes even though he was employed only sporadically in various unskilled jobs.

Unlike Mickey, Jake had an effective antidote for the anger and hard feelings over the lawsuit—a happy and rewarding home life with his wife and daughter, as well as a promising career. The joys, challenges and accomplishments of his own life soon enabled him to relegate the entire Quinn affair into a tightly sealed compartment deep within the recesses of his memory, from where it would rarely surface.

After six years with Samuelson & Reid, Jake was considered one of the firm's rising stars. His work ethic, self-discipline and penchant for exhaustive preparation served him well in the legal profession. More than those attributes, however, it was his people skills that impressed the firm's senior partners. He came across as confident, without being brash. He was personable, in a low-key way, and unfailingly polite and professional, even in situations that were rife with conflict and tension. To the outside world, he was calm and even tempered at all times, the inner intensity well hidden. He related well to everyone— bosses, peers, judges, juries, and most importantly from the firm's perspective, clients. His time was in high demand, and he was considered a lock for partnership in three or four years.

Amanda's professional life was equally promising, and even more demanding in terms of working hours. Following completion of her fellowship at Northwestern, she had joined a fledgling medical practice on Chicago's Near North Side. She had also accepted a position as a part-time professor at the medical school, which enabled her to keep one foot in the academic world while still spending the bulk of her time building her practice and seeing patients.

Amanda approached her medical practice like she had everything else in her life—with drive, passion, organization and efficiency. Not only was she a highly skilled physician with a wonderful bedside manner, she had a knack for building strong relationships with the right people in the medical community. Her positive and energetic personality, coupled with the confidence, intellect and talent that she naturally and effortlessly projected, quickly impressed the medical practitioners, administrators and academics whose influence mattered when one was trying to establish a reputation and a practice. As a result, her practice flourished and soon came to be regarded as the premier geriatric practice in the city. Within a few short years, she had been named in the local newspaper as one of forty women under forty who were making a difference in their respective fields in the Chicago area.

Despite their demanding schedules, both Jake and Amanda made family time a priority. Although late meetings and conference calls were sometimes unavoidable, Jake continued his efforts to keep evening hours sacred. The highlight of his day was walking into his home after work and watching his five-year-old daughter streak across the living room exuberantly yelling "Daddy!" and throwing herself into his arms. Unfortunately for Amanda, medical emergencies did not limit themselves to standard working hours, and she often found herself pulled away from her family when duty called at inconvenient hours. She felt conflicted and guilty on those occasions, but she knew it was unavoidable in her profession. Jake was understanding and supportive, and Anna adored him, so they were fine together whenever she was called away.

Juggling everything was stressful, but on balance, they made it work. Life was full, but fulfilling. Most evenings, they were able to eat dinner as a family at a reasonable hour. In the spring and summer, they would take an evening walk or bike ride through the neighborhood. They had moved from their downtown condominium to Jake's old neighborhood on the South Side, in search of more family-oriented surroundings, where Anna would have no shortage of playmates her own age. The neighborhood was full of parents and children taking evening strolls, or playing or visiting in front yards, so the McShane family found their evening walks to be a great way of casually socializing with friends and neighbors, as well as an opportunity for fresh air and exercise. Weekends revolved around soccer games, birthday parties, and the myriad of other activities that filled the social calendar of a five-year-old girl.

Anna and Jake continued their bedtime reading ritual, and it had become a special time for both of them that they sorely missed on occasions when Jake was traveling or working late. Although she was only in kindergarten, Anna had begun reading already and it was a great source of pride for both of them when she read to her father rather than the other way around. After reading time, Jake and Amanda would tuck Anna in, and then have a precious hour or so to themselves. They called it their "couch time," as they would sit on the sofa in the family room and catch up.

Before turning in for the evening, Jake would quietly sneak into Anna's room to kiss her goodnight as she lay sleeping. He would often look at her quietly for a few moments, caressing her hair or cheek, and offer a silent prayer of thanks for the precious little girl that had become such a major part of his life. Later in the evening, he would frequently lie in his bed staring at Amanda after she had drifted off to sleep, thinking the same thing. He was luckier than he had ever dreamed of being. He found it hard to imagine that life could be any better.

CHAPTER 31

R ick closed the door of his office after having escorted his new client to the elevator. "Yes!" he shouted, raising both arms into the air triumphantly.

He picked up the signed retainer agreement that was lying on his desk. The ink was barely dry. He delighted in performing the simple mathematical calculation in his head. The first part of the equation was typical: thirty-three percent of any favorable settlement; forty percent of the award if the case went to trial. It was the next part of the equation that thrilled him. Forty percent of what? One hundred million perhaps? Maybe even several times that. This was the case he'd been waiting for his entire career. He was in the big time now, and the whole world would be watching as he worked his magic.

In the two years since the Quinn trial, Rick's career had been skyrocketing. Soon after that trial, he had scored several other good-sized verdicts in personal injury and medical malpractice lawsuits. His successes fed on themselves. Each favorable trial outcome generated publicity—he made sure of that. The publicity brought in more cases. As his courtroom successes mounted, defendants became loath to litigate against him. That produced nice settlements—easy money.

Last year produced his biggest verdict yet. He sued a major fast food company after one of its employees sexually assaulted a teenaged customer in a restroom. It turned out that the perpetrator had been hired despite having had a prior history of sexual assault. Unfortunately for the company and the victim, the company had failed to check references or do any sort of criminal background check.

The employer had been eager to settle, but Rick persuaded his client to take the case to trial, so that the sins of the company could be put on display for the entire world to see. Besides that, he believed he could work the jury into a righteous rage, setting the stage for a large punitive damages award. That was precisely how it played out. The jury rendered an award of eight million dollars. Rick enjoyed his forty percent take, but he relished the publicity even more.

After that, a number of prominent plaintiff firms began sending feelers his way. Recruiting this talented young trial lawyer would be a major coup for any plaintiffs' firm. For the most part, Rick had no interest. He was doing quite well on his own. There was only one firm that was attractive enough to lure him away from his own increasingly lucrative and successful practice.

Sullivan & Leach had established itself as one of the premier class action law firms in the nation. Class action litigation was a burgeoning business for plaintiffs' lawyers, and that's where the real money was. By representing thousands of plaintiffs in a single lawsuit, the potential award could be enormous. Even though the amount that actually worked its way into the hands of the injured parties was often paltry, the legal fees were based on a percentage of the entirety, which frequently was a staggering figure. Because of the lucrative rewards for successful class-action attorneys, hundreds of plaintiffs' firms wanted in on the game. Only a small handful had the resources and know-how to truly master it, and Sullivan & Leach was among the very best.

Rick had met Jack Leach, the firm's founder, at a luncheon seminar relating to the new federal laws designed to limit class action litigation. Leach had actually sought him out. A week later, after a round of golf, the deal was sealed. Rick was in, as the twenty-second attorney with Sullivan & Leach.

That was just six months ago, and since then, Rick had unquestionably pulled his weight. He had strong-armed the city into a sizable settlement after one of its buses ran a red light, broadsiding another vehicle and making the driver a paraplegic. He also brought in several promising medical malpractice cases and a handful of employment cases involving wrongful termination and workplace discrimination that were still pending.

Despite those successes, he had been waiting for the big case—the kind that had class-action potential and would draw national attention; the kind that would enable him to combine his own considerable skills with the vast resources now at his disposal at Sullivan & Leach; the kind that would catapult him to instant notoriety, and make him really, really rich. An hour ago, that case had just walked through his door.

"Jake, come look at this," Amanda called from the living room, as Jake quietly closed Anna's bedroom door after putting her to bed. Amanda was watching the ten o'clock news on TV. There was Rick Black, talking to a roomful of reporters at what appeared to be a planned press conference.

"We believe that US Health has engaged in widespread and systematic fraud in its billing practices," Rick said to the reporters. "Overcharging, billing for services that weren't provided, furnishing unnecessary services at exorbitant rates—it's been occurring on a massive scale. The amount of money involved is staggering. We may be talking about hundreds of millions of dollars. We intend to put a stop to these egregious practices and ensure that patients who have been unknowingly victimized are made whole." Rick spoke forcefully and passionately. He seemed credible and convincing. He went on to explain that his firm would be asking the federal court in Chicago to certify this lawsuit as a nationwide class action, so that his firm could seek redress for victims all across the country.

"What do you make of that?" Amanda asked.

Jake flipped the channel, and caught the same footage on two other stations. "US Health is a major client of ours," he said. "It's a gigantic company. They have hospitals, surgical centers, and outpatient clinics in more than thirty states. They bring in over ten billion dollars in revenue and serve nearly 900,000 patients each year. This could be a huge case."

As a medical professional, Amanda was generally familiar with US Health. The company had created significant waves in the medical industry as it underwent explosive growth through its voracious acquisition of hospitals and other medical businesses over the past decade. "I thought Rick was a solo practitioner," said Amanda. "The caption on the TV screen referred to him as a partner with some law firm."

"Sullivan & Leach. I didn't realize Rick had joined them. It's a real powerhouse plaintiffs' firm," Jake explained. "They've developed a reputation as one of the premier class action firms around. They really have that kind of litigation down to a science."

"Do you think the case has any merit?"

"Who knows?" Jake mused. "I hope not. I know some of their senior management team fairly well and they seem like well-meaning, ethical people. I wonder if we'll be representing them."

Jake's question was answered promptly the following morning. He was summoned into the office of Demetrius Giannakis, the firm's managing partner, and the person who was primarily responsible for the firm's relationship with USH. Upon entering Demetrius's plush office, Jake recognized Paul LaDuke, USH's General Counsel, whom he knew well, and Dr. Bernard Parkerson, the company's president, whom he had met only once. After shaking hands, Jake sat down.

"Did you see the news, Jake?" Demetrius asked.

"Yes, I saw it on television last night and in this morning's paper."

"We've been asked to represent USH. At Paul's specific request, you and I will lead the team. As of this moment, we have no higher priority than this."

Jake felt the kind of nervous excitement he used to feel before stepping onto a basketball court before a big game. He also knew that when Demetrius said that he and Jake would be leading this effort, that meant it would be mostly Jake. Demetrius was a big picture guy, used to dealing with relationships and politics rather than actually trying cases. That said, he had a keen intellect and a wealth of experience, so his involvement would undoubtedly be helpful.

"I understand you went to law school at Stanford," Dr. Parkerson said brusquely. He was stocky, of medium height, with the bearing of a military man. Jake had heard that he was a West Point graduate, who placed great emphasis on academic pedigree, and surmised that Paul or Demetrius must have provided Jake's background.

"Yes sir," Jake replied.

"I did some research on the plaintiffs' attorney last night," said Parkerson. "He went to Stanford, too. Do you know this guy?"

"Yes, I know him pretty well. We spent a fair amount of time together during law school."

"Is he a friend of yours?"

Jake thought about the Quinn trial. "No. We're not friends. We played basketball together in school. I haven't kept in touch with him since we graduated."

"So what are we up against?" Parkerson demanded.

Jake thought carefully. "A very tough, capable adversary. He's smart and resourceful. He's aggressive. We should expect some serious hardball tactics. And he's great in front of a jury. All in all, I'd have to say that he may be the most naturally gifted trial lawyer I've ever laid eyes on."

"Shit! What a goddamned mess," sputtered Dr. Parkerson. "Gentlemen, we need our best, too. Whatever it takes. You will have full and unfettered access to our people, our facilities, our records, whatever you need. We need to make this go away as quickly as we can, with as little pain as possible. I'm counting on you to make that happen."

CHAPTER 32

R andy Kraft closed his office door and read every word of the article in the morning *Tribune*. Then he read it again. He felt a sense of power, knowing that he'd put the wheels in motion to bring this disaster down upon his employer. The company deserved this. It was sweet and satisfying.

He had been a loyal soldier for USH for over twelve years, and manager of the Accounts Receivable Department for five. He routinely worked twelve-hour days, and was happy to do it. When USH acquired a new business, as it had done countless times in recent years, he was the one who ensured that the Accounts Receivable systems of the acquired company were properly integrated into USH's system. Based on all of those conversions, he knew the company's billing systems better than anyone. Billing was the lifeblood of the company, after all. He was the guy that kept the bills going out, which in turn kept the money flowing in.

When the Assistant Controller position opened up, Randy believed he was a shoo-in. His tenure with the company was far longer than any other candidate. He was intimately familiar with the various accounting functions within the organization and the hardware and software systems that supported those functions. He knew the people, too. And yet the job went to Alberto Garza, a gladhander who had been with the company barely two years. They told Randy that technical proficiency wasn't enough, and that the position required someone with better leadership skills. It just wasn't right, Randy told himself. He had earned that position. He felt cheated and betrayed. The company would pay for this insult, one way or another.

Randy first encountered Rick Black when Black had brought a malpractice lawsuit against USH a little over a year ago. Randy had been subpoenaed to appear for a deposition to explain a series of medical bills. Mr. Black had made an impression on him. That guy was a shark, if there ever was one, and he proved it by muscling USH into a two-million-dollar settlement.

Rick had been more than happy to meet with Randy after Randy called him and briefly explained his situation. According to Rick, the fact that Randy had been passed over for promotion did not give him much of a legal claim. He was a thirty-six-year-old white male, and therefore had no ammunition for any discrimination allegations. But, Rick pointed out, there were other possibilities, if he was patient and played his cards right.

Rick explained that if Randy sent a written communication to senior management complaining about wrongdoing within the company, then the company was prohibited by law from retaliating against him. That was a great way to obtain job security. More importantly, from Randy's perspective, from that point forward, any adverse action against him by the company could be considered unlawful retaliation. If that happened, he would have a claim with some real teeth. So he just had to identify some improper activity on the part of the company and call it to management's attention.

That was easy. Randy knew that the company's billing system was a mess. Countless customers received invoices containing mistakes, some of them pretty egregious. This was due to the fact that the company was continually acquiring new businesses, each having different billing and accounting systems. As a result, numerous billing systems were in use at any given time and there was an ongoing effort to merge the acquired companies' systems into the standard USH platform. There were inevitably bugs that had to be worked out whenever they handled a system conversion, and until that happened, errors were commonplace. Randy had already raised this issue several times, but the company had not provided the staffing and financial resources necessary to adequately address these issues.

The lawyer's interest had really picked up when he heard that. Rick suggested that Randy send an e-mail to his bosses, alerting them to these serious billing problems, and even drafted it for him. Randy had asked Rick if he could sue USH based on these billing irregularities. Because Randy had never been a patient of USH, Rick explained that Randy himself had no standing to bring a lawsuit alleging fraudulent billing practices. However, there definitely was a basis for bringing a class action lawsuit against the company on behalf of many of its patients, and Randy could help him do that. It was clearly justified, Rick pointed out, in light of all the patients that were being overcharged. And, once the company realized that Randy's knowledge would make him a dangerous witness, they might not want to keep him in his present role. Then he'd have them. If they fired him, or transferred him to another position, he'd have a strong whistleblower's claim. If they were afraid to fire him, they might try to entice him to leave voluntarily— with a generous severance package. It was beautiful! He could position himself for a nice payoff, but even if that didn't happen, he could see the company punished. And they deserved it.

The first step had been sending the memo that Rick had written for him. He had done that, and now enjoyed the protected status of a whistleblower. The next step had been to find clients for the lawsuit. Rick explained that he had no way of knowing which patients had been overcharged, and that even if he had that information, the ethical rules of the legal profession would not allow him to directly contact those patients to solicit their business. That was where Randy could help. Having access to all of the company's billings, he was in a perfect position to identify erroneous invoices. He could find a way to make sure that some of those patients wound up in Rick's office.

Now everything was coming together. Randy put the newspaper back in his briefcase. He would take it home and keep it, like a trophy—a testament to his power and accomplishment.

CHAPTER 33

It was Friday afternoon, four days after he had filed the USH lawsuit and held his press conference. Rick sat in his office, pleased with how well the week had gone. Due to the firm's extensive network of media contacts, the lawsuit had received considerable attention all week long in every major market in the country—television, radio and newspaper. His firm had also run full-page newspaper advertisements in every market where USH did business, alerting USH patients to the possibility that they may have been overcharged, and the fact that Sullivan & Leach was prepared to represent them if they had. There would be no charge to those patients except for a percentage of any recovery. All they had to do was contact the firm to sign a representation letter. The ads provided a toll-free phone number to call for further information as well as the Internet address for the website the firm had established to provide information about the lawsuit.

The calls were pouring in, and the firm was well-prepared to handle them. It had mobilized the call center it had used many times before in similar situations. The phones were manned around-the-clock—six operators on staff from 8 a.m. until midnight, and two handling the night shift. The operators answered routine questions about the lawsuit and obtained permission to send representation letters to the callers. They contacted people who had requested information through the website, again with the ultimate goal being to obtain more representation letters.

A small army of clerical support worked closely with the phone operators to send out the representation letters. They kept meticulous records, which enabled them to follow up with contacts who did not return the letters promptly. They also generated detailed reports showing how many calls had come in, which USH business was involved, how many representation letters had gone out, and how many had been returned.

The early reports were even more encouraging than Rick had dared to hope for. Over one thousand representation letters had been mailed, and it had been only four days since the lawsuit was filed. Most people took some time to react to something like this. It would take awhile for them to dig up their medical bills and try to decipher them. Those people would eventually call. The firm's advertising blitz would continue and news would spread by word-of-mouth. Thousands more would sign up, making it a cinch that the court would certify this case as a class action. When that happened, Sullivan & Leach would be representing every patient who was overbilled by USH, whether they had responded or not, unless they affirmatively elected to opt out of the class, which almost no one ever did.

Rick had barely slept all week. He'd given countless interviews to reporters from all over the country. When he wasn't speaking to the media, he was returning phone calls to potential clients who had questions that the call center was unable to answer. He should have been exhausted, but he wasn't. He was elated. He felt like celebrating, and since the long week was about over, that's what he intended to do. But first, there was one more task to accomplish; one more set of wheels to put into motion. He asked his secretary to send in Mr. Fowler, the visitor who had been waiting patiently in the reception area.

"Fowler!" Rick strode across the office, smiling brightly and extending his hand. "We're in business, pal. This is going to be a big one!"

Fowler shook his hand, but did not return the smile. Rick took no offense, because he'd never seen the man smile. He was all business.

Rick had worked with Fowler several times in the past, when he needed an investigator who was highly skilled, resourceful, and not afraid to bend a few rules to get what he wanted. In fact, Rick was pretty sure Fowler didn't consider himself bound by any rules. His past was a mystery, but Rick knew better than to pry. Fowler would not have been forthcoming, and Rick was better off not knowing certain things. He suspected that Fowler had once worked for the government, in some sort of covert operations capacity, but now he was strictly freelance. He worked alone, and he worked for cash. He was expensive, but he was worth it. He got results. Just as importantly, he was discreet. Rick was confident that Fowler would keep confidences, no matter what, and that neither danger, legal threats nor torture would unseal his lips. That was just part of his makeup.

Fowler got right to the point, as he always did. He spoke little, and when he did, he was economical in his use of the spoken word. "What's the mission?" he asked.

"For starters, I need to know who I'm up against. I like to know my enemies." Rick handed Fowler a copy of USH's most recent annual report. Inside the front cover was a photograph of the company's officers. "I want to know everything there is to know about these guys. Have they been involved in any prior business scandals? Did they do drugs in college? Any extramarital affairs? I want to know anything and everything that might be harmful or embarrassing to these guys. If they ever got a parking ticket, I want to know about it."

"No problem. What else?"

"Their lawyers—these guys." He handed Fowler a picture and a short biography of Jake McShane and Demetrius Giannakis, along with a printout of the Samuelson & Reid website. "Same thing. I want any dirt you can find on them or their firm. Find out who they've represented. If we can't find dirt on the lawyers, there's a decent chance that they've represented some bad apples in the past, and that kind of information may be useful. Dig into the courthouse records, particularly the criminal records, and see if you can find any connection between these guys and some scoundrels."

Rick knew that hacking into computer systems and navigating complex databases was one of Fowler's specialties. He didn't look like a computer geek. To the contrary, he looked more like a biker. He wore a black leather jacket, black jeans and black cowboy boots. Although he appeared to be in his mid-forties, his perfectly coifed hair was snow white, in stark contrast to a very ruddy complexion. He was fit and muscular. Just plain scary looking, Rick had often thought, but a master of gathering information.

"Anything else?" Fowler asked.

"Yes, after you dig up whatever information you can find, I want you to follow this guy closely." Rick pointed to Jake's picture. "I want to know where he goes, and who he talks to. He's careless. We may get some clues as to their strategy."

"What makes you think he's careless?"

"I know this guy. We went to law school together. He's always been sort of naïve, too trusting. When we were first-year law students, he had his entire semester's worth of work wrapped up in his study outlines. He was at the library studying and left them just lying there on the desk while he went out for a snack." Rick paused.

"And?"

"And I taught him a valuable lesson." Rick laughed heartily, relishing the memory. "He panicked so badly I thought he might just give up and drop out of school. Anyway, my point is that any normal person would be guarded enough to keep track of something that important. Intellectually, this guy is smart. But he's careless. If we watch him closely, it may pay off somehow."

"Anything else?"

"Yeah, one more thing. Can you get into USH's e-mail system?"

CHAPTER 34

T hree weeks had gone by since the USH lawsuit was filed. Jake had virtually taken up residence at USH's corporate headquarters since that time, reviewing mountains of documents and interviewing countless employees, trying to develop an understanding of the past history and present state of USH's billing practices. He was waiting outside of Demetrius Giannakis's office, while Demetrius was finishing up a meeting with the governor. It was an election year, and the governor was making his rounds with the city's power brokers, enlisting their support. Demetrius Giannakis was on everyone's list as one of the most powerful and influential members of the Chicago legal community.

To Jake's surprise, Demetrius called him into his office while the governor was still there, and made introductions. Both men were all smiles and polished charm as they said their farewells. Immediately after the governor had departed, Demetrius's smiling countenance abruptly became dark and impatient. Jake had requested this meeting to apprise Demetrius of his preliminary findings and had warned Demetrius that they were troubling.

"So, what've we got?" Demetrius asked curtly.

"Well sir, I'm afraid it's a bit of a mess. They—"

"Don't editorialize. Just give me the facts," Demetrius demanded.

Jake composed himself. He had rarely worked with Demetrius before being assigned to this case, and he was beginning to understand why the firm's associates were intimidated by him. Although he oozed charm when dealing with clients and politicians, the tall Greek with the hawk-like features was known to be a brusque and impatient bully with the firm's younger attorneys.

"Here's what we're dealing with," Jake began, coolly and firmly. "As you know, USH has been growing at a tremendous pace over the past ten years. They've gone from owning seventy-five facilities in five states to over six hundred facilities in thirty-four states. Their focus has been on growth through acquisition, and they've had great success on that front. Their revenues have skyrocketed, as has their stock price, because of the phenomenal success of their acquisition program. They've devoted their best people, their resources and their attention to that aspect of the business, and some of the back-office functions have not received the attention they need."

Demetrius threw up his hands. "Look, I don't need a dissertation on the history of USH. I'm well aware of it. Tell me about their billing practices."

"I was getting to that. Two years ago, the company installed a new software system to handle customer billings. Unfortunately, it was implemented before they had ironed all the bugs out. On top of that, there has been an ongoing effort to convert the billing systems of the newly acquired businesses into the USH system. That involves a great deal of complex programming, as well as a huge amount of data entry. A lot of errors were made in the process."

"What kind of errors? And how many?"

"First, there are mistakes caused by simple human error in the data entry. The task of inputting this massive amount of information into the new system is enormous. They don't have adequate staffing to do this quickly and with good quality controls. They have a number of temporary employees assigned to the project, but they're working very long hours and their competency is marginal to begin with. Here's an example of what can happen." Jake handed Demetrius an invoice. "This is a bill relating to a knee surgery. It was a fairly routine procedure to repair a torn ACL, which took less than two hours. The invoice shows that the patient was charged for twenty-two bags of IV fluid. That's an obvious error—someone simply hit the keystroke twice. The quantity should have been two, not twenty-two."

"Okay, so there's some quality control issues and human errors involving data entry. What else?"

"There are other problems resulting from the programming and the attempt to merge different billing systems. These are more widespread and more concerning. For example, when a certain procedure is performed at hospital "A", there may be a standard group of services and supplies that are provided. However, that bundle of goods and services may be different at hospital "B." They're not identical in every hospital. USH is trying to standardize that throughout their network, but they're not there yet. As a result, when the bill is generated using the USH system, it assumes a group of services and supplies that may be different than what the customer actually received, particularly if the facility in question is new to the USH network. The customer may wind up paying for items he didn't receive. Similarly, the billing systems of the various hospitals use codes that are not identical from one facility to the next. The USH system may translate a code from the newly acquired facility inaccurately, and again, a customer could be charged for something he didn't receive."

"I assume that sometimes the customer is better off, and is charged less than he should be?"

"No question about it, although I'm not sure we'll get much credit for that. USH's prices are generally a good deal higher than the businesses it acquires. What frequently happens is that a patient received certain services at a facility before it was acquired by USH. The billing is not generated until after the acquisition, and the billing reflects USH's pricing structure, which is not what was in effect at the time and place the patient was treated."

Demetrius was getting visibly more agitated. "What a goddamned mess! What about the specific examples cited in the complaint. Are the facts accurate?"

"I'm afraid so, every one of them. As you may recall, one complaint involves a patient who was double-charged for various items in her hospital room—tissues, latex gloves, petroleum jelly. Those items are supposed to be included in the price of the room, but due to a programming error, she was charged for each of them separately, in addition to paying for them as part of the room charge. The complaint also included an allegation that a patient was charged an exorbitant rate for an antibiotic that she allegedly did not receive and wouldn't have used because she is allergic to it. That allegation appears to be true as well. Her medical charts clearly indicate she is allergic to that drug, and that the doctor canceled the order for it. Then there's the allegation involving the Turner baby."

"Which is?"

"That the family was charged $300 for a circumcision allegedly performed before the baby left the hospital."

"Is there something unusual about that?"

"Yes—the baby was a girl."

"Son of a bitch," Demetrius muttered in disgust as he dialed Paul LaDuke, USH's general counsel. "Find him, and have him call me immediately," he demanded, after being informed that Mr. LaDuke was traveling.

"How many individual patients have actually been harmed?" Demetrius asked. "With health insurance as prevalent as it is, I would think that it's mostly insurance companies that get stuck footing the bill when there's an overpayment."

"There's no question that many insurance companies have been overcharged," Jake replied, "but there are far more individual patients who were victimized, either because they had no medical insurance or because they had to pay deductibles or co-payments, even when they did have insurance. Sullivan & Leach will be representing most of the insurance companies too, but that will be a separate lawsuit. They'll push the lawsuit for the individual plaintiffs first, because a jury is much more likely to react emotionally and award large punitive damages when the plaintiffs are a bunch of little people with compelling individual stories. Then, if the verdict goes their way in that case, it gives them a lot more leverage in their case involving the insurance companies."

Within minutes, Paul LaDuke called and proceeded to receive a serious tongue lashing from Demetrius. Jake had never heard one of the firm's lawyers speak this way to a client before. Demetrius was ranting. Two reasons occurred to Jake. First, Demetrius didn't like the idea of his firm being on the losing end of a high-profile case, and this one was shaping up to be a loser. Second, he was setting his client's expectations and protecting the firm from possible criticism. He was making it abundantly clear that USH had gotten itself into a royal mess and that the best legal counsel on earth could not protect them from a costly adverse judgment.

"Are you aware that you've got serious problems with your billing systems, Paul?" Demetrius had raised his voice, almost to the point of yelling.

"We're not perfect, I realize that," LaDuke replied, sounding defensive.

"You're far from perfect. What have you been doing about it?"

"We're taking a serious look at this, I can assure you, and we have been for some time. We established a task force over a year ago, and they've made various recommendations. Basically, the recommendations involve a full-scale audit, using an independent auditing firm, and then, once we identify mistakes, we would proactively follow up with the affected patients, providing a refund or billing adjustment to anyone that's been overcharged. Does that sound like a sensible approach?"

"It makes perfect sense, only you should've done this a long time ago."

"Won't it help our legal position that we've been looking into these issues and have been developing plans to address them? We've been trying to do the right thing. I'm completely confident that you won't find the slightest evidence of any intentional wrongdoing."

Demetrius gave Jake a look, indicating that he wanted to hear Jake's thoughts on that point. Jake chose his words carefully. "From what I've learned, I agree, Paul. I have seen absolutely no evidence that anyone working for USH did anything remotely fraudulent or inappropriate. And the fact that you've taken measures to address this is good. That will be a major part of our defense. What hurts us is the fact that we haven't actually implemented the plan and started issuing refunds. The plaintiffs will try to use that against us. They'll argue that this demonstrates that USH had knowledge of this problem for a long time, and did nothing."

Demetrius jumped in again. "Paul, listen to me. Fix your goddamned system—now! Whatever resources it takes, get it done. Get that auditing firm in there immediately. We need to identify any and all errors ASAP and start issuing refunds—immediately!"

"I understand, Demetrius. We'll get right on it."

"Good. Just one more thing, Paul. This plaintiffs' lawyer has a source, someone who knows your organization. That's obvious. There's no way that six people with billing errors involving USH facilities just happened to call this guy out of the blue at the same time. I don't believe in coincidences like that. That son of a bitch solicited them somehow, and he ought to be disbarred, but we'll never prove that. But the fact is, someone has to be feeding him information. He's got an ideal batch of clients with very compelling stories. I want you to think about that. Who would be in a position to serve up those cases? Find out if there are any disgruntled employees or former employees who have access to that kind of information."

The door to Demetrius's office opened and Jake's secretary timidly stuck her head inside. Demetrius shot her a look of irritation, as he continued talking into the speakerphone. It was clearly inappropriate to interrupt a meeting with Demetrius Giannakis and Kimberly ought to know that, Jake thought. She beckoned to him urgently. "Judge Trainor's clerk just called," Kimberly whispered. "There's been some development with the case. He wants to discuss it with counsel for both sides immediately. She wouldn't say what it was about, except that it was urgent."

Judge Trainor, who'd been assigned to the USH case, was known to be a very slow, deliberate judge. Neither Jake nor Demetrius had known him to order an unscheduled hearing on short notice.

"This can't be good," muttered Demetrius.

CHAPTER 35

Nearly five years had gone by since his incarceration began. To Jerome, it seemed like a lifetime, but the day was finally here. He had survived, and now he was free. It had been a bleak and depressing existence, but he had managed to avoid the many forms of abuse that were common inside the prison walls. He had established his reputation early on as one very dangerous character. An intense dedication to weightlifting had added bulk and definition to his already massive frame, so the other inmates gave him plenty of room.

There had been ample time on the inside to contemplate his future, yet he had difficulty envisioning where he would be and what he would be doing after his release. One thing was certain: He would never go back to his old way of life, where he was always broke and had no hope of any income except what he could steal or what he could scrounge up selling small quantities of drugs. That was a dismal existence with no future, and it was not for him. He had a way to start down a different path now. He didn't know where it would lead, but it would be a definite improvement over what he had known.

Shooter would be there to pick him up and take him back to the apartment at the church, where Jerome could live with him until he got on his feet. The athletic program that Shooter had been developing for Reverend Lonnie was thriving, and Shooter had advised Jerome that the Reverend had given him permission to hire Jerome as a part-time assistant. It wouldn't be much money, Shooter had said, but would be gainful and legitimate employment, which could be a stepping stone to something else.

Another opportunity had been pitched to him as well. Snake said that the road had been paved for Jerome to join the Street Sultans. For a guy with Jerome's ability, he could easily prove himself and become a full-fledged enforcer in no time. That would mean good money, drugs, women, and above all else—respect.

It was an easy choice.

CHAPTER 36

J ake entered Judge Trainor's courtroom with a sense of trepidation. Rick was there, and it was the first time they had seen each
other since the Quinn trial two years earlier.

"Looks like you drew the short straw on this one, Jake. Even the
world-class lawyers at Samuelson & Reid can't do much with facts
like these. All you can do is hope for a merciful jury."

"They've made some mistakes, Rick. There's no denying that. But
these aren't bad guys, and it's not a bad company. I haven't seen the
slightest evidence of any intentional wrongdoing."

"You will, my friend. Just wait until we really get into discovery.
Actually, you may not have to wait that long. I think Judge Trainor's
about to give you a pretty good indication of what you're dealing with."

Before Jake could inquire further, the judge entered the courtroom,
followed by his court reporter. Jake had dealt with Judge Trainor
numerous times in the past. He was one of the more seasoned federal
judges in the city, and was known to be strong-willed and forceful. He
took his responsibilities seriously, and expected the attorneys practicing in
his courtroom to do the same. Aside from Jake and Rick, there was only
one other person in the courtroom. Probably a reporter, Jake surmised.

"Gentlemen, thank you for being here on such short notice," said the
judge. The stern tone in his voice matched the uncharacteristically grave

look on his face. "Information came to my attention this morning that is extremely disturbing, and requires immediate action. Mr. McShane?"

Jake had no idea where this was heading, but his stomach was quickly in a knot. "Yes, Your Honor?"

"Can you explain this e-mail to me? It was sent yesterday by USH's General Counsel." The judge handed Jake a short e-mail that appeared to have been sent by Paul LaDuke at 4:33 p.m. the previous afternoon. It was addressed to "All Department Heads." It was succinct and to the point: *"As you know, USH maintains a records management policy that establishes a retention period for each category of document created by our company. After a document reaches its life expectancy, it is to be destroyed. This helps to ensure that we can efficiently manage our records and avoid paying storage costs for outdated records that are no longer needed. We have not been very diligent in adhering to this longstanding policy. On the advice of outside counsel, Samuelson & Reid, I am requesting that you immediately examine all documents within your department to confirm compliance with this important policy. Any documents whose established life has been exceeded should be destroyed immediately. Thank you in advance for your prompt compliance with this directive. Paul."*

Jake's knees weakened as he read the e-mail, and then read it again.

"Would you care to explain that communication, Mr. McShane?" The judge's demeanor was intense, and his voice, ominous.

Jake was at a loss. "I can't explain it, Your Honor. I haven't seen this before and I don't know anything about it. I can assure you, I will investigate immediately." This was a disaster and Jake knew it. It looked like a thinly disguised attempt to destroy evidence.

"I'm sure I don't need to explain to you that this is a very serious matter, Mr. McShane. Spoliation of evidence will not be tolerated. Within forty-eight hours, I expect a complete accounting of any documents that have been destroyed. Then I will decide what to do about this. If I learn that any documents are destroyed by USH from this moment forward, I will direct a finding of liability on all counts. I may do that anyway. In that case, the only question for the jury will be to determine how much to award in punitive damages. And, if I learn that any attorney encouraged or participated in the destruction of evidence, there will be severe sanctions. Do I make myself clear, Mr. McShane?"

"Yes, Your Honor."

"I will see both parties back here in forty-eight hours."

Jake left the courtroom feeling chastened and panicked. What had Paul been thinking? This looked like the act of a guilty company trying to cover its tracks. And why would Paul have stated that Samuelson & Reid had given such instructions? That was absurd. Unthinkable. Nothing upset a judge or jury more than a deliberate attempt by a highly placed corporate official to order a cover-up or destruction of evidence. If that happened, the best case would be that the judge would allow the jury to draw the inferences most favorable to the plaintiffs' case. The worst case—which seemed more likely— would be the result threatened by Judge Trainor, known in the profession as a "death sentence." That would mean that USH loses, without a trial. Even if it were spared that fate, Judge Trainor would almost certainly be skeptical, if not downright hostile, to USH from here on.

"What the hell is this?" Demetrius exploded as he read Paul's e-mail. Then, glaring at Jake, he continued, "Our firm is mentioned in this e-mail. What did you say to them about document destruction?"

"I had just one brief conversation with Paul right after the lawsuit was filed. He assured me that there would be no document destruction, and that their records policy had been dormant for some time, so there was nothing to worry about."

"Obviously, there is something to worry about! Maybe Paul didn't interpret that conversation the same way you did. When the stakes are this high, you can't just assume the client understands your instructions. You need to make goddamned sure that they do!"

They tracked down Paul LaDuke on his cell phone. He was still in New York. Demetrius dispensed with any pleasantries and got right to the point. "Paul, we've got a crisis on our hands. It relates to the e-mail you sent out yesterday."

"What e-mail?" Paul sounded confused.

"The e-mail that urges all of your department heads to start destroying documents."

"What? Destroying documents? What are you talking about?"

"Read it to him," Demetrius ordered, looking at Jake.

Jake obliged, reading the e-mail slowly, and enunciating carefully, so that Paul could hear every word.

"And my name is on that?" Paul sounded incredulous.

"Yes, Paul," Jake replied. "It went out under your name at 4:33 p.m. yesterday."

"Son of a bitch! I can't believe this! Listen, guys, I assure you, I sent no such e-mail. I've been in meetings in New York all week and haven't sent an e-mail in three days. Besides, do you think I'm crazy enough or stupid enough to order a massive document destruction right after a major lawsuit is filed?"

Jake and Demetrius exchanged worried glances. "Listen, Paul," said Demetrius, his voice steady yet urgent. "Judge Trainor is beside himself. He is close to issuing a death sentence here. Whatever you've got going on in New York will have to wait. You need to get the word out immediately that there must be no document destruction—none. Anyone who received that e-mail must be instructed to disregard it. It is absolutely imperative that you stop this in its tracks right now. And I do mean imperative. And Paul?"

"Yes?"

"I suggest you get your ass home, pronto. This ship is listing badly. It may be starting to sink. We need all hands on deck."

"I'm on my way."

"And Paul, one more thing."

"What's that?"

"Find out who the hell is sending out e-mails under your name."

After hanging up with Paul, Demetrius gave Jake a harsh look. "I'm not sure what's going on over there at USH, but you make damn sure our firm is not drawn into anything improper. I don't want to see our name surfacing in connection with anything like this, ever again," he shouted waving the e-mail. Then he put his palms on his desk and leaned across toward Jake, and said in a low, threatening voice, "I'm holding you personally accountable."

CHAPTER 37

❧

"Jake, it's been way too long. Johnny here. I'll be at Riley's Pub tonight. I was hoping we could get together for a beer. Got a surprise for you. Hope to see you there—any time after eight o'clock."

Jake erased the recorded message. It was Wednesday, for Chrissakes. Didn't Johnny realize he had a life, and a very busy one at that? He couldn't just go out drinking beer in the middle of the week like they used to. He was in the midst of a huge case—the biggest of his career. It had been four months since the case was filed, and he had been completely immersed in it. And it was going badly.

On the other hand, there was no denying that it was good to hear Johnny's voice. They had seen very little of each other over the past couple of years. Perhaps a little midweek break would do him good. He always seemed to have a better perspective on things after spending time with Johnny. Amanda wouldn't mind. Even though quality time with her and Anna had been scarce over the past few months, she would understand his need for a break and had always encouraged him to keep in touch with his old friends. Besides, Johnny seemed eager to tell him something. Just one quick beer, he told himself.

Jake walked into Riley's promptly at eight o'clock. He hadn't been there in quite awhile, but it looked exactly the same. It was more crowded than Jake had expected for a Wednesday evening. He had become so entrenched in his own routine—awakening early, working a long day at a demanding job, and then spending time with his family in the evening—that he had forgotten how many people still spent their evenings at watering holes like this one.

Johnny had arrived just minutes before, and Jake found him at the bar ordering a beer. He ordered one for Jake as well, and then ushered him to a booth near the back. They saw several old friends and acquaintances as they walked through the bar, but Johnny hurried past them with only the briefest of greetings. That struck Jake as unusual for his normally gregarious cousin. Clearly, something was on his mind.

They sat down in the booth and Johnny asked about Amanda and Anna. He then asked about life at the firm, but shortly into his response, Jake could see that Johnny seemed to be distracted, and was barely listening. Jake stopped himself in midsentence. "OK, pal. We can get back to my boring life later. You look like a kid on Christmas Eve. What's this big surprise you mentioned in your message?"

Johnny grinned. "Guess I don't have much of a poker face, do I? Well, here it is: Congratulate me!" He hoisted his beer mug. "I'm engaged."

Jake stared at Johnny in open-mouthed disbelief. Johnny had always seemed completely content with his freewheeling, single lifestyle. Being self-employed, he was never burdened by bosses or restrictive working hours, and while Johnny had always had plenty of girlfriends, he'd never dated anyone seriously since high school, as far as Jake knew. He hadn't even realized Johnny was seeing someone now and had difficulty grasping the concept of Johnny settling down and getting married.

"Who's the lucky girl?" Jake stammered when he was finally able to speak.

"Corey Miller," Johnny replied, grinning even more broadly as he shared the news.

"Corey? Are you serious? What about Danny Flynn?"

"She left him almost a year ago."

"Are you sure about this, Johnny?" Jake realized that his question sounded judgmental and disapproving. He caught himself before Johnny could respond. "I'm sorry, Johnny ... I'm just ... stunned. I had no idea you were even seeing her." He grabbed Johnny's hand and shook it vigorously. "That's great! Fantastic! Congratulations!" Jake did his best to seem enthused, while trying to hide his misgivings.

"Thanks, pal," Johnny replied. "I wanted you to hear it directly from me. No one else knows except our parents. And Jake, to answer your question—I've never been more sure of anything in my life. She's the only girl I've ever loved. You remember how inseparable we were when we were teenagers. We talked about getting married right out of high school, but I just wasn't ready. That's why we split up. Unfortunately, she couldn't wait, and married shithead a year later." He nodded toward a table across the bar, where Jake could see Danny Flynn, drinking by himself. "I've never stopped loving her, Jake."

"This may sound like a stupid question, but are they divorced yet?" Jake asked.

"They've been separated for nearly a year, and Corey's filed for divorce. It'll become final any time now. And I'm not the reason they split. I was working at a house on her block about a year ago, painting the outside and remodeling the kitchen. I was there for a few weeks, and sometimes Corey would walk by with her kids and we'd chat. One day she walked past by herself, and I could see that she'd been crying. She told me that she'd separated from Danny, and then really unloaded. She talked about how abusive Danny was to her and the kids, not physically, but definitely verbally and emotionally. She said he was out drinking every night, which I knew, and that he was a mean and nasty drunk. Hell, he was just as bad when he was sober. It just broke my heart to listen to that. It tore me up inside, but I didn't feel it was my place to get involved. I felt helpless. All I could do was suggest that maybe some counseling might help. She told me that it was way beyond that and she felt that what she needed was a divorce lawyer. I didn't see her again for a couple of weeks after that, so I decided to call her just to see how she was doing. She'd been so distraught that I was really concerned. She sounded a lot better when

I called her. She told me that she had filed for divorce and made up her mind to start over again and felt good about the decision. I ran into her a short time later at a party and we spent several hours reminiscing about old times and laughing a lot. Then I asked her out, and one thing led to another, and here we are. We'll probably wait awhile—so the kids can get to know me better and get used to the idea of being separated from their father. Once we think they're ready, we'll tie the knot. I've never been this happy in my life, Jake."

They talked about the wedding plans, and about Corey's kids and the challenges of becoming a stepfather. Johnny asked about Jake's job and his high-profile USH case. Jake kept his responses brief. This was Johnny's night, and the focus belonged on Johnny and his future.

"What about your job situation, Johnny? Are you planning any changes?"

"I'm hoping I won't have to, but I don't know. I love the flexibility I have. It gives me the freedom to do the things that are really important to me, like my activities with the disabled kids. I don't know what else I would do, professionally speaking. I'm good at what I do now, and I enjoy it, but I doubt I could support a family of four on what I make." Johnny seemed pensive, as if he had given this issue a great deal of thought, but had yet to figure it out.

"Johnny, I've always said that you are the most naturally gifted person I know. You can do anything you put your mind to."

"Well, it's a little late for some things, Jake. We're over thirty now. I can't very well start over and go back to school."

Jake was silent for a few moments. "Do you ever wish you had stayed in school, and accomplished more?"

Jake intended it as an innocent question, as he was genuinely curious, but he didn't like the way it sounded.

"I don't regret anything about the path I've chosen," Johnny answered curtly. "And I suspect my definition of accomplishment differs from yours, and from that of a lot of other people. Let me ask you a question, Jake. What have you accomplished in your life that you're most proud of? And don't be modest—be honest. List anything that comes to mind—big things as well as little things—whatever comes to mind when you think about your accomplishments."

Jake pondered the question for a few minutes.

"Okay, here are a few that come to mind, in no particular order: getting straight A's in college and graduating first in my class; scoring in the 99th percentile on the law school admissions test; getting into Stanford Law School; graduating from Stanford Law School; getting hired by Samuelson & Reid ... let's see, what else? ... teaching myself to play guitar; being voted best all-around athlete in high school ... I guess those things would be on my list."

Johnny laughed. "I'd forgotten what a high achiever you are." Then he turned serious. "Don't take this the wrong way, Jake. I certainly don't mean to diminish your accomplishments. How could I? They're pretty damn impressive, by any measure. Here's my point," he said leaning across the table. "If someone had asked me what I just asked you, my response would be completely different. I wouldn't think about what I'd done for myself. I would think about what I've done to make things better for others. That's what's important to me. I can't change the world, and I'm not out to. When I'm with those disabled kids, I see the joy I can bring them just by spending time with them, telling jokes, really talking to them and treating them like they matter. That's what it's all about for me. If I were to go in a different direction professionally, I'd have to find something that allows me to continue doing that in some way."

Jake looked sheepish. "I feel like a schmuck. You got me bragging about myself, and now I look like an idiot. I guess I misinterpreted your question. I—"

"No you didn't, Jake. You gave me an honest answer to a very straightforward question. It's similar to what most people would say, although their accomplishments would pale next to yours. The only point I was trying to make is that I'm different than you, and than a lot of other people. If I change directions with my career, I need to find something that allows me to be who I am, something that's consistent with my priorities."

Jake smiled ruefully. "Suddenly, my career path doesn't seem very meaningful. I wonder how much value lawyers like me really contribute to our society."

"No offense, pal, but I've often wondered the same thing. Think of all the talented, energetic people in your profession. They spend most of their time fighting each other. I can't help thinking that the world would be better off if all that brainpower and energy were directed toward something constructive—science, medicine, education – anything, other than court-condoned combat."

"You're probably right," Jake mused. He stared thoughtfully at his beer for a few moments. "Can I change my answer to your question? The thing that makes me most proud and happy about my life is that I was able to convince Amanda Chang to marry me."

"Amen, brother. You're one lucky son of a bitch, and so am I. Here's to Amanda and Corey." They raised their glasses and drank. As he did so, Jake noticed Danny Flynn stumbling in their direction.

"Hi Danny," Jake said casually, relieved to see that Flynn was just walking past them on his way to the men's room.

"Piss off, McShane. Both of you," Flynn snarled without changing his pace. A few minutes later, he emerged from the restroom and was standing before them. He looked terrible. He'd aged ten years since Jake had seen him last. "Stay away from my wife, McShane, you hear me?" Flynn said, glaring at Johnny and slurring badly.

Jake tensed immediately, but Johnny seemed completely relaxed. "I think you've got that backwards, Danny boy," Johnny said in a casual voice. "She's not your wife anymore. She's divorcing you. And she's got a restraining order against you—you're the one that needs to stay away."

Jake tensed. In high school, Danny Flynn had been one of the toughest guys around. He'd been the muscle-bound football player who never backed down from a fight, and instigated plenty of them. He was overweight and out of shape now, but old habits die hard, Jake thought. It wouldn't take much to set this guy off, particularly in his highly inebriated state.

Danny scowled and pointed his finger at Johnny, swaying badly from side to side as he did so. "You stay away from her, McShane. Stay away if you know what's good for you or I swear you'll regret it." Malice emanated from the bloodshot eyes. "Stay away from my wife!" He glared for another moment and staggered away.

Jake breathed a sigh of relief. "You're in a delicate situation, Johnny. Be careful."

"I can handle it," Johnny replied with cool confidence.

Jake eyed his cousin nervously. "I hope so."

CHAPTER 38

USH was a company under siege. It faced challenges on all fronts. The media was relentless in its portrayal of the company as the new poster child for corporate greed and corruption. Patients were outraged. Admissions had dropped significantly in the months since the lawsuit was filed, as patients were gun-shy about getting cheated. Revenues were dropping fast, which was causing the stock price to plummet, sending investors heading for the exits. Regulators were now investigating to determine whether federal or state laws had been violated. All of this was causing serious morale issues among the company's employees, who were forced to listen to scathing criticism of their employer and its leadership from their friends and neighbors, as well as the media.

Damage control was the immediate mission. Senior management and legal counsel collaborated to develop a strategy to minimize the legal exposures and business fallout. The company's auditors were instructed to begin the massive effort of reviewing every bill generated over the past three years, and comparing each bill to the patient's records in an effort to identify any discrepancies. Where overcharges were identified, refund checks would be sent immediately to the patient. For those patients who did not care to wait while that process was being carried out, the company had established a customer response center that could be contacted through a toll-free phone number or through the Internet. Those customers could have their file reviewed promptly by an independent auditing firm retained solely for that purpose, and again, if any overcharge was identified, the customer would receive a prompt refund, with interest. In cases where a billing error worked in the customer's favor, USH chose not to make any attempts to recover the shortfall, because of the risk of compounding the negative customer relations problem.

Through this process, the company hoped to demonstrate to its clientele, the regulators, the media, and ultimately, the court, that it was taking proactive measures to do the right thing by its customers. From a legal perspective, the hope was that exposure to monetary damages in the lawsuit would be significantly reduced. Patients who were made whole arguably had no claim left to litigate. At least that was the theory. Plaintiffs' counsel was working hard to convince patients not to accept those refunds, telling them that the court could award substantial punitive damages, thereby enhancing their recovery potential.

The lawsuit had been mired in the muck of class action discovery for eighteen months now. The case was document-intensive, and complying with the plaintiffs' discovery requests was proving to be a monumental undertaking. USH was required to produce every patient invoice for the past three years, along with every patient file having any activity during that time period. That amounted to literally millions of records. To make matters worse, the records were not housed in a central location. Many of the facilities that had been acquired in recent years had not yet gotten around to transmitting their billing records to the corporate headquarters in Chicago. The files documenting a patient's treatment were typically kept at the location that had provided the services.

Largely because the records were so widely dispersed, USH and its attorneys had dodged a bullet at the outset of discovery. No documents had been destroyed by the time the e-mail bearing Paul LaDuke's name had come to the legal team's attention. By acting quickly, they had been able to rescind the destruction order and avert a major calamity.

The incident was still a disaster in some respects, although not nearly of the magnitude it could have been. The *Chicago Tribune* had run a story about the document destruction order, which was another very public black eye for the company, as well as its law firm. The judge refrained from imposing sanctions upon receipt of a sworn affidavit from Paul LaDuke stating that no documents had been destroyed, that Samuelson & Reid had not recommended any such destruction, and that he had not transmitted the e-mail in question. Nevertheless, Judge Trainor had clearly become hostile and skeptical toward USH and its case, and made it abundantly clear that the slightest irregularities in connection with the discovery process would be dealt with severely.

For that reason, Jake took no chances. He enlisted the assistance of a dozen associates at the firm and an army of paralegals to help gather and review all of the documentation USH was required to produce. They had to ensure that they had acquired from every USH facility all patient files having any activity during the past three years. Then they had to review all of those records to determine what was relevant and responsive to the plaintiffs' discovery request. It was a hopelessly impossible task, since there were millions of pages of documents to be produced. To avoid any risk that they could be accused of withholding evidence, Jake's instructions to his team were "when in doubt, produce it."

Jake had argued vigorously that the plaintiffs' discovery request should be limited to a period of one year prior to the filing of the lawsuit, since all of the named plaintiffs were treated within that time period. Anything beyond that was purely speculation, he argued, and given the enormous time, effort and money it would take to comply, such a fishing expedition was not warranted. Rick had pushed for a much longer discovery period—six years. He argued that there was a high likelihood that the billing problems had existed for a considerable period of time, and that only through a thorough examination of the relevant records could that be determined with any degree of certainty. The judge compromised, deciding on a three-year time period, and stated that he would consider expanding it if that discovery confirmed problems throughout that extended period. More significantly, he had certified the case as a class action and ruled that the class would include all patients who had used any USH facility during that three-year period whose bills were inaccurate.

From Jake's perspective, this exercise was a glaring example of the inefficiencies and wastefulness of the American litigation system. The end result was that USH produced truckloads of documents. The time and effort required to locate all of the necessary documents, transmit them to the legal team, have them reviewed and catalogued by the attorneys, photocopied, boxed and shipped to the plaintiffs, was mind-boggling. It cost USH millions of dollars just to complete this exercise. Jake knew that the plaintiffs' counsel would not even bother to look at most of these documents. They already had the evidence to prove that billing problems existed, and in fact, USH had agreed to stipulate to that. The real point of the exercise, Jake knew, was to harass his client and force it to spend enormous sums of money. It was the plaintiffs' hope that, as the costs of litigation mounted, USH would be more favorably inclined to stop the bleeding by agreeing to an exorbitant settlement.

Nevertheless, USH and its attorneys had no choice but to comply, and after eighteen months and two extensions to the discovery deadline reluctantly granted by Judge Trainor, the effort had been completed. The parties had been summoned to court for a status conference. Jake expected it to be a routine hearing to set the trial date, finalize the witness lists and schedule the remaining depositions. As the hearing commenced, the judge confirmed that agenda and indicated that he was pleased that the document discovery had finally been completed. Before he could go on, Rick interrupted.

"I'm sorry to have to say this, Your Honor, but there are some issues regarding the document production that I must bring to your attention."

"What kind of issues?" The judge was clearly irritated.

"Your Honor, we have serious questions about whether the defendant has complied in good faith with our discovery requests. It appears that relevant information is being withheld. We have just begun a review of the documents provided, and we have already identified some very troubling deficiencies. I have three invoices here that came to me directly from other sources. All of them appear to contain billing errors and not one of these was produced in defendant's discovery. And that's just for one location—Evergreen Memorial in Boulder, Colorado. Lord knows how much more of this we'll find as we review the remaining documents. I should also mention that these invoices relate to services performed two and three years ago. I am therefore renewing my request that the class period be expanded to six years, and that defendants be ordered to produce for that entire period the documents identified in our original discovery request—all of them." He stared pointedly at Jake.

Jake was stunned. He had not expected this.

"What about this, counsel?" the judge demanded sharply, looking at Jake.

"Your Honor, to my knowledge, we've produced everything in our possession that was requested," Jake replied. "Several truck-loads of documents have been produced. Perhaps plaintiffs' counsel overlooked these particular invoices. I can't imagine that they have had time to thoroughly review the thousands of files that have been produced."

The judge looked at Rick. "Your Honor, the boxes are clearly labeled and a complete index has been provided," said Rick. "We have located all of the boxes pertaining to this particular facility and reviewed every scrap of paper in those boxes. I assure you, these invoices are not there."

Judge Trainor looked exasperated. "Mr. McShane, I assume you kept a log of what was provided to the plaintiffs?"

"Yes, Your Honor."

"Then I suggest you review that log very carefully. I want to know by the close of business today whether these invoices were produced. If they were not, you've got serious problems. I will expand the class period to six years, and I will impose sanctions against you and your firm. Do I make myself clear?"

"Yes, Your Honor," Jake replied meekly.

As they went through the remainder of the judge's original agenda, Jake tried hard to focus, but his head was spinning as he groped for explanations. How could this have happened? Who had reviewed the Boulder documents? Had he missed any obvious categories of documents when they made their requests of the staff? Had a box or a file been misplaced? He needed answers, and he needed them fast.

Jake's investigation brought him neither comfort nor answers. The bills that were produced in court were in the files in the USH billing department, exactly where they should be, but they were not included in the discovery log. There was no evidence to confirm that those invoices had been produced. Jake spoke with litigation team members who handled that portion of the document production. They explained their procedure. They had taken the file drawer in question in its entirety. They were adamant that every invoice in the file had been copied, logged, boxed and sent to Samuelson & Reid for final review. The legal assistant who reviewed the files for the hospital in question insisted that she removed no documents whatsoever from those boxes. According to Jake's team, every invoice in the file drawer in question was copied and sent to the plaintiffs. The only explanation his team could come up with was the possibility that the three invoices in question had been temporarily removed from the file drawer prior to the photocopying. The USH employees who had access to those files could provide no reason why that would have been the case, since the invoices in question were old and inactive.

Judge Trainor made good on his harsh promise. He ruled that the class period was expanded to six years, and gave USH just sixty days to supplement its document production to cover the expanded period. During that time period, the parties were to complete any remaining depositions. USH was to produce a report to the court, to be signed by its general counsel as well as its outside law firm, summarizing the procedures they followed in their effort to comply with the plaintiffs' document request, and explaining to the court why it should believe that the results of that effort were thorough and reliable. In addition, Judge Trainor issued sanctions against Samuelson & Reid, which included a formal reprimand entered into the record of the proceedings and a $20,000 fine.

Demetrius was livid when Jake reported in by cell phone from the courthouse. He demanded that Jake report to his office immediately. The tall Greek was standing in his office doorway fuming when Jake arrived. He ushered Jake into his office and slammed the door.

"I can't tell you how upsetting this is," he shouted. "This firm has been sanctioned by a federal judge. I won't have it! It's completely unacceptable! As a representative of this firm, you are accountable! How could this happen?"

Jake explained the efforts he had undertaken earlier that day to get answers, and that no good answers were forthcoming. He began to explain in detail the process his team had gone through to ensure that their document production was thorough and reliable, but Demetrius cut him off.

"I don't care to hear the details of your process!" Demetrius shouted as he paced angrily about his office. "Whatever process you followed, it was your responsibility for overseeing it and ensuring it worked. Obviously, it broke down!"

"I'm not convinced that it broke down, Demetrius."

That stopped him in his tracks. "What is that supposed to mean?"

"You once said that you don't believe in coincidences. Neither do I. Think about it. We produced millions of pages of documents. Within three days, Black shows up with three invoices that allegedly were not provided to him. Where did he get those invoices? Out of the millions of documents, what caused him to check those three so quickly? And it just so happens that each of those invoices contains an obvious error in the hospital's favor. While we know that there were many cases involving inadvertent overcharging, the majority of the bills are accurate and there are also plenty of cases where the customer was undercharged. What are the odds that all of this is just coincidence? Remember Paul's e-mail? They have help on the inside; I'm convinced of it."

Demetrius paused for a moment. He took a step toward Jake and pointed a finger at his chest. "I don't want to hear excuses, and I'm not interested in some phantom insider. If there is such a person, find him! Whether there is or not, this discovery response was botched. As a result, the class period has been expanded, and our client will spend another fortune on additional discovery. On top of that, our firm has been sanctioned, on your watch! I suggest you think hard about your approach to your work and whether you have what it takes to represent this firm." He opened the door for Jake, signaling an end to the meeting. "Consider this a potentially career-limiting development."

CHAPTER 39

Randy Kraft walked into the Art Institute of Chicago around noon. With the aid of a museum map, he made his way to the American Artists wing. There were few visitors, and he easily spotted Rick Black in front of Grant Wood's *American Gothic*, just where he said he would be.

"This has always been one of my favorite paintings," Rick said casually, as Randy sidled up next to him, nervously glancing around to see whether anyone was watching them.

"Why do we have to meet here?" Randy asked. "What if someone sees us?"

"Relax, Randy," Rick whispered. Then, in a slightly louder voice, he pointed at the couple in the painting and said, "Did you know that this couple never actually posed together? In fact, they were never even a couple. The woman model was the artist's sister and the man was his dentist." He continued in a quieter voice, "I can't have you visiting my office, or calling. Remember that you are not a client of mine, not yet anyway, and it's very important that you keep that in mind and act accordingly. So what's on your mind?"

"I'm getting really nervous, Rick. That lawyer—McShane—he keeps coming to see me, and he's asking a lot of questions."

"That's perfectly normal. Your deposition is tomorrow, and he wants to be prepared. He wants to know what you know. Just stick to your story. What kinds of questions is he asking?"

"At first, it seemed like pretty routine stuff. Where records are kept, the history of our billing systems, how to interpret billing codes, that kind of thing. Lately, he's really been pressing about who has access to those records, whether any of those people might be disgruntled, and whether I think any of our people might be sharing information with outsiders. He suspects something, I'm sure of it, and I'm getting really nervous about this deposition."

"Well, don't be. Just stick to your story, like we discussed. I'll be the one asking the questions, so just relax. Everything is proceeding exactly as planned; in fact, even better than I could have hoped for."

"Really?" Randy looked doubtful.

"Really," Rick assured him. "Look, those three invoices you sent to me were a big help—huge. It'll really make a difference in the litigation. As for you, you're positioned just like we discussed, and after tomorrow afternoon, it will be even better. There's nothing they can do to you, Randy, so just stick to your story and relax."

Randy Kraft was to be the last witness deposed. His deposition had been scheduled previously, but Rick had asked to postpone it several times, claiming he had scheduling conflicts.

Jake had met with Randy numerous times since the litigation began. Randy seemed nervous and uptight, not the kind of employee who would make a good witness, but his testimony would be critical on several key points. Randy knew the company's billing systems and their history better than anyone. He could explain the root causes of the problems. He would testify about the inevitable challenges that arose when an acquisition-oriented company tried to merge hundreds of different billing systems and the kinds of things that could go wrong despite the best efforts of numerous well-meaning employees. Randy would also be able to testify about meetings that had been convened on multiple occasions to address these problems and plans that were developed to do so. Unfortunately, those plans had not been implemented prior to the filing of the lawsuit, but Jake hoped that Randy would help convince a jury that there was nothing nefarious at work involving USH's billing practices, and to the contrary, the company had been taking measures to proactively address whatever problems had been inadvertently created.

Since Randy had been subpoenaed by the plaintiffs, Rick would be the one questioning him. Jake was not surprised that Randy appeared nervous and agitated, since he had always appeared that way during Jake's meetings with him.

After some preliminary questions about Randy's personal and employment history, Rick inquired about Randy's role in the efforts to integrate the various billing systems. He had Randy identify the types of problems that came to his attention and homed in on when Randy learned of those problems as well as the measures taken to address them. Randy answered as Jake expected. He indicated that he had been diligent about bringing issues to his superiors' attention, and that a number of meetings had been convened to formulate a strategy for dealing with those issues. Jake knew that Rick would then try to elicit information indicating that USH had been remiss in not following up on those problems in a timely manner.

"Mr. Kraft, when did you first bring your concerns about USH's billing problems to your superiors' attention?" Rick asked.

"Nearly four years ago."

"Were your concerns addressed at that time?"

"I was asked to meet with our Controller and our Internal Audit Department."

"Then what happened?"

"We met a week or so later—me, Tom Lusky, who was our Controller, and the guy from Internal Audit. I explained to them the kinds of problems I was seeing. They asked me to pull together some examples, which I did, within a few days. I forwarded the information to them, and they said they would follow up. I believe they assigned a couple of internal auditors to do some samplings of billings from different locations."

"Then what?"

"Then nothing. I didn't hear anything more from anybody. About a year later, I raised the issue again by sending an e-mail to the guys involved in that first meeting. I copied Andrew Klein, our CFO, on that e-mail. Another meeting was called. It was attended by the same people who attended the first meeting, except that the CFO was there this time. He instructed us to work together to develop an action plan for addressing these issues. He said I should take the lead, since I was most familiar with our systems. He said it was important that we develop a thorough step-by-step plan to rectify any errors that had occurred in the past and to fix the systems problems to prevent future mistakes. He said that the first order of business should be fixing the systems so that we weren't compounding the problems, and that all of the resources of our IT department were at my disposal."

None of that testimony was news to Jake. He heard that before from Randy and others.

"Were there any other meetings addressing these issues?" Rick asked.

Randy hesitated and glanced at Jake, then quickly looked away. "Shortly after that meeting—the same day, I think—I met privately with the CFO, Mr. Klein."

Jake sat up straight in his chair. He had not heard this before.

"What happened during that meeting?" Rick asked, matter-of-factly.

"Mr. Klein told me that fixing our systems to prevent any additional errors should be my focus. He said don't worry about rectifying any past errors. He said he wanted a plan in place to address past issues in case anybody asked about it, but that he had no intention of ever implementing that plan. He said that old bills got stale quickly, and as time passed, people weren't likely to raise a stink. He said he couldn't justify giving away that much cash when no one was even asking for it."

Jake dropped his pencil. "Let's go off the record, counsel." he said crossly. "I need a moment with my client."

"Sure thing," said Rick.

Jake escorted Randy to a private conference room down the hall. "Randy, what the hell are you talking about? Are you saying that

Andrew Klein told you to deliberately avoid rectifying past errors? You never mentioned a word of that before!"

Randy looked panicked. "You never asked me about that," he replied weakly.

"Bullshit! We've spoken at least a dozen times about the meetings relating to your action plan, and I've repeatedly asked you to tell me everything relevant about that effort. How could you leave something like this out? What's going on here, Randy?"

"I guess I just thought it might hurt our case, so I kept it to myself."

"Goddammit Randy, you can't do that! This could be devastating. What else haven't you told me?"

"Nothing else," Randy stammered. "I've told you everything."

"Tell me everything about your meeting with Klein. Right now!"

Randy repeated exactly what he had just stated in the deposition. "That's all there is. I've told you everything."

The court reporter knocked on the door. "Are you guys ready? We're approaching the end of the allotted time."

They returned to the deposition room. Randy was sweating. He loosened his tie. "I'm sorry, gentlemen," he said in a shaky voice. "I'm not used to this. I think I'm having an anxiety attack. I don't know if I can continue."

"I'm just about finished, Mr. Kraft. Only a few more questions, okay?" Rick sounded gentle and reassuring.

Randy nodded.

"I haven't seen Mr. Klein's name on any recent company materials. Do you know where he is now?" Rick asked.

"He's deceased. He took medical leave from the company and then died about a year ago. Leukemia, I think."

"I see. Just one more question. I want to be sure I've got this straight. You've testified here today that USH knew about rampant billing problems almost four years ago, that it convened several meetings to discuss those issues, but that it made no actual effort to rectify any errors on bills sent to its patients. You've also testified that the company's CFO specifically informed you that the plan was to fix the systems issues to avoid future mistakes but to avoid addressing any prior mistakes at all. Is that accurate?"

"Yes, sir."

"I have no further questions."

Jake asked Randy to accompany him back to his office. There was a tense silence between them as they walked the six blocks across downtown Chicago. Once there, Jake ushered Randy into a large conference room and instructed him to take a seat. Jake sat directly opposite him, and did his best to maintain his composure.

"Randy, that didn't go well, and that's an understatement!"

"I know, I know ... I'm so sorry, Mr. McShane. I screwed up ... I'm sorry."

Randy stared down, elbows on the table, hands behind his head. Jake could see that he was near tears. It would do no good to berate him or make him feel worse. He needed this guy's cooperation. He needed to know everything Randy knew. He also needed to know why he had never mentioned the meeting with Klein before.

"Listen to me, Randy. Listen very carefully," Jake said, calmly but firmly. "Your testimony will be a key element of this case. It is a matter of the utmost importance that you tell me everything you know about the company's efforts to deal with its billing issues. I mean everything. I will decide whether it's helpful or harmful, and what to do with that information, but I need to know everything you know. Is that clear?"

"Yes."

"Was I not clear on that before?"

"You were, but like I said, I thought that information might hurt us, and I was afraid I might get into trouble. I was just following orders, but I still thought that if this came out, I'd be in big trouble. Then, this morning, one of the last things you said to me before the deposition was to tell the truth, so when Mr. Black asked me that question, I felt like I had to answer it."

"Randy—"

"But I should've told you first, I know. I'm sorry, I'm really sorry." Randy's voice quavered and his hands were shaking.

Jake realized that a vigorous interrogation while Randy was in this state would not be productive. "Okay, Randy, I need you to shake this off. Put it behind you for now, but go home and think very hard about anything that might be relevant to this case that you may have neglected to tell me. We'll get together tomorrow morning to talk further. Just one more question ..." He waited for Randy to look up at him. "Have you had any direct contact with anyone from the plaintiffs' side—lawyers, investigators or anyone else?"

Randy froze momentarily. "Just today, in that deposition," he stammered. "Nothing other than that. "Why? Does someone think that I'm talking to the other side?"

"Just asking. It's a question I have to ask everyone. I'd be remiss if I didn't."

CHAPTER 40

R ick Black looked out at Lake Michigan from his posh office on the sixty-third floor. After nearly two years, the USH trial was about to begin, and he was finding it difficult to contain his excitement. This was the case that would catapult him into the upper echelon of trial lawyers. It would solidify his standing with Sullivan & Leach and make him one of the most sought after lawyers in the nation. He would attain celebrity status. He would be feared and respected.

It was his case. He had seen the opportunity and capitalized on it. Between his own talent and initiative and the firm's vast resources, he had developed this into a case with mind-boggling potential. It was not a question of whether he would win. That was a given. USH could not deny billing errors, and it would be ordered to make restitution. That alone would likely cost the company twenty-five or thirty million dollars. The only uncertainty was whether Rick could convince a jury that USH's conduct was sufficiently egregious that punitive damages should be awarded. That could make the case worth $100 million, maybe more. But he had to show the jury that the company engaged in some intentional wrongdoing. That's where Randy Kraft's testimony was essential. And that's why Rick was worried.

Randy was clearly feeling the pressure. That was evident during their meeting at the Art Institute and it was even more evident at Randy's deposition. Rick had done his best to calm the nervous little man, but he was one very fragile witness. And after Randy's surprise testimony, Jake McShane would be bearing down on him hard. According to Randy, he already was.

There was too much at stake to leave things to chance. This case could be a once-in-a-lifetime opportunity, and Rick was not about to put blind faith into a skittish witness like Randy Kraft. He had to take control. He had to eliminate or minimize the chances of anything going wrong with Randy. That meant finding a way to alleviate the pressure on him. That was why Fowler had just arrived at his office.

"We're gearing up for trial in the USH case, Fowler. I've got one major problem, and I need your help with it. It's extremely delicate."

Fowler's face was expressionless. "That's my specialty. What's the problem?"

"The problem is USH's lawyer, Mr. McShane. He's very close to mucking up my case. I need him distracted, or better yet, I need him off the case. If the defense has to assign another lawyer to this case, it'll be all they can do to get up to speed on the big picture. They won't have time to sniff out the little details that McShane is getting close to. So I want McShane out of the picture. *Capiche?*"

"No problem. Anything else?"

"I don't have to tell you how sensitive this is, Fowler."

"No, you don't."

"And I don't need to know your methods. I just need results and I need them fast."

"Consider it done."

CHAPTER 41

Trial was less than a week away. Jake was in heavy-duty preparation mode, and had been for several weeks. That meant he was at the office by 7:00 a.m. most mornings and seldom got home before midnight. He barely saw his family. Amanda was understanding—she knew that was the life of a trial lawyer. Anna was less understanding. Her seven-year-old mind couldn't fathom why her Daddy missed their bedtime reading ritual night after night, and rarely called her on the phone after school like he used to. Jake felt guilty and neglectful, but powerless to do anything about it. He promised himself he would make it up to them once the trial was over.

On Tuesday evening, Jake returned to his office at eight o'clock after an all-day preparation session with the trial team. He quickly glanced through a stack of phone messages. One in particular caught his eye. "Darnell Tucker called at 4:15—urgent," the message read. Jake thought about Shooter. It had been a long time. The guy must be in trouble with the law again. Like everyone else, Shooter would have to wait. He couldn't focus on anything other than the trial right now.

Shortly after 10:00 p.m., the phone rang. Thinking it must be Amanda, Jake answered it on the first ring.

"Hello?"

"Is that you, Stanford?"

Jake recognized the caller immediately. Only one person had ever referred to him by that nickname. He was instantly annoyed. He didn't have time to deal with this guy.

"Hi Shooter. I'm in the middle of something right now. Can I get back to you?"

"No, man. This can't wait. We need to talk."

"Are you in trouble again?"

"No—you are." There was an urgency in Shooter's voice.

"What are you talking about?"

"Some dude came around here today, asking about you. I know trouble when I see it, and this guy is trouble."

"Who was he?"

"I don't know, man, but he was spooky. He was a big dude, with white hair, like an old man, but he wasn't very old, and his face was really red. He had an accent—like he was from the South somewhere. There ain't too many guys that can scare me, but this guy gave me the creeps."

"Doesn't sound familiar to me. What did he want?"

"He said you were being considered for some honor from the State Bar and that he was doing a background check. Said he learned that I was a former client of yours, and he had to go through the drill, you know, talk to your clients to see if they were satisfied with your representation. He asked me about my case, what I knew about you, if we kept in touch, that kind of stuff."

"What did you tell him?"

"I didn't tell him shit. I told him you helped me out of a jam once, a long time ago, and that I had nothing else to say. I knew he didn't work for no State Bar. Anyway, I thought you should know. Like I said, this guy ain't right. He was scary."

Jake's curiosity turned into concern. "Thanks for calling, Shooter. I don't know what to make of this, but I appreciate the heads-up."

"You watch your back, Stanford."

"I will." Jake was about to hang up, but caught himself. "Hey, Shooter?"

"Yeah?"

"How are things with you?"

There was a pause. "Good, man, real good. Got a great job. I've met some good people. Things worked out well for me. I'll tell you about it sometime."

"I'd like that. Thanks again for calling."

"No problem. Like I said, you be careful." He hung up.

Jake thought for a moment, then picked up the phone and called home.

"Hello?" His wife's voice sounded sleepy.

"Hi, sweetheart. I woke you, didn't I?"

"I must've drifted off here on the couch. What time is it?"

"It's about 10:30. I'm on my way home. I love you."

"Love you, too. See you soon."

There was no point in alarming Amanda, especially at this hour, Jake thought. He needed more time to sort this out. He would talk to Demetrius in the morning.

CHAPTER 42

S hooter was glad he had reached Jake the night before. He was convinced that the white-haired "investigator" was up to no good, but he had done all he could. The guy had not returned, and Shooter didn't expect him to.

The evening's basketball games had just finished. As was his custom, Shooter lingered with the teenaged ballplayers in the parking lot afterwards. This was what Reverend Lonnie called rap time, which Shooter saw as one of the most important aspects of his job. It was a time to visit with the kids and just talk, about whatever came up. There was no agenda, other than to get to know the kids and have them get to know him. That built trust. Sometimes Reverend Lonnie joined him, but most nights Shooter was on his own—just him and a bunch of teenagers. Sometimes the kids would ask about his past, or Reverend Lonnie's. That was an opportunity to impart life's lessons without sounding preachy or forcing it upon them. That's when they might really listen.

There were six of them hanging out with Shooter that evening. Four of them he knew fairly well, the other two, Lamarcus and Rashid, were newcomers. They talked tough and acted tough. They were loud and boastful, not unlike he had been at their age. Shooter's instincts told him they were trouble, but he had learned patience, and had come to view tough cases as a challenge. It was kids like these that needed direction most.

After nearly an hour, Shooter was ready to lock up the gym and call it a night. As he played with the keys in his pocket and started dropping hints that it was time to move on, three cars careened around the corner and screeched to a halt. Doors flew open and bodies leapt out before the cars had even reached a stop.

Shooter assessed the situation in an instant. "Y'all split," he yelled to the kids gathered around him. "To the gym—now!" No further encouragement was needed, as the young ballplayers bolted to the gym. Shooter held his ground, as the screaming mob raced toward him waving tire irons, chains and knives. He kept his hands in his pockets, and walked slowly toward them, trying to look as casual as he could. He knew that any word or action perceived as a challenge would be a serious mistake.

"Out of the way, motherfucker! We want Lamarcus Jackson," said a large bald man leading the pack. Gangbangers seeking revenge for something, Shooter surmised.

"This is a church. It ain't a place for violence." Shooter replied, in a voice that was loud, but calm.

"Church, my ass! Where's Jackson?" The bald man brandished a shiny switchblade, inches from Shooter's face.

Shooter's impulse was to thrash this punk, but there were too many, and they had weapons. More important, it was no longer his way. He had vowed to himself to set the right example for his kids.

"You heard of Lonnie Cole?" Shooter asked the group. "This is his church. Like I said, this ain't a place for fighting. We don't want no trouble here. Why don't you—"

Two gunshots rang out. Another gangbanger emerged from the crowd, a silver handgun pointed toward the sky. He lowered the gun and pointed it directly at Shooter. "The next bullet is for Lamarcus Jackson. If you don't get his sorry ass out here, it'll be for you!"

Shooter's mind raced, as he desperately tried to find words that might defuse the situation. He raised his hands, palms outward, in a gesture intended to show that he was unarmed and not looking for trouble. Suddenly, sirens blared nearby. The crowd made for their cars and the man with the gun glared at Shooter, then turned and sauntered back toward the street, gun at his side.

"This is a church," Shooter yelled after him. "Don't come back, unless you're coming to pray!" The man whirled quickly and fired a single shot. Shooter gasped, as pain seared his abdomen, the force of the blow knocking him backwards and off his feet. He tried sitting up, and slowly peeled back his shirt so that he could examine the wound. He could see blood gushing from a hole just beneath his ribcage. He felt a burning sensation, but worse than that he could feel that something was torn up inside. The world began to move in slow motion. He saw faces looking down at him. He saw Reverend Lonnie standing over him, saying something, but it was just sound. He couldn't understand the words. Then the sounds ceased, and he heard no more. The faces became blurry, and started to fade. Then all was black.

CHAPTER 43

The evening following Shooter's phone call, Jake was working late again. He was tired, having gotten little sleep the previous night as he pondered the strange phone conversation. He had decided to tell no one. He didn't want to alarm his family unnecessarily, and he knew the police would do nothing, since there had been no actual threat. He also decided not to tell Demetrius, because he wasn't sure it had any bearing on the USH case, and Demetrius would undoubtedly question him about the source of this information. Jake was not eager to call attention to the fact that he had represented a former drug dealer with a felony record. Reporting the matter to Judge Trainor also seemed like a bad idea. The judge was already hostile toward Jake and his firm, and might consider such a report to be some sort of ploy, perhaps an attempt to make unfair innuendoes and disparage the opposing side. Besides, there was no evidence whatsoever that Shooter's information had any bearing on the USH case, and Judge Trainor would certainly point that out. He couldn't risk antagonizing the judge any further.

The most logical explanation in Jake's mind was that the opposing side was looking for dirt on him. He had never been involved in a high-stakes lawsuit with a powerful plaintiffs' class action firm, and for all he knew, this could be standard procedure for them. If that were the case, he had nothing to worry about—there was no dirt to be found. Perhaps they wanted him to know that some sinister looking figure was asking questions about him. Maybe their motive was to scare him and distract his attention from the case. That was precisely what was happening, and if he informed others of the situation, the distraction would only grow. So he concluded there was nothing to be done but to follow Shooter's advice to remain vigilant.

By ten o'clock, Jake decided to call it quits for the evening. He was exhausted and had a pounding headache. It had been another fifteen-hour day of intense trial preparation, and he was operating on very little sleep. He took the elevator to the basement level and exited at the parking garage. The garage was deserted, as it normally was at this hour. Jake felt an aching, numbing fatigue overtaking him as he trudged toward his car, unfocused and oblivious to his surroundings. He climbed in and started the engine.

"Turn off the ignition." The voice came from the back seat. Jake was instantly jolted into a state of alertness by a rush of fear and adrenaline.

"Do not turn around." Jake glanced into the rearview mirror, and saw a man wearing a black ski mask that completely concealed his face. He held a gun, pointed at the back of Jake's head. His voice was neither angry nor threatening. It was perfectly calm, and completely devoid of any emotion, which made it all the more chilling.

"Listen carefully, Mr. McShane. My instructions to you are very simple: Drop the USH case. Find some excuse, but make sure that your involvement with that case terminates immediately. I will be watching. I can get to you at any time. And don't try to be a hero. I'll be watching your family, too."

Jake was trembling, partly out of fear, and partly out of rage at this intruder and at his own helplessness.

"Do as I ask, Mr. McShane, and you will never hear from me again. Ignore my request, and I promise, you will regret it." He opened the rear door. "Stay right here for ten minutes. Do not leave a second earlier. After that, you can go home to Amanda and Anna. And one more thing—tell no one about our little conversation." The door slammed and he was gone.

Jake stared straight ahead for several minutes, then tentatively looked around. The garage was silent and empty. He was shaking so badly he didn't know whether he could drive. He took several deep breaths to calm himself. He could focus on only one thought: his family. The fact that this maniac knew Amanda and Anna by name chased all other thoughts from his mind. A feeling of dread and terror gripped him as he struggled to understand what was happening. Then another realization struck him as the creepy voice replayed itself in his mind. The man had an unmistakable Southern drawl.

CHAPTER 44

Jake sat in the parking garage for a full fifteen minutes after the man in the ski mask had departed, then he raced home. The exhaustion he'd been feeling thirty minutes before was long gone, replaced by a state of high alert and high anxiety. He sped through the city streets trying to decide what to do next, but his attempts to think clearly were overcome by a feeling of dread and panic, knowing that his family might be in danger.

Amanda was sleeping when Jake arrived at home. She awoke when she heard him speaking loudly on the kitchen telephone. He sounded agitated.

"Problems with the case?" she asked sleepily. Then she looked at him more closely. He looked pale and shaken. "Jake, what is it?"

He hesitated, then told her everything—the call last night from Shooter, the incident in the parking garage and the phone conversation he had just had with the police. Amanda listened in stunned silence.

"Jake, this is really scary. What should we do?"

"I don't know. I can't seem to think straight. The police are on their way. I better let Demetrius know, too."

It was past eleven o'clock, and Jake didn't relish the idea of contacting Demetrius at home with this news. He was confident that Demetrius would be irritated, but he was under standing orders to contact Demetrius, day or night, whenever there was a significant development in the case. To Jake's surprise, Demetrius's reaction was one of genuine concern rather than annoyance. He made no mention of the case, and focused solely on the safety of Jake and his family.

"I know the Chief of Police personally, and I'm going to call him right now," said Demetrius. "I'll have them station some officers outside your house immediately. Can I do anything for you? Would you like me to come over?"

"No, I don't think that's necessary," Jake replied. "The police are on their way, but thanks for offering, Demetrius."

"Let's meet in my office first thing in the morning, at eight o'clock. I'll have the police there. And then we're going to pay a visit to Judge Trainor."

Jake was happy to see Demetrius spring into action, since he felt paralyzed. He had reservations about approaching Judge Trainor with this information. He had no proof of anything, and the judge might be skeptical. But he was happy to let Demetrius do the thinking on this point. His thoughts were scattered. The adrenaline was wearing off and exhaustion was setting in. The police arrived within a matter of minutes and Jake repeated what he had already told them by phone. They assured him they would remain parked right outside for the remainder of the evening.

Jake spent another night with very little sleep, tossing and turning, realizing full well that if someone had a goal of distracting him on the eve of trial, they were doing a fine job.

At eight o'clock the next morning, he entered Demetrius's office. Walter Tomczak, the Chief of Police himself, was there, along with a man named Webster, whom Tomczak introduced as his finest detective. After introductions had been made, Tomczak said, "I have personally contacted Judge Trainor, and he's asked all of us to meet in his chambers immediately. He has summoned opposing counsel as well. The judge thought it best that all of us hear your story at the same time, Mr. McShane."

Demetrius was clever, Jake thought. It must have been his idea to have the Chief of Police call Judge Trainor. The judge would be more likely to receive the news with an open mind if it came through that channel rather than through his law firm.

By eight thirty, they were all crowded into the judge's comfortable but cramped quarters. Rick Black arrived a few minutes later, and seemed surprised by the group that was gathered there. Judge Trainer looked uncharacteristically somber as he commenced the meeting. "Gentlemen, as some of you know, there was an incident last night that is of the utmost concern to me and to this court. It is also a matter of serious concern to the police, and of course, to Mr. McShane and his family. Jury selection in the USH trial is scheduled to begin tomorrow, and opening arguments are scheduled for Monday. It is my duty to protect the integrity of that process. This trial must be orderly, and free of any distractions or prejudicial influences, but of even greater importance is the safety of the participants. Issues have arisen that are very troubling. I need to know about these events, so I can determine what impact, if any, they will have on this trial. I believe it best that all of us present hear about these events at the same time, so no one feels that anything is taking place behind their back. This will enable all parties to provide whatever input they have about how we should proceed."

Rick looked confused. "Excuse me, Your Honor, but I'm in the dark here. I have no idea what you're talking about. Could someone please enlighten me?"

"I'm sorry to keep you in the dark, Mr. Black," said the judge. "I haven't heard the complete story myself yet. Mr. McShane, I'd like you to brief all of us. Tell us everything you can remember about last evening's events."

Jake recounted the story in as much detail as he could remember. He felt every eye staring at him intently as he spoke. Webster took copious notes. He stopped Jake when he had reached the point in his story where the intruder walked away from the car.

"Did you watch him as he walked away?" Webster asked.

"No, I stared straight ahead, until I felt it was safe to look around."

"So you didn't get a look at his size, his build, the way he walks, anything like that?"

"I'm afraid not."

"And you never saw his face?"

"No. Like I said, he was wearing a dark ski mask that completely covered his face."

"So we have no description and no witnesses."

"No."

"What about his voice? Was there anything distinctive about it?"

"He had a Southern accent. Georgia or Alabama maybe, I'm not sure. And that leads me to something else." Jake described the call he had received from Shooter the night before last.

"That may help. There could be a connection, and maybe we can get a good description from this Shooter guy. Where can I find him?" Webster asked.

"I don't know. I hadn't heard from him in years, but he called me several times earlier this week. My secretary should have his phone number."

"Good. I'll get somebody on that right away. Excuse me for a moment." Webster made a call on his cell phone and gave someone instructions to find Darnell Tucker and set up an appointment for later that morning.

Chief Tomczak stood up and looked around the room. "Here's what I'd like to know: Who would do this? Who has enough at stake in this trial to want to cause trouble for the defendants? Are there plaintiffs that stand to collect big dollars here?"

Judge Trainor leaned back in his reclining chair. "I've been asking myself the same question since I first heard about this. This case has thousands of plaintiffs, Walter—anybody that might have been over-billed by USH. The amount of potential recovery by any particular individual is not likely to be significant. We're talking about a few hundred dollars in most cases, maybe a few thousand for some. Even if punitive damages are awarded, no single plaintiff is going to get rich off this."

Then he looked at Rick. "The biggest winner from a financial stand-point would be Sullivan & Leach, Mr. Black's law firm. However, I'm sure the attorneys at that firm do quite well financially, and would have no need to stoop to tactics like this. Besides, they would know that I would personally see to it that any attorneys involved in something like this would not only be disbarred, they'd be criminally prosecuted and sent to jail." He looked steadily at Rick as he said this.

"Unfortunately, as we all know, there are plenty of kooks out there," Rick pointed out. "There's been a lot of publicity surrounding this case. It's an emotional subject for many people. A former patient may have very hostile feelings toward the company, even if he doesn't have a great deal of money at stake in the trial. A former employee may hold a grudge and want to see the company punished. Anything is possible."

"I'm afraid Mr. Black is right," Chief Tomczak said. "It could be anyone. We don't have a lot to go on."

Webster's cell phone rang. The group waited in silence as he took the call. Webster listened intently, then terminated the call, looking gravely at the group. "Darnell Tucker has been shot, early yesterday evening. It appears to be some sort of gang incident, but who knows? He's alive, at least for now, but he's not in good shape."

An elderly woman opened the door, and waved a newspaper at Judge Trainor. "I thought you might want to see this, Judge."

He beckoned her in, and she handed him the paper, pointing to an article on page three. "Dammit," the judge muttered, handing the paper to Chief Tomczak.

"Shit!" Tomczak exclaimed sharply upon looking at the headline. It read, "USH Counsel Threatened On Eve of Trial." "Some reporter must have picked this up on the scanner last night when the officers were dispatched to Mr. McShane's house."

A grim silence possessed the group as the paper was passed from person to person. Judge Trainor broke the silence. "I will not have this trial become a media circus," he announced with resolve in his voice. "And I will not allow anything to interfere with the fairness of these proceedings. I would hate to delay this trial any further, but you are the person scheduled to try this case, Mr. McShane, and you are the person most directly affected by these developments. I'd like to hear from you. What should we do here?"

Jake had been hoping the decision would be made for him. He didn't want to irritate the judge by requesting a delay. Moreover, he wanted the trial over with, and he was ready to try the case, or at least he thought he was, until last night. "I don't know that I can answer that question, Judge," Jake replied hesitantly. "I'm ready to try this case, but I have to consider the safety of my family. I'm sorry, but that needs to come first."

"Of course it does," replied the judge. "Walter, what can we do here?"

"The Chicago Police Department is at your disposal, Judge. We can assign around-the-clock protection to Mr. McShane and his family. We will station two officers at his house, we can escort his wife to and from work and his daughter to and from school. I know how important this trial is, and the safety of Mr. McShane's family is even more important. We'll take care of you, Jake." He put his hand on Jake's shoulder as he said this.

"Thanks, Chief. I appreciate that." Then looking at Judge Trainor, Jake continued, "Your Honor, I know we need to make a decision and move on, but I really need to discuss this with my wife. May I have a little time?"

"Certainly, just let me know by the end of the day. If you're not comfortable proceeding, I understand. If that's your decision, I'll postpone the trial for several weeks so that your firm has time to get another attorney up to speed. I assume you would have no objection, Mr. Black?"

"None at all, Your Honor," Rick replied. "I understand the seriousness of the situation, and we will do everything we can to accommodate the court and Mr. McShane."

"Thank you—all of you," Jake said, looking around the room. "I really appreciate your concern."

Chief Tomczak looked at him. "You know, Jake, this may actually help," he said, pointing to the newspaper. "Whoever did this will know that we're watching closely now, and it may scare him off."

That brought Jake little comfort. "I hope you're right," he replied, and then excused himself to return to Amanda, who had stayed home for the morning. A uniformed police officer drove him to his house.

Anna was snuggled up to Amanda on the couch when Jake walked in. Anna was reading and Amanda was doing her best to appear interested and disguise her worry. Jake kissed them both and gently asked Anna to read in her bedroom for awhile so that he and Amanda could discuss some grown-up business. Anna put on a pout-face, but immediately broke into laughter, as Jake lifted her up, flung her over his shoulder and carried her off to her room.

He returned and sat down next to his wife on the sofa, then did his best to recount the entire conversation that had just occurred in Judge Trainor's chambers. When he finished, he took his wife's hands in his and asked, "What should I do, Amanda? I will walk away from this case if you want me to. You and Anna come first."

"Do you really think we're in danger?"

"I've been asking myself that question over and over. My gut tells me no. Someone may be trying to scare me or distract me, but it really seems implausible that someone would actually try to hurt us. Who would have the motive to do that?"

"Who has the most to gain if your client loses?"

"That's just it. There's a ton of money at stake here, but no single person stands to win a whole lot. Rick's law firm may cash in big, and Rick is certainly capable of dirty tricks, but I don't think he'd do anything like this. So, logically speaking, I think there's little risk. But then I think about Shooter …"

"But that was gang-related, isn't that what the detective said?"

"Yes, but they haven't had a chance to fully investigate yet."

"And the police assured you they would protect us?"

"Around-the-clock protection for the duration of the trial."

Amanda thought silently for a few moments. "If you back down and withdraw from this case, that means some bad guy gets away with manipulating the system. You've put your heart and soul into this case. You're ready to try it, and you would do a great job. If you think this is most likely nothing more than a scare tactic, and we're going to have the Chicago Police Department watching over us, you have my full support if you feel like you should try this case. I hate the idea of giving in to intimidation and letting some scoundrels get their way."

"Are you sure?" Jake asked. She seemed more confident than he was.

"Yes, I am sure. If there are any further problems, we can reconsider. But for now, let's not give in to these scare tactics. It's just not right."

"Okay." Jake nodded slowly trying to work up the same conviction his wife had just demonstrated. "Okay, I'll handle it. We will proceed as planned. Jury selection starts tomorrow, and the trial begins on Monday. With a little luck, this will all be over in less than two weeks."

Jake called Judge Trainor's clerk and told her to inform the judge that the trial could proceed as planned. He would be handling the case.

CHAPTER 45

Shooter was in bad shape. The bullet had damaged his spleen and a kidney, and he had lost a great deal of blood. It had been touch and go the previous night, mostly because of the bleeding, but Shooter was tough, and he had pulled through. For Jerome, the sight of his brother lying near death in a hospital bed, connected to a massive array of tubes and machines, was almost more than he could take. Shooter had always been the rock in his life, the only person he could count on and the only person he'd ever really looked up to. He was the toughest guy in the neighborhood. He was a god on the basketball court. He was smart. He was a leader. People liked him. More important, they respected him. Shooter had begun a new life, and his future looked promising. The fact that a bullet had nearly robbed him of that future shook Jerome to the very core of his being. But the doctors said Shooter would survive. Jerome left the hospital feeling a profound sense of relief.

He also left with a feeling of resolve. Since leaving prison, Jerome had felt reasonably certain of the direction he would take. He had just needed some time to readjust to life on the outside. Now, after seeing his brother lying in a hospital bed, nearly dead from a gunshot wound he didn't deserve, he knew what he had to do. It was time to start his new life. He would not go back to the way things were. He had an opportunity to do something different, and his destiny was entirely within his own control. His path was clear. He too would become a man worthy of respect.

CHAPTER 46

Attorneys for both sides spent the better part of Thursday questioning prospective jurors and conferring with their high-priced jury consultants, trying to decide which candidates were acceptable and which were not. The press was not allowed into the courtroom during this process, but they were waiting in force outside the federal court building when the lawyers emerged. Rick had made sure that the media was well aware that the long-awaited trial was about to begin, and the media was eager to begin its coverage.

Jake looked out over the sea of reporters, with their cameras, microphones and notebooks. Their attention was focused on Rick Black, as he expressed his gratification over the fact that the day of reckoning for USH had finally arrived, and that thousands of patients who had been cheated were about to receive justice. Jake barely paid attention. He was scanning the faces, looking for a big white-haired man with a reddish complexion. When he saw no one with white hair, he looked for any large middle-aged man with a red, pink or ruddy complexion, assuming that the hair easily could have been dyed. Still, he saw no one fitting that description.

Then something caught his eye. A gaudy white Cadillac with a maroon top and gold trim was parked at the curb, just beyond the group of reporters. A large black man slouched against the car, legs crossed, muscular arms folded across his chest. He was young, probably in his early twenties. He clearly was not a reporter—he was dressed more like a gang member—but he was watching the activity outside the courthouse with keen interest. It didn't fit.

After finishing his speech about the quest for justice, Rick climbed into a dark Mercedes that had been waiting for him, and the throng of reporters dispersed. Jake began walking the three blocks back toward his office. The muscle-bound black man was still there, and seemed to be watching him. This definitely was not the man Shooter had encountered, nor was he the man who held the gun on Jake in the parking garage. He had seen the hand holding the gun—it was white. Who was this character? For some reason, he struck Jake as menacing and dangerous, but he wasn't sure why. His image was etched in Jake's mind as he hurried back to his office. He was just being paranoid, he told himself. He had no reason to suspect this guy of anything. He needed to put it out of his mind. He needed to focus. He could not afford to let himself get distracted.

CHAPTER 47

The next day was Friday. Judge Trainor heard several pre-trial motions regarding routine evidentiary matters, which took less than an hour. Jake had the rest of the day to prepare for the week of testimony ahead.

He felt ready. As in law school, he believed in preparing well in advance, so he could spend the final day or two relaxing and developing the right mindset, rather than cramming and escalating his stress level. He planned on spending an hour or two over the weekend fine-tuning his opening statement, and would spend the rest of the time relaxing with family and friends. As luck would have it, St. Francis, his former elementary school, was holding a reunion picnic for all alumni at the forest preserves southwest of the city on Saturday. It would be a great way to reconnect with old friends and clear his head before starting the trial. Amanda would welcome the social time; Anna would love the kids' activities that were planned; and it would be an opportunity for Johnny and Corey to celebrate their marriage with plenty of good friends from the neighborhood. They had gotten married in a private ceremony in Puerto Rico the week before and had just returned.

Jake's sister, Peggy, was planning on attending the picnic with her nine-year-old twin girls, and offered to drive. The McShanes were happy to hitch a ride, since Anna adored her older cousins and would enjoy riding with them as much as she enjoyed the picnic.

The parking lot at Carlson Woods was jam-packed when Peggy's minivan arrived shortly after noon. Jake was immediately glad they had come. He recognized numerous old friends before they had even made it out of the parking lot, and was reminded how lucky he was to have grown up in such a social, close-knit neighborhood.

The parking lot led to a large open field, surrounded on three sides by dense woods. A group of men were warming up on a makeshift softball field, preparing to begin what would be the first of many spirited ballgames throughout the day. A lively volleyball game was in progress, and several enterprising teenagers were erecting a badminton net. Swarms of kids ran everywhere.

A large crowd was gathered under a pavilion, where kegs of beer were wedged into large tubs of ice, attracting a never-ending line of thirsty picnickers. Johnny and Corey were sitting at a picnic table adjacent to the beer line, greeting the steady stream of well-wishers who stopped by. Jake felt a twinge of nervousness when he observed that Corey's former husband, Danny Flynn, was among the revelers; however, Danny seemed to be minding his own business and keeping his distance from Johnny and Corey.

Jake and Amanda worked in a game of volleyball and one of softball, but spent most of the day just strolling the area, visiting. Amanda was once again amazed at the social fabric of Jake's old neighborhood and the fact that he seemed to know virtually all of the hundreds of people in attendance. Jake, in turn, was impressed at how easily Amanda fit in and how comfortable she was in this setting even though she knew almost no one. He stayed by Amanda's side for the entire day, not because she would have been uncomfortable otherwise, but rather because it felt so good to be with her. Their time together had been far too scarce during the preceding weeks as Jake was gearing up for trial. Now, as he spent a leisurely afternoon together with his wife, under a sparkling September sky, surrounded by old friends, and not thinking even for a moment about USH, he experienced a sense of fun and joy that had been missing for a long time. Life was good again. He was relaxed.

The atmosphere was festive throughout the day, and the beer flowed freely. The flow accelerated as the afternoon turned into evening. Jake had abstained, as he always did when he was in trial-preparation mode. He couldn't afford to feel tired or sluggish. Johnny and Corey, on the other hand, found this to be the perfect occasion to celebrate their recent nuptials. They had been drinking heavily all afternoon, and as the pavilion transformed into a dance floor, they showed no sign of slowing down. Jake watched as Johnny lost his feet trying to perform an acrobatic dance move, and sprawled to the pavement. He lay there, looking up at the faces around him, laughing uncontrollably. Jake walked over and helped Johnny to his feet. "Hope you don't plan on driving home, pal," he said.

"Hell no. A man's got to know his limitations, and I know mine. There are plenty of people here that can give me a lift. How about doing your favorite cousin a favor? Drive my car home for me?"

"Only if you can guarantee it'll make it that far," Jake replied with a grin. Johnny drove a 1968 Bonneville that he kept looking in mint condition, although it required constant maintenance.

"That dreamboat will drive forever. Enjoy the ride!" Johnny tossed Jake his car keys.

Dusk was falling, and Jake and Amanda decided to call it a day. The roads in the area were dark and narrow, and not well marked, so they hoped to be well on their way before nightfall. Anna begged to ride home with her cousins and spend the night at their house, and Peggy happily agreed. Despite their best intentions to make a quick exit, Jake and Amanda found themselves stopping repeatedly on their way through the parking lot to say their good-byes. As a result, they were not able to escape before dark.

The old Bonneville looked better than it drove. The handling was stiff, and the acceleration poor, but Jake was in no hurry. He had no desire to put any strain on the tired old vehicle or to risk their safety on the dark, winding two-lane road. Several cars had left the picnic at around the same time. Jake slowed to allow them to pass safely, and two of them did. In his rearview mirror, he could see the headlights of a third vehicle approaching from behind. Again, he slowed, but this vehicle did not pass. It appeared to be a large sports utility vehicle, and was soon following much too closely for Jake's comfort. The SUV's high beam headlights reflected harshly into Jake's eyes from his rearview mirror. Jake reduced his speed, and the SUV pulled up alongside him, but did not pass. The Bonneville rode much lower than the dark SUV, so Jake was unable to see the driver. He wanted no part of this game, knowing that oncoming traffic could round a bend and be right on them in an instant.

He slowed further, trying to force the SUV to pass him, but still it did not pass. It maintained the same pace as the Bonneville, until suddenly, without warning, it veered directly toward them. Instinctively, Jake jerked the steering wheel hard to the right to avoid a collision. In the seconds that followed, Jake could see that his headlights were no longer illuminating the road, but were shining directly into the woods, which seemed to be rushing toward him at warp speed. The Bonneville pitched violently, its front tires losing traction as they sailed over the roadside drainage ditch. Jake heard the sound of crunching metal and shattering glass, and his momentum hurled him violently forward. For a brief instant he was aware of intense pain searing through him. Then all awareness ceased.

CHAPTER 48

Rick Black jogged along Lake Michigan, one of many runners, walkers, bicyclists and rollerbladers crowding the concrete path adjacent to the lake. To anyone who might see him, he was just another fitness enthusiast enjoying a perfect Sunday afternoon. They would be oblivious to the fact that he was a man on the threshold of greatness. Tomorrow, he would begin the case that would rocket him to the pinnacle of his profession, and open the door to obscene wealth. The world would be watching, and he was ready. All of his talents and experience, his drive and his ambition, his craftiness, resourcefulness and killer instinct, would coalesce and be prominently displayed for the legal profession and the rest of the world to see during this trial. It was his trial. Without him, there would be no USH lawsuit. He and he alone had developed this lawsuit into what it was. He was proud of that. He felt powerful, and the feeling was intoxicating.

Certainly a bit of luck was involved—he'd stumbled upon a case that was a surefire winner. But he was not a big believer in luck. Successful people created their own lucky breaks and knew how to capitalize on them. He was perceptive enough to see the possibilities in this case, and resourceful enough to develop it into a case with almost unthinkable financial potential. And, it was a case he could not lose. The only thing in doubt was the magnitude of the victory.

From the start, the case had developed as well or better than he could have hoped for. Everything had gone smoothly, and according to plan. Well, almost everything, and it was the "almost" that was eating at him now.

Randy Kraft was his key witness, the gateway to huge punitive damages, perhaps hundreds of millions of dollars. So much was riding on this squirrelly, little guy, yet Rick was not confident that he had the necessary level of control over this key element of his case. Fowler had not delivered—McShane was still on the case. McShane had been distracted, however, and had lost precious time. More importantly, McShane had not spent any further time with Randy, and Rick needed Randy to be calm and free from probing attorneys as the trial was commencing. Nevertheless, he was frustrated with Fowler, and surprised. Fowler was a perfectionist, and he was relentless. He prided himself on his ability to deliver results.

Another jogger fell in beside Rick as he passed Navy Pier. "I was just thinking about you," Rick said as he stared straight ahead. "I've never known you to leave a job unfinished. Last I heard, Jake McShane was still on this case. You must be slipping."

"Then your information isn't current. I suggest you tune in to the news. I can assure you, McShane will not be in court tomorrow." Fowler picked up his pace and vanished into the crowd.

CHAPTER 49

J ake struggled to open his eyes. A sensation of profound groggi-
ness overpowered him as he tried to fight his way to consciousness. Even in his semi-conscious state, he could feel pain. His
entire body ached, but there was a sharper, burning pain in his left leg,
and a deep throbbing in his head. With great effort, he willed himself
awake and looked around. It was difficult to focus, but he soon realized he was in a hospital. He had no idea what or who had brought
him there.

He felt detached from his surroundings. Everything seemed distant.
He heard noises, but his mind was not processing them. He felt the
powerful pull of sleep overtaking him again. Then he recognized a
sound—it was a voice and it sounded familiar. He felt the touch of a
hand on his head. He looked toward the voice. It was Peggy. "Jake?
Jake? Can you hear me, Jake?"

His sister's voice pulled him back from the brink of sleep. "Peggy,
where am I?" he whispered hoarsely.

"You're in the hospital, Jake. They brought you in last night. You
were unconscious. You've been in surgery all morning."

As his eyes began to focus, Jake could see that his left leg was in
a cast. "What happened?" he asked, still dazed and struggling to stay
awake.

Peggy hesitated. "You were in an accident, Jake," she replied, her voice breaking. "A car accident ... on the way home from the picnic."

Jake's memory flooded back. He remembered the SUV cutting him off. He remembered the headlights shining into the woods, and the Bonneville veering off the road. For a moment, that was all he remembered. Then he remembered that Amanda had been riding in the passenger seat next to him. He was wide awake now, a feeling of panic surging through him.

"Where's Amanda?"

Peggy looked at him, unable to speak, as tears streamed down her cheeks.

"Where's Amanda?" Jake demanded, his voice rising, as he fought through the pain to sit up straight. Peggy's shoulders began to shake with heavy, silent sobs. She breathed deeply, trying to find her voice. "Jake, I'm sorry ... I'm so sorry ..." Peggy grasped his hands and looked at him through tearful, bloodshot eyes. "Amanda's dead."

The words struck Jake with the force of a stunning physical blow. He felt faint and dizzy. His stomach turned. This couldn't be. He must've heard Peggy wrong. He desperately hoped that he had heard her wrong, as he stared at her uncomprehendingly.

"What?"

"She's dead, Jake. She died in the crash, at the scene of the accident."

He heard the words, but every fiber of his being resisted their meaning. "Are you sure?" His voice trembled as the horrific reality began to take hold.

Peggy nodded. The pain etched on her face left no room for doubt.

Jake shook his head slowly. He gasped, barely able to breathe, eyes darting around the room as if looking for a way to escape the unthinkable reality. He tried to cry out, but there was no air in his lungs. He covered his face with bandaged hands, as tears rushed forth and his entire body was wracked with uncontrollable sobs. Peggy threw her arms around her brother. They held each other tightly, desperately, crying for a long time, as they contemplated the cruel reality that had transformed his happy, orderly life into unmitigated anguish and chaos in an instant.

The days and weeks that followed were a blur. Jake's grief was all-consuming and utterly debilitating. He couldn't think. He couldn't focus. Any form of human interaction was painful. His friends, family and colleagues showered him with kindness and concern, but that only heightened his pain and sense of loss. He wanted to be left alone, to think about Amanda, to miss her, and to continue loving her. He spoke to her constantly in his thoughts, sometimes aloud, hoping that somehow she could hear him.

Spending time with Anna was the only activity that could bring him out of the depths of immobilizing grief. She needed him, and he was determined to be there for her and to help her cope with this ordeal that no seven-year-old child should have to endure. At first, Anna had been inconsolable. She had cried almost nonstop for three days, curled up into a fetal position in her bed or on the floor. He could do little but hold her during that time, as she remained largely unresponsive to everyone, including him. When she spoke, she continually asked him, "Why?" and "What will we do without Mommy?" He wished he knew how to respond to those questions, but he had no answers. He was asking himself the same questions. After those first three days, Anna faced the world bravely. Jake spent as much time as he could with her. Looking into that brave little face brought him some comfort. She resembled her mother so, and he could see Amanda living on through their daughter. However, it also was a constant reminder that Amanda was gone, and it broke his heart to know that this precious little child would grow up without her mother.

When he was with his daughter, Jake could be strong. He forced himself to set aside his grief in Anna's presence, or at least hide it, so that he could provide her with some sense of stability and security. He realized that their time together did him as much good as it did her, because she gave him a sense of purpose.

When they were not together, his loss tormented him. He spent hours by himself, sitting in his living room chair, thinking about things he and Amanda had done together, and things he wished they had done. He couldn't stop thinking about her, nor did he want to. At night, after Anna was in bed, he sat on the couch where he and Amanda had spent so many evenings. Sometimes he prayed. Sometimes he spoke to her. Mostly he just stared into the darkness, feeling numb.

He rarely ventured outside of his house. Getting around on crutches was difficult, and gave him an excuse to stay at home and avoid human contact. Sometimes the physical pain distracted him from the anguish he felt in his soul. More often, however, it served as a brutal reminder of the accident and of his loss.

Anna had returned to school two weeks after Amanda's funeral. Jake thought that returning to her routine quickly might bring a sense of normality to Anna's life and that keeping her occupied would prevent her from dwelling on her loss.

He believed that returning to his own routine might provide the same benefit, but he just wasn't ready. He had taken a leave of absence from the firm. He had told his bosses that he needed some time, but he didn't know whether he would need a few weeks or a few months, or whether he would return at all. The firm had been very supportive, and assured him he could take as much time as he needed.

One evening, about six weeks after the accident, Jake sat in the dark in his living room chair, staring out the window. He heard the sound of little footsteps approaching from Anna's bedroom. "What are you doing, Daddy?" Anna had gone to bed an hour earlier, but she looked wide-awake.

"Hi sweetheart. Can't sleep?"

She shook her head and climbed onto his lap. He put both arms around her and held her tightly.

"What are you doing?" she asked again.

"I was just sitting here thinking."

"I've been thinking too. That's why I can't sleep."

"What were you thinking about, little girl?"

"I was just feeling sad, Daddy."

"Because you miss Mommy?"

She nodded her head and looked up at him. "Yes, that makes me sad. But mostly I feel bad because you seem so sad all the time."

Pain and guilt seized him. He thought he'd been acting positive and normal around his daughter, yet her little seven-year-old mind could see right through him. He wished he could think of the right thing to say, but words eluded him. "I'm sorry," was all he could manage, fighting to keep the tears at bay.

"Daddy, it really helped me when I went back to school. I still miss Mommy, but it makes things seem normal again. Maybe you should go back to work. I think it will help you feel better."

Jake looked at his daughter, and imagined a seven-year-old Amanda. She would have said the same thing. He smiled, feeling a surge of gratitude that he still had such a precious soul in his life. "Sometimes I can't believe how smart you are, Anna McShane. That's probably good advice. It's been over a month now. Do you want me to go back to work?"

Anna nodded. "I want you to be happy, Daddy. I think it'll help."

He kissed her on the forehead. "You are such a special little girl, and I love you more than you'll ever know. Thanks for the advice, kiddo." He held her and they sat together in silence for a long time. She snuggled into his chest and closed her eyes. "Let's go to bed," he whispered after awhile. She didn't hear him. She was already fast asleep, and he carried her to her room.

CHAPTER 50

Jake dropped Anna off at school in the morning and then drove into the office. It had taken the words of a seven-year-old child to motivate him, but it felt right.

He spent most of the morning greeting colleagues who stopped by to welcome him back. He was touched as they extended their condolences again and inquired about his well-being, but it made for a difficult morning. Those well-meaning comments drew his attention back to his loss. By late morning, however, he was able to dive into the files on his desk with a sense of eagerness and purpose.

Upon hearing that Jake had returned, Demetrius Giannakis stopped by to pay him a visit. Jake felt honored, since the managing partner rarely lowered himself to visiting the office of an associate attorney. He conducted business in his own office and expected the associates to come to him when summoned. Demetrius greeted Jake warmly, and offered to brief him on the USH case whenever Jake was ready. Jake asked to be updated immediately, and Demetrius complied.

The USH trial had been postponed for sixty days, partly to provide Jake's firm adequate time to get another attorney up to speed, and partly to allow the publicity to subside. Jake's accident had attracted tremendous media attention, and speculation regarding foul play was rampant. The police had interviewed Jake twice, but he was unable to provide any useful information. He was certain that someone driving a large, dark SUV had deliberately run him off the road, but he had not seen the driver, and could not even guess as to the make and model of the vehicle.

The police published a sketch of the big white-haired man based on Shooter's description, and described him as a person wanted for questioning in connection with the accident. The introduction of this sinister looking mystery man to the story fanned the flames of the media frenzy, but no helpful leads emerged.

After completing his update, Demetrius said, "Jake, I'd love to get you back involved in the case. No one is as close to it as you are, and your continued involvement would be invaluable—in whatever role you'd like to play. Our plan is to have Jim Anderson and Nancy Fox try the case, and it would be a huge benefit if you could help them prepare."

"I'm at their disposal," Jake replied. "I really want to get back to work and I'd love to see this case through."

"Any chance you'd like to jump back into the saddle and take the lead?"

Jake looked down and spoke quietly. "I don't know, Demetrius. To be perfectly honest, I don't know if I'd be up to it. Let me think about it."

"I understand, and I will certainly respect your decision. But the trial's just two weeks away, so you better decide quickly."

Jake spent the next two days with the lawyers who had been assigned to fill in for him. Jim Anderson and Nancy Fox were two of the firm's finest litigators, but trying to master such a complicated case in a few short weeks was a hopelessly impossible task. While they might be able to develop a working knowledge of the most basic elements of the case, there was simply no way they could be expected to attain the level of knowledge Jake had amassed by living with this case on a daily basis for the past twenty-eight months.

Jake was besieged by guilt and conflict. He was clearly in the best position to try this case. Although he'd been away from it for six weeks now, he knew every detail and nuance, yet that wasn't enough.

He would need to bring the highest degree of focus and intensity, and he was not sure that he was ready for that. Even more concerning, he was a single parent now. Anna needed him. He could not risk his safety or hers. Part of him wanted to believe that handling this trial would not put him in any real danger, but there had been too many unnerving coincidences. What would Amanda advise? He asked himself that question repeatedly, and desperately groped for the answer. He just couldn't find it.

CHAPTER 51

Kenny Oliver put down his Bible and picked up the newspaper. There was another article about the upcoming USH trial. He had been following the case closely because he knew both attorneys. He knew Rick Black through the Quinn case, and he had known Jake McShane since childhood. His conscience troubled him whenever he thought about the Quinn case. He knew what he should do, but he felt ashamed and afraid. He looked at his Bible again. Maybe he could never make it right, but he should do what he could, before it was too late.

Thirty minutes later, he rang the doorbell. Jake McShane answered and seemed startled by his visitor. Kenny looked nervous and shuffled his feet. "Hi Jake. I know you probably don't want to see me, but can we talk for a minute?"

Jake could not fathom what might bring Kenny Oliver to his doorstep, but his anger over their last encounter outweighed any curiosity. "This isn't a good time, Kenny. I'm putting my daughter to bed."

"Okay, sorry to bother you, Jake. But will you call me sometime soon? I want to talk with you about something important."

"Sure, Kenny. I'll call you sometime." He began closing the door.

"It's about Rick Black."

Jake halted and then opened the door. "Okay, Kenny, come on in."

Jake ushered Kenny to his kitchen table and asked Anna to continue reading without him. Under the bright kitchen light, Jake could see that Kenny looked pale and emaciated. "Are you okay, Kenny?"

"Actually, no, I'm not. I'm dying, Jake. I've got a brain tumor. It's inoperable."

"Jeez, Kenny, I'm really sorry."

"It's okay. I'm at peace with it." He smiled sadly. "Funny, isn't it? It takes dying to be born again. But, that's okay. I found God while there was still time. And I want to get right with Him before my time comes. That's why I'm here."

"I'm not sure I understand, Kenny."

"That lawyer you're up against—Rick Black—he's bad news, Jake. He may be a good lawyer, but he's not a good person."

"What are you talking about?"

"The Quinn case—it was a complete scam. Mickey didn't do nothing wrong. Nothing at all. Me and Larry made all that shit up. Every bit of it. And the lawyer encouraged it."

"Rick Black told you to lie?"

"Yeah—well, not exactly. He was careful not to come right out and tell us to lie, but he made it real clear what he wanted us to do."

"What do you mean?"

"Here's what happened," Kenny explained. "Larry was pissed that he got fired. He wanted revenge. He met Rick at a bar one night and talked with him about filing a lawsuit. Rick told Larry what kind of cases could destroy a guy's reputation and make a jury really mad. Larry made up a story right along the lines Rick described, and then Rick coached him on how to tell it. He even made up a lot of the details for Larry—made them up out of thin air when he didn't like Larry's story."

"How did you get involved?"

"Larry comes to me and says he has a great case if he can get a jury to believe him, but all he has is his word against Mickey's. He says if another witness told a story about what a bad guy Mickey is, the jury would really turn on him and we could make big bucks. I told him I didn't have any dirt on Mickey. He said it didn't matter, we could just make it up. Said his lawyer had given him a few ideas. So we talked about it. At first, it was just me and Larry, and I thought Larry was just being Larry—you know, full of shit. But then I met with Rick and he got me believing I could make some real cash. So I took a few things from some of the old ladies on the delivery route and put them in Mickey's office. Then I made that video. You know the rest."

"Why would you do that, Kenny?" Jake demanded, his voice rising. "Didn't you think about Mickey? Didn't you think about how wrong that was and how much harm it might cause?"

"I should have, but I didn't. I just blocked it out of my mind when Larry and the lawyer talked about how much money I could make. I made over two hundred grand, Jake. Do you know how many years I'd have to work to make that kind of dough? So I let myself get talked into it. I knew it was wrong, but I just blocked that out of my mind— until afterwards. The more time passed, the worse I felt about it. I know I should've come forward sooner, but I was afraid. Rick told me that people go to jail for fraud, and I was scared. I didn't want to go to jail. Then I got cancer, and everything changed. I found the Lord, and I knew I had to come clean about what I did. Then I heard about your accident, Jake, and I knew this guy would do anything to win his case. I couldn't stand by and do nothing when he could be involved in something like that. I had to tell you what I knew. I don't know what you want to do with this information, but I'll help in any way I can."

"I may want you to testify in court, Kenny. Would you be willing to do that?"

"Absolutely."

Jake tapped his fingers on the kitchen table as he processed this information. He had always suspected that the Quinn case was a set-up, but it was still hard to believe that an attorney, particularly one of Rick's caliber, could orchestrate such an outrageous fraud. Kenny had said that Rick never actually told him to lie. That fit. But for either Rick or Larry to pay a witness to provide false testimony seemed far too brazen and reckless, even for Rick. An attorney caught doing that would unquestionably be disbarred.

"Kenny, there's one thing I still don't understand. How did you get paid? A lawyer can't just pay you for testifying."

"Rick didn't pay me. Mickey did."

"What? I don't get it."

"Rick set it all up. After the verdict came in, Mickey appealed. Shortly before that, Rick had sent Mickey a draft of a lawsuit he said he was going to file, as my lawyer. The lawsuit said that even though I quit, it was the same as being fired—constructive discharge, Rick called it. In other words, I had no choice but to quit because of the bad things going on at the store. Anyway, Rick didn't actually file the lawsuit because then it would be a public record and he wanted to keep this quiet. He got Mickey to settle both Larry's lawsuit and my claim for a total that was less than the jury verdict. So Mickey saved a little money and Larry and I got paid separately—by Mickey. Rick said everything would be squeaky clean that way."

The outrage Jake had felt over the Quinn trial had lain dormant within him for a long time. It boiled up anew. This was personal now. One way or another, Rick Black would be held accountable. He would see to that.

CHAPTER 52

Two days later, Jake entered Judge Trainor's courtroom. He still had not decided whether to take an active role in trying the case. He was strongly inclined not to, but today's business was a simple evidentiary motion, and he was in the best position to handle it. The discovery deadline had long since passed, and witness lists had been finalized, but Jake was requesting permission to add one new witness.

Rick bustled into the courtroom two minutes before the hearing was to commence. He was startled to find Jake there.

"Jake, it's great to see you," he said warmly, extending his hand. "I'm so sorry about Amanda." He sounded as if he meant it.

Jake took Rick's hand and shook it. "Thanks, Rick," he replied coolly. He took a step toward Rick, still gripping his hand firmly. They were eyeball to eyeball, and Jake stared hard at Rick for several seconds without speaking. He tightened his grip on Rick's hand and said in a low voice, "I have to ask you something, Rick. Did you have anything to do with the accident or the other threats I've received?"

Jake felt Rick recoil, but maintained a tight grip on Rick's hand. For the briefest instant, Jake sensed a flash of fear in Rick's eyes. Rick glanced down for a split second, then returned Jake's gaze.

"I can understand why you'd feel compelled to ask that, Jake, given the media coverage, and all the innuendoes from the reporters. I assure you, I would never have any part in something like that. I was as shocked as anybody—stunned. Again, you have my deepest sympathies."

Jake released Rick's hand. "I had to ask," he said as he turned and walked over to the counsel table.

Judge Trainor entered the courtroom. He, too, seemed surprised to see Jake. "Welcome back, Mr. McShane. Please accept my deepest sympathies on your loss," he said in a kindly tone.

"Thank you, Your Honor."

Judge Trainor continued, "I understand you're here to request permission to supplement your witness list. Obviously, it's very late in the game. Is there some compelling reason why I'm just now hearing of this?"

"Yes, Your Honor. This witness came forward just two days ago. He has information that I believe may be highly relevant."

The judge peered at Jake over the rims of his spectacles. "Who is he, and what is the nature of this information?"

"His name is Kenny Oliver, Your Honor." Rick was clearly surprised and seemed about to blurt out something, but thought better of it. Jake continued. "The nature of his testimony is as follows: Mr. Oliver was a witness in a previous trial handled by Mr. Black. Mr. Black represented the plaintiff in that case. This witness will testify that Mr. Black encouraged both him and the plaintiff to provide false testimony and fabricate evidence. He will—"

"This is outrageous, Your Honor, and entirely inappropriate." Rick shot Jake a hostile glance and continued, in a voice filled with contempt. "This is an obvious attempt by Mr. McShane to divert attention from the real issues in this case. USH has no defense, so they are trying to turn the jury against the plaintiffs by making scurrilous allegations against me personally, which are both unfounded and defamatory. There is no truth whatsoever to such allegations, and in any event, that trial hasn't the remotest degree of relevance to this case. This is nothing more than an underhanded ploy. The defense should be sanctioned for employing such unprofessional and mean-spirited tactics."

"Those are serious allegations, Mr. McShane," said the judge. "However, I'm inclined to agree with Mr. Black. He's not on trial here. The State Bar would be the appropriate forum for dealing with such matters. What relevance does that testimony have to the USH case?"

"It has significant relevance, Your Honor. This case will turn largely on the credibility of Mr. Black's witnesses. If there is evidence that he has persuaded witnesses in other cases to be untruthful, the jury is entitled to hear that evidence as they weigh the credibility of his witnesses in this case."

"Do you have any evidence that witnesses in this case are being encouraged to provide false testimony?" the judge asked.

"No, Your Honor, but if there is a past history of such behavior, we can't rule it out here. The jury can decide how much weight to give this testimony."

Rick was seething. "Your Honor, any relevance at all is sheer conjecture. Allowing the jury to hear that testimony would be highly prejudicial."

"I agree," said Judge Trainor. "Any relevance is remote at best, given that there is no evidence of similar conduct in this case. And it would be highly prejudicial. Your motion to call Mr. Oliver as a witness is denied, Mr. McShane." The judge left the courtroom, a troubled look on his face.

"That was a cheap shot, pal!" Rick called out angrily over his shoulder as he stormed out of the courtroom.

CHAPTER 53

Present Day
Sunday Afternoon—One Week Before
The USH Trial
Suburban Chicago

Jake stood in the middle of the street, outside the cemetery, watching the Cadillac careen around a corner and vanish from view. His impulse was to race back to his own car and give chase, but he realized that would be futile. The guy would be long gone. Besides, he had come to the cemetery for a reason, and his business was still unfinished.

Horns blared at him as cars whizzed by in both directions. When traffic cleared, he hustled off the median strip and back toward the cemetery as fast as he could manage on his crutches. Once inside the cemetery gate, he stopped to catch his breath. His gaze fell upon a nearby granite bench and he sat down to collect his thoughts and wait for his heart to stop pounding.

After a few minutes, he rose and moved slowly back toward Amanda's grave. When he had been standing there just minutes before, he had felt paralyzed by an unabating grief. That grief had not left him, but the paralysis seemed to be giving way to a sense of urgency and resolve, propelling him onward. He vowed that he would not let himself be intimidated or distracted by the thug in the white Cadillac, whoever he was. He forced himself to focus on what had brought him to this place: an overwhelming desire to be near Amanda, and a desperate hope that being there would help him find the answer that thus far had been beyond his grasp.

"I miss you, sweetheart," he said softly, looking down at the grave, not knowing or caring whether anyone saw him talking to himself. "I miss you so much." His voice was shaky, but he was dry-eyed now, trying to speak clearly and with a sense of purpose. "I wish I had done more to show you and tell you how much you meant to me—how much you still mean to me. I've loved you with my whole heart from the moment we met and I will never stop loving you—never. I will try my best to do what you would want me to do, and be what you'd want me to be. I'm really trying, but it's so hard. I hope you can hear me … I wish you could guide me … help me find my way."

Jake looked up and took several deep breaths, trying to regain his composure. He tried to visualize Amanda standing there beside him, and imagine what she would say if he spoke with her about his present situation. They had known each other so well that he was good at anticipating her thinking on most issues. Amanda would encourage him to go back to work and get on with his life, he was certain of that. She wouldn't even have to ask him to be a good father to Anna, because she would know that he would. But what about the trial? What would her guidance be? It was only one week away, and he was torn by indecision. Part of him desperately wanted to try this case, but he wasn't sure he had the necessary fortitude. He had been unable to feel passion or intensity for anything since the accident. In fact, he had barely been able to function at all. But then Kenny Oliver had shown up on his doorstep, and kindled a burning desire to stop Rick Black—a desire to beat him, embarrass him and expose him for what he was: a dishonest, conniving, unscrupulous pirate. But the analysis didn't stop there. He had to think of Anna. He couldn't put himself or her in danger. As a result, conflict raged within him, and it steadily intensified as the trial drew nearer. If he only knew what Amanda's advice would be, his decision would be clear.

As he struggled with that question, he vividly remembered their discussions about the flaws and vulnerabilities of the American legal system. Amanda was passionate in her belief that the system could work if the good guys made the integrity of the system their personal responsibility and challenged the abuses and the abusers whenever and wherever they manifested themselves. It would take courage and conviction, she had said, but those who had the opportunity to stand up for what is right had a responsibility to do so when confronted with unethical behavior. Attorneys who lacked the courage and conviction to do that were part of the problem.

As Jake thought about those conversations with Amanda, he could almost hear her speaking to him. A sudden and unmistakable sense of clarity settled over him. He knew what she would say about the trial, beyond any doubt. She would not only say that he had her permission to try the case, she would say that he had a duty to do so—a duty to his client, to his profession and to himself. And she would be right. He needed to try this case.

The complicating factor was that he also needed to think about his daughter. Her safety was paramount, and as a single parent, he had a responsibility to be mindful of his own safety to a much greater degree than he had before. The Chief of Police himself promised around-the-clock protection for both Jake and Anna. That would be a nuisance, but the trial would not last more than two weeks. Jake decided to have another conversation with Chief Tomczak to discuss security measures in greater detail. If he felt confident in the Police Department's ability to protect him and his daughter, he would try the case. He thought about Rick Black, and the revelations provided by Kenny Oliver. He thought about Amanda, and the advice she would have given. His fears about lacking the intensity and fortitude for the trial were melting away. He felt excited about moving past the indecision and leaping back into trial preparation mode.

He bent over and put his hand on the wet grave marker. "Thank you, sweetheart," he said. "Thank you for sharing your life with me and for always being there for me. I'll do my best to make you proud." He stood up and blinked away the tears, then headed back toward his car. He drove through the cemetery's front gate and stared at the spot where the Cadillac had been parked. His newly found feeling of resolve was tempered by his vision of the sinister looking character behind the wheel of that Cadillac. He knew that face from somewhere, and his inability to place it gnawed at him. "Who are you, you son of a bitch?" he muttered to himself. "Who the hell are you?"

CHAPTER 54

The case of Barnes, et al. versus United States Health Corporation commenced promptly at 9 a.m. on Monday, November 10th, in the Federal District Court for the Northern District of Illinois, before the Honorable Justice Peter Trainor. Opening arguments were presented by Richard T. Black for the plaintiffs, and Jacob J. McShane for the defendant.

Rick went first. He informed the jury that they were about to hear a tale of unbridled corporate greed, on a grand scale. According to Rick, there was nothing innocent about USH's conduct in this case. For years, it had been aware of significant billing problems, and took no remedial action. It knowingly allowed inflated invoices to be generated and transmitted to its customers, counting on the fact that few customers would raise issues due to the fact that the invoices were hopelessly confusing. Even worse, its senior management team made a conscious and deliberate decision to avoid addressing these issues, so that the company could continue to enjoy the ill-gotten gains generated by its fraudulent and deceitful billing practices. According to Mr. Black, there was a carefully orchestrated plan to continue generating excessive invoices for as long as the company could get away with it. This was conduct worthy of the jury's contempt and deserving of the most severe punishment.

When it was his turn, Jake felt ready. He was approaching this case with a confidence borne out of complete mastery of the facts and issues. His opening argument was simple. He candidly acknowledged to the jury within the first sixty seconds that USH had made mistakes that resulted in overcharges to many of its patients. Establishing credibility with the jury was critical, so he did not try to sugarcoat the problems. The thrust of Jake's message was that, although serious billing problems existed, there was no intentional wrongdoing. To the contrary, when these problems were brought to management's attention, management devised a plan for addressing them. That plan included making voluntary restitution to any clients who had been inadvertently overcharged. Jake also emphasized that the company had implemented a widely publicized program pursuant to which any customer having doubts or questions about an invoice could submit the invoice to an independent auditing firm, and if an overcharge was confirmed, the patient would receive a full refund, plus accrued interest. Therefore, Jake pointed out, a fair and effective mechanism was already in place to make all affected customers whole. Under those circumstances, Jake argued, there was no basis for awarding any punitive damages.

By the conclusion of the opening arguments, the issues had been clearly framed, and it was evident that the case would turn on how the jury interpreted the company's reaction to its billing problems. The jury would be asked to decide whether USH was slow and inept, but well meaning, or whether it was out to deliberately defraud its patients for as long as it could get away with it. The answer to that question would determine whether punitive damages were awarded. If they were, the case could cost USH upwards of $100 million, perhaps several times that.

To the extent that Jake harbored any doubts about whether he had the emotional fortitude and intensity level to try this case, those doubts vanished the moment the trial began. He felt sharp and ready to focus on this trial from start to finish, having dealt with all distractions in the days leading up to it. He had discussed safety issues at length with Chief Tomczak, and gotten comfortable with the Police

Chief's assurances that he and Anna would be adequately protected. Anna would be staying at Peggy's house, with two uniformed officers hovering nearby, around the clock, and escorting her everywhere she went. Jake would likewise have constant police protection until the trial was concluded. USH assisted by having its Corporate Security Department install state-of-the-art alarm systems and video surveillance equipment at both Jake's home and Peggy's. The deployment of these resources, coupled with the fact that there had been no further threats or incidents, left Jake feeling sufficiently comfortable to concentrate on the trial.

The trial was expected to last two weeks. The entire first week was consumed by Rick's presentation of the plaintiffs' case. He began with a parade of witnesses who testified that they had been patients of USH and had been overcharged. Each of the six plaintiffs named in the original complaint testified about the facts of their particular case, and three additional witnesses told similar stories. The jury heard about charges for procedures that were never performed and charges for supplies that were never provided. They heard about double billing. They heard about charges that were grossly in excess of the hospital's own published billing rates. They heard about charges for physicians and technicians that had no contact or involvement with the patient. And they heard about the circumcision fees charged to the parents of the baby girl. Throughout this testimony, Rick repeatedly elicited comments from the witnesses about what they perceived as outrageously high charges and incomprehensible invoices.

This testimony began early Monday afternoon and lasted through the end of the day on Tuesday. It was long and tedious, but a very effective way of educating the jury about the magnitude and nature of the billing problems at USH. They also saw flesh and blood victims of those problems. By the time Rick had finished with those witnesses, he had done a masterful job of demonstrating to the jury that the mistakes were both rampant and egregious.

On the third day of the trial, Rick called several present and former USH financial executives, including its Chief Operating Officer as well as its Vice President of Corporate Development, who had over-seen the company's expansion program. Through their testimony, with the aid of various charts and graphs, the jury learned about the rapid growth of USH over the past seven years. They were informed that the company's highest priority during that time period had been growth through acquisition. They were informed that the annual revenues had grown 400% over that time, its annual profits had increased by over 500%, and the stock price had soared. Both the COO and the Vice President of Corporate Development grudgingly acknowledged that executive bonuses were tied closely to revenue growth and stock price, and that they personally had profited handsomely from the company's achievements in those areas.

They were also forced to admit that integration of the back-office functions of the newly acquired businesses, such as billing systems, was not given the same level of attention that revenue growth and acquisitions had enjoyed. Over and over, the jury heard Mr. Black mention that the company's annual revenues were currently over $10 billion and its profits nearly $3 billion. The jury also heard him ask repeatedly what it would cost to promptly and thoroughly address the problems with the company's billing systems. They never heard a straight answer.

After that, Rick got to the heart of his case. He produced an array of present and former employees who had knowledge of the company's billing systems, and continually pressed them about when the company became aware of the problems. The totality of that testimony strongly indicated that the company had knowledge of significant problems for two full years before it implemented any remedial measures. Although several witnesses referred to plans developed in meetings that were convened to deal with these issues, they each acknowledged that no such plans were actually implemented before the lawsuit was filed. While none of those witnesses provided any testimony to suggest any deliberate misconduct, their collective testimony painted a picture of a company that had knowledge of serious problems, yet clearly neglected to deal with those problems, to the detriment of the company's patients.

When testimony concluded late on Friday, plaintiffs' counsel had only one remaining witness—Randy Kraft. Jake surmised that Rick was saving his most damaging witness until last, in the hope of leaving a powerful impression on the jury when he concluded his case.

Jake had his weekend completely mapped out before he left the courthouse Friday afternoon. He planned on relaxing that evening and catching up with Anna. He would meet Peggy and the girls at her house at six o'clock for pizza and board games. Saturday, he would spend the entire day preparing for next week and then take Anna to see a movie after dinner. Sunday, he would spend time preparing Randy Kraft and several other witnesses for their testimony.

Jake's police escorts accompanied him to Peggy's house, where he observed another patrol car parked conspicuously in her driveway. He was comforted by their presence, but still felt himself resenting the intrusion on his privacy. However, the fact that he had gotten through the entire first week of the trial without incident made it easier to forget about them and focus on his daughter.

After spending Friday evening with Anna and his nieces, Jake returned home feeling more relaxed and lighthearted than he had in some time. Playing board games and working on jigsaw puzzles with a seven-year-old child seemed more important and rewarding than anything about the high-stakes trial that had been consuming him. It brought him much needed perspective.

He went to bed early, exhausted from the grueling demands of the trial, and was immediately asleep. In the middle of the night, he awoke with a start and sat bolt upright in bed. He had been dreaming of the muscular black man in the pimped-out white Cadillac. Recognition sprang into his mind and jarred him into consciousness. He knew the face. He had not seen it in nearly five years, and had seen it only twice before it had recently resurfaced, but he knew it. It was Shooter's brother, Jerome. No longer a skinny teenager, he had grown into a massive young man, but there was no mistaking the face.

This revelation was no source of comfort. Jake's memories of Jerome were unsettling. Their first encounter was on the basketball court at St. Simon's. Anger and hostility had spewed forth from the wild kid, and Jake vividly recalled Jerome's efforts to persuade his cohorts to thrash him and Rick. Only Shooter's influence had been able to prevent that. Their second meeting was in a prison cell. Again, the kid had seemed off-balance and irrational, not to mention belligerent and dangerous.

Why in the world would this guy be following him? It made no sense. What possible connection could he have with the USH case? Jake racked his brain and could think of none. What other reason might he have for following him? He got out of bed and walked to his window. The squad car was parked outside. Its occupants were awake, as evidenced by the orange glow of their cigarettes and the smoke rising out of the partially open window. He returned to bed and slept fitfully until dawn.

Shortly after daylight, he was driven into the office by the two burly policemen who had spent the night parked in front of his house. He continued to think about Jerome as the police cruiser sped through the deserted streets toward downtown. He just couldn't make sense of it. He would call Shooter when he had time. He had heard that Shooter was recovering from his gunshot wound and had been meaning to call him anyway. But that would have to wait. He was in the middle of the biggest trial of his life, and couldn't afford any distractions. He forced himself to put Jerome out of his mind, and renewed his focus on the trial.

After a full day of intense preparation at his office, Jake once again was escorted to Peggy's house. He said hello to Peggy and the twins, and then climbed back into the waiting patrol car with Anna. They had dinner at the crowded food court in the mall, and watched an animated movie at the mall's multiplex theater, a bodyguard at their sides at all times. After that, they were driven back to Peggy's house where he, Anna, Peggy and the twins engaged in a spirited game of charades before bed. Thunder rumbled in the distance as Jake tucked Anna in and kissed her goodnight.

The thunder and lightning grew closer as the police escort drove Jake home. The heavens opened just as the squad car reached his block. He waved through the driving rain to Officers Mraz and Jordan, the patrolmen sitting in the squad car parked in front of his house. From that vantage point, the car's occupants could see both the front entrance as well as the side entrance adjacent to the driveway. Because of the downpour, Jake's driver turned into the driveway and pulled up to within a few feet of the side entrance. Jake exited the vehicle as quickly as he could, but his movement was slow and awkward due to his cast and crutches. He was soaked by the time he arrived inside and shut the door behind him.

Jake hobbled into his kitchen and began flipping through the mail that had piled up on his kitchen counter. A crash of thunder shook the house and lightning illuminated the sky. Seconds later, the lights went out and Jake stood still for a few moments, hoping the lights would return quickly. They did not. He looked toward the luminescent clock on his microwave oven. It was off. The quiet hum from the refrigerator had stopped as well. Apparently, he had lost all electricity.

Jake looked out his kitchen window at the house next door. It was dark, too. From where he stood, he could see the houses across the street through his front window—also dark. It appeared that the storm must have knocked out power for the entire block.

Back at USH headquarters in downtown Chicago, the elderly gentleman monitoring the company's security system noticed that he'd stopped receiving a signal from the alarm system that had been installed at the McShane home. He checked the video monitor linked to that residence. The screen was dark. This was not normal. He followed the instructions precisely and dialed the phone number taped to the video monitor. Within a minute, he was patched through to the squad car in front of the McShane house.

"My connection just shut down. Everything okay there?" the elderly gentleman asked.

"Nothing to worry about," replied the officer. "Just a power failure. The whole block is dark."

"That's strange. We have a battery-powered backup system on our monitors. They should still work even when there's been a power failure."

"I wouldn't worry about it, sir," replied the officer. "I just saw Mr. McShane enter the house ten minutes ago. He's fine. We just had a huge lightning strike—that must be what caused the power outage. The surge probably blew out your security system, backup and all. But don't worry; we've got this place covered. I can see both entrances to the house from where I'm sitting."

Jake moved slowly. Navigating in the dark on crutches, with a wet floor, was treacherous. He made his way to the back door where the security system had been mounted. The pale green lights that were always glowing were now dark. The red power light beneath the surveillance camera was dark as well.

"Damn!" he muttered under his breath, a feeling of uneasiness growing within him. He needed to alert the security guys at USH, and thought he'd better let the police know as well. He moved back toward the kitchen, faster now, and picked up the telephone. It was dead. Thank goodness he had a cell phone. He reached up on top of the refrigerator and grabbed the small flashlight he kept there. He shone it on the kitchen counter, where he had left his cell phone in its battery charger when he'd gone out that afternoon. The charger was empty.

Jake could feel himself breaking into a cold sweat. He knew the police were right outside, and started to make his way toward the front of the house so he could signal them with his flashlight.

Another deafening crash shook the house. As he reached the front window, he saw the squad car pulling away.

"Son of a bitch!" he muttered and tried shining his flashlight at the departing vehicle, to no avail. It was gone.

"Don't waste your time, Mr. McShane. They're not looking in this direction."

He spun quickly and saw a dark silhouette facing him from across the room. The voice continued. "It's called a diversionary tactic. I'd wager that your policemen friends are attending to the car that just exploded up the street." Jake recognized the voice that was at once unnaturally calm and dripping with menace. He had heard it before. The man took a few steps toward him and stopped. As lightning illuminated the room, Jake noticed his snow white hair. "You should have done what I asked last time we met," the intruder continued in a soft Southern drawl. "Unfortunately, you did not, and now we have a serious problem. Move away from the window, please."

Jake stood, frozen where he was, unable to move or speak. His mind raced through his options. He couldn't flee; his cast made that impossible. Fighting seemed like a bad idea. Even if he were healthy, Jake doubted that he would be a match for the intruder. The man outweighed him by thirty or forty pounds, and he looked just plain dangerous. Besides, he might have a weapon. Jake couldn't tell in the darkness. He had to stall until the police returned.

"Who are you? What do you want?" Jake demanded. His voice sounded shaky, and he knew it.

The man walked toward Jake and stopped directly in front of him, staring with cold, unblinking eyes. "I'm the guy who turned out the lights. I'm the one who arranged the little diversion down the street." Lightning flashed again and the big man walked around Jake to the window and closed the curtains.

"You and I are going for a drive, before your friends in blue return. Back door! Move!" He raised a gun, pointed it at Jake and gestured toward the back of the house.

Jake left his crutches on the floor and began hobbling across the living room, moving slowly and limping badly. He had to drag this out as long as he could. Halfway across the room, he stopped and turned back toward the window. "I need my crutches," he said.

"Keep moving—back door—now!" The big man walked briskly across the room, picked up the crutches and shoved them at Jake.

Jake felt a full-fledged panic gripping him as he moved toward the door. There had to be something he could do, but he couldn't think. His mind was frozen with fear. He made it to the back door and looked toward the street as he stepped outside—no sign of the police car. A feeling of helplessness and despair set in, as he felt the gun between his shoulder blades. Then he thought about his daughter, and in an instant, those feelings turned to anger and defiance as a survival instinct took hold. His mind reached a high state of alert. He had no intention of getting into a car with this guy. As he stepped off his doorstep onto the driveway, Jake tumbled hard to the pavement, doing his best to make it look accidental, while buying a few more precious seconds. He kept his face flush against the pavement, trying to look stunned. He saw the big man's boots near his head and felt a powerful hand grab his arm and jerk him upwards.

Then the arm let go, and Jake dropped to the pavement, the side of his skull thudding against the concrete. The next few seconds were a blur of sound and motion. Thunder crashed again and the rain hammered down on him. He sensed a body moving over him at great speed. He heard the impact of flesh meeting flesh, and two loud simultaneous grunts, uttered by different voices. He heard the sound of splintering wood and looked up to see two massive bodies crashing into his neighbor's fence. Jake grabbed one crutch and stumbled to his feet. He watched the two men wrestling ferociously in the mud along the fence line. They struggled to their feet, fists flying. Jake could see that the white-haired man's assailant was a huge, muscular, black man, but he couldn't see his face in the rainy darkness. The black man appeared to be getting the better of the battle, until his feet went out from under him in the mud. He landed on his back and the white-haired man was on his chest in an instant. Jake saw the glimmer of a knife as the white-haired man drew his arm back. Jake swung his crutch with all his strength and watched it smash into the white-haired man's face. The man screamed and the knife flew from his grasp. The black man heaved the white-haired man off his chest and was on his feet in an instant, pummeling his stunned adversary. Jake saw the white-haired man go limp and drop in a heap as a solid blow crashed into his temple. The black man stared down at him, breathing hard, and shoved the limp body with his foot, confirming that he was indeed incapacitated.

The black man was hunched over, hands on his knees, trying to catch his breath. "Thanks, man," he gasped, still staring at his fallen foe. Then he straightened up and looked at Jake.

Jake started, fear and uncertainty flooding back. "Jerome. What are you doing here? What's going on?"

"Shooter sent me. He asked me to keep an eye on you," Jerome explained, panting as he spoke. "This sucker's been following you around. I don't know who he is, but I knew he was trouble."

The squad car pulled into view at the end of the driveway. Jake waved both arms and shouted, "Over here!"

A spotlight illuminated the driveway. Upon seeing Jake outdoors with a large black man dressed like a gangbanger and a motionless body lying prone on the pavement, the officers jumped out of their vehicle and dashed toward them.

"What's going on here?" shouted Officer Mraz, panic etched across his face as he looked from Jake to Jerome, to the white-haired man lying unconscious before him. The thunder was growing distant again, and the rain had subsided.

"Where the hell were you?" Jake shouted back at him. "I was nearly abducted by this bastard!" He motioned at the man on the ground, who had started to stir.

"A car exploded right down the street. We went to investigate. I called it in right away, and we hurried back here as soon as backup arrived. We didn't plan on being gone for more than a few minutes. I'm really sorry."

"Forget about it, I'm okay," Jake muttered. He noticed that his head was bleeding where he had hit the driveway, and that he was shaking all over. He hurriedly explained to the officers what had happened. The white-haired man sat up, a glazed look in his eyes.

"That's the guy from the picture," said Officer Jordan, referring to the sketch that had been drawn from Shooter's description and circulated following the threat made against Jake in the parking garage.

"Yeah, that's him alright," Jerome nodded, blood dripping from his nose and mouth.

"Cuff him, Jordan," Mraz instructed his younger partner. "I'll call another car to take this guy in." He turned and walked toward the car.

"Get up," Jordan ordered the white-haired man, who was still in a sitting position, looking dazed.

"Help me up," the man replied in a groggy voice, holding out his right arm.

Jordan extended a hand and the white-haired man took it. As their hands clasped, the white-haired man sprang to his feet, pulling Jordan toward him with his right arm and grabbing Jordan's firearm with his left, while delivering a vicious head-butt to the bridge of Jordan's nose. Jordan howled with pain, and Officer Mraz came running toward them, reaching for his weapon. The white-haired man pointed his gun directly at Mraz's forehead.

"Freeze!" he shouted.

Mraz complied.

"Drop your weapon."

Mraz hesitated for just a moment, then did as instructed.

"Kick it over here."

Officer Mraz kicked his gun toward the white-haired man, who bent over and picked it up, keeping his eyes and his weapon fixed on Mraz. The white-haired man walked backwards slowly, toward the alley behind the house. "Don't move," he said, keeping the gun trained on the group as he backed away. They saw him disappear around the corner of the garage, and then heard the sound of running footsteps, fading into the darkness.

Mraz bolted back to his car and radioed for help. "Put out an APB," he ordered the dispatcher. "Caucasian, male. Six-foot-four, two hundred thirty pounds, white hair, mid-forties. Dressed entirely in black. He is armed and should be considered extremely dangerous. Last seen on foot heading south at 104th and Hamilton Streets." Within minutes, the sound of approaching sirens filled the air. Three squad cars pulled up almost simultaneously, blue lights flashing.

Jake repeated his story to the officers several times. An unmarked car arrived, and Chief Tomczak sprang out of it and rushed up to Jake.

"Are you okay, son?" he asked Jake.

"I'm alright, Chief." Jake replied. "Just a little shaken up."

"Who's he?" Tomczak asked, looking suspiciously at Jerome.

"He's okay," Jake replied. "He's a friend of mine. Just saved my ass."

"Why don't you two go inside?" the Chief said. "I'll join you in a minute."

Jake and Jerome complied. They could hear a long, loud tirade from the Chief as he berated his officers for leaving their posts, and then losing their weapons.

"Think it's okay if I split?" Jerome asked. "All these cops make me nervous."

"I think you better stick around awhile longer. I imagine the Chief will want to talk with you."

After a few minutes, Chief Tomczak joined them. He was profusely apologetic and embarrassed over the evening's events and promised to double the size of the security detail. One more time, Jake was forced to describe everything he could remember about the incident. When he had finished, Tomczak shook his head and looked at him gravely.

"You're goddamn lucky he showed up," Tomczak said, nodding at Jerome. "I hate to think what might have happened otherwise. By the way, why were you here?" the Chief asked Jerome.

Jerome hesitated, clearly uncomfortable at the prospect of a police interrogation. "Let's just say I owe him. I knew that dude was following him around, so I been keeping an eye on Mr. McShane."

"Well, I'm glad for that. Shit, you did a better job than we did. But, I don't get it. Why—"

Jake cut him off, sensing that Jerome was uneasy with any form of interrogation by the law. "I've known Jerome and his brother for a long time, Chief. That's a story for another time. Look, I've got a busy day tomorrow and a long week ahead. Let's call this a night, shall we?"

Chief Tomczak excused himself, promising Jake that the army of men in blue lingering around the house would stay through the night, and assuring him that reinforcements had arrived at Peggy's house as well. The power company was diligently working to restore power, and reported that the lines serving the entire block had been sabotaged by someone who obviously knew what he was doing. The phone line had been cut as well, so the Chief loaned Jake a cell phone.

Jake and Jerome were left alone in the kitchen, in the eerie light produced by the combination of candles and flashlights.

"I don't know what to say, Jerome. I can't thank you enough." Jake hesitated, then continued. "I still don't get it. The Chief asked the same question that's been on my mind. Why?"

"Like I said, Shooter feels like he really owes you, man. And that means I owe you."

"But why? I don't understand."

"You don't need to understand. Just know that we've got your back. Now, let me ask you something. Why is that dude after you? I've been around a lot of bad dudes and I know one when I see one— that sucker's bad news. What's he got against you?"

"It's got something to do with a trial I'm handling. He wants me off the case. But why, I don't know. I can't make any sense of it."

"Yeah, I know about your case—I've seen you on the news a couple of times and read about it in the papers. How's that going?"

"I don't know yet. We're in the middle of the trial. It should be over after next week, and then maybe that guy will be out of my hair."

"You gonna win?"

"Probably not. It's really more a question of how badly we lose, and there's a whole lot riding on one witness. He's one of our guys, but I think he's lying. If the jury believes him, we're sunk."

Jerome looked puzzled. "Why can't you get him to tell the truth?"

"I'm not sure. He's got some agenda, but I don't know what it is."

"Why don't you let me help?" Jerome suggested. "Let me talk to that dude. I can tell when people are bullshitting me, and I'm pretty good at making 'em tell the truth."

Jake smiled, as he imagined nervous, little Randy face-to-face with an angry Jerome. He was pretty sure Jerome could scare the truth out of Randy. "Thanks for the offer. I have no doubt you'd get results, but I have to do this my way. I'm meeting with this guy in the morning. Maybe I can bring him around."

"Suit yourself. If you change your mind, let me know. I'd be glad to help."

"Thanks, Jerome. Thanks for everything. I still don't understand why you think you owe me. I think it's the other way around now. Anyway, I'm truly grateful."

"No problem, man." He stood up and they shook hands. "I gotta run. And don't worry; I've still got your back. That crazy sucker is still out there and your trial ain't over yet. You be careful."

Jake looked out his back window as Jerome walked quietly into the alley. He saw the glare of headlights and then watched as the big white Cadillac drove silently into the night.

CHAPTER 55

Despite the events of the previous evening and an extremely restless sleep, Jake awoke clearheaded, with a renewed sense of determination. He willed himself to banish those events from his mind for the time being. His enemy, whoever that was, wanted him distracted, and he would not allow that to happen.

With the assistance of Paul LaDuke, USH's General Counsel, Jake spent the morning and early afternoon preparing his witnesses. He would be presenting various corporate officials to testify about the plans that had been developed to address the billing systems issues, and the company's intentions to implement those fixes, even though that had not been accomplished prior to the filing of the lawsuit. He had witnesses to explain the program that had been put in place since the filing of the lawsuit to provide patients with an independent review of their invoices, and refunds plus interest where overcharges were substantiated. He had witnesses to testify that the billing problems resulted from the attempt to integrate numerous highly complicated billing systems, and that there was never any intention to deliberately overcharge anyone.

The key witness would be Randy Kraft, and Jake met with him last. Randy would take the stand first thing the next morning as the last witness for the plaintiffs. He looked more nervous than usual. Jake had Randy's deposition transcript beside him, with various sections highlighted. He had written a list of questions on a yellow legal pad. These were questions he anticipated that Rick would ask, as well as questions that he intended to ask during cross-examination.

Jake looked at the questions in front of him. They had been through this many times before. The answers were always the same, except for the curveball Randy had thrown at the end of his deposition—his claim that he had been instructed by the CFO to deliberately avoid any effort to identify past errors and correct them. That would likely be the single most important piece of evidence in the entire case. The way Randy responded on that point could have an impact of hundreds of millions of dollars. Impulsively, Jake shoved aside his notes, and decided on a different tack.

"Randy, I'll make this short. I want you to listen to me very carefully, okay?"

Randy swallowed hard and nodded. Jake folded his hands in front of him and leaned forward, staring intently at Randy. "I'm not going to sit here and tell you what you should say tomorrow, and I'm not going to tell you how to say it. The only instruction I have for you is the instruction I give to every witness: Tell the truth. That's all you have to do. Don't worry about the consequences; just explain exactly what happened." Jake paused, looking for a reaction. Randy stared at the table, avoiding eye contact. Jake continued, in a voice that was soft, but earnest. "Tell the truth, Randy. You have a legal obligation to do that. The court requires it and both sides deserve to hear it. More important, you owe it to yourself. I've been through a lot lately, as you probably know, and I've done a lot of soul-searching. I ask myself all the time, what really matters, and do you know what I think, Randy? Honesty matters. Goodness matters. Knowing that you live your life the right way matters. You need to be able to look yourself in the mirror tonight, tomorrow and forty years from now, and feel proud of yourself. When you're in a position to honestly reflect on your life, you'll realize that money doesn't matter—fame, power, getting even—those things don't matter. Knowing that you've done your best to be a good person and do the right thing in every situation is what it's all about. In this situation, that means just telling the honest truth on that witness stand tomorrow. Your testimony may impact a lot of people. You owe it to them, you owe it to the court, and most of all, you owe it to yourself, to tell the truth. That's all you need to do, Randy. See you tomorrow."

With that, Jake got up and left the room. Randy continued staring at the table. He said nothing. Paul LaDuke gathered his files and walked toward the door. He turned to face Randy. "Just one more thing, Randy. Like Jake said, you should tell the truth because it's the right thing to do. But if that's not a good enough reason for you, think about this: That young man's wife may have been murdered, and that incident may have had something to do with this case. The police are using all of their resources to investigate. If they think anyone in the plaintiffs' camp had anything to do with that, and if you happen to be working with the plaintiffs in any capacity, you may share in that responsibility. I don't know whether you could be found legally responsible and face murder charges or conspiracy charges, but there is certainly that possibility. Even if you escape criminal culpability, you'd carry a moral responsibility with you for the rest of your life if you had any part in promoting a cause that's tainted by such a crime. Just tell the truth, son, and you'll have nothing to worry about."

Randy Kraft took the witness stand at 9 a.m. Monday morning in front of a packed courtroom. Everyone in attendance anticipated that Rick Black would conclude his case with a flourish, maybe even a bombshell, although they could not anticipate what it might be.

Rick walked Randy through a series of questions and established that Randy was intimately involved in identifying the company's invoicing problems and closely involved in the meetings called to address the problems. In fact, it became clear that no one in the company had greater knowledge of these issues. Rick led Randy through the sequence of events leading up to the meeting involving the company's CFO and its Vice President of Information Technology. He was clearly building up to a climax, the exact nature of which was still unknown to his audience. "Mr. Kraft, what was the outcome of the meeting held on March 29th, the one in which the CFO and the head of IT participated?" Rick spoke in a loud and clear voice as he strutted before his witness.

"They told me that addressing our billing issues needed to be a matter of the highest priority. They said to do whatever it would take to fix these problems ASAP and that I would have whatever financial resources and IT support I needed."

"But then you had a subsequent meeting with the CFO a short time later—alone—is that correct?" Rick continued his pacing and glanced at the judge and jury as he asked the question.

"No."

Rick stopped his pacing and turned quickly toward his witness.

"Excuse me?" His tone was sharp.

"That is not correct. There was no subsequent meeting with the CFO."

Anger and surprise flashed across Rick's face. "Mr. Kraft, listen to me carefully. Is it your testimony that you did not have a private meeting about these issues with Mr. Klein, the CFO, sometime after the March 29 meeting?"

"That is my testimony. There was no subsequent meeting."

Rick was momentarily dumbstruck, then he launched into attack mode. "Mr. Kraft, you gave a deposition under oath before testifying here today, is that correct?"

"Yes, I did."

"You testified during your deposition that Mr. Klein approached you privately after the March 29th meeting and told you to go through the motions, but to purposely drag your feet and avoid fixing any past problems. Do you recall making such a statement in your deposition, under oath?"

"Yes, but it's not true. There was no such meeting. Mr. Klein gave me no such instructions."

Rick was livid. "So, you lied under oath at your deposition? Or are you lying now, Mr. Kraft?"

"I'm telling the truth now. I only made up that story during my deposition because you asked me to."

"Objection!" Rick yelled, his face contorted with rage.

"Mr. Black, he's responding to your questions. You can't object to your own questions," Judge Trainor admonished him.

Rick looked down, struggling to control his anger. He walked aggressively toward the witness stand and glared at Randy. "So, you are admitting here that you committed perjury, by knowingly lying during your deposition?"

"Only because you asked me to."

Rick bit his lip to keep from exploding. "And you expect the jury to believe your testimony here today, the testimony of an admitted perjurer?"

"I'm telling the truth as I sit here today."

Rick turned his back on the witness and walked quickly back toward the counsel table. "I have no further questions for this witness," he said with obvious disgust.

A buzz rippled through the courtroom, as whispers and glances were exchanged over this unexpected development. Judge Trainor pounded his gavel. "Quiet please!" he ordered. "Your witness, Mr. McShane."

Jake approached the witness stand. "I have only a few questions, Mr. Kraft. I need you to be perfectly clear on this point. The only instructions you received from Mr. Klein, the CFO, were to fix the problems as quickly as possible and to pay refunds to anyone who had been overcharged, and he told you that you would have whatever resources you would need to accomplish that, is that correct?"

"That is correct."

"And why did you testify differently during your deposition?"

"Objection!" Rick shouted.

"Overruled," Judge Trainor replied. "You opened that door yourself on direct, Mr. Black. The witness may answer."

"Mr. Black encouraged me to tell that story."

"I have no further questions."

"The witness is excused. We will take a short recess. I want counsel in my chambers, immediately," said Judge Trainor.

Rick and Jake followed the judge into his chambers. Rick began talking before they had sat down. "Your Honor, I have serious concerns about what's going on here. I think the defense has obviously gotten to this witness and influenced his testimony. They are clearly trying to taint the jury by attacking me with these malicious allegations. They're trying to detract attention from—"

Judge Trainor raised a hand and interrupted. "Enough, Mr. Black. I have serious concerns here, too, but I'll remind you, you called this witness. If his testimony today is truthful, I don't need to tell you what kind of trouble you'll be in with the State Bar. Unauthorized secret meetings with a member of the defendant's management team; encouraging fraudulent testimony; this is very disturbing."

Jake spoke up. "Your Honor, I am renewing my motion to call Kenny Oliver as a witness. He's the person who will testify that Mr. Black encouraged him to be untruthful in another trial. You denied my motion previously on the grounds that there was no similar issue in this case. Now there is."

Rick looked like he wanted to strangle Jake. "You've already ruled on that, Your Honor. It's much too late in the game to be adding new witnesses. It's a blatant attempt to make me look bad in the eyes of the jury. That story is false and malicious, and it would have a prejudicial effect on these proceedings. Moreover, it simply has no relevance to the issues in this case."

"To the contrary, Your Honor, this is highly relevant," Jake argued. "Mr. Kraft's testimony is critically important in this trial. The jury must decide which of his stories is true. Today he's claiming that his deposition testimony was false and encouraged by Mr. Black. Mr. Oliver will testify that he had almost the exact same experience with Mr. Black. The jury needs to hear that in order to fairly evaluate Mr. Kraft's testimony."

Rick jumped to his feet. "Your Honor, if Mr. Oliver is allowed to testify, I will move for a mistrial. Whatever relevance that testimony may have is outweighed by the prejudicial effect it will have upon the jury. I'm not on trial here. USH is."

Judge Trainor looked gravely at Rick. "Mr. Black, I too am concerned about the prejudicial effect this may have on the jury. I am equally concerned about the substance of this testimony. But I cannot deny the relevance. We will hear Mr. Oliver's testimony. After that, you may move for a mistrial if you wish. I may declare a mistrial on my own, but we will hear the testimony. It is relevant. And we will hear this witness before we hear any others. How soon can you produce him, Mr. McShane?"

"I'll try to reach him immediately, Your Honor. Perhaps he can be here as early as this afternoon."

"With all due respect, Your Honor, I'll need time to prepare for this witness," Rick said.

Judge Trainor became impatient. "I will not delay this trial any further. How much time could you possibly need, Mr. Black? If what he's saying is true, then you already know what happened. If it's not, then there won't be much to talk about, will there? See if you can reach him, Mr. McShane. If he's available, we will adjourn for the afternoon and resume tomorrow at nine o'clock. That gives you the rest of today to prepare."

Jake telephoned Kenny Oliver at home, and he answered on the first ring.

The next morning, the courtroom was filled to capacity by eight thirty. Legions of media types who arrived too late to find a seat in the courtroom milled about the corridors just outside. The place was abuzz with rumors and speculation and a clear sense that something dramatic was imminent.

At five minutes after nine, Kenny Oliver was sworn in. Before Jake asked the first question, Rick stood up. "For the record, Your Honor, I renew my objection to this witness, on the grounds of relevancy and prejudice."

"Your objection is duly noted, Mr. Black—and overruled. You may proceed, Mr. McShane," said Judge Trainor.

Jake approached the witness stand. He dispensed with the customary background questions and got right to the point. "Mr.

Oliver, did you previously testify in another trial where Mr. Black acted as legal counsel?"

"Yes."

"Tell us about that case, please."

"Well, this friend of mine, Larry Doyle, filed a lawsuit against the grocery store where we both worked. He claimed the owner sexually harassed him and then fired him when he wouldn't go along. Mr. Black was Larry's attorney."

"And what was the nature of your involvement?"

"Larry was afraid he might lose the case. He didn't have any evidence to back up his story. That's because it was all bullshit ... uh, I mean nonsense ... he just made it up. So all he had was just his word against the boss's. I met with Larry at a bar one night. He told me that he had a chance of winning a huge pile of money in this lawsuit, but he needed a little help to make this a sure thing. He said his lawyer told him to find another witness who could make the boss look like a real scumbag."

Rick jumped to his feet. "Objection! That's hearsay."

"Sustained," Judge Trainor pronounced. "The jury will disregard the witness's statement about the content of any conversation between Mr. Black and Mr. Doyle. You may proceed, Mr. McShane."

"So what happened next, Mr. Oliver?"

"Me and Larry talked about some possible ideas for a story. We finally agreed that I'd tell a story about how the boss was stealing from some of the old ladies we delivered groceries to. We agreed that we'd go talk to his lawyer the next day."

"What happened then?"

"I chickened out. The next day, it just seemed like bar talk, you know, something guys would scheme about over a few beers, but never actually follow through with. I told Larry that the plan was crazy. Those things never happened and I couldn't just make up a story like that and expect a jury to believe it. Besides, it just didn't feel right."

"How did Larry respond?"

"He got really pissed ... uh, excuse me ... angry. He said I could make more money from this case than I would earn in five years. He said I shouldn't worry about the story. He had a lawyer that would help us turn this into a very believable story. He said his lawyer was really good, and he wasn't one to let the facts get in the way when there was a lot of money to be made."

"Objection!" Rick yelled again.

"Overruled," Judge Trainor replied.

"Then what happened?"

"I still didn't want to do it. Then I got a call from Mr. Black. He said he just wanted to talk. Just talk, that's all. So I went to see him. He said that if I were to testify, and tell the story that me and Larry talked about, there would be easy money, and lots of it. He told me I could be so much more than just a delivery boy in a grocery store. He told me it was insulting, how little they paid me. If I had a story to tell, this could be my ticket to a new life."

"And what was your reaction?"

"I started thinking about my dead-end job, and feeling bad about my situation. I began warming up to the idea. He really made it sound like it was something I should do, like I owed it to myself. But I told him I didn't have any evidence, so why would anyone believe me?"

"And what did Mr. Black say?"

"He said, no problem, just go out and get the evidence. He said that if some valuables from the old ladies' apartments wound up in the boss's office and I had pictures, the jury would go crazy and we'd score big."

Rick was red-faced with rage, and on his feet again. "Objection, Your Honor! This is outrageous and ridiculous. It is a blatant character assassination that has nothing whatsoever to do with these proceedings. This witness should be excused and his testimony stricken from the record!"

"Sit down, Mr. Black! Your objection is overruled. If you have issues with this testimony, you may bring them out in cross-examination."

"So then what happened?" Jake asked.

"I took some jewelry and other things from some of the old ladies' apartments and planted them in the boss's office. Then I filmed them and brought the recording to Mr. Black. Before I gave it to him, I asked him how I was going to get paid. He said that he and Larry agreed that my cut would be ten percent of the jury verdict, but we had to be careful about how I got it. He said he couldn't pay me directly for my testimony, and neither could Larry. So, what he would do would be to threaten a lawsuit against the store and the owner. I would quit, and the lawsuit would claim that I was constructively discharged, you know, forced to quit because my only other choice was to do something against the law. After the jury verdict came in, he would get the defendant, Mr. Quinn, to settle both cases. He'd make it worth Mr. Quinn's while by agreeing to settle both my case and Larry's for something less than the jury verdict. The settlement agreement would be confidential. We would never actually have to file the lawsuit, so there would be no public record. And that's how it played out. I got $220,000 to settle my case."

Jake looked at Rick, who fumed in silence. "I have just one more question, Mr. Oliver. Did Mr. Black, as your attorney, encourage you to provide false testimony in that case, and promise to reward you for doing so?"

"That's exactly what happened," said the witness. "The whole idea about creating the evidence—actually stealing from the old ladies, and then filming it—that was his idea."

"Your witness," Jake said to Rick, sitting down, his heart pounding at the implications of this testimony.

Hostility and rage were etched into Rick's face as he glared at Kenny Oliver from his seat. The courtroom was utterly silent. Every eye was riveted on Rick, as he rose and walked menacingly toward the witness, looking like he might strike him.

"As I understand it, Mr. Oliver, you have just told this courtroom that you knowingly provided false testimony under oath, for your own personal gain, is that correct?"

"That is correct, and I'm not proud of it."

"Of course you're not. Committing fraud and perjury is nothing to be proud of. Think back carefully on our conversations, Mr. Oliver. Did I ever once instruct you to lie?"

"I don't recall if you ever used words like 'I want you to lie,' but you definitely encouraged me to do that and even helped me develop the story."

"Answer the question, Mr. Oliver," Rick said. "Did I ever tell you to lie?"

"I think I just answered that question."

"No, you didn't. It's a yes or no question. Your Honor, I ask that you instruct the witness to answer the question posed to him."

"Answer the question, Mr. Oliver," Judge Trainor directed.

"If the question is, did you ever specifically state that you wanted me to lie, the answer is no, but—"

"Thank you, Mr. Oliver. That's all."

"—you encouraged me to. You helped cook up the scheme and you encouraged me to lie," Oliver shouted.

"Move to strike, Your Honor." Rick shouted back.

"The jury will disregard the witness's last statement," Judge Trainor instructed.

"One last question, Mr. Oliver. By your own account, you are an admitted perjurer. Why should the jury believe you here today?"

Kenny Oliver paused and looked down. "Because I'm dying," he said in a soft voice. "I have an inoperable brain tumor. I have no reason to lie today."

Rick grimaced at the response. He had just asked one question too many and he knew it. "I have no further questions for this witness," Rick muttered, looking scornfully at Kenny Oliver as he took his seat.

Jake rose. "Your Honor, I would like to recall Randy Kraft to the stand." The judge looked surprised. Rick looked like he was about to object but the judge cut him off with a look.

"Very well, call Mr. Kraft."

Randy Kraft walked into the courtroom and was reminded that he remained under oath.

"I have just one additional question, Mr. Kraft," Jake said. "You testified yesterday that Mr. Black encouraged you to provide false testimony in your deposition. Did he indicate that there would be some financial reward in it for you if you did so?"

"Yes. He said that after the trial, I should quit and claim that the company was retaliating against me for my testimony. He would threaten to bring a wrongful termination lawsuit and we would make big bucks."

"Objection, Your Honor! This has gone on long enough!" Rick was shouting, a fit of rage clearly overtaking him. "This is nothing but a malicious, underhanded ploy by the defense to besmirch my character and divert the jury's attention from the real issues in this case. I'm not on trial here—"

"Sit down, Mr. Black," Judge Trainor ordered sharply.

Rick ignored him. "I'm not on trial here," he shouted again. "The defense has produced two witnesses who are both admitted perjurers. Their testimony should be stricken—"

"Sit down, Mr. Black, you're out of order!" Judge Trainor shouted angrily.

Rick shouted back. "With all due respect, Your Honor, these last two witnesses have irreparably tainted the fairness of these proceedings. The prejudicial effect of their testimony has made it impossible for this jury to render an objective verdict. I am moving for a mistrial."

Judge Trainor rose to his feet. "Sit down, Mr. Black, that's enough!"

Rick looked like he was about to say something else, then thought better of it and took his seat.

Judge Trainor sat down, folded his hands and stared down at his desk, as he took a few moments to compose himself. He heaved a deep, audible sigh and looked up. "Much as it pains me to do so, I must agree. I am declaring a mistrial." He hesitated, then looked at the jury. "Many people have invested a great deal of time and effort into this trial—the parties, their counsel, the witnesses, and the jury. They deserve better than this. Unfortunately, I have no choice. The integrity of these proceedings has indeed been compromised. Therefore, I am dismissing this case, without prejudice. The plaintiffs are free to request a new trial; however, if they do so, you will have no part of it, Mr. Black. It is the allegations about your misconduct that compel me to declare a mistrial, and the taint that surfaced here would follow you into any subsequent proceeding. I must say, I find those allegations deeply disturbing. You're right, Mr. Black, you're not on trial here, and it is not my place to pass judgment on you. However, as an officer of the court, I feel I have an ethical duty to turn this matter over to the State Bar's Ethics and Disciplinary Committee for further investigation. I sincerely hope these allegations turn out to be unfounded. Conduct of that nature has no place in our profession. If the allegations are substantiated, I assure you that I will do everything within my power to see that you never practice law in this state again. Case dismissed!" He pounded his gavel and walked out.

The courtroom exploded. Excited voices chattered urgently on cell phones, spreading the news. Cameras clicked and flashed. A hoard of people crowded around Jake, all seemingly talking at once. He didn't hear any of them. He was lost in his own thoughts, trying to comprehend what had just happened. This had been an exercise in damage control, yet the case had just been dismissed without any adverse judgment. That was something that neither Jake nor anyone else had considered even a remote possibility. The plaintiffs could seek another trial, but what impact would these events have? It would take some time to sort out all of the ramifications, but at least for now, there was no question that this was a stunning victory for USH.

Rick sat in his chair, looking like a dazed prizefighter trying to get his bearings after being knocked out. After several minutes, he looked around at the sea of reporters snapping pictures and hoping for a quote. He stood up and abruptly walked past them, muttering "No comment."

CHAPTER 56

Jake stood outside the school as the bell rang and hordes of young students poured out. He spotted Anna chatting happily with a couple of classmates, one on either side of her. He watched silently, his heart warming at the sight of his young daughter, looking and acting like a perfectly normal, happy, well-adjusted seven-year-old.

One of her classmates pointed in his direction, and Anna looked up. "Daddy!" she squealed, and sprinted toward him. "What are you doing here?" she asked, her face beaming with delight at the unexpected surprise. Then, for a moment, her demeanor abruptly darkened. "You didn't get fired, did you?"

Jake laughed. It seemed strange; it had been so long since he had laughed. "No, little girl, I didn't get fired. The trial is over. I came to bring you home."

Anna's eyes widened. "Really? Home?"

Jake nodded.

"Yea! I'm going home! I'm going home!" she shouted exuberantly, to no one in particular, and to everyone.

That night, they snuggled together on the couch, like they used to. Jake attempted to read to Anna, but it soon became clear that she just wanted to talk and cuddle. He put the book down.

"Tell me about your trial, Daddy."

Although he expected that she would not understand much, he explained what the trial was about and how it concluded, in terms he hoped a child could understand. Anna listened with keen interest, looking intently at her father with dark, intelligent eyes—Amanda's eyes.

"And it's all over now?" she asked, when Jake had finished his story.

"Yes sweetheart, it's over."

A look of concern crossed her face. "Will you have another trial soon?"

"I don't think so."

"So we can get back to having a normal life?"

"Yes, little girl. We will get back to having a normal life. I promise."

The next morning, Jake looked at the headline in the morning paper with a sense of wonder. "USH CASE DISMISSED" was plastered across the front page in large bold print. His eyes wandered over the opening sentences of the article:

> "In a shocking turn of events, Judge Peter Trainor dismissed the class-action lawsuit against US Health Corporation yesterday. The dismissal was prompted by evidence of misconduct on the part of plaintiffs' counsel, Richard T. Black. A witness testified that Black encouraged him to provide false testimony against the company in exchange for the promise of future financial rewards. When Black challenged the testimony, the defense produced a witness who testified about a similar incident involving Black in another trial. Judge Trainor ruled that the testimony was sufficiently inflammatory that, true or false, it was likely to taint the fairness of the proceedings. The State Bar is investigating, and considering disciplinary action against Black. The State's Attorney's Office is considering possible criminal prosecution. And most ominous of all, sources indicate that Black is considered a "person of interest" in a homicide

investigation relating to the death of the defense counsel's wife in a suspicious auto accident."

Jake walked Anna to school, then drove to work, arriving late, around 9:30. "Your phone has been ringing off the hook," said Alice, handing him a thick stack of messages. "People have been stopping by since I got here. Mr. Giannakis wants to meet with you in his office at ten o'clock. The people from USH will be there." Then, pointing at the messages she had just handed him, she said, "That message on the top is from a Mr. Leach. He said it's extremely urgent, and asked that you call him as soon as you arrive. I told him you were very busy this morning, but that I would pass along the message."

"Thanks, Alice," Jake replied, quickly shuffling through the messages. A number of them were from reporters, some were from colleagues, two were from Demetrius and the one on top read, "Jack Leach, of Sullivan & Leach. Please call ASAP." Jack Leach was one of the founding partners of Sullivan & Leach, and one of the nation's premier trial attorneys.

Although it was widely considered to be unwise for the firm's associate attorneys to keep Demetrius Giannakis waiting, Jake decided to call Leach first. It would be helpful to know what was on his mind before meeting with Demetrius and the USH executives.

After a lengthy conversation with Mr. Leach, Jake reported to Demetrius's office twenty minutes late. He expected the managing partner to be irritated with him for his tardiness, but Demetrius smiled broadly as he walked in. USH's general counsel, Paul LaDuke and its president, Bernard Parkerson, were seated on the leather sofa near the windows of his spacious office. "Here's the miracle worker! Hail, the conquering hero!" said Demetrius pumping Jake's hand.

LaDuke and Parkerson rose to their feet. "Masterful job, Jake," said LaDuke. Absolutely masterful!"

The normally reserved Dr. Parkerson was all smiles as well. "Congratulations, counselor! Well done!"

The four men spent some time rehashing the courtroom events of the previous two days, like sports fans basking in the glow of victory in a big game. Presently, Demetrius changed the course of the conversation. "Gentlemen, there's no question that we won a significant battle, but as I was explaining before you arrived, Jake, the war isn't over." Turning to Jake, he continued. "Paul and I have been explaining to Bernie that the plaintiffs are free to seek a new trial, and almost certainly will do so. It's also possible that plaintiffs' counsel might be more receptive to reasonable settlement terms in light of these developments. We thought it would be wise for the four of us to discuss our options now rather than waiting for the plaintiffs' next move."

"As a matter of fact, they've already made it," said Jake. "I just finished a long conversation with Jack Leach. That's why I was late getting here," he added, looking at Demetrius.

"You mean *the* Jack Leach?" LaDuke asked.

"Yes, that Jack Leach," Jake replied.

Parkerson gave Demetrius a dark look. The jubilant mood evaporated in an instant.

"What the hell did he want?" Demetrius demanded.

Jake looked at the three suddenly somber faces staring at him. A sly smile crossed his face. "Lighten up, guys," he said. "It was a good conversation."

"Out with it, goddammit!" said Dr. Parkerson, still looking troubled.

Jake enjoyed the fact that these three powerful men were squirming with nervousness. "First, Leach wanted me to know that he has taken over the USH case. Rick Black will no longer be involved. In fact, Rick Black has been asked to leave the firm." Jake paused for effect.

"That was smart of them," Demetrius muttered. "Go on!"

Jake continued. "Mr. Leach said that he was interested in discussing settlement, so I told him I would be happy to hear him out."

"What do they want?" demanded Parkerson.

"Well, he huffed and puffed for a while, and made some ridiculous demands. I turned him down cold, and it quickly became apparent that they just want out. This case has given his firm a huge black eye. If they try it again, it'll keep their name in the press, with a big bright spotlight shining on that black eye. And, their star witness—their ticket to punitive damages—just self-destructed and came over to our side. So here's the deal: We pay no punitive damages; we pay no attorneys' fees to their side; we simply agree that the auditing and refund program we implemented will remain in place for two years."

"That's it?" LaDuke asked.

"That's it," Jake replied. "It's something we're already doing anyway, voluntarily, but we would agree to a stipulated judgment that requires us to keep this program in place for the next two years. Of course, they'll try to spin this as a victory for their side. They'll make a big splash in the press about how every aggrieved patient will be made whole, and they'll try to take credit, but they're really just trying to save face for themselves."

Demetrius stood up. "That's not a settlement. That's a surrender! They're waving the white flag!"

Jake nodded. "It's over." Dr. Parkerson collapsed back into his chair and heaved a huge sigh. "Thank God!"

Paul LaDuke and Bernard Parkerson stared at their lawyers in stunned silence for a few moments as the news sank in, then launched into a new round of high-fives and fist pumps. A flurry of hasty phone calls followed, to the chairman of the board, the public relations department and a variety of other senior corporate officials. After a few moments, LaDuke put down his cell phone, wandered over to the window and then looked out, pensively. "So, after all this, the plaintiffs' lawyers don't get a dime. And not one of their clients will get rich either."

"Oh, I don't know about that," Jake replied. "Someone is bound to figure out that they may be able to recover big bucks by suing Rick Black and his firm for malpractice."

Demetrius shook his head and chuckled. "Wouldn't that be sweet?"

Jake lingered in Demetrius's office after LaDuke and Parkerson had left. Despite his elation over the outcome of the case, he felt a twinge of sadness as he thought about his former classmate. "What a waste," he said, shaking his head slowly. "Rick Black is one of the most talented people I've ever met. He's got a brilliant mind, tremendous communication skills and boatloads of charm and charisma. He is without a doubt the most naturally gifted lawyer I know. He had everything."

"Not everything," Demetrius corrected him. "He had no moral compass. That's what got him lost."

CHAPTER 57

Word of the USH outcome spread quickly through the firm. For the rest of the morning and into the afternoon, a steady stream of well-wishers stopped by Jake's office, offering their congratulations. His colleagues were effusive in their praise, convinced that Jake's brilliant lawyering had produced a victory no one had expected. Jake didn't feel brilliant. He believed he'd done a good job of playing the cards that were dealt to him, but just like in poker, a great deal of luck had been involved.

By late afternoon, he craved solitude. He closed the door to his office and unplugged his telephone. He sat there for a long time, relishing the silence.

Sometime later, Alice opened his door hesitantly and peeked in. She found Jake, sitting alone in the quiet office, weeping. He looked at her, unashamed, as tears cascaded down his cheeks. Alice stepped inside, closing the door quietly behind her. "A trial can be draining, can't it?" she said softly.

"It's not that, Alice," Jake replied in a voice that was barely audible. "I just miss her. I should be able to share this with her." As he spoke, Jake looked at the picture of Amanda on his desk.

Tears of sympathy welled up in Alice's eyes. "I know you do." She patted his shoulder and walked out, closing the door quietly behind her.

Jake wept harder, as he picked up Amanda's picture. If she were still with him, he would think about packing it in and doing something different with his life. Perhaps they would move back to California. Perhaps he would choose an entirely different career path—something more meaningful. In the overall scheme of things, was he doing anything to make the world a better place? What had he just accomplished anyway? He had won a fight for a client, but what difference did it really make? The client wasn't exactly innocent here. Was society any better off? Well, maybe a little. After all, there might be one less pirate loose on the high seas by the time the State Bar had finished with Rick Black. Maybe he deserved some credit for that, and maybe that would prevent future miscarriages of justice. Amanda would say that the good guys needed to stand up to the bad guys if there was to be any hope for justice in our fragile legal system. On that front, he had done his part.

Jake composed himself and informed Alice that he was leaving early. She advised him that Demetrius had called to invite him to dinner. Jake reluctantly dialed Demetrius's extension.

"Jake, I think a celebration is in order. And, I'd like to spend some time with one of our finest litigators to discuss the bright future he has with this firm. Can I take you to dinner tonight?"

"I'm sorry, Demetrius, can I take a rain check? I really appreciate the offer, but I've some pressing personal business I need to attend to." Jake knew it was not politically correct to decline a dinner invitation from the managing partner; however, he simply was not ready to have a serious discussion about his career path.

"No problem. I understand," Demetrius replied. "I know you've had to put your personal life on hold for awhile, so do what you need to do. We'll get together and celebrate sometime soon, maybe next week."

"Thanks, Demetrius. That would be great."

An hour later, Jake pulled up in front of a large, newly built gymnasium, next to an old but well-maintained church. The gymnasium's newness stood in stark contrast to the dingy, boarded-up buildings and dirty streets in the surrounding neighborhood. The parking lot outside the gym was devoid of vehicles, but bustling with activity. Two side-by-side basketball courts adjacent to the parking lot were in full use, and dozens of young boys and girls were scattered around the lot, throwing footballs, jumping rope or just hanging out. Many of them stared at the white man in a suit getting out of his vehicle, and the other car that had driven up directly behind him, which was obviously an unmarked police car.

Jake moved toward the basketball courts. He was in a walking cast now, navigating without the aid of crutches, and walked with a pronounced limp. The crowd appeared to be mostly high school age, with a smattering of younger kids mingled in with them. Many of them eyed Jake suspiciously.

As he neared the basketball courts, Jake saw a big man with his back to him, reprimanding a teenaged basketball player in a loud voice. "Hey man, it's okay to play rough, but don't play dirty! Understand? Watch those elbows!" The big man noticed the eyes of the players looking past him, and he turned around.

"Hi Jerome," said Jake.

The big man smiled. He seemed different—the scowl and the attitude were gone. "Well, look who's here. Boys, this is Mr. McShane. He tries to pretend he's a hot-shot lawyer, but he's really a basketball stud." He gestured at Jake's cast. "When are you going to get that thing off so you can come up here and show these boys how the game is played?"

A skinny teenager in a Chicago Bulls jersey eyed Jake skeptically. "Shit, I bet I could take that dude left-handed."

Jerome laughed. "Like hell you could, Mouse. He'd put a whupping on you, just like he did on Shooter."

The kid looked incredulous. "That dude whupped Shooter? No way, man. I ain't never seen anyone could whup Shooter. Not this dude, that's for damn sure."

Jake smiled. "Well, I'm out of practice and out of shape, but once I get this cast off, I plan to get my game back. I'll be around." Then, turning to Jerome, he said, "I came by to see Shooter. Is he here?"

"Yeah, he's inside resting. Come on, I'll take you."

They entered the gym and walked across the shiny hardwood floor, then entered a small office. A doorway from the office led to a small but comfortable looking apartment. Jerome walked in without knocking and yelled loudly, "Hey Shooter, you got company."

"Send 'em in," Jake heard a voice shout back from another room. Shooter was sitting up in bed, reading. He looked the same, except that he was wearing glasses.

"Stanford!"

"Hey Shooter," Jake replied. "You look good. How are you feeling?"

"Better every day. It was rough for a while—I lost a kidney and my spleen. But God gave me two kidneys, and who really needs a spleen? Anyway, I'm just starting to feel normal again. I'm still kind of weak, and need lots of rest, but I'm getting stronger. I plan to start shooting the roundball again soon. Hey, I heard about your case. Mistrial, huh? That's a good thing, isn't it?"

"Yeah, it's a good thing. It's finally over. It's been an ordeal."

Shooter's face turned somber. "I'm sure it has. I read about your accident. I'm really sorry about your wife. I've been praying for you."

"Thanks, I appreciate that. I also appreciate the heads-up about that white-haired creep, and the fact that you had Jerome looking after me. I don't know what would've happened if Jerome hadn't been there to save my neck last weekend. I wanted to come by and thank you in person—both of you."

Jerome had been lingering in the doorway. "Aw, don't worry about that. We owed you. I'll let you two catch up. Later!" he called out as he left the room.

"That's the second time he's said that," said Jake. "I don't get it. Why does he think you guys owe me something?"

Shooter stared at Jake, looking surprised that Jake didn't seem to comprehend. "Man, you changed my life, and that helped me change Jerome's. We're both on a righteous path now. We're doing something positive. And it was you that got me started on that path."

"I did?"

"Remember the speech you gave me in that jail cell?"

"Vaguely."

"Well, I remember every word of it, and it changed my life. You told me you'd help me out, but only if I promised to get my act together and do something positive with my life. I promised you that I would. I spent four days in that jail cell, promising God the same thing—if only I could have another chance. Then you came through. I got that chance, and when that happened, there was one thing I knew for sure—I needed to keep my word. It took me awhile to find my path, but I eventually found it here with Reverend Lonnie. He's making a difference in the lives of a lot of people around here, and he gave me a chance to do the same thing, working with these kids. I can relate to them. I've been where they are, so they'll listen to me. I get them off the streets, with sports. That gives me a chance to get to know them and try to steer them in the right direction. Not everyone listens, but some do, and that makes a difference."

"I'm really happy for you, Shooter. And pretty damn impressed, too. But you deserve all the credit, not me. I certainly don't feel like you owe me anything."

"Like I said, it was you that started me in the right direction, and that brought me here to Reverend Lonnie. He's a special person, Stanford, and he's taught me some things. When I first met him, I couldn't believe how he had his act together. He had everything—women, fame, money—and he gave it all up. He wouldn't go back for a second. He says that if you want to change your life and become a righteous man, you need to do two things. First, you make atonement. If there are people in your life you've hurt, you try to make it up to them. If you can't make it up to the person you've hurt, then do something helpful for somebody else. Second, you've got to realize that it's not about you. You need to put aside your pride and your ego and your selfish ambitions, and focus on making life better for others. That's Lonnie's secret to leading a good life, and finding a sense of purpose and peace. I've seen how it's worked for him, and now it's working for me."

"How does Jerome factor into this?" Jake asked. "And why was he following me around?"

"Jerome's had a tough life—lots of bad breaks. Our father left us when he was eight, and that was hard on him. He was devastated—mad at the whole world. As he got older, he got wilder. He got into a lot of fights, and started hanging around with the wrong crowd. I did my best to look after him, but he was always out of control. And on top of all that, he just had bad luck. When he got busted with that big stash, I thought he had some part in killing that drug dealer—the Priest. As it turned out, he was just in the wrong place at the wrong time. One of his pals, this guy named Freddie, was a small-time dealer who wanted to go big-time. Jerome was with him one day when Freddie went to make a buy from the Priest. Jerome didn't know it, but Freddie had other plans. He shot the Priest, and planned to steal his entire stash, but the Priest shot back. Damn fools wound up killing each other. Jerome's waiting outside, so he goes in after a few minutes and sees those two dudes dying on the floor and a big suitcase full of drugs, so he takes the stash and runs. You know the rest. He did almost five years. Talk about bad luck! Anyway, I visited him in prison almost every weekend, and tried to show him the way. I told him about my life and how it had changed. He'd always looked up to me, so I thought maybe he'd listen. I'm not sure it really sank in until he got out and saw my work here. Then it started opening his eyes, but I could tell he still had doubts. I was afraid he'd go back to his old ways. Then I got shot, and that changed everything."

"How?"

"This may sound crazy, but I think it was the best thing that could have happened. It was a turning point. I think it was a little push in the right direction from God."

"You've lost me."

"When I got shot, Jerome's immediate reaction was to get revenge. Most of the kids that hang out here had the exact same reaction. That's just how people think around here. I told Jerome no way. If we took that path, it would send the wrong message—that violence and revenge are acceptable. I had a perfect opportunity to send a very different message: forgiveness, and turning the other cheek."

"And Jerome saw the light, just like that?" Jake looked dubious.

"Hell no, he didn't see at all, not at first. That wasn't the way things worked in our world. If someone hurts you or disrespects you in some way, you make them pay—otherwise you lose respect. That was Jerome's reaction, and he wasn't about to let it drop."

"But somehow you changed his mind?"

"Jerome was just like I used to be. I thrived on respect. I didn't have nothing else, but people respected me, and that made me feel like I was important. They respected me because they thought I was a bad-ass, and because I could play basketball. And Jerome always wanted to be like me. He craved respect more than anything. I told him I had it all wrong. I had a lot of time to think about my life when I spent those four days in jail, and even more since I've gotten to know Reverend Lonnie, and I came to realize that respect ain't worth shit if it's from the wrong people and for the wrong reasons. Respect shouldn't be the goal—look at Reverend Lonnie—he's not motivated by what others think of him. That would be an ego thing, and that's not what he's all about. I told Jerome I was on a new path—the only respect I needed was self-respect, and that comes from living your life the right way."

"I'm impressed. You must be acquiring the persuasive powers of a preacher. So you actually got through to him at that point?"

"I don't think so—not really. But when Jerome saw how important it was to me, I think for the first time he really understood that I'd truly changed, and that I was on a good path, so he was willing to honor my request and promised me there'd be no revenge. Then I told him about Reverend Lonnie's formula—the one I just described to you. I told him that you really changed my life and that I wanted him to help me watch over you—that would be his form of atonement. He still really didn't buy what I was saying, but he agreed to do it because he saw how important it was to me. Well, he took the assignment to heart and started feeling like he was doing something important—and something good. And that feeling began to open his mind and his heart. I've really seen a difference in him over the past two months, and that's been the most gratifying thing in the world to me. I am eternally thankful. Maybe you didn't even realize it, but you helped me get on the right path, and that eventually helped Jerome do the same. We owe you, Stanford. We will always owe you. Thanks, man."

CHAPTER 58

Monday morning, the week after the USH trial concluded, Jake was summoned to the office of Demetrius Giannakis. Chief Tomczak was there, sipping coffee, as Jake arrived. "The Chief has been filling me in on your old law school buddy," said Demetrius. "I thought you'd like to hear this."

Jake looked at the Chief. "Absolutely," he said. "What's the latest?"

"As a result of all the media attention, as well as a little prodding from my office, both the State Bar and the State Attorney's Office have moved quickly on this one," said Tomczak. "They met with Black last week and really put the screws to him. They made it abundantly clear that not only was his law license in jeopardy, he was likely to face serious criminal charges as well. That could mean prison time and financial ruin."

"So how did he respond?" Jake asked.

"The man is a born negotiator, and knows when it's in his best interest to cut a deal. He realized that the only way he would receive any leniency whatsoever would be if he cooperated fully. So he opened up and started talking."

Jake looked surprised. "What's he saying?"

"First, he admitted that everything Kenny Oliver said about the grocery store trial was true. He still says he never actually told anyone to lie, but he acknowledges that he indirectly encouraged the plaintiff and Oliver to do so. He told them what kinds of claims would really win the jury over, and lo and behold, those guys would tell him that's exactly what happened. So he never used the words 'I want you to lie,' or 'I want you to make up a bullshit story,' but they all knew exactly what they were doing."

"What a devious bastard," Demetrius muttered, shaking his head.

Tomczak continued. "As for the USH case, he admitted having secret meetings with Randy Kraft, and that the two of them concocted a scheme just like Randy told the jury. Black acknowledged that it was critical to his case to have a witness who would testify that there was intentional misconduct on the part of USH, and Randy was willing to play that role—until he had that last-minute change of heart on the witness stand."

The Chief stopped momentarily to let that information sink in. "But it gets worse," he said, looking more serious. "Black admitted to hiring that white-haired goon who's been following you around. He didn't want to give up his name at first. He seemed scared of the guy. But after some strong-arming from the State's Attorney, he said the guy's name is Fowler."

Jake looked stunned. "I don't know what surprises me more—that he would do that, or that he would admit it."

"He didn't have much choice. Our people put a lot of pressure on him. They let him know that we had some solid leads on Fowler. We were able to lift some fingerprints off the knife he lost in your driveway, and got good DNA samples from the blood on Jerome Tucker's clothes. They told Black that Fowler was a prime suspect in your wife's murder. If that was his doing, and there was any connection between Black and Fowler, Black himself could be looking at felony murder charges. They reminded him that Illinois is a death penalty state, and that if he had any hopes for leniency at all, he'd better fully cooperate. They also told him that, even apart from the accident, there were grounds to bring criminal charges on any number of other fronts, based on his conduct in the USH case as well as the grocery store case. That little weasel, Randy Kraft, apparently was pretty paranoid and secretly taped most of his conversations with Black. There's some pretty incriminating stuff on those tapes. I guess Black's survival instinct kicked in, and he decided to do what he could to save his own ass. He knows he'll have to kiss his law license good-bye, and he's hoping that his cooperation will keep him out of jail so he can retire young and enjoy his millions."

"So exactly what did he ask Fowler to do?" Jake asked.

"According to Black, all he asked Fowler to do was scare you off the case. He thought you were getting close to cracking his key witness, and that if you were off the case, your replacement wouldn't have time to really focus in on Randy Kraft. Even if you didn't quit, he knew you'd be distracted, which might achieve the same result. He claims that he never instructed Fowler to assault you, and he insists he had nothing to do with your car crash. He was adamant about that. Oh, there was one more thing. Apparently, Fowler hacked into USH's e-mail system and sent out an e-mail under some big shot's name, ordering that documents be destroyed. He thought that would get the judge really pissed at you guys."

"No shit. It worked," said Demetrius.

"What do we know about this Fowler character?" Jake asked. "That creep is still out there somewhere."

"He's still a bit of a mystery," Tomczak replied. "I doubt that Fowler is his real name. Black said he was introduced to him at a seminar in Birmingham, Alabama, sponsored by some class action law firms. He was described to Black as a resource who was highly skilled in many areas—surveillance, intelligence gathering, computer hacking, elec-tronics—basically a guy who could be trusted with highly sensitive projects, and who got results. Although it was communicated deli-cately, Black was also led to believe that Fowler helped with assign-ments where persuasion was the objective. In other words, blackmail, coercion, intimidation—you get the picture. Black's impression was that he worked in some sort of military intelligence capacity years ago, but who knows?"

This discussion was making Jake increasingly uneasy. "Is there any hope of finding this guy?" he asked.

"Keep your fingers crossed," Tomczak replied. "The FBI is running the fingerprints and DNA through their database. That may tell us who he is, especially if he's ex-military or government. As far as where he is, we may have a good lead. Fowler and Black communicated through disposable cell phones. If Fowler still has his phone, we may be able to get a satellite trace on it. Our technicians are working on that as we speak. In the meantime, we'll keep our security detail at your house, but I can't imagine you'll have any more trouble. The trial is over. He has no reason to bother you now. Hell, he's probably long gone."

"I'm sure you're right," Jake said. He did his best to sound positive, but Fowler's image and his spooky voice hovered in his mind like an ominous storm cloud.

CHAPTER 59

"Mickey? It's Jake McShane."

"Jake! How are you, lad? It's great to hear your voice."

The voice on the other end of the line sounded strong and upbeat, the familiar Irish lilt giving it an almost musical quality. Mickey sounded like his old self, not like the beaten, shell-shocked wretch that Jake had seen at the conclusion of his trial.

"I just put some newspaper clippings in the mail, but I wanted to call you first and share some news that you'll appreciate."

"I'm all ears. News from Chicago is always welcome down here."

"It involves some people you know—namely, Rick Black, Kenny Oliver, and Larry Doyle."

There was a long silence on the other end of the line. "I'm not sure I want to hear it, to be honest, Jake. I've done my best to put that sordid episode in my past."

"I understand, Mickey, but you'll appreciate this news, I promise."

Jake proceeded to tell Mickey about the USH trial that had concluded the week before, with particular emphasis on the testimony provided by Kenny Oliver on the final day.

Another long silence followed when Jake finished the story. "So what does this all mean? What happens now?" Mickey asked, pain evident in his voice from the reopening of old wounds.

"First, it means that the entire South Side will know that you were the victim of a despicable fraud. To the extent people around here had any doubts about your character, this will exonerate you. Your good name will be restored. Second, Rick Black will be disbarred, and he'll probably face criminal charges. Larry Doyle may be prosecuted, too. They could wind up in prison, and there's a good chance they'll have to forfeit every penny of their ill-gotten gains. Third, you've great ammunition for a lawsuit against them. You may be able to recover everything you've lost, and then some."

Mickey sighed. "I don't believe I'll be filing any lawsuit. Our system of justice failed me the last time around. I don't want any part of it."

"But Mickey, after what they did to you, they should be held accountable, and you deserve to be made whole."

"No Jake, I won't do it! My last experience with our legal system almost destroyed me. Besides, I can never be made whole. Aside from the financial consequences, that trial cost me everything that mattered to me: my good name, my business, my friends, and perhaps most importantly, my faith in people. Until then, I really didn't understand how the culture of greed had become so prominent in this country. I didn't understand the decline of our value system. That experience turned me into an angry and bitter person. It changed the way I looked at people. It changed me. It robbed me of the essence of who I was. It was a time of darkness and despair for me, but I'm past it now, and I have no desire to open up that part of my life again."

"I understand," Jake said with quiet resignation. "I would just hate to see those scoundrels escape justice."

"And so would I, Jake, but it looks like justice will be done through the State Bar and the criminal court system. I don't need to get in the middle of that. Like I said, I'm past it now. I've got a new life here in Florida. I'm a deacon at my church, and I find it truly rewarding. It's what I'm meant to be doing now. I didn't plan it this way, but there's a certain symmetry to all this. I'm a preacher and a counselor now, and I'm in a position where I can influence people. I can help them understand the importance of honesty and personal responsibility, and the evils of greed and selfishness. I can't do anything to change the flaws in our legal system, but maybe I can make a difference by changing a few hearts, so perhaps some good can result from that awful experience with Rick Black and Larry Doyle. I'm at peace now, Jake. I really am. I won't look back."

"It sounds like you've a good situation there, Mickey. I'm really happy for you. Will you be coming back to Chicago for a visit anytime soon? There are plenty of people here who would love to see you."

"I don't think so. Some hurts are too deep. I'll never forget the looks people gave me after the lawsuit was filed. I gave my heart and soul to that neighborhood, and they abandoned me. I won't go back."

"I'm sorry to hear that. But remember this: You did make a difference, Mickey, to a lot of people. Your generosity, your goodness, your dedication to the community ... You were such a wonderful example for so many of us. Think about all those employees who worked for you over the years and watched you live your values every day. You showed us that honesty, integrity and service matter a whole lot more than the numbers on our paychecks. You've made more of a difference than you'll ever know."

"Thanks for the kind words, lad. It does this old heart a world of good to see that some of the young people who grew up at the store have grown into such fine human beings. I do appreciate the call, Jacob. It gives me some closure on that part of my life. But I'm not going back. My life is here now."

Jake knew Mickey was right, and was saddened by that realization. He realized he would likely never see his old boss again, and struggled to think of something meaningful to say; however, words eluded him as he choked back his emotions. "I'm glad I know you, Mickey," he blurted out clumsily. "You take care."

"Goodbye, Jake."

CHAPTER 60

The big man took a swallow of Jack Daniels as he looked at the newspaper article describing the McShane accident. That was not the result he had intended. This was a mess. That goddamned McShane! It was time to put an end to this. He knew what he must do. He caressed the revolver in his hands. He opened the chamber and looked thoughtfully at the bullets. He took another long drink, then he walked to the garage, climbed into his black SUV, and started the engine.

CHAPTER 61

It was Thursday evening, three days after Jake had learned of Rick Black's confession. He had just put Anna to bed and was sitting on his living room sofa, looking out his front window at a violent thunderstorm. It had been less than two weeks since Fowler's ghostly silhouette had appeared in his living room in the midst of another storm. An eerie and unsettling feeling of déjà vu crept over him. He turned on the lights, and walked around the house, trying to assure himself that nothing was amiss. He checked the doors. They were locked. He looked out the windows, and saw nothing unusual. Still, he couldn't shake his nervousness.

Fowler was still out there somewhere. The police had yet to find any trace of him. Jake knew that, logically speaking, the man should be long gone, like Chief Tomczak said. He would have no reason to linger in the area, particularly in light of all the media attention. But that logic was not enough to erase the terrifying memory, which seemed to be rekindled anew with each flash of lightning and crash of thunder.

There was a lull between thunderclaps, and he heard a soft knock on the front door. He froze, and listened. The knock came again, louder this time. Jake peered out the living room window and could see a large man in a dark raincoat, leaning toward the door with his head down, trying to avoid the wind and rain. He couldn't see the man's face.

"Who is it?" Jake yelled through the door.

The man outside yelled something in reply. Jake could hear irritation in the voice, but couldn't make out the words.

"Who is it?" he asked again.

"It's Walter Tomczak. For Chrissakes, Jake, open the door!"

Jake recognized the voice and quickly opened the door, apologizing profusely for keeping the Chief of Police standing in the rain. Tomczak stepped inside, wiping the rain out of his eyes.

"I'm sorry to drop by so late, and unannounced, but I just received some news that I thought you'd want to know about." The Chief's manner was grave, which immediately put Jake on edge.

"Come on in, Chief. Have a seat," Jake said motioning to the sofa.

Chief Tomczak remained standing. "We found Fowler. Actually, his real name is Scott Radford. He was a former Green Beret, who worked in some sort of covert operations capacity. He left government service under suspicious circumstances about twelve years ago, and seemed to vanish from the face of the earth after that. Speculation is that he became a mercenary overseas for awhile and then turned up back here in the States three or four years ago. Since then, he's been doing freelance work for people like Black and other shady characters. Anyway, I came here to tell you that we found him. Our trace tracked his cell phone to a four-block radius, and we blanketed the area with undercover officers. One of our guys spotted him coming out of a convenience store and tailed him. He spotted the tail right away, made for his car and took off. There was a high-speed chase and we had eight cars converging on him. He ran into a tollbooth doing about a hundred and twenty. He's dead, Jake."

"I guess I should feel relieved, shouldn't I?" Jake asked quietly. "I wish you could've interrogated him, though. There are still some unanswered questions."

"Maybe not, Jake. There's something else. Normally I wouldn't show this type of thing to anyone other than the next-of-kin, but I thought you should see it." He handed Jake a note written on wrinkled notebook paper in shaky handwriting.

"Danny Flynn was found dead in his garage earlier today," the Chief said. "A handgun was at his side, but he never used it. He died of asphyxiation in his SUV. He sat in the garage with the engine running. That note was found next to him."

Jake read the note:

> "*Time for me to check out. Got no reason to live. Tell Jake McShane I'm sorry. It was me that ran him off the road. I didn't mean to. It was Johnny's car. I thought he was Johnny. Tell my wife she's a cheap unfaithful whore. Tell Johnny McShane to go to hell.*"

"That bastard!" Jake said. "That mean-spirited, cowardly bastard. He got off way too easy. He should be rotting in jail for the next fifty years. He took the coward's way out."

Jake was crumpling the note in his fist without realizing it. Chief Tomczak gently grabbed his hand. "I'll need that, Jake. It's evidence."

Jake handed the note back to the burly Chief of Police. Tomczak put his hand on Jake's shoulder. "I'm sorry, son. I know this must be hard. I better go inform the ex-wife."

It was hard. Jake had known that someone deliberately had forced him off the road and caused Amanda's death. But learning the identity of the killer put things in a different light. He now had a target for his rage, but it was a target beyond reach. His thoughts turned to Johnny and Corey.

"Do you plan to share this note with Corey, his ex-wife?" Jake asked.

"She needs to know what happened," the Chief replied. "She's not the next-of-kin, since they're divorced, but she's the mother of his kids."

"I understand, Chief. She should know that Flynn committed suicide. But can you let me decide when and how to tell her about that?" he asked, pointing to the note.

The Chief hesitated. He folded up the note slowly and put it in his pocket. "Sure, Jake. It's against protocol, but after all you've been through, it's the least I can do. I'll keep this as evidence, and leave it to you to decide what to tell them."

"Thanks, Chief."

CHAPTER 62

J ake was back in his office the following morning. He had been
finding it difficult to focus since the conclusion of the trial, and
last night's news had him feeling even more distracted. He spent
some time reviewing the drafts of the USH settlement documents, but
quickly realized he had neither the energy nor the concentration for
that task, so he decided to spend the day catching up on the numerous
phone messages that had piled up during the trial.

By late afternoon, he had returned all of the most pressing calls and
started wading through those that were less urgent. He played back
his recorded messages, jotting down names and phone numbers, and
stopped when he heard a familiar voice. *"Jake—Johnny here. Just
heard about the USH result. I'd like to buy the city's finest lawyer
a beer. Give me a call."* The message had been left a week earlier,
but Jake had been too preoccupied to return the call. The thought of a
rendezvous with Johnny at one of their old Western Avenue hangouts
was appealing—like old times. And, after Chief Tomczak's visit the
previous evening, he had another reason for meeting with Johnny.

Jake made arrangements with Peggy to have Anna go directly to her
house after school and spend the evening with the twins. He arrived at
Riley's Pub at seven o'clock, and found Johnny already there, sitting

in his usual spot near the back. A bottle of champagne in an ice bucket was waiting for him.

Johnny made a congratulatory toast, and then pressed Jake for a play-by-play account of the trial. He listened with rapt attention as Jake recounted the highlights, from start to finish.

"After all the preparation, and then the intensity and drama of the trial, I imagine it's hard to put it behind you," Johnny observed. "Do you still find yourself thinking about it all the time?"

"Surprisingly, no," Jake replied. "It's such a relief to have it over. I don't think about the trial or USH much at all. But it really has caused me to do a lot of reflection, not about the case itself, but about the people involved, and about myself. This case brought me into contact with people that really left an impression on me—some good, some bad. I try not to think about the bad ones, because I get angry and bitter when I do. But I can't stop thinking about some of the good people that have crossed my path."

Jake paused and pensively stared at the champagne he was swirling slowly in its glass. "I've seen some striking examples of how one person's life can touch so many others in a positive way. I've been thinking a lot about Mickey Quinn, how our legal system failed him, and how egregiously wronged he was, and how despite all that, he's been able to rise above it. I think about the lessons I learned as a kid working in the store, his commitment to making life better for others, the sense of dignity and hope he's been able to maintain even after all he's been through. What an amazing man! I also think about Shooter, and his brother, Jerome. They grew up just a few miles from you and me, but they were born into a different universe. They were surrounded by poverty, gangs, drugs and violence. They didn't have a loving mother and father who were always there for them. They both spent time in prison, and yet the two of them rose above that adversity. They straightened their lives out, and now they've devoted themselves to steering other underprivileged kids in the right direction. They tried to give me credit for putting them on the right path, but I think I've learned more from them than the other way around."

Johnny listened quietly. He could tell that Jake was speaking not just to him, but also to himself, trying to sort through his thoughts and emotions.

Jake continued. "I think about Amanda in the same way: all the students she inspired, the patients she comforted, the clinic she founded, which is flourishing and doing so much good for so many people. She, and Mickey, and Shooter—they all made a difference. They've touched a lot of lives and truly made the world a better place."

"It's funny, isn't it?" said Johnny softly, "How one person can impact so many others, often without even realizing it, and their goodness radiates to an ever-widening circle of people."

Jake continued staring at his drink and nodded slowly. "That seems so obvious, but I'm only now just getting it. Last time we were here, you told me I was living the life of a selfish bastard—putting my own desires and ambitions above everything else. You said—"

"I don't think that's quite what I said," Johnny protested.

"Well, it was something close to that, and you were absolutely right. I've been way too focused on my own personal accomplishments and achievements. Shooter put it in slightly different terms, but he made the same point. He said that he'd spent most of his life trying to earn respect, and that took him down the wrong path. He pointed out that if we're trying to earn respect and admiration, we're really being self-centered. Respect from others shouldn't be a goal in itself. It should be a byproduct of living the right kind of life. The goal should be living your life the right way—by really focusing on others. I think most people accept this conceptually when they think about it, but how many of us make it a guiding principle in our life that affects all of our interactions and everything we do? For some people, like you or Amanda or Mickey, living that way is as natural as breathing. For others, it takes real effort. I know it doesn't come naturally to me, but after our previous conversation, I had made up my mind that things would be different. Amanda was doing so much good for so many people, I was determined to find a way to put her first in my life—I mean really first. I would've changed jobs. I would've taken her back to California to be near her family. I would've supported her career anyway I could."

Jake's eyes began to fill with tears, and he lowered his voice to a whisper to keep it from breaking. "She deserved all that and so much more, and I never got to do that for her." He paused to keep control of his emotions. "This is so hard, Johnny. It wasn't supposed to be this way. We were supposed to grow old together. I feel so ... cheated."

Johnny leaned across the table and put his hand on Jake's forearm. "You're right, Jake. It's a terrible tragedy. Nothing can change that. I know you miss her desperately, and your life will be entirely different than you expected. But think about this: Most people will never have what you and Amanda had—never! Think about how great it was that she came into your life. She was such a special person, and of all the men in the world, she chose to spend her life with you. And when you look back on your life as an old man, you'll be so grateful for the time you had with her. And she'll always be a part of you, Jake. Not just because of the memories, but because she had a profound impact on your life. She shaped the way you look at things, the way you think and the way you act. She gave you your precious little girl, who is so much a part of both of you. You have every right to grieve over her loss—and you should. You have to, in order to get through this. But you should also realize how tremendously blessed you are to have shared part of your life with her."

"I do realize that, Johnny. I really do," said Jake, wiping his eyes with his sleeve. "And I know I'll get through this. But do you know what scares me more than anything?"

"What?"

"This thought first hit me like a ton of bricks when I watched Amanda's burial, and I've never been able to shake it. What if there is no God and no afterlife, and she's just gone, and her spirit no longer exists anywhere, in any form? That thought absolutely tears me up inside. I want so badly to know that somewhere, somehow, she lives on. She deserves to. She deserves so much. She didn't deserve to die in that car wreck."

"I believe that Amanda lives on in some way that we can't fathom, Jake. I believe it as strongly as I believe you're sitting across the table from me."

"But do you believe that because you want to, or because you really think it's true?"

"Both, I guess. Our existence just makes more sense to me that way."

"I want to believe that so badly, I really do. Maybe it's the lawyer in me that questions everything, but part of me fears that we live with those beliefs because the thought of our loved ones being truly gone in every sense is just too difficult to bear."

"That's where faith comes in, pal. It provides answers when hard evidence and logical reasoning fall short. There's nothing wrong with having doubts. Faith isn't the absence of doubt—it's a choice we make—a choice to believe in spite of our doubts. And I choose to believe."

Jake nodded his head slowly and sighed, "Thanks, Johnny. Thanks for always being there for me."

"Anytime, pal." They finished their drinks and headed toward the exit. On the sidewalk in front of the bar, Johnny stopped and asked, "Can you stand a little good news?"

"I sure could use some," Jake replied.

"You can go home and tell Anna she's going to have a new second cousin."

Jake's mind felt sluggish, and he stared blankly at Johnny for a few moments until comprehension clicked in. "Corey? Is she pregnant?"

Johnny nodded happily.

Jake gave his cousin a high five, followed by a rough bear hug. "That's great, Johnny! That's fantastic! I'm really happy for you. That's the best news I've heard in a long time. Anna will be thrilled!"

There was something uplifting about seeing Johnny beaming with joy, and realizing that, despite all his grief, he could feel that joy himself and share in it. Jake felt an emotion that he had not felt in some time, and it was heartening just to know he could feel it again. He felt hope.

As they walked toward the parking lot, Johnny rattled the car keys in his pocket and eyed his cousin, looking serious again. "So, Jake, you mentioned on the phone that you had some news about Danny Flynn?"

Jake thought about the suicide note. Johnny was as happy as Jake had ever seen him. Corey was embarking on a new life with an optimism and hope that had long been missing. If he told them that Flynn was responsible for Amanda's death, they would be torn with guilt. They shouldn't be, but they would.

Jake avoided Johnny's stare and looked up at the streetlight. "Aw, I'd heard a rumor, but it turned out to be nothing. The less we think about that lowlife, the better."

"Yeah, ain't that the truth?" Johnny replied. He climbed into his car and gunned the engine. "Catch you later."

CHAPTER 63

Six Months Later

J ake was awake early again. Sleep did not come easily of late, and when it did come, it was fitful and unsatisfying. Last night was no exception.

He crept quietly to Anna's bedroom, silently opened the door, and peered in at her. For some time now, he had found himself doing this before he went to bed at night and as soon as he awoke in the morning. He often found himself doing the same thing in the middle of the night, when sleep was beyond his reach. Seeing her that way brought him a sense of comfort that otherwise seemed sorely lacking in his universe.

He tiptoed to her bedside and caressed her cheek, ever so gently, so as not to awaken her. Her eyelids fluttered, but did not open. A smile formed on her face and she reached for his hand. "Hi Daddy," she whispered hoarsely, eyes still closed.

"Good morning, little girl," he answered, annoyed with himself for having awoken her, yet pleased that they were sharing this moment.

"What day is it today?" she asked, struggling to open her eyes.

"Sunday."

She was still for a moment, then suddenly wide-awake, popping into a sitting position. "Let's go to church today! Remember how much fun it was when we used to go?"

He stared at her, surprised, yet intrigued by her request. "We haven't been in a long time. I'm surprised you still remember it."

"I don't remember much. What I remember mostly is the music. It made me feel happy all over. Can we go again, like we used to, with Mommy?"

He smiled at the memories, which flooded back in vivid detail. He could see Anna, as a three-year-old, squirming out of the crowded pew the moment the music started. The aisle became her private dance floor, as she twirled around and around, curls flopping, skirt billowing, eyes cast skyward, with a look of pure joy on her smiling face. She would spin in circles, wider and wider, becoming increasingly unsteady until dizziness caused her to flop down in a heap. She would lie still for a few moments, laughing quietly to herself until the world stopped spinning, and then she would hop up and continue the routine.

Jake had always found that routine to be a pleasant distraction from the service that rarely inspired him. Those in the nearby pews usually seemed as amused by the distraction as he was, so he never felt the slightest desire to interfere with the little floorshow, despite the stern looks of disapproval from the humorless ushers. Clearly, the three-year-old Anna had found church to be an uplifting experience. That impression still lingered somewhere in the recesses of her memory, and burst into her heart with such exhilaration that Jake found himself mustering up as much forced enthusiasm as he could, saying, "What a great idea. Find your best dress and let's go."

Despite Anna's eagerness, a feeling of uneasiness and trepidation soon overtook him. Sunday morning Mass had been a regular part of his life with Amanda during the early years of their marriage. It was one of the few constants during a week that was otherwise too busy and unpredictable to lend itself to anything resembling a regular schedule. Although he didn't share Amanda's deep commitment to the church, he went willingly because it meant so much to her. He also found it to be conducive to reflection and meditation, the opportunity for which was all too scarce during the remainder of the week.

As he pondered these thoughts, his apprehension grew. He found himself staring into the bathroom mirror, straightening his tie for far too long, taking deep breaths and trying to collect himself. He feared that attending Mass without Amanda would be a harsh reminder of how deeply he missed her. He feared that the loneliness and crippling sense of loss would overwhelm him once more, just as he was starting to be able to lock it away. And yet, despite those fears, some part of him wanted to believe that he might actually find some solace and comfort within the old stone walls of St. Francis Church.

"Do you plan on dancing in the aisle, like you used to?" Jake asked his daughter as they pulled into the church parking lot.

"No Daddy, I'll behave myself," she replied, laughing at the fuzzy memories.

They walked hand-in-hand through the courtyard toward the church. As they walked, Jake felt as if he were taking in the scenery for the first time. He noticed the religious statuary throughout the garden: a large statue of St. Francis, beckoning some unseen creatures; the statue of Mary cradling the Baby Jesus, with a look of pure serenity clear and unmistakable on her stony visage; and most prominently, the stone Celtic cross in the middle of the circular fountain, a reminder to all of the Irish heritage that was so pervasive in the neighborhood.

The church itself looked exactly as it always had: an imposing structure of gray stone, towering above all the surrounding buildings, with a bronze cross extending toward the heavens from the top of the steeple. The old building brought back a flood of jumbled memories, bridging the present with the past, remote and recent. He remembered going to Mass with his father every day before school as a small child. He remembered making his first communion with 160 other second graders. He even remembered the date—May 8th—because Sister Joan insisted it would be the most important day of their lives. He remembered the terror he felt at the prospect of facing the unseen priest in the confessional, which he forced himself to do every Saturday despite the dread and fear. God was part of his everyday life then. His faith was absolute and unshakable, a source of meaning and inspiration. With a sense of guilt and remorse, he realized how much it had faded.

Such were his thoughts as he and Anna seated themselves near the statue of the Blessed Virgin, where he and Amanda had always sat. With the first strains of the opening hymn, all of those disjointed thoughts evaporated, and a single subject came into sharp focus: Amanda. He remembered their wedding day, and how he began trembling all over when the organ struck the first chord and she slowly glided up the aisle toward him. He remembered feeling blessed beyond his wildest dreams to be embarking on a life together with Amanda Chang. He remembered their vow to stay together "till death do us part." In his mind, that implied lifelong companionship and growing old together.

The sorrow he'd worked so hard to keep dammed up within himself threatened to come crashing through once again. He would not allow that to happen. He missed her desperately, and she was never far from his thoughts, but on some level, he had grown accustomed to life without her. He would not give in to the paralyzing grief and self-pity he had struggled so hard to overcome. She would not want that.

He needed to move on with his life, and he was determined to do so in a way that would make her proud. He would strive to approach life like she did—with cheerfulness, warmth and a deep and genuine desire to make a positive difference in the lives of others. He would strive to see the good in people. He would keep her memory alive for their precious child, so that she, too, could benefit from her mother's wisdom and spirit. He would always miss Amanda, but living that way would allow him to honor her memory and give him a sense of purpose. Living that way would keep her spirit living on through him.

Through his musings, Jake heard Father George leading the congregation through the Apostles' Creed. "We believe in God, the Father Almighty, maker of heaven and earth ..." He thought about that statement, and about his own journey through the realm of faith. As a child, it had been an integral part of his existence. God was as real and as present as the air he breathed and the earth beneath his feet. As he grew into adulthood, faith was relegated to some distant corner of his mind, as his time and thoughts were consumed by the demands and pressures of a busy life. Faith had faded, yet it was still there, somewhere. There had been little reason to question it—until that moment in the cemetery, when he watched Amanda's casket being lowered into the ground. Doubt assailed him like a blast of icy wind. What if the notions of a benign Creator and an afterlife were nothing more than fantasies created by the human mind to protect against a pain that would otherwise be unbearable? What if Amanda's existence—her soul, her spirit, her conscious being, her essence—had utterly and completely perished in the wreckage of Johnny's car on that dark, wooded roadside? That thought horrified him— not because of the implications it held for him regarding his own mortality—but because of the implications it held for her. She deserved to live on, and the possibility that she was simply gone for all eternity and had no further existence of any type was too painful to contemplate.

He remembered Johnny saying, "I choose to believe." Johnny was right—faith was a choice. For some, the choice was easy—it was made almost without thinking. For others, it was a struggle, and sometimes an agonizing one. He was struggling, and had been since that moment in the cemetery. His doubts tormented him, almost to the point of physical pain. He craved answers, and resolution.

Father George droned on, but Jake was barely aware of the sound of his voice. He found himself praying, trying to channel every ounce of his being into some connection with the Almighty. "Please God, Almighty Father, please hear me … I will cope with this loss. I will make the best of my situation. I'm not concerned about myself. I'm asking you to take care of Amanda." Anguish filled his heart and clouded his thoughts. He forced himself to concentrate on his prayer. "Lord, I realize that I have no right to ask you for anything, but I can't help myself. There is one thing I must ask of you … I need to know that she is okay and that somewhere, somehow, her spirit lives on. Let me know that her existence did not end in that car crash…. Please God, send me some kind of sign, however subtle, and I will see it, and never doubt you. Please … I need to know … please … please …"

He stopped and thought about the silent prayer that just gushed forth. As he did so, another feeling began welling up within him, forcing aside the feelings of doubt and desperation. It began as a twinge of guilt and shame over the request he had just made, then quickly transformed into something else: awareness; and then gratitude. On an intellectual level, he had always known how fortunate he was to have shared part of his life with Amanda. However, the sorrow over losing her was overpowering, and had prevented him from deriving any comfort from that realization.

He continued his prayer. "Lord, forgive me for my doubts and my weaknesses, and my selfish desires. I know I have been truly blessed to have had Amanda in my life as long as I did. That was a gift far greater than I ever expected or deserved. I thank you for that with all my heart. She was always so able to see the goodness in this world. I can see how blessed I was to have shared ten years with her. I will try to never forget that, and to live my life with a spirit of gratitude for that tremendous gift. I will strive to keep her spirit alive, by learning from her example, by trying to live my life as she lived hers, and touching other lives the way she did. And as for faith, I may not be able to vanquish all traces of doubt, but I choose to believe. I will believe in you, and I will believe that somewhere, somehow, Amanda lives on. I know that I will live a better life by believing that. I choose faith."

He looked up at the crucifix hanging above the altar, and finished his silent prayer.

The church was silent except for the rustling of missalettes, and the sound of someone's cough echoing through the cavernous structure. Father George had finished his sermon and asked the congregation to offer a silent prayer of thanksgiving. Jake's eyes drifted toward the window, and he watched the elm trees swaying silently in the gusty spring winds. Despite his resolve to have faith, he still found himself yearning for some sign that his prayer had been heard, and some part of him half expected to see something unusual—a sudden ray of sunshine or perhaps a colorful bird. He saw nothing, yet he kept staring, until he noticed an urgent tugging at his sleeve, which snapped him out of his trance-like state. He turned toward Anna and leaned down, so that she might whisper in his ear. She stood on her tiptoes and kissed him gently on the cheek. Then she looked up at him with bright, adoring eyes, and in her most earnest voice, whispered, "I love you, Daddy!"

The End

4944159R00215

Made in the USA
San Bernardino, CA
16 October 2013